BLING

ERICA KENNEDY

◆

Bling

MIRAMAX BOOKS

BLING

INTRO

◆

LAMONT SAUNTERED INTO THE GRILL ROOM like he owned the place.

"Mr. Jackson," the maître d' greeted him warmly. "Mr. Greene is waiting at your usual table."

Lamont gifted him with a courteous half-smile. Their usual table was the *best* one in the midtown Manhattan restaurant where the power players converged.

A dark-skinned man with an imposing build and a cocksure swagger, Lamont Jackson was not conventionally handsome. Rather he had that well-groomed sheen particular to rich, image-conscious men. He cut a formidable swath as he strode through the room in his favorite Brioni suit, chin up, acknowledging fellow members of the media elite with friendly nods, the masculine scent of his Bulgari cologne lingering in his wake. He derived a soul-deep satisfaction from being watched, being known. He felt their eyes upon him as he approached Irv Greene, the sixty-six-year-old chairman of Augusta Music who had been ranked number ten on last year's *Entertainment*

Weekly Power 100. After his own record label had achieved its best year to date, Lamont had landed in the magazine's annual "honorable mention" spot at 100.5. An insult. He would have preferred not to have been mentioned at all.

Lamont consulted his Patek Philippe as he slid into the booth. "Am I late?" Irv Greene was a stickler for punctuality. It was something he and Lamont had in common.

"No," Irv said cordially, not bothering to get up. "Right on time."

They enjoyed a warm professional relationship. There was no need for formality, though if Lamont had arrived first he would have instinctively stood to greet the music industry legend. They ordered lunch and made small talk until Irv finally addressed the unspoken topic hanging in the air.

"So it's true," he announced between bites of salmon.

"Really?" Lamont attempted to sound surprised, even though rumors had been swirling for a month. "They want you out?"

"Yeah," Irv said. "The fuckers." He leaned over and in a confidential whisper said, "So everyone knows already, huh?"

"Well, not everyone."

"What are people saying?"

"Listen," Lamont said. "HMG can't ask you to step down. They have no cause."

"None," Irv agreed immediately. "It's a forced retirement." He was reconciled to the fact that he was being pushed out as the head of Augusta, where he had been cranking out hits for more than thirty years.

"What bullshit," Lamont spat, truly outraged. Even at thirty-eight years old, as the CEO of Triple Large Entertainment, the hip-hop label he'd founded in a joint venture with Augusta, Lamont was feeling the heat from younger moguls-in-training.

"Bullshit it is," Irv sighed. "But we operate in a world that worships the young and exiles the old." He shrugged. He'd been wrestling with the dilemma for a month and had let go of the anger.

Technically, Lamont had to report to Irv but mostly he was the master of his own ship. Irv wasn't going to tell Lamont, an African-American who had the pulse of urban culture, how to run a hip-hop label. Irv had been one of Lamont's most vocal supporters to the higher-ups at HMG, the German conglomerate that owned Augusta. The same fuckers who were trying to push Irv out of his job.

"You remember the first time we had lunch here?" Lamont reflected. "Nine years ago. When we were working out the joint venture."

"I remember it like it was yesterday," Irv said. "You had on jeans that were too baggy, Air Jordans, a yellow hooded Morehouse sweatshirt, and you kept taking calls on a cell phone that was the size of a brick. I was embarrassed to be seen with you!"

Lamont didn't want to be reminded of *that*. "But remember what you said to me that day? People were just starting to realize hip-hop wasn't a passing fad. I said the Germans at HMG were racist and the only reason they wanted to get in bed with me was because green was the only color that could blind them to my own."

Irv nodded. "And I said, 'I'm a Jew from Canarsie. You think they like me better? To them we're both niggers. Accept it and move on.'"

They both chuckled at the recollection.

"It was the best advice I'd ever gotten," Lamont said. "Still is." He'd learned so much from Irv. How to handle corporate politics, how to groom and break an artist, even how to dress. Lamont looked at Irv now, casually attired in a white shirt, no tie, what was left of his dark brown hair elegantly slicked back. The shirt was so crisp, so sturdy, so blindingly white it almost had a celestial glow. Where did you even buy a shirt like that? And how much did it cost?

"You also said," Lamont continued the trip down memory lane to massage Irv's ego, "'You make hit records, we all make money and everyone's happy.'" A thoughtful pause. "You've been producing hits for thirty-five years, Irv. You've made them a lot of money. You're still at the top of your game. It's not right what they're trying to do. That's what everyone's saying."

Irv smiled and raised his glass in appreciation.

"So what's next?" Lamont asked casually. Self-serving to the bone, he was more curious about what this shake-up meant for *him* than his mentor.

"Golf's not my thing," Irv said. "Might start my own label. I can write my own ticket."

A deferential "Of course."

"And they're still deciding on my replacement." The pause was so pregnant it was expecting triplets.

Say it, Lamont silently urged. *Say it.*

Irv Greene looked across the table and smiled genially. "If it were up to me the job would be yours today. But I do know you're at the top of their list."

Lamont leaned his considerable girth back on the leather banquette and pushed his plate of risotto away, taking a moment to compose himself so his deep baritone would not sound too eager in reply. He felt like jumping up in the packed dining room and shouting "I'm ready!" but he only shifted slightly and when he spoke, he sounded cool and calm. "You know, I've been thinking of branching out," he said. "Doing some R&B shit. I have some things in the works right now."

"Wonderful," Irv enthused. "That's what you need to do. Show the Nazis you're not a one-trick pony." Irv wiped his mouth with the cloth napkin. "There's still a lot to be worked out before I leave. Everyone's going to be watching you, Monty. Show 'em what you can do."

As soon as Lamont hopped into the back of his Mercedes Maybach, he called Daryl McHenry, his all-purpose whipping boy. They'd already spoken about the brilliant idea that had come to Lamont last night. Daryl was just waiting for the word. Lamont had three for him. "*Call the girl.*"

◆

On the Come Up

◆

CHAPTER 1

Excuse Me Miss

"'CAUSE WE AIN'T NOBODY," LaToya said.

Lakeesha turned from peering out the window of the Chester-field Hotel, annoyed because her question—"Why they got us staying in this bum-ass hotel?"—had been a rhetorical one. There was no view. Just another hotel across Thirty-seventh Street. And from what little she could see, the rooms over there were nicer.

"I know," Keesha said. "But still…we didn't even get a limo from the airport."

"We didn't need a limo," Mimi said, busily straightening up. "They sent a car and it was fine."

"Why are you cleaning up Kenny's room?" Keesha said, stretching out on the perfectly made bed.

"Because I already finished with ours," Mimi said. "I can't just sit around, doing nothing, waiting for the phone to ring. It's driving me crazy." They were sharing the adjoining room but they were camped out here because their manager, Kenny Hill, would get the call—at

3

the hotel since his cell-phone service had been interrupted for non-payment—and they wanted to be there when he did.

"Let's eat," Keesha said. "That'll give us something to do." She picked up the room service menu. "We can order food, right?" She frowned over at Toya. "They pay for that?"

Last night after their audition at the Triple Large offices they had gone to Planet Hollywood for dinner, hoping to spot some celebrities, unaware that it was a tourist trap populated by auto-graphseekers like themselves where no celebrity would ever be caught dead.

"I don't know," Toya said wearily. Keesha was always looking for a free meal, literally and figuratively, and it got under Toya's skin that she was so simpleminded. "You need to ask Kenny."

"Where's he at anyway?" Keesha said. She twirled one of her long microbraids. "It don't take that long to buy a pack of Newports."

Mimi didn't care about the low-budget accommodations or that there had been no limo yesterday. Keesha thought this whole trip was going to be like an episode of *Making the Band*—she was obsessed with that show! Kenny did nothing to dissuade her from thinking it was going to be limos, parties, and Cristal bottles popping, but why on earth would anyone do that for them? They *were* nobodies. But they had come here to change that.

They'd all met at Performing Arts School of Toledo. They joked they were like TLC, whose *CrazySexyCool* album was one of their all-time favorites. Keesha, big-boned and equipped with a razor-sharp tongue, was the crazy component. Toya, a round-faced girl with a heart-warming smile and a degree of self-assurance that belied her years, was the cool. And Mimi...well, she wasn't wild like Keesha and she didn't possess Toya's innate confidence, so sometimes she felt she got the sexy slot by default.

No doubt, Mimi was pretty. Since she was a baby everyone had remarked on it. But in her usual baggy gear, sexy she was not. Tight jeans and midriff-baring tops invited attention, and as a biracial girl in a predominantly black school, she already stood out enough. All she'd ever wanted was to blend in. Her mother, Angela, was Italian, and Mimi couldn't remember her Haitian father. Jacques Bertrand had run out on Angela a year after their only child was born, and the annual birthday cards that had arrived (late) with no return address stopped arriving altogether after Mimi's eighth birthday.

She kept the details of her home life to herself as she did most things, managing to pull straight As while dodging the taunts of "white girl" and "high-yellow heifer." As if she thought she was better than the other girls. Just like many of them, she was raised by an overworked single mother, she rode the bus to school from the bad side of town, and the clothes over which they ran a disapproving "you think you cute" eye were paid for by the after-school jobs she'd been juggling since she was fourteen. She never made her looks an issue, they did.

Toya, however, was different. She made that clear only two months into freshman year, when Nichelle Griffin had stormed over to Mimi in the cafeteria and began to lay into her for coming on to her boyfriend (even though it had been Nichelle's wannabe teenage lothario who had been coming on to a completely uninterested Mimi). Toya, who Mimi knew only casually, had calmly looked over her shoulder from the next table and said, "You just mad because you *wish* you had that long hair. Go get yourself a weave and shut the hell up." Keesha, always spoiling for a fight of any kind, had jumped up to enter the fray but Nichelle had slunk away before she could.

Toya, Keesha, and Mimi had been friends ever since.

Later that year, their group was formed. They named it Heartsong. They debated endlessly about what kinds of songs they should sing, what kind of group they wanted to be. Keesha and Toya were into hip-hop. Mimi's tastes fell more on the soul side. She idolized those female artists whose songs stirred something inside her more than an urge to dance. Her mother had harbored dreams of being a singer way back when and music was the only constant in their unstable lives. From Aretha to Alanis Morissette, Sarah Vaughan to Sarah McLachlan, Mimi would close her eyes and try to mimic their every inflection, pretending she was them, not a girl from Toledo who wouldn't recognize her own father if she passed him on the street.

That was how she got through performing onstage. She became someone else—whoever's song she was belting out. She was pretending to be Beyoncé on the night they met Kenny at a local talent show; Heartsong had just won the top prize and three hundred dollars for their rousing rendition of "Bills, Bills, Bills," the Destiny's Child hit.

A lanky dark-skinned man of thirty-four with droopy eyes and a seemingly permanent deposit of white crust in the corner of his mouth, Kenny Hill's name was one they recognized from flyers posted all over town. A part-time club promoter, he told them he knew every musician, nightclub owner, and DJ in Toledo. Which in retrospect, they realized, wasn't saying all that much. He proffered a business card that read simply "talent manager" and they didn't know to ask him for any credentials beyond the promises he made. He talked about getting them a record deal and he didn't ask them for money, and so it was that Kenny Hill became their manager.

He had arranged for them to sing backup on demos at Wildside Studios in exchange for free studio time to record their own music. He kept telling them that he was setting up auditions with labels but nothing ever panned out. And they'd graduated high school two years ago! The day after they tossed their caps, Mimi's part-time job at the discount emporium Sav-Mart became full-time, Toya was doing hair at Black Roots (without a license), and Keesha wasn't doing much of anything except hanging out with her crazy-ass drug-dealer boyfriend.

They'd finished their demo, using tracks Kenny bought from a local producer and singing generic R&B lyrics that Kenny had written himself. Kenny Hill—club promoter, talent manager, songwriter. Jack of all trades and master of none.

When he finally got a callback from Triple Large Entertainment a week ago, he didn't tell the girls right away that they had a chance at a recording contract. Instead he'd gotten everything in order—wrangling four coach plane tickets to New York, two $99-per-night rooms at The Chesterfield—before he strolled into Wildside Studios and crowed triumphantly, "Pack your bags, girls. We're goin' to New York!"

CALL THE GIRL? Why did Lamont always have to be so dramatic? Daryl wanted to call the girl but he couldn't even remember the bitch's name! La-something. Lavonne? No, LaToya. Or maybe that was the other one. He'd already asked Lamont's assistant and the receptionist if they remembered the name of the "pretty one" because he couldn't find the group's bio and attached photo. With all the groups that had come through the office in the last few weeks, no one could remember a damn thing about any of them. Now Daryl rummaged through all the useless office memos on his desk in search of the package the manager had left with him the other day.

Daryl's office was tiny. So was he. But what he lacked in size he more than made up for in self-aggrandizement. He was five foot five and three-quarters of an inch, but whenever anyone dared to question his height he'd pull out his driver's license. *Bam!* Five foot seven. People always took that as gospel, as if the DMV actually measured folks.

His office would have felt larger if he'd cleared out the half dozen boxes of demos he was supposed to listen to as the A&R rep of Triple Large Entertainment. When he first got the gig he didn't even know what A&R stood for. "Artist and repertoire" he was told. He still didn't entirely understand, but he'd figured out he was expected to discover new artists and work on their development once they were signed. That he could do, although he really wanted to be a producer solely and forget the office bullshit.

He rarely got around to assessing the volumes of material that found their way into the midtown office. Most artists who got signed had already made names for themselves on the street or were affiliated with an established hip-hop clique. The next big thing rarely arrived unannounced via the United States Postal Service. Nevertheless, Paul Mankewich, the label's V.P. of A&R, stayed on Daryl's ass about listening to every single submission.

A strapping, floppy-haired white guy in his mid-thirties, Paul Mankewich made six figures and his own hours. He was nicknamed "Witchy" because he had successfully cultivated so many R&B and hip-hop acts at various record companies that people said he could work "black magic." Twenty-three-year-old Daryl didn't have an official title. He was usually called "the A&R guy," which he preferred to being called Witchy's assistant. Though affable to most, Witchy cracked the whip on his departmental subordinate—mostly, Daryl believed, as a form of insurance. If Witchy failed to meet his monthly beat-up-on-Daryl quota, Witchy was guaranteed to receive a few lashes from the HNIC himself, Lamont "Fat Man" Jackson.

Daryl idolized and despised Fat Man with equal fervor. Some days he wished he were standing tall in Lamont's four-hundred-dollar shoes, making big moves and bigger bank. Other days he hoped Lamont Jackson would keel over and die from a massive coronary and spend all eternity rotting in hell.

A few months ago, Fat Man had put out the call that they'd be branching out into R&B. They were hoping to find the next Destiny's Child. In the past two months, they'd seen twenty-seven groups. None of them got past their first song. After an audition two days ago of three white girls with varying degrees of pink hair who called themselves Shades, it was obvious Witchy was digging at the bottom of the barrel. Lamont had turned to Witchy and said, "Mr. Mankewich, why do I feel like I'm a judge on *American Idol*?" Daryl had fallen back on Lamont's sofa and laaaaaughed. It was a joy to see Witchy catching some flak for a change, but the most hysterical part was that Lamont *was* beginning to resemble the fat guy on the show.

And then this group Heartsong—the worst fucking name!—had come in yesterday. Daryl had only listened to their demo as a favor to Meagan, Triple Large's certified hottie receptionist. She'd urged him to listen to it, saying the manager was a friend of her cousin's friend.

"Oh well, I'll give it the VIP treatment right now!" Daryl had clowned. Like he cared. It was certain to be garbage, but if it brought him one small step toward getting some pussy from Meagan, it was worth a listen. And, what did you know, it wasn't bad. Not bad at all.

Witchy was heated when he found out Daryl had flown them in without consulting him. One of the girls, the one with the long braids, had to be twenty pounds heavier than she'd been when the bio picture was taken. And the manager was annoying as hell! Daryl had to shove him out of Lamont's office as he tried to sell him on two other hip-hop acts he managed. The group's audition didn't seem to ignite much enthusiasm in Lamont although he didn't say that he straight-up hated them, which was his response to most of the twenty-seven who'd come before.

This morning Lamont had called Daryl—at the crack of dawn—to say maybe they didn't need a group after all. Actually his first words were "Where the hell is Witchy?" Daryl rolled over, looked at the ungodly hour and yawned, "At home sleepin' maybe?" Lamont grunted his disapproval, then told Daryl he'd had a moment of revelation. He'd decided they needed just one girl. A solo artist. He wanted to meet with the lead singer of Heartsong. "The pretty one," he'd said.

Daryl finally found the bio picture sticking out of a stack of magazines on the floor. Mimi. That was her name. He looked at his fake Rolex. Damn! It was already 4:15 and Lamont wanted her down there by 5:00. He picked up the phone and dialed the hotel.

This chick could be his first discovery. And if a signing came out of this, he wouldn't let Witchy or Fat Man forget it.

◆

CHAPTER 2

If I Ruled the World

LAMONT CLIMBED THE WINDING STAIRCASE to his home gym, thinking, *Lamont Jackson, Chairman of Augusta Music.* Had a nice ring to it. He'd be able to sell Triple Large to Augusta but he'd still retain control of the label he'd founded as well as run several others. How much would the deal reap? Sixty million? No, Triple Large was worth seventy-five at least.

He stepped onto the treadmill and poked a few buttons. He usually worked out in the evening after coming home from the office and before going out for dinner and whatever else the night offered. But today he'd come home right after his lunch meeting with Irv. One of the perks of being a top dawg—you didn't have to account for your whereabouts to anyone.

These workouts were often the only time he spent alone in an entire day. At the office he had his minions swarming around and his faithful assistant, Imani, hovering nearby. At night, out at the most exclusive clubs, his entourage was always surrounding him. When traveling in his

Maybach or Suburban (money green, fully loaded), his driver, Carlos, was at the wheel. And when he finally fell asleep in this TriBeCa triplex, there was almost always a gorgeous babe in bed beside him.

He had tried working out with a highly recommended personal trainer, but the guy had annoyed him and was fired after two sessions. Anyway, he had gotten the information he needed and could continue the exercise regimen without some faggot Richard Simmons wannabe counting off repetitions and applauding him afterward like he'd just run the New York City Marathon. He had nothing against a little ass-kissing—as long as his ass was the one on the receiving end. It was actually one of his favorite things. But he got more than his fair share of that every day. And he'd gotten an uncomfortable feeling that *that* guy had wanted to kiss his ass for real.

Besides, working out alone gave him a chance to decompress and think. The thought that was going through his mind right now was, *I need a hit.* A blinding success story that would prove—to Irv Greene, to the heads of HMG, to the world—that he deserved the top job at Augusta.

Nine years ago, he had been one of hip-hop's corporate trailblazers, founding Triple Large Entertainment long before rappers were starring in movies, shilling for Sprite, and mingling with high society. His early track record as a label head had been unimpressive. The first few artists he'd released had come and gone without much fanfare and been summarily dropped from the label.

Then three of his acts achieved gold-record status—and selling 500,000 albums had still meant big success then. How far the bar had risen in only a few years. Now a record that was merely gold-certified meant one with lackluster sales. Lamont didn't allow the word "failure" to be uttered by anyone within his ranks. In a slumping industry where music downloading had become an escalating problem and major labels were regularly laying off hundreds of employees, posting profits was more difficult and more important than ever.

Lamont's first big success was Flo$$, a raspy-voiced West Coast rapper who wove biblical sayings into his rhymes about his ghetto fabulous lifestyle. He became the label's resident sex symbol despite the fact that he had one prosthetic leg. He'd lost his left leg below the shin after a car accident when he was sixteen and claimed to have had a near-death experience and found God. Flo$$ gave a whole new meaning to the term "hip-*hop*." His debut, "Prophet & Flo$$," came close to selling 500,000 copies, although his bio said it was certified gold anyway.

Radickulys, Triple Large's hip-hop comedian, rapped about girls, parties, and, mostly, himself. Lamont had come up with the name following the "phonetic spellings are cooler" tradition that the younger rappers seemed to favor. He thought Radickulys was an improvement over the rapper's original moniker, Big D.I.C.K. He could just imagine MTV having a heart attack over that. Dicky's first album, *Ha Ha*, made some noise with two hit singles but Lamont was disappointed with its performance. Two million copies sold of the rapper's second effort, *No Foolin'*, more than made up for any bad feelings.

But it was a plasma-obsessed rapper named MC Grimy who had taken Lamont and TLE to the next level. Grimy's first album, *Bloodhound*, went gold; his second, *Hematoma*, went platinum, selling a million copies in total; his third, *Code Red*, sold two million in its first two months; and his next, *Crimson Tide*, was the TLE all-time best-seller, at four million copies to date. When Lamont learned that Grimy had taken an I.Q. test as a child and scored a staggeringly high

140, Lamont started calling Grimy his "thug genius." He was pleased when that nickname got picked up in the press. It appeared in large type next to Grimy's head when the toned rapper was featured, shirtless and splattered with blood, on a controversial *Rolling Stone* cover. (Controversial, in large part, because Grimy had shown up for the photo shoot toting a cooler containing four hermetically sealed bags of human blood of unknown origin.) Thereafter, Lamont's publicist let it be known that Lamont himself had coined the term.

Grimy's success had really put the company on the map. The Triple Large imprimatur meant something now. When a new album was released from the Triple Large stable, hip-hop consumers, 80 percent of whom were suburban white kids, took notice. Flo$$'s second album, *Gimme the Loot*, had gone double platinum. *O Negative*, Grimy's latest LP, had just reached three million. And, from the looks of the first-week sales numbers, Radickulys's *Strayt Clownin'* was on track to do even better.

The R&B- and hip-hop-infused movie soundtracks TLE produced had become a business unto themselves, and Lamont had formed a separate division around them, Triple Large Trax. Ten soundtracks released in the last five years, and they'd all gone at least platinum.

With his label dominating the industry, Lamont was firmly lodged in the top tier of the crop of new black moguls. But he didn't want to be one of. He wanted to be king. The one and only. And as the new chairman of Augusta Music, that's what he would be.

*   *   *

BY THE TIME the girls' late-afternoon snack arrived, Keesha's nerves had gotten the best of her and she was in the bathroom vomiting up lunch.

It was then that the phone finally rang. But it was the phone in their room, not in Kenny's, as they'd expected. While Toya tended to Keesha, Mimi walked through the adjoining door to answer it. It was probably her worrisome mother. She'd already phoned twice today.

"Can I talk to Mimi?" said the caller.

"This is."

"Hey. It's Daryl from Triple Large. Kenny there?"

"No," she said, excited to be hearing from him. "He went out."

"Good. Look, meet me downtown at five o'clock. Eighty-six Walker Street. Don't say shit to Kenny. Not a word."

"I don't know if we can get there by five. Keesha is kind of sick right now."

"No, just you. Don't say anything to them yet either. Tell them you have to meet a friend or something. I'll explain when you get there. Eighty-six Walker. I'll meet you downstairs. Take a cab. I'll pay for it."

"But what—" Mimi began.

"Don't stress me," Daryl cut her off, "just get down there by five. You're already runnin' late!"

Mimi hung up the phone and stared at it. What was going on? If she were to tell the God's honest truth, she hadn't expected them to call. At least, not to say they wanted them. The audition hadn't gone very well. They'd all been so nervous. Keesha's voice cracking was the low point. But she was trying to remain optimistic, for herself as much as for the other girls.

Yesterday, Lamont Jackson, the head of the label, hadn't said "good-bye" or "thanks for coming" or "nice job." Nothing. He'd picked up his telephone before they were out the door and started dialing as if their performance had been an unwanted interruption in his daily business routine. The last to file out, she'd looked back at him. The phone to his ear, he caught her glance and finally cracked a small smile. Of encouragement or pity? She wasn't sure.

Lamont had seemed to be channeling his thoughts to Daryl, who had done all the talking. Daryl had said they'd have an answer today. "Yea or nay," he'd told Kenny. *So which does this call mean,* she wondered. *Yeah or nay?* And what was all this "come alone" business?

When she walked back into Kenny's room, Keesha was lying on the bed with a wet rag on her face, moaning like she'd just given birth. "Are you okay?" Mimi said, kneeling beside her.

"No," Keesha moaned.

"Was that your mother again?" Toya asked.

"Um, no," Mimi said hesitantly. "It was some guy. The son of my mom's friend. He lives here. He wants me to come meet him right now. At this place just around the corner."

Too much detail. She was lying—poorly—and for what? The address Daryl had given her wasn't the address of the office. Despite Daryl's fierce warning, she wished she could talk to Kenny first before she did anything. Where the heck was he? He'd left almost two hours ago! And why couldn't he pay his cell-phone bill?

"What place?" Toya questioned.

"Um…" Mimi said, trying to come up with a name, but she didn't know New York so she just turned and walked back into their room, hoping Toya wouldn't ask again.

"Mimi, what if they call?" Keesha whined.

"Not 'if,'" Toya corrected. "They said they'd call today."

"Well, they might say they want us or they might say they don't," Keesha countered, getting her energy back.

"I'll call you guys in an hour," Mimi said, changing out of her sweats as Toya watched from the doorway.

Mimi went to the closet and considered her clothing options. She couldn't wear the tight stretch jeans and cropped peasant top that she'd worn yesterday for the audition. Toya and Keesha had worn the exact same outfit, so Daryl would surely remember it. Besides, that look was a tad hoochie for her personal taste. During their search for the perfect audition attire, Keesha and Toya had nixed her more conservative suggestions.

"You don't even know this guy," Toya complained. "Forget him."

"I can't." Mimi held up the black turtleneck with the bell sleeves that she had worn on the plane. "I already told him I would come, so..." She shrugged.

Yes, it would be the turtleneck with army-green cargo pants, and her leather boots with the platform heels instead of the slutty high heels Kenny had insisted they wear yesterday.

"Is he cute?" Toya said.

"Who?"

"The guy. The guy you're meeting."

"I don't know. I've never met him." She was already lying, so best to leave it at that.

Mimi went into the bathroom and momentarily thought about telling Keesha and Toya the truth as she pulled back her wild mass of chestnut brown curls into a neat ponytail. She put on her favorite dangling silver-and-turquoise earrings, even though they stretched her lobes, because she loved how they chimed with every step she took. She didn't have time for all the makeup Kenny had ordered them to pile on yesterday. Just a little concealer to cover the rash of pimples that seemed to be multiplying on her forehead.

No, she decided as she applied some cherry-flavored lip gloss, she wouldn't tell them. She'd do this alone as Daryl had said, find out what was up, and then report back. Kenny had to be the problem. Seeing him in that plush New York office, sporting his best nylon track suit, had made it glaringly obvious how small-time he was. When he had tried to give Lamont a demo of a male hip-hop group he was representing, it was obvious that Lamont was not the least bit interested. Kenny kept saying, "Just listen to the first track. It's on fire!" Daryl had almost been forced to shove him out of Lamont's office.

I'm the lead singer, Mimi told herself. *I can handle this.* Imagine if she could come back and tell them they had a deal!

"Okay." Toya finally relented—a little late as Mimi was already grabbing her knitted poncho and suede hobo bag and heading for the door. "Maybe he's cute. And maybe we're gonna get signed. And maybe we're gonna move here and maybe we'll be famous and maybe he'll be your man!"

"Let's not get ahead of ourselves," Mimi said, shooting Toya a smile as she walked out the door.

◆

CHAPTER 3

Can't Knock the Hustle

FOR TEN MINUTES DARYL HAD BEEN STANDING in front of the glass tower in midtown that housed the Triple Large offices with his arm outstretched as available cabs whizzed by. He'd rushed out without his coat and it was too cold to be out here in just a sweatshirt. The cold was the one thing he hated about moving up here from South Carolina. It took damn near till June for the weather to break.

Cabs never stopped for him; he knew he should have given himself more time. And he would have, if Lamont's cornball assistant hadn't made him wait while she put together some package for him to take to Lamont. "He needs to see it tonight, Daryl!" she'd insisted. *Then call the messenger service, girlfriend, 'cause I gots to go!*

So now he was going to be late and Lamont wouldn't stand for that. He thought about throwing up the hood of his sweatshirt to cover his cornrows, but that might just make him seem more menacing. He was damned if he did, damned if he didn't. Story of his life.

A cab slowed to a stop in front of the building, and Daryl saw the blond woman passenger handing money to the driver. Daryl crowded the door and tried unsuccessfully to open it. He wasn't going to accept that "off-duty" shit that these towelhead cabbies always tried to pull.

He glanced up the street for a split second, thinking he saw a cute new TLE intern heading up the block, and when he turned back around the cab was taking off, knocking him off balance and nearly running over his foot! The taxi stopped at the next corner to let the blond woman out. She walked back toward the building, conspicuously avoiding Daryl's glare.

To add insult to injury, Daryl looked down and noticed a smudge on one of his brand-new white-on-whites. Oh hell no! He bent down to inspect the damage to his Nike and decided not to mess with it and risk making it worse than it was. He rose and saw that a white man had hopped into the cab.

This was the shit that Lamont needed to see! This was why he had to order cars on the company account. Lamont was always complaining about that, calling it "blatant abuse of company policy."

"It's a necessity, yo" had been Daryl's response.

When Lamont pointed out that no one else in the office ordered town cars to get around, Daryl decided to drop it. Most of Triple Large's employees were female. Fat Man's own harem. They didn't have to deal with this bullshit. Cabs would stop for them, no problem. And the other guys in the office probably took the subway. Daryl wouldn't know. He didn't socialize with *them*. He only hung with other industry playas on the rise. Though the price of admission to get into Lamont's inner circle was high, he was the only cat in the office who had membership—other than Witchy, who'd waltzed right in just because he'd discovered a couple of successful groups and stayed there by being the ultimate yes-man.

To join this elite hip-hop fraternity, for over two years Daryl had been a virtual indentured servant with a round-the-clock list of menial chores to do. It was not uncommon for Lamont to call Daryl at three in the morning to tell him his car needed a washing. And he didn't mean wash it "at your earliest convenience." It was understood that when Lamont told anyone to do anything, he meant *now*.

But Daryl had made it in, winning some respect along the way for being able to withstand the pressure. Most who thought they could hang disappeared once they found out how much work was required to become part of the crew. But the menial chores and public mockery that used to rain down on him constantly were only intermittent these days. Too bad the other guys who'd tried to infiltrate the TLE circle couldn't suck it up because the end rewards were well worth it. Now Daryl was a producer of hit records. Well, one so far. If "Say Whaaat," the new Radickulys single, hit big, he'd see some serious cash.

So why should I have to take the subway? Daryl wondered spitefully. And why should he have to pay out of his own pocket for using the corporate car service? He considered himself the oil in the Triple Large machine. The other employees were replaceable. He deserved preferential treatment.

Even though he was sure he'd soon be making more money than he'd ever dreamed possible, he couldn't roll like he wanted to. Not yet. In preparation for his eventual jump in tax brackets, he had toured some pricey apartments with a real estate broker, telling the woman he was looking for "somethin' fly." That bony white bitch had held tight to her purse and kept a pinched little smile on her face the whole time and all the doormen at the buildings they visited had looked at him like he was some common thug.

Or had they? Sometimes he felt like he was becoming para-noid—he had to cut down on the weed! He had noticed that Lamont would be at a party stone-cold sober while everyone around him was drunk or high. And Lamont would be having as much fun as the rest of them, if not more. Fat Man had told him he'd tried everything *once.* Daryl realized he had to keep his mind right if he was going to make it to the top.

But he was so out of his element rolling with Lamont, who could talk shit with street niggas one minute and take a meeting in a board-room on Madison Avenue the next. Lamont, who'd commit fouls that no one had the guts to call during his pickup b-ball games at his Hamptons spread, then head into town for his favorite snack, bagels and lox. The regular pickup players were Lamont's big-money "net-working" pals. Some were white, some were black, and there was one Asian Internet gazillionaire who looked like a college freshman and dressed like one, too. They all had two things in common—none could ball and they were all self-important dicks. They followed Lamont's cue and treated Daryl like gum stuck to the bottom of their sneakers, never inviting him to the post-game chowdowns. For the longest time, he'd thought it was bagels and "locks" and he couldn't figure out what that meant. Then one weekend he was sent to Twice Upon a Bagel to pick up Lamont's lunch and the secret of the lox was unlocked.

Daryl wished he had Lamont's social dexterity, but having grown up in a trailer, drinking Kool-Aid out of old peanut butter jars, it was a difficult quality to master. When Dicky, his childhood friend—

turned–rap star, had brought him up to New York close to three years ago, it was like being called up from the minors. At the time, Daryl's most treasured possession had been a fourteen-carat-gold Mickey Mouse pendant and he'd worn his hair in sloppy braids that made him look like Celie from *The Color Purple*. He thought he was fly but Dicky, who'd always had an innate sense of cool, disabused him of that notion. Dicky took him shopping for all the proper hip-hop gear—throwback jerseys, fitted baseball caps, jeans and sweatsuits by Sean John, Akademiks, and Rocawear, and the newest kicks.

Now that he had worked his way into the Triple Large crew, things were looking up. But not far enough.

Daryl threw up the hood of his Phat Farm sweatshirt and shoved his balled fists into its front pocket. Keeping Imani's package tucked firmly under one arm, he headed for the nearest subway station, cursing under his breath the whole way.

MIMI WALKED OUT OF THE HOTEL and a cab stopped for her right away.

"Hey, where you going?"

She turned around to find Kenny standing by the hotel entrance, sucking on a Newport in the chilly air. He'd just returned from having a lap dance at Stilettos in Times Square.

"To meet a friend," she stammered, opening the taxi door.

He squinted at her. "What friend?"

"Go upstairs," Mimi said without meeting his gaze. "They'll tell you. I'll be back soon." She slammed the door and the driver asked her where she wanted to go.

"Eighty-six Walker Street," she said, glancing toward the entrance of the hotel.

Kenny stubbed out his cigarette and looked back at her. He held his hand up to his ear in a gesture that she instantly knew meant "Did they call?"

As the driver pulled off, Mimi shook her head and averted her eyes, mouthing the word "No."

A BEAD OF SWEAT rushed down Lamont's forehead. He wriggled his nose and picked up his pace on the treadmill, his eyes glued to the three flat screens hanging on the wall in front of him. The televisions were a recent installation. Lamont hated flipping back and forth between channels. He might miss something. The TVs were tuned, as always, to BET, MTV, and CNN. He tried to catch *Moneyline with Lou Dobbs* whenever he could. Lamont's personal motto was "If it don't make dollars, it don't make sense." The three screens were like his own customized stock ticker flickering with cultural currency.

He pounded the conveyor belt until his white Nike T-shirt was clinging to his damp, protruding belly. He cut off the treadmill, stepped down, and grabbed a bottle of Dasani from the refrigerator in the small upstairs bar. Guzzling the ice-cold water, he snatched a fluffy white towel from the basket next to the massage table and stepped out onto his terrace to cool off for a minute. Taking in the panoramic view, he savored a momentary feeling of satisfaction.

This deck had more square footage than the entire apartment where he had grown up in the Marcy projects in Bed-Stuy. He looked out and spotted the Brooklyn watchtower. He hadn't been over to the old neighborhood in a while. Not since he'd convinced his father to move to an upscale retirement community in Florida. The warm weather was better for his father's chronic joint problems.

Lamont Sr. called the records his son produced "jump up music." "Every time you see one of these videos, they're always hopping around like jumpin' beans! Can't none of those kids stay still?" A civil servant for thirty-nine years, Lamont Sr. would often preach: "A man can make good money, but all that money can't make him a good man."

Simply saying, "I'm proud of you, son," wasn't his father's way. Lamont's beloved mother picked up the slack with a pride in her eldest son that bordered on idolatry. Now that Pops was living in Florida and Mama had her own luxurious condo uptown, there was no need for him ever to go back to the old 'hood. Manhattan was Lamont's 'hood now.

He stepped back inside, whipped off his T-shirt, and tossed it in the laundry hamper—which could have been more accurately described as a trash can. His obsession with cleanliness—bordering on neurosis—meant he wore his gym clothes one time only. His housekeeper had orders to dispose of the clothing she found in the gym hamper.

He lay down on the exercise mat and bent his legs at the knees. Time for crunches. He liked to do this part of his workout shirtless so he could keep an eye on his midsection.

He had always been a bear of a man—six feet of solid masculine bulk with shoulders worthy of the NFL. Firm and toned. But, in the last year or two, his arms had gotten a little flabby and his midsection had expanded to unacceptable dimensions. He knew it wasn't solely due to an overindulgence of his wicked sweet tooth. He'd never had to work this hard to stay in shape in his twenties or even in the earlier half of his thirties. He couldn't believe he was almost forty years old. Playing basketball had always been workout enough to keep him in shape. But not anymore.

He clasped his hands behind his head and strained to raise his upper body. The first one was always the hardest. He felt like quitting after fifty reps but he soldiered on to complete the full three hundred, hating every damn one. He had no choice. That old-man gut had to go.

WHEN THE CAB PULLED UP AT THE ADDRESS Daryl had given her, Mimi looked in her bag for money. Daryl appeared out of nowhere and yanked the door open.

"You late," he aggressively greeted her, handing a ten-dollar bill to the driver. He sounded out of breath.

"Sorry," she said, as Daryl hustled her past the doorman, through the lobby, and into the elevator of what looked like an expensive hotel.

"Lamont don't like folks to be late," he said, fingering one of his cornrows, which had come loose at the bottom.

So is that where we're were going? Mimi wondered. *To see Lamont?*

Daryl rushed down the carpeted hallway like a harried traveler desperate to make a connecting flight. Mimi glimpsed at his blotchy reddish-brown complexion and wondered if he had some kind of skin disease. He didn't say another word to her until they reached the last door on the hall. It was already ajar so he didn't bother to knock.

Before they crossed the threshold, he turned to Mimi and asked, "Ready?"

That scared her. Ready for what? But she nodded, anxious to hear whatever Lamont Jackson had to say.

CHAPTER 4

◆

Hypnotize

"MONTAAAAAAAY!" Daryl bellowed into the cavernous apartment. Getting no reply, he dashed upstairs.

Mimi took a seat on the small sofa at the end of the entrance hall and removed her poncho. *This apartment has stairs,* she marveled to herself.

A few minutes later, Daryl returned. "Go up and wait in the livin' room," he instructed her. "He'll be right out."

Mimi had thought she *was* waiting in the living room. She began to head upstairs when Daryl hollered after her, "Shoes!"

He pointed to the shoes lined up neatly by the front door and said, "Lamont don't like dirt." He was lucky that Lamont had been in the shower just now and hadn't caught him upstairs with his sneakers on.

"And, hey," Daryl said, "don't be touchin' him, grabbin' him or nothin'...aiight?"

That struck Mimi as odd. Why would she want to grab Lamont?

Seeing her puzzled expression, Daryl explained, "Don't be tryin' to shake his hand or nothin'. He got a thing about germs."

Mimi nodded, pulled off her scuffed boots, and then walked slowly up the stairs to the main floor of the apartment. It was a massive open space with a wall of glass along one side looking out over the city. The kitchen had not one but two huge, gleaming refrigerators. The sheer size of the place took her breath away. She was amazed that all this was hidden inside a six-story building on a quiet city block. It was like opening a door and expecting to see a walk-in closet but finding a ballroom instead.

At the top of the stairs, across from the kitchen, stood a long, massive dining table made from slabs of the most beautiful wood she had ever seen. There was a spiral staircase leading to yet *another* floor. She wanted to go up and check it out but Daryl had said to wait here. At the far end of the room there were two huge sofas covered in cream-colored suede, two impossibly large brown leather chairs, an ebony concert grand piano, and a collection of ethnic-looking objects and tiny statues arranged on a low glass coffee table. Everything was expensive-looking, but she wasn't sure if she liked it. Nothing looked like it had ever been touched.

She walked over to the fireplace to examine the array of framed photos displayed across the mantle. Lamont with Naomi Campbell. Lamont with Mariah Carey. Lamont with Latrell Sprewell. Lamont with Bill Clinton. Lamont with...a white guy she couldn't identify. They were both laughing in the shot and the other guy's head was tilted so far back, it was hard to tell who it might be. She picked it up to get a closer look.

"Eminem," Lamont said, walking up behind her.

Startled, she quickly set the picture back down in its place.

"That was at his last album-release party," Lamont explained. "I had just told him he should have called his album *Nigga on the Inside*."

She laughed because she could tell he wanted her to. But standing this close to him made her uneasy. So did being in this apartment.

"Have a seat, sweetheart," he said, walking to the kitchen. "Pellegrino, Diet Coke, cranberry juice, Red Bull?" he inquired politely, his face obscured by the heavy stainless-steel refrigerator door.

"Um, cranberry is good."

He filled two huge goblets—one with juice, one with water—and took a seat next to her on the sofa.

"This place is really"—she searched for the right word—"big."

"You like it?"

"Yeah!" she said with more enthusiasm than she felt. "It's really...nice."

"Bethany did it," he said.

"Bethany?" He'd said the name as if Bethany was some friend of hers. Was that his girlfriend?

"Bethany Oglethorpe," he clarified and took a swallow of water. Another weight-loss tip from the annoying trainer. Drink gallons of water.

"Right," she said although she had no idea who or what he was talking about.

"She's an interior designer," he informed her. "Does all the celebrities."

"Right," Mimi repeated, wondering if Lamont considered himself a celebrity. She'd never heard of him until last week.

"But do you really like it?" he asked, looking around. He'd

bought the place for $3.8 million and paid Bethany an arm and a leg to do it up right. Elegant and masculine had been his only design directives. But did it look weird? Sometimes he walked in late at night, stood in the middle of the living room, and felt like gutting the whole place.

"*Metropolitan Home* called the decor 'eclectic,'" he said facetiously when she didn't answer. The only reason the wacky, overcharging design diva was worth her fee, in his opinion, was because a Bethany Oglethorpe–curated apartment generated press all on its own.

Mimi had no idea that *Metropolitan Home* was the name of a magazine. And did he say "electric"? She didn't know what he meant by that so she just smiled.

"So how old are you?" he asked, moving on.

"Almost twenty-one."

"Almost?" He smiled. Most of the women he knew—and some of the men—were trying to shave a few years off their real ages. Only a kid as young as this one wanted to round *up*. "I'm not going to card you."

Mimi managed a smile, though every word that came out of his mouth made her feel more uncomfortable. But his mouth, she decided, was the most attractive thing about his dark-chocolate face. He had full, sexy lips. The rest of his face was kind of flat, like someone had smashed it in and it had never bounced back. His close-cropped hair was going gray at the temples and before he slouched down on the sofa—*was this real suede?*—she'd detected a tummy jiggling under his T-shirt.

"So is Mimi short for something?"

"Marie," she said.

Lamont fixed his gaze on her. She really was a beauty. Compared to the other girls in her group, she was practically a supermodel.

"Actually, it's Marie-Jean," she began to babble. Why wasn't he saying anything? Coming here alone might have been a mistake. She should have brought Kenny! "With a hyphen, you know."

Lamont crossed his arms and began having visions of what she could be. At first, he had thought their audition was going to be another "Next!" situation, like the twenty or so groups that had come before them. But when Mimi sang her solo verse, it was like the other two girls had disappeared. And then it came to him in a moment of divine inspiration. He didn't need a girl group. He just needed one girl he could mold into a pop superstar. And when he accomplished that, the Augusta job was going to be his. No one called him a one-trick pony!

"But everyone calls me Mimi," she continued, waiting for him to speak. "But you already know that. Right. So Marie-Jean was my father's mother's name. My dad was Haitian."

Lamont continued to stare at her. Would her hair look decent if she shook out those mousy brown curls? He liked what he saw other-wise—the café au lait skin, the long legs, and, yum yum, those juicy lips that had a natural rosiness. Her dark sweater, which looked like it needed a serious dry cleaning, made it hard to determine if she had anything going on up top and her baggy pants made it hard to see what was going on from behind. She was almost five foot nine, he guessed. As a connoisseur of models, he could determine a woman's height within an inch at a glance.

"Let your hair down," Lamont commanded.

Mimi blinked several times. "What?"

"Let me see what you look like with your hair down," Lamont said with some irritation, because he didn't like to repeat himself. It wasted time.

Mimi tugged the band out of her hair and shook her curls out.

"Okay," Lamont said neutrally, throwing his feet up on the ottoman. "So, sweetheart, this group you're in is called..." Before she could reply, his attention turned to something buzzing in the pocket of his gray cashmere sweats. He pulled out a cell phone, looked at the caller ID screen, and tossed it onto the table.

"Heartsong," Mimi answered brightly.

Lamont smirked. "Your manager come up with that?"

"No," she said, slightly offended. "I did."

"And you're proud of that I can see."

"Well, we want to sing songs that, you know, mean something," she said, trying to read his manner to decide what she should say next. *I can do this,* she told herself. "Songs from the heart," she continued, as full of herself as she could manage. "We don't want to be singers who just look good. We want to touch people with our music."

"Touch people," he said, and let out a noise that sounded like he couldn't decide whether to sigh or laugh. "Honey, you can't touch people"—this time he spit out the word "touch" as if it were a piece of lint stuck on his tongue—"unless they hear your music. And people won't hear your heartsongs unless they buy your record, which no one will do if they don't hear your songs playing on the radio first. And you won't get any radio airplay if you can't steal the program-mers' attention away from the fifty other singles that come their way every week. And even if your songs are on the radio every hour on the hour, people won't be interested in laying out their hard-earned cash for your album if they aren't interested in *you*. So don't turn your nose up at looking good, baby, because at this moment, looking good is your best asset."

Though struck by his cold assessment, she managed to say, "Really? I thought my voice was."

Her naïveté amused him. "Neck and neck, I'd say." He looked down and noticed a hole in the heel of her sock.

Mimi noticed him noticing, his brow creasing as if he could not understand how someone could actually be walking around in the world with holey socks. He probably had socks that cost more than her boots!

"I think you look spectacular today," Lamont said sweetly, leaning over to pat her hand gently as she repositioned her foot to hide the offending hole. After Daryl's stern warning, she instinctively pulled her hand away at his touch. She thought he looked momentarily offended. "That shit you had on yesterday was booty! Looked like something you bought on sale at Target."

No one in Toledo used the term "booty," but she could tell he meant it was tired, tacky, or something along those lines. She thought so, too, but Kenny had insisted.

"Is Jean your last name?"

Another phone rang and she paused, thinking he might get up to answer it. He didn't move an inch or glance away and it stopped ringing. "No," she said. "My full name is Marie-Jean Castiglione."

As she pronounced her last name, he looked like he had just gotten wind of a foul odor. "Damn, baby, that is a mouthful! That sounds like some mafia shit."

His cell phone started vibrating on the table. Again, he looked at the caller ID but did not pick up.

Good, Mimi thought, *pay attention to me*. He was going to offer them a deal! She could feel it. Why else would he ask her here and spend this much time? She wished he would just get down to it.

"I like the name Mimi," he said, almost to himself. "But I like Marie-Jean, too. The Haitian thing."

He silently considered all this as the house phone began ringing again. He looked over, idly watching four of the six lines flashing like Christmas lights. After the third ring Lamont's placid facial expression changed abruptly. "ANSWER THE MOTHER-FUCKIN' PHONE!" he roared in a tone so harsh that Mimi actually leaned away.

The phone stopped ringing.

"Damn, I got it!" Daryl shouted from downstairs seconds later. "Got three lines goin'. It's Imani. Want it?"

"No," Lamont boomed. "I'll hit her back in a minute." He looked directly at Mimi and in a soft voice that Daryl couldn't possibly hear, said, "I'm in an important meeting." He stared at her, then broke out into a wide grin. "Well, Mimi," he said. "Welcome to the Triple Large family." He stretched his hand out in her direction.

She didn't take it. She instinctively put her hands up to her face, shaking with excitement. "You mean we're signed? You want us!"

"We?" he snapped. "I don't see any we in here."

"What do you mean?" she sputtered, eyes wide. "I thought you called me because you didn't like Kenny, our manager."

"You're right. I don't like Kenny."

"*We* don't either," she stammered. "Not really. But he was the only person we knew in Toledo." She began jabbering faster and faster and Lamont just let her go. "I mean I'm the lead. I can make decisions and we can get rid of Kenny. I know he's an amateur..."

"And so are your two little friends," Lamont said smoothly. "I'm signing you, Mimi, as a solo artist. You have the voice, you have the look. You have it. They don't. Forget them."

She was dumbstruck.

He slid closer to her on the sofa. She smelled sweet and clean, like a mixture of Dove soap and licorice, and he felt a stirring in his groin. "Now," he commanded as if contracts had already been signed, "we have a company apartment. You'll stay there. It's completely furnished. If you want you can move in tomorrow and send for your things. Or you can go home, get everything settled, and we can wait until next week."

She looked down at her unpolished, bitten-to-the-quick fingernails. She hadn't heard a thing he'd said since "forget them." Forget Toya and Keesha? How could she do that?

"Talk to me," he said evenly.

She didn't know what to say.

"You want a contract, don't you?"

"Yes," she said softly. "But for the group." She looked at him pleadingly, moistness rimming her brown eyes.

"I know they're your friends, honey," he said soothingly, "but they aren't as talented as you. It might sound harsh but this is a harsh business. If you want to do this, and I can see that you do, you have to recognize that."

Mimi inhaled sharply. She felt like he could see her heart beating. He was right. She did have the best voice. They all knew that but that was why she was the lead! Doing this without Toya and Keesha had never entered her mind. They were a group.

Sensing he was making headway, Lamont pulled out the line that worked like a charm with every woman he'd ever wanted to get into bed. "You're special," he cooed, pausing to let the words take effect. "Talented." Another pause. "And beautiful."

She was flattered, but she heard herself saying, "I can't." The words sounded lame, even to her. She couldn't even imagine going solo. It would be like shedding her security blanket and she was not ready to do that. And Toya and Keesha would be devastated. She couldn't do it. She wouldn't.

"What a shame," Lamont said, his friendly tone cooling. She would come around but he didn't have all day to play guidance counselor to this child. He had a massage scheduled for six.

"They're my best friends," she said, flushing with anger. If he was so tough, why couldn't he tell Toya and Keesha to their faces that he didn't want them?

Lamont wanted to tell her how many times the supposed best friend of some girl he was fucking tried to give him some pussy on the sly. And that chunky girl with the braids? Lucretia, Laquifa, or whatever? She had "ho" written all over her. He was quite certain that if she had been called for a meeting here today, she would have sucked his dick and swallowed if she thought it would earn her a solo deal. He'd received oral favors for a lot less.

"I know for a fact," he said sharply, "that if either of those girls were here in your place right now they would jump at this chance and never look back."

Mimi smirked. He knew that "for a fact," did he? Toya and Keesha would never dump her to take a solo deal...would they?

"But it's just that..." Mimi began, unsure of what she wanted to say.

Lamont looked at her expectantly. He knew she'd be thanking him later for advising her to drop the dead weight. Right now, however, he had an overwhelming urge to strangle her. Was she really so naïve as to throw away a solo deal in order to spare the feelings of two no-talents, just because they all used to jump double Dutch together?

"And what do I say when they find out I got a deal without them?" she said as defiantly as she could. Without her, there was no group. How could she ever face them?

"Hey, that's on you," he said. "Maybe they can do background vocals." He stood up.

Mimi remained seated, her jaw firmly set.

"You're not going to get a deal somewhere else," he said, sensing she might be trying to come up with alternatives to his proposal. "Not with those other two girls hanging around your neck like cement blocks." He loomed over her, speaking with a stinging finality. "Maybe that fake-ass manager told you different, but I'm telling you the truth."

Mimi knew his assessment of Kenny's managerial skills was dead-on. Kenny didn't have much juice.

"Does he have other labels interested?" Lamont asked, 100 percent sure that the fake-ass manager did not.

"I'm not sure," she said, her eyes darting nervously around the room. "He might."

"He doesn't," Lamont snapped. "Truth is, I could pull two girls at random off the street who look as good as those other two and they'd probably sound better."

Mimi shot him a wounded glare on behalf of her girls. God, he was awful! How could he talk like that about Keesha and Toya? They were cute enough and their voices were good, if not great!

Lamont stood over her, wondering if this girl was ever going to come around. The meeting was over. He helped her up, wordlessly leading her downstairs, where Daryl was manning the phones. He glanced at the clock on the wall. It was three minutes past six. Where was his masseuse?

"I have to think about it," Mimi said shakily. This couldn't be happening. Not this way. It was supposed to be the three of them, together.

"Great," Lamont said easily. "You have till tomorrow." He stepped close enough to speak to her without Daryl's overhearing. "Mimi, listen to me," he murmured. He put both of his hands on her cheeks and stooped a little to look directly into her eyes. "Toledo is no place for a girl like you. You're golden, honey, and you don't even know it. This is the way it has to be. Trust me." He kissed her on the forehead. "I'm a star-maker, baby," he said with a huge grin. "And, believe me, you are going to be a star!"

Corniest line in the world, but that was the kind of Hollywood movie bullshit that he knew she wanted to hear.

"HEY, CONGRATS," Daryl called out, hurrying down the hallway after Mimi, her bag on his shoulder and her poncho and boots in his arms. She'd forgotten everything, wandering out into the hall like a sleepwalker. "You can call me Daryl but my peeps just call me Country D 'cause I'm from down south," he said.

The elevator doors opened and she seemed to float inside.

"Mimi. That's a hot name!" he continued, following her. "I groom acts so I got a big say when it comes to details like that. Names and shit. I produce, too."

Mimi did not respond. Daryl was beginning to think she was deliberately ignoring him. She'd had plenty to say to Lamont, the big bossman. But she couldn't say shit to him? *The minute you get a deal, you turn into a diva, huh?* Who'd listened to her group's crude demo? Him! Who'd brought it to Lamont's attention? Country D! If it wasn't for him, she wouldn't even be here!

Arriving downstairs, she hurried out of the elevator, but the coolness of the lobby tile startled her back to reality. She turned around just as Daryl dropped her boots, bag, and poncho to the elevator floor.

Daryl strode through the lobby, thinking, *If this uppity chick thinks I'm going to play houseboy to her Cinderella she's out of her pretty little head!*

He walked out to Lamont's Suburban, with the 3LARGE license plate, which was idling by the curb. After pulling on her boots in the lobby, Mimi followed.

"Yo, shoot her up to the Chesterfield on Thirty-seventh," Daryl said, rousing Carlos from his catnap. "And be back by eight to get Monty for dinner."

"The Chesterfield," Carlos muttered. "Where's that?"

"On Thirty-seventh, nigga!"

Daryl was simmering. Lamont never let *him* floss around town in his whip! "I'll call you tomorrow to touch base," Daryl said gruffly and turned to head back into the building, leaving Mimi to struggle with the door. Daryl knew Carlos, a quiet man with menacing eyes, never performed any official chauffeur duties. He was just a thirty-six-year-old b-boy on parole whose full-time job was safely shuttling Lamont around town.

Mimi slid onto the seat, a grim look on her pretty face. The back windows were half open and the crisp air felt good. Raising her pouty lips up to the opening in the window, she called out, "Country D..."

Oh, the princess had something to say? At least she had addressed him correctly. He'd come up with the nickname "Country D" a few months ago, but it didn't seem to be catching on at the office.

"Yeah," he huffed, hoping she wasn't going to hit him up for some cash. Money matters had to go through Lamont.

"Thank you," she said quietly.

"No worries, baby," Daryl managed to say nonchalantly though he was caught off-guard by the genuineness of her tone. Thank you? No one he worked with ever said that to him, unless they were being sarcastic.

The Suburban took off and Mimi settled back, thrilled and panicked, Toya's words spinning in her head. *Maybe we're gonna get signed and maybe we're gonna move here and maybe we're gonna be famous...*

Maybe. But how could she tell them that, as far as Lamont was concerned, there was no more *we?*

CHAPTER 5

◆

Get By

LAMONT'S DRIVER HADN'T SAID ANYTHING TO HER. He was chatting on his hands-free cell the whole time. The drive back to the hotel gave her time to consider her options.

Option number one: Tell the truth. "Lamont thinks you have no talent and I should go solo and forget you." Not really an option at all.

Option number two: Focus on the positive. "Lamont wants to give me a solo deal but he wants you guys to sing backup. Isn't that great?" Toya might go for that but she could hear Keesha's voice already...and it was saying, "I ain't no backup singer!"

Option number three: Put the decision into their hands. "Lamont wants to give me a solo deal but it's on you. If you don't think I should do it, we'll stick together and try to get a deal as a group. If Kenny got us one audition, he can get us another." A possibility, except for the fact that their trip to New York had made it clear Kenny needed to be subtracted from the equation.

When she walked back into the hotel room, she still hadn't

decided what to say. Keesha was curled up in one of the double beds, Toya was staring mindlessly at the television, and Kenny was in his room, bent over the phone like he was praying to it.

"No call yet," Toya said, managing to be simultaneously glum and optimistic.

Mimi sighed, trying to sound disappointed.

"How was your date?" Keesha said.

"It wasn't a date," Mimi replied.

"Was he cute?" Toya said.

"No," Mimi answered, picturing Lamont. She had to tell them. She went into the bathroom and looked at herself in the mirror as she quietly rehearsed options two and three. But Kenny was still around so she'd have to wait.

By the time they'd gotten to the airport the next day she realized there was a fourth option: Say nothing. Go home and start over. If Lamont wanted her, another record label would, too. And Keesha and Toya *did* have good voices. They were a group and that's what they would continue to be.

TWO NIGHTS LATER, Lamont was sprawled out in what some considered to be the choicest piece of real estate in all of downtown Manhattan: the center banquette at Swirl. The booth was big enough to hold seven people comfortably, but the way Lamont and his cohorts spread out, there was only room for four. The center banquette was the perfect vantage point from which to see the entire lounge. And more important, from which to be seen. The crowd was strictly A-list—well-known actors, models, and cool media types who looked like models.

Lamont had invested a small amount of money in the place because he'd gotten to know the owner, Gustav, when Gustav had managed Cognac, a hot spot a few years back. Even though Lamont's monetary investment was negligible, people would say, "Hey, Monty, let's go to *your* club," as if he had poured his life savings into the place and built it from the ground up with his own power tools.

Tuesday was hip-hop night, so there was more color to the room than usual. When Lamont and crew showed up for a late dinner, the prime table was waiting for them.

"Wassup my niggas," squawked Nate Gibbs, Lamont's lawyer and closest friend, as he joined Daryl, Lamont, and Witchy in the booth. "My niggas and Witchy," Nate jokingly amended his salutation.

Witchy was a well-liked member of the crew because he had mastered the art of race-mixing. He got all the inside jokes, he could play the dozens with the best of them, he appreciated black women (he'd dated plenty of them), and when talk turned to racial politics he could add his own insightful but never condescending two cents. Even though he was a highly successful record executive in New York, Witchy was, in an almost literal sense, the black sheep of his family. The rest of them had shortened their surname, Mankewich, to the more ethnically ambiguous Mann. His venture capitalist father was a staunch Republican, his mother was a society matron. But with Lamont and crew, Witchy was accepted and respected (most of the time). He never mentioned his family or the fact that he'd been raised in Marin County, one of the richest, whitest enclaves in America. All anyone knew was his oft-told story that listening to Public Enemy's *It Takes a Nation of Millions to Hold Us Back* in 1988 had forever changed his life and incited him to "fight the power"—at least, in a way that was lucrative enough for him to purchase a loft in SoHo.

Nate, a forty-year-old fair-skinned brother with gray eyes and a bald spot on the top of his head that Lamont frequently advised him to treat with Rogaine, sat next to Witchy. He nodded at Daryl, who was looking as sullen as usual. "That's a fly sweatsuit, Daryl. Rocawear does infant sizes?"

"It's a men's small, muthafucka," Daryl snapped. "But when I copped it, I ran into your girl comin' out the boys department with some jockstraps for you."

Nate looked at him blankly. No one bothered to respond.

Lamont's eyes ping-ponged around the room. He waved at a raven-haired actress chilling in another booth. She was one of the stars of a hit show on HBO. He'd never seen the show and couldn't recall her name. But she was a somebody, so she merited a wave.

"So your search for a new act finally bore fruit," Nate said. He was already readying Mimi's contracts. "About time."

"Yes, Daryl's discovery," Lamont said, more to make a point for Witchy than to give Daryl any props.

Normally, Daryl would have taken this opportunity to toot his own horn, loudly, but tonight he was uncharacteristically quiet, acknowledging the remark with a stiff nod.

"Mimi our Haitian mami," Lamont said. "She'll be back in town in a couple of days. We can sign the papers then."

"What does she look like?" Nate asked. "She hot?"

"At this point, more like lukewarm," Lamont said noncommittally. "She needs some work. But she has the potential to be a real looker."

"We'll get her all shaped up," Witchy said confidently.

Daryl tapped away at his two-way pager, adding nothing to the hot-or-not evaluation.

"Travis!" Lamont cried when he spotted Travis Peters, the author of the most widely read gossip column in the city. "Travis!"

"Hey, fellas," Travis said as he approached the table.

"Have I got a scoop for you!" Lamont said, as excited as if he were about to hand the scandal hound color photos of Tom Cruise tongue-kissing another man. "I just signed a new artist. Mimi Jean. Amazing voice and hot, hot, hot. A real looker."

"A female rapper?" Travis asked with slight interest.

"No," Lamont corrected, "a singer. She not hip-hop. She's hip-*pop*." Lamont noticed Travis wasn't writing. "You getting this?"

Travis dutifully started scribbling in his notebook. "A singer? Great," he said. "Maybe I can run a little something about her."

"She's pop meets R&B, but with a real hip-hop edge," Lamont continued. "Sort of like J.Lo." He didn't like the way that sounded and immediately added, "But she can really sing."

"Great," Travis said, still scribbling.

"And you know being down with TLE, I mean, there's no better place for her to be. She has instant credibility in the hip-hop world..." Lamont went on for another twenty minutes, big upping himself and his label and managing to work in the impressive sales figures of all of his artists. He did this pitch so often it was like he had a press release on CD-ROM in his head and all he had to do was hit PLAY and open his mouth.

Travis stopped taking notes fifteen minutes into Lamont's PR spiel. "Great," he finally said. For a writer, Travis said the same thing a lot.

"So what day is Mimi coming back?" Lamont questioned Daryl as soon as Travis had ambled away.

The music was getting louder and Daryl had his nose buried in his two-way. To get his attention, Lamont dipped his fingers in Daryl's water glass and flicked a spray of drops into Daryl's face.

Daryl looked up angrily, wiped at his face, then snapped his pager shut. He was used to Lamont's childish ways. One minute Lamont would be barking out orders, the next cackling and spinning around in his two-thousand-dollar office chair like a kid on an amusement park ride. And Daryl knew all about the secret stash of candy bars in Fat Man's plush office.

"I asked you what day Mimi's coming back. I want her to sing the hook on that song with Phat E for the soundtrack. We need to get going on that."

"Um, I don't know. Maybe Wednesday." *Or maybe never,* Daryl thought.

Mimi had called him yesterday morning before he had a chance to call her. Their conversation had been brief:

"I'm at the airport."

"Your flight ain't 'til two."

"We're taking an earlier one."

"So you're goin' home to get your stuff together. Cool."

"No, I'm going home."

"Yeah, what day you wanna come back?"

"I can't take the deal."

"What?"

"I can't take the deal. Not solo."

"What!"

"I'm going home. I'm not coming back."

"Are you high?!"

"Thanks though."

Then she hung up.

MIMI SLIPPED INTO THE BOOTH at Winky's Diner in Toledo and announced, "Let's move to Atlanta."

Toya looked up from the menu. "Excuse me?"

"I've been thinking about it," Mimi said. "Let's move to Atlanta."

"Move to Atlanta and do what?" asked Keesha.

"Get a new manager first of all," Mimi said, closing Toya's menu in order to have her undivided attention. They ate here three times a week and Toya always ordered the same thing. "Then get a record deal. Get a new life."

Mimi's mother, Angela, came over to take their orders. She gave Mimi a peck on the cheek. "Usual, ladies?"

"Yeah," Toya said. "Bacon cheeseburger deluxe."

"Make that two," Keesha said.

"Make that three," Mimi chimed in. "But hold the bacon. No swine for me."

"We don't know anyone in Atlanta," Toya pointed out as soon as Angela had left.

"And why Atlanta?" Keesha asked.

"There's more of a music scene there," Mimi said. "We can meet people. And the same jobs we have here we can get there."

"Keesha doesn't have a job," Toya said.

"But unlike you two," Keesha volleyed back, "I got a man and I'm not leaving him."

"No, he'll probably be leaving you when he goes to jail," Mimi sniped.

"Don't hate because you're lonely," Keesha responded airily.

"I'll stay lonely before I get caught up with a drug dealer," Mimi retorted while Toya nodded and uh-huhed.

"He's getting out of that," Keesha muttered.

Mimi and Toya both had the same thought: *That's what they all say.*

"And what about you?" Keesha said. "Moving to Atlanta will put you closer to your man."

That idea hadn't even occurred to Mimi. "Who . . . Jamal?"

"Yes, Jamal," Keesha said. "You've only had one man in your life."

"He's my ex-man."

"Well, he's at Georgia State. You want me to leave my man while you're trying to get back with yours?"

Since Mr. College Football Star had dumped her, Mimi hardly thought about him anymore. The last time she'd come across a picture of them together, taken during the happy days, she'd only thought about how much she couldn't stand him now. Then she'd burned that picture like she'd done all the others.

"I am not," Mimi said persuasively. "Not at all. I'm over that jackass."

Toya and Keesha exchanged skeptical glances and then it was cheeseburgers all around.

CHAPTER 6

◆

Heat

IT WAS A LITTLE AFTER SEVEN IN THE EVENING and Lamont
was padding around his office in silk boxers and stocking feet. Two
dark suits were draped across the sofa. He'd just showered, applied
deodorant, shaved, slapped on some cologne. The private bathroom
tucked inside his expansive office was a must. With so many social
functions to attend in the evenings, it was a hassle to have to go all
the way home to change. And he had to get clean before he *got clean*.
He didn't want to feel funky underneath one of his impeccable
Italian suits.

Whenever he found something truly sharp, he'd buy two of it—
suits, shirts, ties, shoes, cuff links. One for home. One for the office.
His ex, Kendra, used to cluck, "You spend more time getting dressed
than any woman I know." He'd tell her, "Image is everything, baby. If
you spent more time cultivating your own, maybe you'd be a *working*
actress."

Reaching for a wooden hanger, he held an Armani up to the

light. So gray it was almost black. Maybe with the silver tie? No, it almost looked like a tux and this event wasn't black tie. The Armani would be trying too hard. The navy Zegna would be better.

Just as he was pulling up his pants, Imani burst in.

A pretty, earthy sister who sported long, neat dreads, Imani Spears was the one person he truly could not live without. Theirs was the longest, drama-free relationship he'd ever had with a woman other than his mother.

Seven years ago, she'd arrived to interview for the job of reception-ist dressed to *re*press, wearing a knee-length black skirt, a white but-ton-up shirt, and sensible loafers. Lamont hired her on the spot. She was a middle-class chick who liked hip-hop and Lamont didn't want some ghetto bitch answering the phones while snapping gum and being rude to people—which was what got the first receptionist fired.

Imani quickly proved to be invaluable. She showed up early every day, stayed late without complaint, manned the phones, made sure Lamont's itinerary was taken care of, and, though she was a tiny little thing, verbally checked any of the rappers who rolled in acting a fool. Within a year, she was allowed to hire another receptionist and she became Lamont's exclusive personal assistant. No one else was allowed to ask Imani to do anything for them. She belonged to Lamont.

Lamont's assistant now had an assistant of her own, twenty-one-year-old eager-to-please Vicki, who was not allowed to address Lamont directly and who stayed in her cubicle in the deep recesses of the office until summoned.

Lamont was not embarrassed to be caught by Imani hopping around half-dressed with his hairy barrel chest on display. Neither was Imani. She'd seen it all many times before. Anyway, there was a crisis brewing.

She urgently picked up the phone on Lamont's coffee table and held it in his direction. "Daryl," she informed him, taking the call off hold. "He's in jail."

"What'd you do?" Lamont growled accusingly, holding the receiver with his shoulder as he zipped up his trousers.

"I didn't do shit," Daryl said defensively.

Lamont knew that was a lie. He put the phone on speaker and continued to dress, slipping into his white YSL shirt. Imani picked up the lavender silk tie from the sofa and Lamont stood in front of her. He never could make a perfect knot like she could.

"We got into a fight on One twenty-fifth," Daryl related breathlessly. "We was comin' out of Sylvia's and we…"

"Who is we?" Lamont interrupted.

"Me and Dicky."

Imani paused in adjusting the knot and she looked up at Lamont. They both exhaled heavily. Daryl getting locked up was a minor annoyance, but one of the label's stars who had a newly released album riding high on the charts was a real issue. Or a serious problem, depending on the charge.

"How the fuck did you let Dicky get locked up!" Lamont snapped.

Imani knew exactly what her boss was thinking. Dicky had major press scheduled for this week. "He's taping One oh six and Park tomorrow," she reminded him.

"He's got BET tomorrow," Lamont snapped at the speaker phone. "How'd you let this happen?"

"*Let* it?" Daryl cried. "I was tryin' to break the shit up! We saw this cat on Lenox sellin' bootlegs of Dicky's album. Dicky started stompin' the CDs and shit, they get into it. I was tryin' to pull him off, next thing I know po-po got us both clinked up. One of them pigs knocked me on my head. They won't gimme no medical attention or nothin'. I'mma sue."

Now that Lamont had the details he felt relieved. This dust-up would make the papers for sure. Whenever one of his artists got into a scrape with the law, he'd say, "Is it gonna sell records?" If so, he didn't see the problem, as long as they hadn't killed anyone. This was just a harmless fistfight. Anything wrong with a little old-fashioned man-to-man combat? Not in his book. And Radickulys's image was getting a bit too clownish. This would make it known that, despite his fun-loving demeanor, he was no punk.

"Where's Dicky?" Lamont said, unconcerned about any lumps that might be forming on Daryl's head.

"They got him in some kinda special holding cell," Daryl griped. "Even in jail they got a VIP!"

Imani noticed line two ringing. She went to pick up the other phone on Lamont's desk.

"Th...th...tha—"

"What?" Lamont snapped, recognizing Daryl's nervous stutter as a sign of real trouble. "Spit it out!"

"Th...that ain't all," Daryl spat. "I had a...a...a heater on me. They got me on that."

"What!" Lamont raged. "Why the *fuck* are you carrying a gun?"

"Protection!"

"From who?" Lamont snarled. "The dwarf patrol?"

"It's Dicky," Imani said, holding the other phone.

Lamont hung up on Daryl and took the other phone from Imani. "I heard what happened, yo. Don't worry. That motherfucka was stealing from you. From us. Taking food out of our mouths. He deserved to get his ass beat. Imani's on her way. Admit to nothing."

Lamont handed the phone back to Imani and finished dressing. He pulled open the drawer that held his shoes. He selected the black leather lace-up short boots by Bruno Magli. *O.J. tarnished a perfectly good brand,* he thought as he laced up.

By the time he threw on his cashmere overcoat, Imani had gotten herself ready to leave and walked with him to the elevator. There was no need to discuss the bail arrangements. Imani knew the routine. Grimy had been arrested twice—for marijuana possession and for carrying an unlicensed gun. Flo$$ had been locked up for driving under the influence with a suspended license. She'd already placed a call to the criminal defense attorney the label had on retainer and he was meeting her at the precinct.

"'Night, sweetheart," Lamont said, strolling to his waiting car. "Call if you need me."

"Don't worry," Imani said, always agreeable, even when heading off for a long night at central booking. "I won't."

Lamont arrived at the Peace Games benefit just in time to have his picture taken on the red carpet with Irv Greene. One of Irv's pet charities, the organization funded workshops for public school children on how to handle conflict without resorting to violence.

Lamont straightened his tie, then stepped between Irv and some really hot actress on whose *very* lower back he smoothly placed his hand, and smiled wide for the cameras.

MIMI SAT AT THE KITCHEN TABLE and decided to test the waters. "I'm thinking of moving to Atlanta."

Angela Castiglione, a haggard woman of thirty-eight who looked ten years older, turned her tired brown eyes away from the coffeepot. "By yourself?" she said nervously.

"No," Mimi said. "With Keesha and Toya." It was going to take some convincing but she was confident that she could wear them down.

"What about Kenny?"

"If we keep waiting on Kenny to do something for us we'll be waiting for the rest of our lives."

"He got you that audition in New York," Angela pointed out, gulping her ninth cup of coffee for the day.

"And they haven't called us back," Mimi said, anxious to change the subject.

She was starting to feel like a complete imbecile for turning down the deal. Ever since she'd returned from New York she couldn't stop imagining what it would be like to be solo. She'd never allowed herself to dream *that* dream. For so long, she'd been dealing with other people's attitudes—"you think you cute" or "you think you white" or "you think you hot shit just 'cause you can sing"—that downplaying her natural assets had become second nature, a defense mechanism almost. So she'd never thought about being on her own. That was selfish. That was for a girl who thought too much of herself. And being out there on stage alone, without her girls on either side, was a bone-chilling prospect.

But Lamont believed in her. Lamont said that she had "it." *I do?* Lamont wanted to make her a star. *He did?* And Lamont knew what he was talking about. He was no Kenny.

"Kenny is full of promises he can't keep," Mimi stated firmly. "There's nothing for me here."

"I'm here," Angela said pointedly.

Mimi walked to the refrigerator to escape her mother's sad puppy-dog eyes. If Angela could have pursued her own dreams of being a singer, maybe neither of them would be here. But when Angela got knocked up and found herself abandoned by Mimi's father, she'd settled into a life of just scraping by, surviving instead of thriving.

"Well, you'll still have Jerry," Mimi called out sarcastically. Jerry Morelli, Angela's current squeeze-turned-permanent-fixture, was a squat, hairy Italian with greasy hair and a lecherous stare. Every time he laughed—*he he he*—it sounded like he'd just remembered a dirty joke.

"Leave Jerry out of this," Angela said, quick to protect the first man she'd ever been able to hold on to.

With a pint of ice cream in hand, Mimi went over to the couch, flicked on the television, and sulked.

Angela had a blind spot when it came to men. After years of romantic disasters, Mimi wondered why her mother still couldn't see worth a damn. The men who had come into her life over the years were no better than Mimi's deadbeat dad. Black, white, Latin, Angela had an equal-opportunity knack for attracting losers. They ranged from bad to worse, each sub-par in his own unique way. One was married, a fact Angela hadn't figured out—even though she was never allowed to call him at home—until his wife had called Angela looking for him. Another guy had punched her so hard he'd broken her eye socket. And then Angela had apologized for making him mad!

Sometimes Mimi played surrogate boyfriend, buying her mother a Hallmark card or flowers on Valentine's Day when she knew no one else would. Sometimes she was a best friend, listening to Angela prattle on like a lovesick teenager about some worthless guy and then consoling Angela when he didn't call. After the phone got turned off one time too many, Mimi started taking care of paying the bills and put her mother on a strict budget.

But she was tired of being her mother's mother. She had her own life to live. Let Jerry take care of Angela. He was another dud but at least he hadn't gotten physically abusive. When Mimi had caught him reading her diary once, he'd calmly shut it as if he'd been leisurely enjoying a good novel. "A singer?" he'd laughed. "Keep dreamin', kiddo." Angela thought he was charming. Mimi thought he was a world-class perv.

Right on cue, they heard a key unlocking the front door. Jerry had recently moved in. One more reason Mimi had a burning desire to move out.

"And here he is," Mimi said quietly, as the creaky door swung open. "Your Prince Charming."

◆

CHAPTER 7

Rebel Without a Pause

AFTER COMPLETING A MARATHON ROUND of phone inter-views in the conference room, Radickulys stopped in to see his pal Daryl. As he pushed a pile of rap and car magazines to the floor so he could sit in the lone office chair that was wedged between Daryl's desk and the wall, Daryl said, "Yo, did you see your review in *XXL*?"

"It's here?" Dicky's impressively picked-out Afro flapped back as he dove into the magazine pile.

Daryl's phone rang and he answered it with "What's poppin'?" Wrong move. It was Imani, Lamont's kiss-ass assistant. Her name meant "faithful" in Swahili, but the only person she was unfailingly faithful to was Lamont.

"Didn't I tell you not to answer the phone like that?" she scolded.

"What *you* want?"

"If Lamont hears you answering the phone that way, it's going to be your ass!"

It was a point of pride for Daryl that he could often get under her skin enough to elicit some expletives. He wished she'd said "fucking ass." Funny how she never said a curse word within earshot of Lamont.

"When you answer the phone, say 'Daryl McHenry,'" she instructed. "That's all. Not 'Who dat.' Not 'What's good.' You sound like a damn fool."

There was nothing Daryl would have loved more than to give Miss Manners a swift kick in the ass. It was bad enough he had to entertain Dicky in this windowless hole *that used to be a fucking storage closet!* He didn't want to sound all corporate and shit.

He and Richard "Dicky" Garnett had grown up together in South Carolina. Dicky, now twenty-five, was two years older than Daryl but he'd been left back twice so they'd wound up in the same grade in school. No academic role model that Dicky, but he was hands-down the coolest and funniest cat south of the Mason-Dixon line. He'd been the star of their high school, always drawing a crowd by spitting clever verses—which Daryl fed him before-hand—to snap on other guys or to compliment the pretty girls. Now he was a star for real with platinum sales, endorsement deals, more hot chicks than he could juggle, a plush condo in Fort Lee, New Jersey, and the brand-new limited edition Sean John model of the Lincoln Navigator which included a Jacob the Jeweler clock in the dashboard.

Daryl watched Dicky intently reading his album review. No more than a paragraph or two, but it still might take Dicky a while to get through. His reading comprehension wasn't the best but he was undeniably good-looking—well-built, with a silky goatee, hooded bedroom eyes, and charisma to spare, so Dicky didn't spend much time worrying about his borderline illiteracy. If Daryl were to disturb him right now, Dicky'd be the first to snap on himself: "Damn, nigga, chill. You know I can't read!"

After being summoned to New York by Dicky three years ago, Daryl had fallen in line and stayed humble. He'd hustled behind Dicky on the road, secured women for the crew, and taken the fall when a bag of weed was discovered on their tour bus by border cops as they'd crossed over into Canada.

Winning over Lamont was harder. For his first six months on the scene, Daryl had to address him as Mr. Jackson while Dicky called him Monty or "my nigga." But he'd made it to the next level, and catering to Fat Man's every whim—including cleaning his sneakers with a toothbrush for five bucks a pair—had paid off. Daryl had finally gotten his shot at producing and he'd received official writing credit on "Strayt Clownin'" after having ghost written some of Dicky's first album and even more of his second. Daryl's goal was to be bigger than P. Diddy, but like the legions of industry up-and-comers who were envious of the unstoppable Diddy mojo, all he did was bad-mouth the hardest-working brother in the biz.

Daryl eyed the enormous diamond jester's crown hanging from a platinum chain around Dicky's neck. That's what he needed. Some fucking ice! A necklace, a watch, a pair of three-carat stud earrings maybe—or damn, not even a pair, just one, diamonds of any sort. But he had to send money down to his parents every month to take care of his four younger siblings so there wasn't much left over for nonessentials. He was embarrassed to be ice-deprived around Dicky but he played it off like he didn't care. Last year, after Dicky got his Reebok dough, he'd offered to buy Daryl a sick watch that cost two times Daryl's salary at this A&R job. "Nah, homie, you know I like to keep it low-key," Daryl had said, turning it down even though he wanted it and how. He told himself he'd get that and more on his own one day. One day very soon!

"I *said* what...you...want?" Daryl repeated into the phone, slowly and sharply.

"I need to speak with you," Imani said.

"We *speak*in' right now."

"No, I need you to look at something. Please come to my office."

Imani had a desk all the way on the other side of the floor, right outside Lamont's stately office. Their spacious executive suite was behind glass doors. Daryl wanted to tell her that just because she wore dreads and got invited to every industry party didn't make *her* cool. She only got into those parties because everyone knew getting in good with Imani meant they'd go to the top of Lamont's callback list. She didn't even have a man to bring as her plus one. As far as Daryl was concerned, she was just a twenty-seven-year-old college dropout who'd worked her way up from receptionist to executive assistant by puckering up to Lamont's fat ass.

"You know, Imani, you shoulda been a school principal," Daryl said to ruffle her feathers. "You woulda been good at that."

"And you missed your calling too, Daryl," she retorted crisply. "You should have been one of Santa's elves."

Stuck-up bitch! "I'm in a meetin'. I'm leavin' in five," Daryl said and picked up another line that was flashing before she could utter another word.

"Talk to me," he answered expansively. It was Mecca, the cutie he'd met at Radickulys's album-release party and almost slept with a few nights later, after they'd shared a cheap Chinese dinner and a flick. She was only eighteen but truly talented between the sheets. And she knew how to cornrow! She'd hooked him up on all fronts.

He got Dicky's attention and put her on speaker. "Wassup, girl," he said in an intimate whisper. "When you gonna lemme get into some of that good stuff again?"

"Am I on the speaker phone?"

"Ain't nobody in here but me. I gotta run out to an important meetin'," he said, winking at Dicky, hoping to impress her and his homeboy simultaneously. "I'm tryin' to get my stuff together."

"So you still want me to braid your hair later?"

Looking at Daryl's messy cornrows, Dicky bugged his eyes out and nodded his head in the affirmative. "Fo' sho'," Daryl said, really hamming it up. "My shit is gettin' raggedy. Swing by the office, 'round seven, and we can get some grub first."

"Definitely. If I come up there, maybe I can get that new Radickulys CD!"

Dicky, smiling wide enough that his one diamond-and-platinum tooth showed, childishly pumped his crotch in the air while Daryl thought, *Groupie!* The first thing she'd said to him when she learned he worked at Triple Large was, "Can you get me into a video?" *Sho' nuff, girlfriend, but fuck me first!* As a no-name producer and no-title-having assistant who was often strapped for cash, he had to work a lot harder than Dicky to pull chicks. Hell, Dicky didn't have to work for it at all. He had to beat these starstruck bitches off him day and night. Daryl stayed in close proximity so he could help himself to the overflow.

"You know why I want you to braid my hair?" Daryl said, flashing Dicky a smile that said, *Peep the game, playa.*

"Because I do neat parts?"

"No, 'cause..." Imani barged in to find the two guys leaning mischievously over the phone, just as the words, "I love to be between your legs" slipped from Daryl's lips.

"Daryl!" Imani exclaimed.

Dicky couldn't hold it in any longer and howled with laughter.

"Daryl!" the humiliated girl on the other end of the line wailed.

Daryl quickly grabbed the receiver, bobbling it like a hot potato, but when he got it to his ear all he heard was a dial tone. Dicky doubled over, howling even louder.

"In a meeting, huh?" Imani rolled her eyes and gave Dicky a friendly peck on the cheek.

"These," she said, fanning a sheaf of papers in Daryl's face, "are studio bills that are going way over budget. You better look at these and come up with some answers, boy."

"They 'sposed to come to me," Daryl responded angrily.

"Yes, they are and they did. But have you submitted them for payment?" She nodded toward a stack of mail on the floor behind Daryl's desk. "You don't even open half your mail. The studio called me about it and I had the past due invoices faxed over."

"I'll take care of it."

"You better."

Dicky's head moved back and forth like he was at a tennis match. He enjoyed having a box seat for these frequent battles. Imani served up a lot of aces.

"Does Witchy know 'bout this?" Daryl asked.

"Not yet."

"Lamont?"

"No," she warned. "But if you don't take care of it in a timely manner, he will!"

Imani turned to leave. She had to get to her screenwriting class at NYU. Lamont was paying for it. Two years ago she'd gone into his office and told him she was thinking of going back to school full-time. She'd timed her announcement for the precise moment when he was fully engrossed in reading the cover story *Black Enterprise* had done on him called "Triple Large and in Charge." He was pissed because they'd underestimated his net worth. When she told him she might have to quit, he kept reading and said, "Go at night. I'll pay. You're not quitting." It had worked exactly as she'd planned and now she was on the second draft of her first screenplay.

Though she was in a hurry, she remembered something and spun around. "What day is Mimi coming back?"

"Um, Friday I think." It had taken Daryl two days to dig up Mimi's home number. He'd lost another day being in jail and then he'd called and left a message with some guy who'd answered. Mimi hadn't yet returned his call.

"Give me the number. I'll call her," Imani said officiously. "We need to make her plane reservations."

"I'm handling it!"

"Are you or aren't you?" Imani said, picking a piece of lint off her black wool pencil skirt. "You told Lamont she was coming back on Thursday. Now you say it's Friday, *you think.*"

All of a sudden, Dicky seemed to get real interested in an article. Daryl knew why. The name Daryl McHenry meant nothing around here. He had no clout. None. He knew it. Dicky knew it. But they didn't talk about it.

"Friday," Daryl declared firmly. "I'll call the travel agency and make the reservations."

Again, Imani turned to leave.

Get to steppin', bitch, Daryl silently commanded.

"And," she said, halting to toss off one last directive, "make sure you tidy up the apartment in preparation for her arrival. Including the bathroom. Spotless, you hear me?"

It killed Daryl for his boy to hear that. Dicky was a star and Daryl was Lamont's slave. He was forced to take a stand. But before he could come up with a snap, Imani had swanned off.

"Whatever," he shouted weakly, and then tried to get Mecca back on the line.

◆

CHAPTER 8

Sky's the Limit

"FOR THE LAST TIME, we are not moving to Atlanta," Toya said, sitting on the couch in the lounge of Wildside Studios. They'd just finished singing background on yet another demo. After all the free background work they'd done, Kenny was finally getting them paid. A pittance. They'd never even heard back after the Triple Large audition. Toya knew, out of all of them, Mimi would be the most hurt, but she hadn't even mentioned it.

Ever since they'd come back from New York a week ago, Atlanta was all Mimi talked about. Used to be that Mimi was the quiet one. The first time they'd performed at a talent show, she'd come down with such a severe case of stage fright that they almost had to pull out at the last minute. But Toya had seen her toughen up a lot over the years. Being in the group had a lot to do with it. Mimi had a beautiful voice but it took hearing applause from other people for her to appreciate it. And then after they gained a rep, all those catty girls from school who had once hated on her were out in the audience applauding, too. Mimi had always had a strong backbone, though—with that flaky mother of hers, she had no choice. It had just taken a while for it to show itself.

Now look at her. She was all ready to pack up and move to Atlanta, a place where they didn't know a soul. Toya wasn't going anywhere. Her entire family was in Toledo and she wasn't about to move to Atlanta to scrape and struggle, chasing some impossible dream. And after what Keesha had told her that afternoon, Keesha wasn't going anywhere either.

"Why are you so desperate to move to Atlanta all of a sudden anyway?" Toya asked.

"Toledo does not breed stars," Mimi said.

Keesha was slumped down at the end of the couch, and Toya shot her a look as she said, "Yeah, but Keesha can breed here."

Mimi looked quizzically at Toya, then she turned and caught Keesha making a face at Toya behind her back. "What does that mean?"

Keesha smiled nervously. "Well, I have some good news."

No, Mimi thought. *Please do not say what I know you are about to say.*

"I'm not getting fat," Keesha said. "I'm pregnant!"

Mimi looked at Toya as if she needed confirmation. Toya kept her eyes directed forward at the television and mumbled, "Don't look at me."

Mimi turned back to Keesha. "But you're not going to have it."

"Mimi!" Toya admonished in Keesha's defense.

"Hell, yes," Keesha said, terribly hurt. She rubbed her belly. "I'm keeping my baby."

"You better congratulate her," Toya said. "And stop being so selfish."

Selfish? Mimi wanted to say. *I turned down a solo deal to stick with the group! And now Keesha wants to have a baby with a drug dealer who already has two other kids and ruin everything!*

"Keesha, you have no job. Your boyfriend is a drug dealer," Mimi said.

"He's getting out of that," Keesha snapped back reflexively. "Anyway, we're getting married."

Toya hadn't heard that part of the news. "You are?"

"Yeah, we're going to shop for a ring tomorrow."

Mimi couldn't believe it. At that moment, she realized she'd been a complete fool. She was always thinking about everyone else—Toya, Keesha, her mother. It was time to start thinking about herself.

"Well, great," Mimi said. "I have some good news, too."

The girls looked at her expectantly.

"I'm signing a solo deal with Triple Large."

"Stop lyin'!" Keesha said.

"I am," Mimi confirmed, a bit haughtily.

"Since when?" Toya demanded, wondering if Keesha's news had sent Mimi off the deep end. Was she making this up?

"Since Lamont Jackson offered me one," Mimi said, thinking that Lamont may have been right. They probably would have dumped her if either of them had been offered the solo deal. Apparently, it was every woman for herself. "That's where I went that day in New York. There was no guy. Daryl took me to Lamont's apartment, this huge penthouse, and he's dying to sign me to a deal. A solo deal."

"And you're going to dump us just like that?" Keesha said angrily.

"No," Mimi said. "I turned them down. For you. But since you obviously don't care about doing this, you go on and have your baby because I'm taking the offer."

"You can't," Keesha wailed.

Toya was surprised by the edge in Mimi's voice. She was acting like Keesha had done this purposely to hurt her. But what was Keesha complaining about? "Keesha, you're pregnant," Toya reminded her.

"But I never said I was quitting the group," Keesha insisted. "I can have my baby and seven months from now everything is back to normal."

"I can't wait seven months," Mimi said, arms folded.

Imani, Lamont's assistant, had called Mimi at home that morning. Imani had been shocked when Mimi told her that she wasn't coming back to New York. Daryl hadn't said anything. Mimi decided that first thing tomorrow, she was going to call her back. God, what if they wanted to take back the offer? What if they thought she was some kind of temperamental diva?

"Look," Toya said before Keesha jumped up to fight. Pregnant or not, she would get into to it with anyone, even Mimi. "I'm quitting the group, okay? So it's all settled. Mimi, go do your thing."

Mimi's anger drained away in an instant. "You mean that?"

"Yes, I've been thinking about quitting for a while. The only reason I went through with the audition is because I knew it meant so much to you two."

"Why didn't you say something?" Mimi asked.

"Same reason you didn't say anything to us about them offering you a deal. Because I knew you'd be upset." Toya took Mimi's hand. "I went to Performing Arts because I liked to dance and it was better than going to the horrible school in my district. And singing in our group was fun, but it was always more like a hobby for me. But for you, Mimi, it's your dream. Lamont obviously thinks you have what it takes to make it come true. And you do. I always knew that. So I say, go for it. "

Mimi hugged Toya then turned to Keesha, hoping for her approval, too.

After years of getting into scrapes, Keesha had learned one thing—to recognize when she couldn't win. After a long silence during which she rubbed her belly, she grudgingly said, "Go on, girl. Just don't forget about your old friends."

"DID I TELL YOU ABOUT SUM WUN?"

Ensconced in a prime booth at Tartan, Lamont had been haranguing Travis Peters for twenty minutes.

"Which someone?" Travis asked, holding his notepad but scanning the room for other people of interest.

"My Asian rapper," Lamont said. "That's his name."

"*What* is his name?"

They had a brief "who's on first"–type go-round until Lamont grabbed the notepad, wrote "Sum Wun" and underlined it. "He's real introspective. A great storyteller. He's gonna be the Chinese Eminem. Album in stores in April."

"Great," Travis said and walked away.

Sometimes Lamont wondered why he needed publicity maven Ally C. on his payroll. He was his own best publicist. But he couldn't spin stories every minute of the day. He was a Bed-Stuy nigga made good and Ally C. was an indefatigable JAP from Lawguyland, as she would say it, but she could get real gangsta when it came to securing pub for her clients. So, in that respect, they were cut from the same cloth.

Lamont watched Travis make his way over to Don Gambino. Sitting with his posse, The Firing Squad, Gambino was guzzling champagne straight from the bottle. A custom-made pair of diamond-encrusted handcuffs dangled from the platinum chain around his thick neck.

Son of a bitch's probably on steroids, Lamont thought nastily. Lamont worked out to stay in shape. Nothing wrong with that. Gambino looked like he was training for an Iron Man competition and, no matter the weather, he wore tank tops or jerseys that showed off his pecs. Which Lamont thought was rather *gay.* Lamont had noticed that since Gambino had taken to appearing in all his artists' videos, his once hairy chest had become totally smooth. Whatever he did to achieve that effect—did he shave it, wax it?—was *completely* gay. The latest word on the street was that Gambino had had liposuction on his stomach and had a weekly high colonic (they stuck a tube up your butt to clean you out!) because it gave his abs a more defined look. If true, Lamont figured the man was one step away from a sex change operation.

But Lamont had to admit that Gambino had done very well with Supa Phat E, the star rapper on his label, Hitz, Inc. That's why Lamont was willing to shell out big bucks to get Phat E for the *Good Lookin'* soundtrack and why he wanted Mimi to work with him.

Now all he had to do was get Mimi back here so she *could* work. Imani had informed him that there was a slight glitch in the program, but he would handle that soon enough.

Travis was scribbling a lot. What did Gambino have to say that was so press-worthy? Lamont called him by his real name, Donald. His surname was Jones. Gambino was a nickname he'd given himself. *These hip-hop new jacks,* Lamont thought scornfully. *Gangstas in their own minds. They all think they're starring in a movie called* Hoodfellas! With his albinoesque fair skin, face full of freckles, and nappy red hair worn in intricate zigzagging cornrows that looked like an alien crop circle, Don Gambino resembled a ghetto Opie more than a member of the Gambino crime family.

All flash and no substance, Lamont had decided long ago. That was the problem with all the dawgs that were barking at his heels. Gambino didn't know anything about the streets. He was straight-up middle class, a graduate of St. Albans prep in Queens. He wouldn't have survived a day in the Marcy projects as Lamont had. Lamont had done it right, attending City College and studying business administration while promoting parties on the side. He'd interned at a now-defunct hip-hop label during college, then after graduation had worked as the label's promotions man for a year before he started managing one of their groups, Ghetto Soldiers. He'd seen all sides of the business and, along the way, learned how to talk the talk with all the white boys. He'd worked his way up and *earned* his success. Nothing had ever been handed to him. Now, after he'd blazed a trail as one of the early hip-hopreneurs, Gambino and those of his ilk wanted to run roughshod over it and acquire a fistful of bills overnight without a solid business plan or one decent suit hanging in their closets.

And they were succeeding. What other industry made you feel old at thirty-eight! For most men, that was an age when their careers were hitting their strides. But Puff had made the *Forbes* magazine

"Richest 40 Under 40," with a net worth of close to 300 million by age thirty! When Lamont had seen that, he'd taken the magazine into the bathroom in his office, locked the door, and let out a primal scream. Gambino, with the revenues of his clothing company, Threadz, growing every year, had a personal net worth of over 75 million. He was twenty-fucking-eight! *Aaaargh!* Lamont had totally missed out on the clothing thing. The garment industry was a totally different ball game and he hadn't had any interest in learning it. But now he saw that his singleminded focus may have been the mistake that left him choking on the glitter dust of these other Negroes. Even if he sold Triple Large one day for many millions, he still probably wouldn't make the *Forbes* list!

Everything was about youth culture these days. The entertainment industry wasn't catering just to teenagers anymore. Last year, Lamont had gone to a conference called "Targeting Tweens" with Verne DeLuca, the advertising guru. He and Lamont were considering forming a company called Triple Large Advertising to market to the urban consumer. Lamont had thought the seminar was called "Targeting Teens" and had wondered why Verne even wanted to go because wasn't that what they both did all day long? But within the first few minutes he got a crash course on this new demographic. "They're ten going on sixteen... not kids, not teens... they're tweens!" the keynote speaker said, looking like he wanted to bust out some pom-poms. "Tweens have become one of the nation's most significant consumer groups. Huge amounts of music, television, movies, games, electronics, fashion, and food are being marketed in their direction—and they're buying! Spending by U.S. tweens will reach nearly forty-one billion dollars by 2005!" Lamont left thinking, *Great, now I have to give a shit about what a ten-year-old thinks?*

The young ballers like Gambino and Damon Dash, the head of the Roc-A-Fella record/clothing/vodka/film empire, always made a show of paying Lamont conspicuous respect but somehow it felt more like disrespect to him. Meanwhile, they all bowed at the altar of Russell Simmons. They acted like "the godfather of hip-hop" had invented the whole shit! Russell was a shrewd businessman and he had retreated from the music scene years ago, after selling his share of Def Jam Records for $100 million. Now he devoted more attention to his clothing line, Phat Farm, and every time Lamont ran into him Russ was either going to or coming from a yoga class. Talk about queer! Lamont thought Russell's semiretirement was a perfect opportunity to step into the godfather's shell-toes and lord over the industry. But the people whose opinions counted had been slow to come around.

Lamont's eyes bore down on Gambino in his Allen Iverson jersey. It didn't matter if you were from Philadelphia or not, all the hip-hop kids rocked number 3 Sixers jerseys because Iverson got down like them. AI's cornrows and the $300,000 worth of ice glittering around his neck, on his wrist, and in both lobes perfectly complemented his fuck-you attitude.

Gambino was a hip-hop *kid* as far as Lamont was concerned. *He's a child, an amateur,* Lamont reassured himself, despite the fact that the "don" was the multimillionaire CEO of his own hip-hop conglomerate. Lamont tried to clear his mind. He knew he conducted these internal dialogues whenever he experienced a flash of self-doubt. The flashes had begun to come so frequently and unexpectedly that he felt like he was suffering from some form of early-onset male menopause.

He now noticed Daryl was also wearing an Iverson jersey that had been concealed under his jacket earlier. Lamont looked over the girl who Daryl was crowding in the corner and decided she had too much flab hanging over the waist of her jeans. She was "semi." He'd let Daryl have her.

Enjoy yourself tonight, playa, Lamont thought. *Because come tomorrow it's ass-kicking time.*

Lamont unconsciously rubbed his gut under his brown cashmere sweater. He was beginning to hate those number 3 jerseys mocking him at every turn. He felt like Michael Jordan guarding Iverson. Once MVP but now fearing one good crossover dribble would have everyone wondering why he couldn't just relinquish his throne gracefully and go play a round of golf.

Gambino caught Lamont's eye and raised his bottle of Cris in salute. Lamont raised his bottle of spring water in return but he didn't budge. There was an awkward moment until Gambino squeezed out of his booth, yanked the brim of his sideways-turned Phillies cap, and headed in Lamont's direction.

That's right, son, Lamont thought. *Kiss my ring.*

◆

CHAPTER 9

Takeover

THE SWEATY, MIDDLE-AGED WHITE MAN threw his basket full of items onto the conveyor belt. Looking at her name tag, he said, "That your real name?"

"Mimi," she said cheerily, beginning to scan his items. "That's me." For the first time in three years, she didn't mind idle chatter from male customers. Soon she'd be out of here.

She had called Imani first thing this morning and was told that both Imani and Daryl were out of the office but that they would call her back tomorrow. When she'd gone to work, she'd imagined the conversation she'd soon have with Herbie, Sav-Mart manager and first-class dick. She had two words for him: *See ya!* But she decided it was better to speak to Imani or Daryl first before doing anything rash. It wasn't official yet.

"Sometimes I see people wearing name tags and think, 'That girl doesn't look like a Diane or a Gwen. Like they picked up any tag,'" the man rambled on, though she wasn't paying him much attention. She couldn't stop daydreaming about being solo. Maybe she could record some of her own songs instead of the mediocre material that Kenny had made them record for the demo. "You ever feel like doing that?"

"Doing what?" she asked.

"Pretending to be someone else."

"All the time," she said, thinking, *Those days are over.* She was going to be a signed recording artist. A *solo* artist. Good-bye Toledo! Good-bye Sav-Mart! And good-bye Jerry!

The man leaned closer and whispered, "You know, I like the sisters."

And good-bye to jackasses like you, she thought gleefully.

"Maybe I'll see you again sometime soon," the sweaty, sister-loving irritant said as he handed her a twenty.

She broke into a wide smile and replied, "Not around here you won't."

She got out of work early by faking an upset stomach and cruised around the mall. Everything looked different. When she saw couples holding hands, she didn't feel the slightest twinge of jealousy. She was going to have songs on the radio and videos on MTV, and Jamal was going to be sorry for what he'd done to her. And New York was a big city. She'd meet somebody better than Jamal in no time. Someone who was going to treat her right and adore her.

She went into a couple of stores and instead of agonizing about making purchases like she usually did, she treated herself. Two pairs of shoes at Nine West and three—count 'em three—pairs of jeans at the Gap. She was worth it.

And then, instead of taking the bus home, she called a cab. Usually she did that only if she was working late at night—and even then, only if she couldn't get a ride from someone at the store.

She wondered what her mother would say. She hadn't told her about it because Angela got hysterical about everything, good or bad. And if Jerry had gotten wind of it, he would have tied her up and taken her back to New York himself and tried to collect a finder's fee.

She decided she'd wait and tell them once she knew for sure. That was her plan. But when the cab pulled up to her house she realized something was definitely up. The limo parked out front tipped her off.

She opened the front door and laid eyes on the oddest assemblage of people she'd ever seen.

Imani was sitting at the kitchen table with Angela, who was holding a mug of coffee in an unsteady hand.

Daryl was perched on the kitchen counter, tapping like mad on his two-way.

The guy they called Witchy, who had been at the audition, was reclining in the armchair, holding the TV remote control and talking on his cell.

At one end of the sofa was Jerry, who for once had the decency to be wearing jeans and a shirt with sleeves, instead of his usual grubby boxers and wife-beater. Lamont was huddled all the way at the other end as if Jerry were covered in anthrax.

She walked in and all six people in the cramped space looked up at her.

"Nice place you've got here," Lamont said in greeting.

Mimi cringed, having a blinding flashback to Lamont's luxurious digs. All the things she had stopped noticing about their ramshackle house came into sharp focus. The clanging radiator. The grease spot on the kitchen wall. The threadbare carpet under Lamont's polished black shoes.

"Mimi, why didn't you tell us?" Angela wailed. "They want you to sign a record deal!"

"I was informed," Lamont said, "that you're having some second thoughts."

Lamont glanced crossly at Daryl, who seemed to be trying to hide behind the kitchen wall. Daryl passed the buck and slapped Imani with a murderous glare. That nosy bitch had to call Mimi when he'd told her not to. And, of course, she'd then gone and snitched to Lamont.

"But we told him you're going to take it," Jerry chimed in.

"Who are *you* to tell them anything," Mimi snapped. She could already see his pupils turning into dollar signs. Ka-ching!

Angela was sitting silently at the kitchen table, afraid to make a peep in front of these people. When they'd rung her doorbell this afternoon, she hadn't known what was going on but she'd tried to be hospitable. Once they'd explained the purpose of their visit, they tried to contact Mimi at work but she had already left and no one knew where she'd gone. Lamont sat down, apparently to wait for Mimi's return, though he hadn't asked if he could stay. Then everyone else settled in because he had.

Lamont didn't look like Angela imagined a "rap person" would. The only hip-hop person she really could identify was Puff Daddy (if the name P. Diddy had come up she would have thought that was someone, or something, entirely different), and when she'd seen him on TV he usually wore lots of gaudy jewelry and a shifty expression. Lamont was wearing a fancy navy pinstripe suit with a crisp white shirt open at the neck and some beautiful jewelry—one diamond earring and a lovely pinkie ring. He seemed very nice and his executive assistant was such a pleasant girl.

Jerry had come home a while ago and been briefed. He confidently declared that this was a good deal Lamont was offering and Mimi should take it. Angela had no opinion of her own but if Jerry said it was good, it must be. He'd been a used car salesman for more than ten years. He knew from deals.

"We brought the contracts," Lamont said to Mimi.

Imani rushed over and put them on the coffee table.

"You can read it all in black and white right here," Lamont reassured her. "We already showed them to your folks."

"Jerry is not my folks," Mimi said as she flipped through the papers. It was all in legal language that she couldn't decipher. And there must have been over a hundred pages.

Lamont was getting antsy but tried not to show it. He'd expected to have things rolling by now. He wanted her in the studio singing on that Phat E record. He wanted the *i*'s dotted, the *t*'s crossed. Done.

The mother, in Lamont's opinion, with her mango-dyed, feathered hair and jowls that drooped like a basset hound, was stunningly unattractive. When she'd opened the door and he'd gotten a load of her, he'd struggled to hide his distaste. Pushing out cute little Mimi had obviously been her finest hour. The Haitian father must have been one attractive dude.

And then this cat Jerry had shown up. He'd thought he only had to deal with the mother! He and Witchy had to back it up and roll out their "she's going to be a big star" shtick all over again.

Lamont restlessly twisted his white-gold pinkie ring (he'd decided platinum was played). It wasn't like he'd had any desire to fly to fucking Toledo! He might have just sent Daryl, but after the mess Daryl had already made of this he couldn't trust him. Neither was

Witchy a sure bet. So he decided to hop on a plane this morning and get it done himself. He made Daryl and Witchy come along as punishment. They were cramped in coach—seated side by side, which pissed them both off—while he and Imani luxuriated in first class.

Lamont hadn't yelled at them. In fact, he hadn't said a word to them directly all day. While he'd often bark, shout, make demands and threats, he wasn't an out-of-control screamer. That undercut one's authority. Like they said: thin line between love and hate. He preferred the silent treatment. He'd found saying nothing spoke volumes. There was nothing worse than being ignored.

He'd brought Imani along for the feminine touch. He didn't want to show up, three guys, barging into this poor woman's house. And, damn, she really was poor. Now that he'd gotten a peek at things, the scene was looking pretty desperate. Mimi was going to turn down the deal to stay *here?* He probably could have shown up with a c-note and a McDonald's Happy Meal and gotten her to sign.

And, by God, they'd *better* be able to catch the last flight home or else there *was* going to be some out-of-control screaming tonight. If he got stuck at some airport motel in this third-rate town, Witchy and Daryl were both going to find a four-hundred-dollar John Lobb shoe stuck up their incompetent asses!

Mimi sat down between Lamont and Jerry on the sofa. "You know I actually called the office this morning," she said, "because I have changed my mind."

Lamont shot death rays at Daryl, who stepped behind the kitchen wall so they'd miss him.

"I thought you would," Lamont said easily, handing her his Mont Blanc pen.

"I suppose I don't have to read all this today," she said, clearly eager to begin her new life. "Just show me. Where do I sign?"

Lamont gingerly held the pages as Mimi signed her name in all fifty-three places marked with SIGN HERE Post-its. He gave her a hug when she was done. Imani told Mimi she'd call her first thing tomorrow to discuss plane reservations and arrange any shipping services she might need.

Lamont didn't like to shake hands with people—germs—but he gallantly went over and shook Angela's hand, then reluctantly shook Jerry's, bidding them a fond adieu before he stomped out.

The others were close behind, practically tripping over each other to get out of the house, though Daryl and Witchy were bracing themselves for the verbal tirade to come. With Lamont, you never knew when the storm would hit.

Jerry and Angela stood in the doorway, smiling from ear to ear. Lamont turned back and waved one last time before he ducked inside the limo.

As soon as the door was closed, Lamont held out his hands to Imani. Having used her superpowers to anticipate her boss's every need, she already had an antibacterial Wet-Nap ready. She slipped off his pinkie ring and thoroughly wiped him down.

◆

All the King's Women

CHAPTER 10

◆

Things Done Changed

THEY HAD HER FAREWELL PARTY AT WINKY'S. Mimi and Toya got tipsy off a cheap bottle of champagne, Keesha got sick from eating too much cake, Kenny, furious that she'd gotten a deal without him, showed up ranting and raving and was tossed out onto the street by Winky himself. Angela cried the whole time, her tears a mixture of joy and sadness.

The next day, Mimi was off to New York. Her first week in the city was already booked solid. Imani had given her an Hermès appointment book as a present and taken the liberty of filling it with appointments.

Mimi had lunch with Allison Beth Cohen, the PR dynamo who ran ABC Publicity, the firm that handled the TLE account. She was an impossibly thin, bleached-blond tornado of a woman who walked very fast but took tiny steps. Everyone called her Ally C., like she was a rapper or something.

She went shopping at Pottery Barn with Imani for some knick-knacks to warm up the company apartment, which turned out to be Lamont's former residence, a spacious one-bedroom co-op on Jane Street in the West Village. Imani said Lamont had been trying to unload it for over three years, but since no one was willing to meet his price it had become a crash pad of sorts for various friends and artists.

She met with a vocal coach, a maniacally cheerful older black woman named Yolanda who flailed her arms a lot. It had taken her aback at first that the label wanted her to see this woman for three sessions a week indefinitely. What was wrong with her voice? After Imani explained that even the most seasoned vocalists worked with coaches "to keep their instruments tuned," she felt better.

There was an appointment with Dr. Regina Lipsky, a sleek woman who wore kitten heels and a white lab coat and proclaimed herself "dermatologist to the stars." "*Which* stars is confidential," she remarked without being asked. Then, again unprovoked, she offered, "Well, Madonna is a *former* client and Versace's dead so there's two. Happy?" She gave Mimi a diamond peel with a little machine that buffed her skin, and put her on antibiotics. Imani scheduled her for a peel every month for the next six months.

Coming the following week, she had a dentist's appointment. Imani said her teeth were yellowish but the dentist would fix that. Mimi studied her smile in the bathroom mirror. Her teeth looked white to her.

Even Lamont, who exuded a "my time is money and you can't afford a split second" air, invited her out on the town. They went to some boutique opening where there were more bizarrely dressed people on display than there were clothes. Lamont looked like he was going to the Oscars. Mimi, who'd used a bit of her advance money to go on a conservative spending spree at Urban Outfitters, looked like she was going to the mall.

And there was a meeting at the office, where she had to sing in the conference room in front of twenty-five members of the staff. She sang "Amazing Grace" a cappella. She sat down in the back corner afterward and ten of the remaining staffers started talking about her like she wasn't in the room. The words "marketing," "positioning," "imaging," and "crossover" were thrown around. There was no mention of her singing. After about twenty minutes, Imani led her out but she realized she'd accidentally left behind the all-important datebook. When she went back in a minute to retrieve it, Lamont was saying, "Should we do something about her nose?" Everyone sitting around the table looked up at her as she reflexively touched her nose. No one seemed embarrassed that she had just heard that awful comment. They actually looked like they were checking out her honker, preparing to give Lamont a full report as soon as she departed. "Not to worry," Imani reassured her when Mimi told her what she'd heard. "Your nose is lovely. I'm sure the idea will be vetoed."

And yesterday a girl named Lena had called to make a date for lunch. "Yo, Monty told me to holla" was her opening gambit. The doorman had just buzzed, announcing Lena's arrival. Now Mimi looked through the peephole of the apartment's front door, waiting for her guest to appear.

LENA WHITAKER BREEZED INTO THE ELEVATOR. Lamont had told her that his new singer Mimi was "really hot." Mimi must be truly beautiful for Lamont to describe her that way. He held women up to a rigid standard of beauty and chased all those model bitches. Or maybe he was just trying to hype Mimi up because she was signed to his label?

Lena wondered if Lamont had ever described *her* as "really hot." Probably not. At five foot four, all tits and ass with only a hint of a waist, she shied away from all the lowriders she saw crowding the stores. Nevertheless, Lena Whitaker was not one to sweat a bitch no matter how fly, and she was convinced she could hold her own with any looker. After all, she had a lovely face—slanted eyes with the longest eyelashes, a cute snub nose, and cheekbones that could cut glass...and the brothers appreciated her thickness.

She was feeling pretty good about her cute thick self today. Her cinnamon skin was still lightly sun-kissed after an exciting getaway to Miami a week ago. That somehow made her feel sexier. Her girl Kiko, a half-Japanese, half-black makeup artist with a ghetto-fabulous flair, was working a photo shoot down there so Lena had jetted down for the weekend. Just to hang. Kiko was wild as hell so it was guaranteed fun. Who knew she'd hook up there?

Crazy G, Crazy G. He was all she could think about now. She'd met him at the album release party for Lady Di, the flashiest and most raunchy female rapper in the game. Her three big hits off her debut album, *Ladylike*, were titled "My Clit," "Ice Me Down," and "On Your Knees, Nigga." The party was at Club Rolexxx, the strip joint where Lady Di used to work (under the stage name Chanel). There were big-bootied girls flipping their weaves while they slithered around poles, offering lap dances that were paid for by Lady Di's record label. It was the best party Lena had ever been to—open bar all night!—and partying was her forte.

Secretly, Lena longed to be outrageous like Lady Di, who looked like a black Pamela Anderson, tousled blond tresses and all, pretty and sexy in an in-your-face way. Lena acted like she was just as confident, but Lady Di, who *Vibe* magazine had dubbed "the goddess of bitch power," didn't have to act.

Crazy G, an unsigned rapper and member of Lady Di's camp, was fine as hell. Tattoos all over his muscled arms, smooth coffee-brown skin, bald head, and the prettiest smile that shone of gold. The kind of thug that made Lena's pussy contract involuntarily.

He'd taken her out to dinner the night after the party to some soul food shack in the Opa-locka section of Miami. It was amazing how they were driving along and then all of a sudden the surroundings changed. They went from greenery to ghetto in one block.

He'd explained that the *G* actually stood for Greg, but professionally it stood for gangsta. "But when it comes to the ladies it stands for game," he'd joked. Lena, who thought it was cool and kind of retro that these Miami cats rocked gold teeth instead of platinum, wanted to jump over the table and maul him right then and there.

The feeling was mutual. "Come on nah, gurl," he'd whispered later up in her room at the Delano when her Cosabella thong was the only article of clothing she still had on. "Let a nigga get some dessert."

He had a tattoo that spelled out Crazy G in gothic lettering on his washboard stomach and it was underlined by a long stab wound. He was such a perfect physical specimen that Lena felt a momentary ripple of shame that she wasn't. Didn't bother Crazy G, who enjoyed himself plenty sucking ferociously on her 34D breasts. But if it was pussy he wanted, it was pussy he got. She let him dive in face-first and he made her come so hard, she went into spasms. People always said black men didn't like to go downtown but Lena had found that to be an urban myth.

He took off his boxer shorts and revealed the biggest dick she'd ever seen, personally or in a porno. She had felt it all night rubbing up against her, but once he whipped it out she was forced to flick on the light. Seeing it from all angles, it was a sight to behold. She wanted to devour it like he'd done her but...what would Lady Di think? He was in Di's camp and tales always traveled. Lena had learned that the hard way. And, fuck what ya heard, she wasn't no ho!

"Oh, is it four in the morning?" Lena had said to him. "I have to get up early for my flight tomorrow." Her flight was actually at three in the afternoon, which meant she'd have to get up around eleven, but that was early for her. "I should go to bed."

"You already in·bed, gurl," Crazy G had pointed out anxiously. "Come on, just suck me."

She'd kicked him out without blowing him or fucking him but she'd gotten hers. And *that* story made Lady Di very proud! Ooh, he'd been heated! But he'd paged her six times the next day and called her every day since, hadn't he?

Lena shuddered to think what Daddy would say if he ever got wind of her dalliance with Crazy G. And there would definitely be more hooking up in the future.

Lena's father, Marlin Whitaker, was an entertainment lawyer— no, *the* powerhouse entertainment lawyer—and now he'd gotten into producing movies, one of which had won an Oscar last year. He was on the board of the Fresh Air Fund, always quick to write a check for any charitable cause, everyone's favorite guy...blah, blah, and blah.

Being Marlin Whitaker's daughter made Lena feel like somebody and nobody at the same time.

He used to try to set her up with "decent" (read: boring) boys, spawn of his stuck-up friends. But her father didn't nose too much into her love life anymore, presumably because he was afraid of what he might learn. She'd only ever really dated one guy, a hip-hop producer named Trevor Banks, though she'd gotten busy with plenty. Her father didn't like the way Trevor's jeans sagged in the seat. For Christmas, Daddy had given him a belt.

Lena had graduated from Meadowcrest, two years behind schedule, because she'd been kicked out of four other private schools. For graduation, Daddy had suggested she go on an all-expenses-paid, year-long overseas trek with a friend so she could, as he put it, "expand your narrow, hip-hop-obsessed vision of the world." To Marlin, popular music meant jazz and Motown soul. Rap was not music. In his estimation, it was insolent noise that glorified criminality, degraded women, and broadcast a negative image of African-Americans to the world.

Sensing that the "find yourself trip" was just a way for him to get rid of her for a year, Lena declined. He was always so busy, busy, busy with his work, work, work and packing her off to India or wherever would make his life just swell. *Slow your roll, Daddy.* Whenever she was in a pinch, she'd invoke the name of her mother, Nancy, who'd died of ovarian cancer during her freshman year. (Marlin had the Nancy Whitaker Research Fund up and running six months later, and the annual gala was a hot ticket on the charity circuit.) The sympathy bid would work and Marlin would back off some but the truth was, Lena had been buck-ass wild well before her mother's death.

She told Daddy she would, in fact, take him up on the all-expenses-paid year off but she'd spend the year in the New York apartment and set her own schedule. What she didn't tell him was that she didn't really have any good friends to invite. Certainly not anyone who'd want to spend an extended period of time traveling in third-world countries with *her*, volatile as she was. After that standoff, Marlin had threatened, "You have one year, Marlena. Get it together or I'm cutting the purse strings. I mean it this time!"

That was eight months ago and Lena hadn't gotten it together in the least. She shopped, lunched, partied, got drunk, and slept late, struggling to get herself up and out of the family's Park Avenue classic eight to do anything at all.

Lena's only real goal in life was to snag a famous boyfriend. Now that she had Crazy G hooked, all she had to do was reel him in. Oh, and one small snag, he needed to become famous. He would. She was sure of it. He was a gifted lyricist, well on his way to stardom. Lena looked at it this way: *Get to the party early before the VIP gets crowded.*

She got out of the elevator and made a left. She'd never been to this place when Lamont had lived here. He'd asked her to show his new artist the ropes in New York and she was happy to do it. This was just what she needed. A new friend. Someone who didn't know how she regularly got trashed in the papers for getting fall-down drunk at some party. Anyway, that was all over. She was turning over a new leaf starting today.

She walked to the end of the hall before realizing she should've made a right. She walked back and as she reached to ring the bell of 7C, the door swung open. And there was Mimi, smiling. Lamont wasn't just hyping her up. She *was* hot.

◆

CHAPTER 11

How We Do

BY THE TIME they'd strolled to a little café called Tartine on West Fourth Street and ordered lunch, Mimi had gleaned a wealth of personal information about Lena Whitaker.

She was a recent high school graduate who was taking a year off "to explore her options." Mimi wondered what her definition of recent was since Lena also said she'd just turned twenty-one. ("You missed my party! It was the shit!") Her father worked mostly in Los Angeles but Lena did not go into what kind of work he did. She lived uptown in her family's apartment with no adult supervision except for her family's longtime housekeeper. Her older sister Alexandra got on her nerves. ("She's getting her MBA from the Wharton School of Business...La di fucking da!") She had a boyfriend, a rapper named Crazy G whom she had met in Miami. She was a hip-hop fanatic.

"Bitch, you gonna eat all that?" Lena shrieked when the waitress put a gargantuan grilled chicken and portobello mushroom sandwich with a mountainous side of fries in front of Mimi.

A woman sitting alone at a nearby table in the tiny bistro glanced over, obviously wondering why this pretty young girl was being called out as a bitch. Mimi winced slightly but Lena just scooped up a handful of fries and prattled on.

People didn't talk that way in Toledo. At least not the people Mimi knew. But she'd noticed a lot of people here did. When Imani had run into a friend as they were leaving Republic, a noodle shop on Union Square, the friend asked if she had found a man yet. She'd replied "Bitch, please." Ally C. had ended a cell phone conversation with a female rapper she represented by saying, "Bitch, don't get me started."

Lamont and his male cronies had a longer list of terms from which to choose when addressing one another: "motherfucka," "money," "pimp," "playboy," "playa." Mostly they just fell back on the timeless "nigga."

Mimi realized that when Lena said "bitch" she was using it as a synonym for "girlfriend." It was all about context. But she wasn't yet used to being on the receiving end of such language, hence her involuntary wince.

"So how do you know Lamont exactly?" Mimi asked. Lena was almost young enough to be his daughter. Were they close friends?

"I *been* knowing Lamont," Lena answered with a self-satisfied smile. Truth was Lamont had taken a seventeen-year-old, party-hopping Lena into his crew as a mascot of sorts because he was hoping to get close to Marlin Whitaker, one of the most respected men in the entertainment industry. She'd managed to maintain her position by keeping Lamont entertained with her wild antics. "I get invited to all the parties." Lena shoveled a forkload of goat cheese salad into her mouth. "Only A-list, nahmean? I know everybody."

"You know who I think is superfine?" Mimi said, hoping Lena knew this person. "That model Omar LaRue. He was in those Tommy Hilfiger ads, you know..."

Lena put up a *go-no-further* hand and exposed a mouthful of half-eaten salad as she said, "I don't just know him. I *had* him."

"Had him?"

"I was fuckin' around with him for a hot minute."

"No!" Mimi choked.

Lena nodded, stabbing at her salad. "Yes."

"I think he's so hot!"

"So did I," Lena said blandly.

"What happened?"

"He kept trying to do me raw." Mimi looked puzzled and Lena thought, *This girl needs to get a translation book if she's going to be rolling with the TLE squad.* "Raw. Without a condom," she elucidated. "And then I find out he gave his ex herpes!"

"No!" Mimi gasped.

"Mmm-hmm," Lena said with a disgusted curl of the lip. "So I ask him about it, nahmean? And this nigga has the nerve to come out with, 'I haven't had an outbreak in two months.' You believe that?"

"Unbelievable!" Mimi snorted.

"So I told him, 'Look, playa, I don't care if the shit is active or inactive. This is information I need to know.'" She sucked her teeth. "Niggas ain't shit. I'm so glad I never let him touch me without a rubber."

"So that was it?" Mimi asked, wondering just how many people Lena had "had."

"Yeah, I kicked his ass to the curb with a quickness. He had a little dick anyway."

"A little diseased dick," Mimi added, gleefully taking part in the man-bashing. Who would have thought Omar LaRue could look that good and be that nasty? Kind of like Jamal. Men were such pigs.

"I saw him on a huge billboard yesterday on Houston Street," Mimi said, pronouncing the street's name as one would the city.

"Where?"

"Houston Street."

"How-ston," Lena corrected. "How-ston. Yeah, I saw it." She leaned toward Mimi and cracked, "And I know for a fact those briefs are stuffed! *Nahmean?*"

"I know exactly what you mean," Mimi concurred, finally figuring out the standard English translation of "nahmean."

The waitress came over for dessert orders and Lena automatically said, "Nothing for me." Mimi pointed out a tasty-looking apple tart in the bakery-style display case and then, without prodding, Lena said, "Well, okay. One for me too."

"I really like your hair," Mimi said, admiring Lena's short Halle Berry–style pixie.

Lena touched it unsurely. "Really? I just had it cut. For the first week I kept thinking it was up in a ponytail, then I would put my hand up there and realize I'm damn near bald." She dove into the tart as soon as the waitress put it down.

"It looks really good on you," Mimi reassured her.

"Thanks. And speaking of hair, we have to do something about yours." Lena pulled a Palm Pilot out of her Louis bag. "I spoke to Rod at James Scott."

"Who?" Mimi interjected, slightly disoriented by all the unfamiliar names coming at her. Rod? James? Scott? *Who?*

Lena looked up. "My hairstylist, Rod Horton, at the James Scott salon. He usually doesn't have immediate openings," she said. "But I told him you were a close friend." Lena smiled at her own pull.

Mimi was getting more confused. This was the first time they'd met. Lena hadn't even known what her hair looked like until today.

"Lamont told me to handle the hair situation," Lena said in response to Mimi's befuddled look. She was thrilled when Lamont told her to befriend Mimi, get her acquainted with the hip-hop scene, and do something about her hair. Now Lena actually had things to put on her to-do list.

"Oh," Mimi murmured. Lamont hadn't said anything to her about "the hair situation."

"He said your hair was too"—Lena made quotation marks in the air—"neo-soul." She paused, then regretfully added, "I see what he means, boo." She tilted her head to get a look at Mimi's bushy ponytail. "Can you even run a comb through that shit?"

"Only when it's wet with a lot of conditioner."

"Yeah, you need a relaxer or at least a good flat iron," Lena said. "Rod will decide. He'll be back from Disney World in a few days."

"He went to Disney World with his kids?"

"He has a few boys," Lena cracked. "But they ain't kids. He went down for Gay Day."

"Gay Day?"

"Yeah," Lena said. "You know how they like to party."

"Right," Mimi said vaguely. Getting her hair relaxed sounded good. She never wore her hair loose because she looked like Chaka Khan. "Are you going to come with me?"

"Sure will." Lena put away her Palm. "What day are you going shopping with Vanessa?"

"Shopping?" Mimi said, lost again. "Who's Vanessa?"

"Boo-boo," Lena screamed as if all this information were front page news known by everyone. "Lamont's sister-in-law! She's taking you shopping."

"She is?"

"No one from the label scheduled with you?"

"No."

"Well, Vanessa could go all day. I can't keep up with her. So I might sit that out."

"Are you friends with Daryl?"

"Wouldn't say friends," Lena answered sourly.

"I don't think he likes me," Mimi said, hoping Lena could tell her what his deal was.

"Don't take it personally," Lena said breezily, having an internal debate about whether she should order another tart. She'd joined the Crunch gym three blocks from her apartment because she wanted to firm up but, in two years, she'd never been able to motivate and get over there. "Does he call you shorty?"

"I don't remember."

"He will," Lena said. "A lot of guys say that. 'What up, shorty,' you know. Whatever, whatever. If anything, it's a compliment. Like, 'What up, cutie' or something. But pay attention the next time Daryl says that to you. He says it with such venom. Like it's a putdown or something. I guess because everyone has been saying that to him all his life. He has a severe short man complex."

"But I try so hard to be nice to him. He's going to be producing my album. How should I deal with him?"

Lena had already decided she and Mimi were going to be best friends but with this question, Mimi scored many bonus points. Mimi was the new hot girl on TLE, the girl that Lamont was banking on, and Miss Thang was deferring to *her*. As Mimi stared at her wide-eyed, Lena gave the question considerable thought. She felt like the all-knowing Wizard of Oz to Mimi's guileless Dorothy. In the distance she heard a dog barking. Toto?

"There's no doubt in my mind that he hates you," Lena said bluntly, which made Mimi's hopeful expression sag. Lena put her hand across the table and softened the blow with, "Because you're very pretty"—that tepid compliment was all she was getting— "Lamont is high on you, and, most upsetting for lil' Country D, you can look down on him. *Literally.*"

Mimi nodded at Lena's sage assessment.

"Don't feel bad," Lena said. "He doesn't like me, Vanessa, Imani, or any of the women in the inner sanctum."

"The inner sanctum?"

"Lamont's people," Lena said impatiently. Did this girl need to have everything broken down to the letter?

With a hushed reverence, Mimi asked, "Are all the women in the inner sanctum beautiful?"

"You have to be," Lena said smugly, proud to be a member and pissed that she was probably considered the least beautiful of the bunch. But, getting back to the problem on the table, she announced dramatically, "Daryl is probably in his filthy little Brooklyn studio apartment putting a hex on you right now."

"What am I going to do!" Mimi cried, as though Lena were a tarot reader who'd just turned over the death card.

Lena pressed the tips of her fingers together. Her nails were painted white with chipping multicolored palm trees, a remnant of her Miami trip. "He *is* a hot producer," Lena very reluctantly admitted.

"He is?"

"Yeah, that song he did for Dicky is retarded!"

Mimi took it from the smile on Lena's face that "retarded" meant good.

"And, on the low, he writes most of Dicky's material," Lena said, snapping for the waitress to bring her a second tart. "There is your bright side. He'll probably give you some great songs. Just kill him with kindness," Lena said, deciding that was the way to go. "I suspect all that boy needs is a little love."

The waitress came over with bill in hand so Lena bailed on tart number two, which she knew she was dead wrong even to think about. Mimi immediately grabbed the bill, saying, "My treat."

Lena hadn't even reached for her wallet. "Thanks," Lena said, scratching at a palm tree on her nail. "I'll get you next time. Things get kinda tight for me toward the end of the month, nahmean?"

"No, not really," Mimi said, putting down three twenties. She barely had enough cash. That was a lot for two sandwiches and some tiny pastries.

"My money doesn't come until the first," Lena explained somberly. She was referring to her monthly allowance, which was deposited directly into her checking account, but judging by her dour expression you'd think she was waiting for food stamps and a welfare check to feed her starving children.

"I thought you said you didn't work," Mimi said, assuming that by money she meant a paycheck and also noting that it wasn't the end of the month. It was the twelfth.

"I don't," Lena said curtly, because the fact that she didn't have any professional goals and didn't aspire to go on to higher education was a sore spot for her. Time to change the subject. "Wanna come over and hang tonight?" She untied the waist of her burgundy FUBU sweats and exhaled.

"Sure," Mimi answered.

"Great," Lena said, throwing on her fur-lined denim jacket over her matching FUBU hooded sweatshirt. "Spend the night if you want. I ain't got shit to do."

"Okay," Mimi said brightly as they walked out. "Let me go over to my place first to get some stuff."

Lena immediately put her arm up for an approaching cab.

"Lena," Mimi protested, "my apartment is only three blocks away. I thought we were going there first." *My apartment.* Mimi couldn't believe she had a place in New York and a record deal. Every night she'd go to sleep hoping she wouldn't wake up to find it was all a dream.

"I know but it's cold," Lena complained. "And I'm full. I can't walk."

Mimi couldn't help chuckling and scooted into the cab behind her. As they waited at a red light, Lena turned to her. "So you never told me. You got a man back in Toledo?"

Mimi rolled her eyes. "Bitch, please."

They laughed.

◆

CHAPTER 12

Queen Bee

VANESSA DE LA CRUZ was gazing into the mirror in her expertly lit bathroom doing what she did best: admiring her own beauty. She brushed a glob of thick Bobbi Brown lip gloss on her collagen-enhanced lips, blotted, shook out her tumble of tawny locks, and admired herself again. Beautiful, gorgeous, beyond. Almost ready to go to Heaven.

She hadn't used any L'Oréal tonight, though the products cluttered her bathroom. A perk of her lucrative contract with the cosmetics company. When they had approached her, she was delighted. When it came to light that they wanted her to hawk antiwrinkle cream, she wanted to tell them to FUCK OFF! She didn't have any wrinkles.... Well, they were only *beginning* to sprout. Since she was supposed to look her age in the ads did that mean they weren't going to airbrush? She was thirty-one and annoyed that she couldn't downgrade to twenty-eight because her adult life was a matter of public record and some nosy reporter would surely call her on it. Oh, to be young again. In her business, she felt like an archeological find.

Vanessa had appeared on the cover of every major fashion magazine—all continents—by the time she was twenty. At the peak of her fame she had, predictably, dated a grungy twenty-something actor and, even more predictably, been dumped by him a year later without explanation. A string of brief and tumultuous failed romances had followed, along with the obligatory rehab stay at Promises that didn't take. By twenty-six, she had fallen out of favor with the fickle fashion flock and, like most models, had no contingency plan whatsoever. Having drunk from the well of fame and privilege, it was difficult to fade away into anonymity.

So she took the L'Oréal job. She had to keep her face out there. But she had her agent negotiate for added compensation for having her face associated with an antiaging product.

On the edge of the sunken bathtub sat Vanessa's best friend, Mustafa, a slightly effeminate, painfully thin native of Senegal who claimed to be a performance artist, though curiously no one, not even Vanessa, had ever seen him perform anything anywhere and he had no identifiable source of income.

"Baby, is that the baby?" Mustafa inquired lazily, flipping through *W.*

"Lupe's got it," she said, unconcerned, referring to one of her illegal immigrant nanny trio. Consuela was weekdays, Lupe was weeknights and Jomadi was weekends, holidays, and travel days. If Vanessa's husband, Alonzo, were here he'd go running. He had extra-sensitive ears when it came to the little one. He could hear that kid fart from three rooms away. It was *bizarre.* Yet when Vanessa would ask him to upgrade her wedding ring, he'd play deaf *and* dumb.

Alonzo was the vice president of hook-ups at Triple Large

Entertainment. That is what it actually said on his business card. Translation: He was the hapless brother of CEO Lamont Jackson. His responsibilities? Doing whatever Lamont said. His annual salary? Very high six figures. Vanessa thought he was a failure.

Alonzo wouldn't be accompanying them to Heaven tonight. He was out of town on some sort of business. Whatever. Marriage didn't really suit Vanessa de la Cruz.

By their fourth date, she'd discovered she was pregnant. They had done the deed on their first, even though Vanessa usually waited until she received an appropriately expensive gift before she invited a man to the paradise that was her pussy. But Alonzo, though not as high profile or rich as the men she'd been dating for a decade, was too sexy to be denied. Tall and ripped, he had short, wavy brown hair, warm chestnut skin, a movie-star profile, and a husky voice that made every stupid thing that came out of his luscious lips sound arousing.

They ran off to Vegas and were married in a $75 ceremony at the Silver Belle Chapel of Love without telling anyone. Except the press. It was so exciting. Vanessa decided to have the baby because—well, all the models were doing it! And she was on the cusp of thirty. Motherhood would be her next act.

She'd appeared on the cover of *FitPregnancy,* in a Gap maternity ad, and, nude in her seventh month, in an *Elle* layout. The accompanying profile (only one page when Vanessa felt she deserved two *at least*) quoted her musing about the rigors of pregnancy ("I've gained nine and a half pounds but the sacrifice is so worth it"), the joy of impending motherhood ("It's a girl and I can't wait to have another little me running around!"), and why she planned on naming the baby Vanessa ("Why should men be able to do that and not women? Carolina Herrera has a junior. I want one too!").

Turned out the amniocentesis was wrong. It was a boy.

Motherhood was the one thing that suited her less than marriage. Pedro Miguel Antonio de la Cruz Jackson was a cranky baby, and Vanessa was used to sleeping in. The round-the-clock nanny rotation took care of that problem. But Pedro, who had olive skin, big hazel eyes, and a shiny mop of sandy-brown curls just like Mommy, always smiled for the cameras, and wasn't that what counted?

Mustafa followed Vanessa as she traipsed into her dressing room, which was designed to look like a chic boutique. She let her long satin robe fall and stood, au naturel, eyeing the racks of clothes and cubicles of neatly arranged accessories. Every public outing was an opportunity to preen, another fashion shoot.

Ashamed of her body? There was no reason. Vanessa was svelte and long-limbed with curves in all the right places. She'd had enough reinforcement from photographers, bookers, and every man she'd ever dated to know that there were no words to adequately describe her physical perfection. Even after the baby. No lipo needed, sweetie.

Vanessa's first order of business after returning from her honeymoon in Cap Juluca, an exclusive resort in Anguilla, had been to hire a contractor to turn the workout space in Alonzo's former bachelor pad (big, and paid for by Lamont) into a closet for her constantly expanding wardrobe. Once married, Alonzo had expected Vanessa to cook and handle other such domestic duties like his mama had done when he was growing up. But when Alonzo had returned home one evening shortly after their lovey-dovey honeymoon, he'd learned that Vanessa de la Cruz didn't serve. She expected to be served.

"I'm hungry," he'd said.

"So am I," she'd responded, not looking up from her copy of *Hola!* magazine.

"What's for dinner?" he'd made the mistake of pressing.

"I don't know," she'd said, peering at him over the top of the magazine with a look of utter confusion. "What?"

When he suggested she cook something, she'd screamed like a banshee, "I'M PREGNANT!"

What did they have in common really? Alonzo thought their son was a blessing from God. Vanessa looked upon motherhood as a noose slowly tightening around her exquisite neck. Alonzo was a reformed bad boy who'd grown out of his hard-partying ways. Vanessa continued to live the life of a rich, unencumbered, socially connected twenty-two-year-old. Alonzo kept imploring her to quit abusing "that shit" for everyone's sake. But "that shit" was the only thing that kept her from confronting the grim reality that she was someone's wife and someone's mother and therefore expected to act as such.

They did have one thing in common: a love of rough sex. That, and the fact that they looked so damn good together, was enough to keep the marriage intact. For the time being.

Dressed in skintight white Frankie B. jeans sans panties, stiletto boots, and a fur chubby over a sheer white camisole, Vanessa struck a pose and waited for Mustafa's usual assessment.

"Perfect, baby," he cooed.

She snorted a line of coke, Mustafa followed suit, then they both donned their shades and were off without a word of farewell to Lupe or Pedro.

◆

CHAPTER 13

Somebody's Girl

"TAKE IT OFF, NESSA!" Witchy shouted.

It was one A.M. and Heaven was fire-hazard crowded. DJ Billie, a rail-thin Japanese girl with long multicolored pseudo-dreads, was spinning. People didn't really dance at Heaven. There was no actual dance floor. The chosen few who made it inside just sat in their seats and bounced rhythmically, waving their hands in the air or shouting out song lyrics. Sometimes, usually very late in the evening, an intoxicated girl would climb up on a table and gyrate clumsily.

Tonight Vanessa de la Cruz was that girl. With each off-balance shimmy, the straps of her silk-and-lace camisole slipped further down her sweaty shoulders.

MC Grimy, TLE's twenty-seven-year-old star, arrived. Lamont had asked him to stop by after his session at a nearby recording studio so they could have a meeting about his still-untitled sixth album. Grimy felt more comfortable in his Bronx neighborhood than in the midst of this A-list madness. He was anxious to get back to his regular habitat, which was sitting in his Escalade lost in a fog of chocolate thai. After peeping the overly trendy crowd out front, four members of his posse, The Dirty Dozen, who were riding with him decided they'd be better off blazing in the truck.

A known celebrity, Grimy had no problem getting through. There were actual pearly gates outside the club and a woman wearing angel wings who was sitting on a high stool with the God-like power to admit or deny entrance to all who approached.

"Where's Monty at?" Grimy asked, taking a seat with Lamont's crew at their banquette. Intently watching Vanessa's performance, no one answered.

A minimalist compared to his hip-hop colleagues, Grimy wore no diamonds, eschewed flashy labels, and kept his hair buzzed tight. Always dressed entirely in black as he was tonight—jeans, logo-less hooded sweatshirt, and work boots—he appeared to be in a perpetual state of mourning. In a way, he was. He had two tattoos—a black teardrop under each eye. One was in honor of his late suicidal mother. The other for his brother, a hemophiliac who'd survived numerous hospital stays only to be stabbed on the street, where he'd bled to death within minutes. Grimy got his record deal a month later.

Grimy had spent his formative years in and out of jail for small-time crack dealing. He told interviewers (when he actually showed up to do press and felt like answering their silly questions) that the time he spent lyrically battling other inmates "in the joint" had helped him sharpen his rhyming skills. "Lot of talented mo'fuckers in there," he'd say. "Just fell short."

A ruffian of the first order, albeit one with a 140 IQ, he regarded "studio gangstas"—including his labelmate Flo$$—with more pity than contempt. "A lot of niggas in this industry—and I ain't naming no names—get caught up trying to be something they ain't just to sell records," Lamont's thug genius had told *Rolling Stone.* "I don't do that. I'm a rapper, not a actor. I never knew my father, my mother killed herself when I was fifteen, my brother got killed a few years later. My reality is gritty enough. I've done wrong in my life, selling drugs, because people told me that was all I could do *right.* I've been locked up, in a *real* prison, so don't send me no video treatment where you got me rapping in a jail cell. There's nothing glamorous about that. I got a second chance. So don't take me back there, not even to pretend. I don't need to pretend. I don't need to *romanticize* shit. Everybody's worried about going platinum, being better, hotter, richer than the next man. But when you're number one ain't nowhere to go but down. I don't sweat the charts and I don't check sales figures. If you want to buy my shit, cool. If not, don't worry about me. I'm gonna be all right."

Mustafa was pulling Vanessa down from her makeshift stage when Lamont returned and spotted his multiplatinum seller. He approached wearing a proud smile, arms spread wide, and bellowed, "My thug genius!"

DJ Billie spotted Grimy and threw on "Buckshots," the hit from his second album that included a chorus of nothing but gunshots. The bullet-popping intro startled a few of the older clubgoers not familiar with the record. Nate, Lamont's buddy and lawyer, gleefully noticed some of them almost dive for cover.

"Where you been?" Daryl asked as Lamont slid down next to Grimy. "You missed Vanessa's little show. Thought we was gonna get a titty flash."

It didn't surprise Lamont. His sister-in-law was a wild thang and her attention-seeking stunts never stopped. Alonzo needed to kick her ass and he made a mental note to tell 'Zo that. At any rate, her titties were old news—he'd seen them poolside, peeking out of flimsy tops during runway shows, in European magazines, etc. He'd go over and make his disapproval known to her in a minute. Right now he had a story to tell.

"Titty flash?" Lamont said, a devilish grin forming. "I got more than that in the bathroom."

Nothing more specific needed to be said. Lamont was known to be an ardent fan of the blow job. Terribly germ-phobic, he wouldn't have unprotected intercourse with a woman until he'd sent her to his own doctor for an HIV test. Blow jobs were a way to immediately satisfy his carnal cravings with only a quick spot check of the mouth area to rule out any visible sores. Since his sexual predilection was well known on the party circuit, women who enjoyed giving such pleasure often approached him out of nowhere. Who knew there were so many?

"Damn!" Witchy said. "Who from?"

They all immediately began scanning the room.

"Her," Lamont said, nodding toward an attractive woman in her early thirties who was making her way through the crowd. "With the pink top."

Grimy's eyes canvassed the room. Whether performing or hanging with his Boogie Down Bronx dawgs, Grimy's ruggedly handsome face usually took on one of three expressions: rage, disinterest, or a temporary weed-induced calm. Unless performing, he spoke in a flat monotone, as though backing his words with any emotion was an arduous task he was not up to. But when he located the woman in question, his eyes flashed and he nearly shrieked. "That old white bitch?"

"She was waiting outside the bathroom when I came out," Lamont said. The guys all huddled around to hear the details over the thump of the music. "I've met her before. Amy...I think her name is. She pushed me back in, locked the door. She just pulled my shit out. Never said a word."

"Did she swallow?" Witchy begged to know, worshipful of Lamont's brazenness and wondering why things like this never happened to him.

"Yes," Lamont happily confirmed. "Yes, she did."

"So," Grimy inquired hesitantly. "You fuck with white bitches?"

"What is wrong with this nigga!" Lamont groaned, throwing his hands up in mock exasperation. "Grimy, you're a rap star. You've never fucked a white bitch?"

Grimy stared at him blankly.

"Not even a dick suck?"

Grimy shook his head. "Nah. I don't get down like that."

"Grimy, Grimy," Lamont moaned dramatically. "You got to get out more, nigga. Try new things!" A low chuckle rumbled around the table. "Grimy, you're kidding me, right?"

Grimy shook his head.

"But you've been all over the world on tour!" Lamont yelled, trying to understand how this could have happened. "You've been to London, Germany, Japan..."

Grimy shrugged.

"Are you telling me," Lamont smirked, "that you go to all these countries and do not sample their cuisine?"

"Wherever I'm at they find me the black chicks," Grimy explained of his posse's international system of rounding up girls for his pleasure.

Lamont squinted at him. "What are you...*prejudiced?*"

Grimy almost grinned.

Feeling right at home as the center of attention, Lamont continued to milk this riff for the crew's amusement. "I was wit chu in Japan nigga," he pressed, lapsing into full-on ebonics because his bit would sound funnier that way. "Ain't no black bitches over there! Not unless they was on vacation! And those cute little Japanese honeys were hoppin' around you like you was a museum piece. All you had to do was sit there and let one of 'em hop on your *dick!* You didn't get *none* of that?"

"Did *you?*" Grimy wondered.

Lamont gaped at him with widened eyes, pretending to take offense, and slipped back into urban sophisticate mode. "I'm an international fucking playboy, money! Of course I got some. You get one with real long hair, it feels like silk, they brush it all over you, their skin's all soft...I'm talking totally hairless, man! They're so tiny you can just flip 'em every which way." Lamont paused to add a visible shiver of excitement for effect. "It's the shit!"

Everyone cracked up except Grimy, who turned up his nose, unimpressed. "I don't like sushi."

That made everyone howl but it was Lamont's instant comeback that slayed them: "How would you know, nigga? You ain't never tried it!"

"The women or the actual food," Nate chimed in. "Grimy's that nigga that goes to Japan and eats lunch and dinner at McDonald's every day!"

Grimy confirmed this conjecture with a nod and added, "Breakfast, too."

"You've been around the world three times over," Lamont said, shaking his head, "but you are one local motherfucka. Seriously, kid, you need to educate your palate in more ways than one."

Grimy looked lost. Educate his *what?* He leaned back into the booth as a flamboyantly dressed man pranced by as if the outfit itself were contagious.

Lamont threw his arm around Grimy's shoulder and pulled him in closer. "You want to know the best thing about all these white women in here?" Lamont scanned the room and cackled at the punchline before he even delivered it. "*None of them want to marry us!*"

A spontaneous burst of laughter rang out from the table.

"They might want Ivy League Nathaniel with his lawyer ass but they don't want any hip-hop niggas like us," Lamont said, conveniently grouping himself, a college graduate who had been raised in a stable, two-parent home, into the same demographic as Grimy, a fatherless child raised on welfare who'd received his high school equivalency in a juvenile lockdown facility. Lamont yoked Grimy around the neck then released him. "I mean, I could pick any one of these white girls in here and decide to make her my girlfriend." He snapped his stubby fingers and waved dismissively. "Send her flowers, take her out, buy her expensive shit. *Play the game.* But if I really did love her and wanted to marry her, you think she would? She would if she was some broad who didn't have shit because I might be a nigga but"—Lamont grinned and tapped his chest proudly—"I'm a *rich* entrepreneurial nigga, ya feel me?"

"Preach!" Nate joked before going over to schmooze with some industry folks. He'd heard Monty talk this bullshit before. So had Witchy and Daryl, who were now trying to molest a girl who'd passed by the table wearing a metallic tube top.

But Grimy cocked his head, all ears.

"I mean, Grimes, you're famous but you're still a nigga from the absolute fucking gutter."

Grimy took that as a compliment.

"You're letting these suburban kids know what it's like down there. You're letting them *safely* experience that. That's the beauty of Grimy."

Grimy basked in the praise.

"But *you* probably couldn't even marry a *minimum wage* white bitch."

Lamont howled with glee. Grimy didn't.

"Unless she really fucking hated her parents!"

"True," Grimy mumbled. "True."

"But these women in here, they're educated, they have their own careers," Lamont rambled. "These women can meet and marry a Wall Street guy. They all want rich men but a rich *white* guy is their first choice. But they want to fuck us for the thrill of it. They want to go to the dark side," Lamont said, wiggling his eyebrows, "and have a story to tell. Or a story just to keep to themselves." He took a big gulp of water and held his fist out to Grimy. "Who am I to deny them?"

Grimy distractedly pounded Lamont's fist with his own while his eyes wandered toward the woman in pink sitting at her table, laughing. She was sitting with two other women and a gray-haired man.

"Who's that guy?" Grimy asked.

Lamont squinted in the table's direction and watched as the

woman possibly named Amy kissed Gustav, his partner in Swirl, full on the mouth. Now he remembered where he knew her from!

Gustav spotted Lamont and waved.

Returning the wave, Lamont casually told Grimy, "Her husband."

Grimy watched this exchange, then, eyes twinkling, asked Lamont, "You know him?"

"Sort of," Lamont said.

Grimy ogled the couple, thinking, *Lamont is the pimp of the century!*

"So," Lamont said, nudging his cash cow in the ribs to pull his attention back to important matters, "how's the album coming?"

CHAPTER 14

◆

Ms. Jackson

VERNETTA LEE JACKSON took a seat in the cozy breakfast nook of her apartment on the twenty-third floor of the Trump International Tower on Central Park West. As she sipped her Earl Grey tea, she wondered what she was going to do about her two boys. One was married, the other needed to be. Both were problems.

She looked at the grandfather clock in her exquisitely furnished living room. It was eleven-thirty. Vanessa was half an hour late and she had not called. Unbelievably rude. Mama Jackson had called a meeting with her daughter-in-law so they could discuss schools for her grandson, PJ. She'd already gotten materials from the best day schools in the city because she knew Vanessa, who was probably at home, still in bed sleeping off a late night, wouldn't bother.

Alonzo, Vanessa's husband, was thirty-four and Lamont Jr. was almost thirty-nine but they were still boys to her and they always would be. Whenever she heard other parents say they loved all their children the same she wondered if they were being truthful or just saying what needed to be said. Mama Jackson had said the same thing many times herself but she wasn't being truthful. She played favorites, but kept it to herself.

It wasn't just that Lamont was her first. He was bright and funny as a baby, walking at nine months (Alonzo was still crawling on his first birthday) and talking a few months later. It took Alonzo so long to utter a word she feared he might be retarded. Lamont's second word—after "Mama," of course—was "gimme." Mama Jackson thought of that now and laughed to herself. "Gimme" should have been his middle name instead of Lavell. That inborn desire to possess things had served him well. He was bagging groceries at Key Food on weekends, making forty dollars pocket change by age ten. He always knew how to get his hustle on. He was a good student and kept out of trouble, which took good negotiating skills living in Bed-Stuy, but he was also a big kid who didn't allow anyone to push him around.

She wished she could have given her kids everything but it was a financial impossibility. Her husband was always spending what little extra income they had on card games and the like. But Lamont Sr. was a decent man and he came home to her every night, which was a lot more than some women could say. She had put herself through nursing school at night while working at a hospital morgue during the day. She just had done clerical work but the aura of death had gotten to her. After a while, she wanted to move upstairs, where people still had a chance at life. No one in her family had ever gone on to higher education. Getting her nursing degree had been the biggest achievement of her life, after giving birth to her boys.

But she wanted more for her children. She hoped she'd be able to send them to prestigious colleges so they could realize their dreams.

She'd gotten Lamont information on the best private schools and hoped he could get some student loans, but he'd decided to go to City College and save her the worry. He was always so thoughtful like that. Now look at him! Lamont had become a success far and above anything she had ever dreamed possible. Knowing his love of money, she had hoped he might become a bank manager or an accountant. A suit-and-tie nigga! That would have put her over the moon. When he had told her he was going to pursue a career in the music industry, she was now ashamed to admit, she hadn't had much faith that he could succeed. But she'd prayed on it. He threw parties during college but she figured that was just a temporary way to make money. She'd considered starting a hip-hop label a risky proposition. Who ever thought of *owning* something? Being his own boss and all that? But if anyone could do it, Lamont could. He made some missteps in the beginning, but she encouraged him to stay the course. "Baby, you'll be the next Berry Gordy," she'd reassure him when he doubted himself.

And that's just what he had become. The hip-hop Berry Gordy. An *Armani* suit-and-tie nigga! God was good, yes He was.

Lamont had told her she could quit working at the hospital once he incorporated Triple Large. She didn't mind the hospital—although she still never went to P. Diddy's Labor Day all-white parties in the Hamptons because it reminded her too much of the life she left behind—but after working on her feet for over twenty-five years, she'd often get shooting pains up and down her legs. Lamont took care of that, too. He found her the best reflexologist in the city and, sure enough, that wonderful man soothed away all the pains.

Thank goodness her ex-husband was too old and infirm to spend Lamont's money or he'd be in Vegas right now hollering, "Let it ride!" But then they had Alonzo to carry on that legacy. Mama gazed out of the window at the treetops of Central Park and shook her head in disgust.

While she had to admit that Lamont had looked like a brown gerbil as a baby, Alonzo could have been on the side of the Pampers box he was so cute. She'd wanted to get Alonzo into that, doing modeling or commercials, when he was younger, but she didn't have the time and wouldn't have known where to start even if she did.

And where have those good looks gotten Alonzo? she wondered sadly.

Lamont had taken care of his baby brother, and Alonzo should have been a lot more grateful than he was. After squeaking through high school, being fired from several low-wage jobs, getting arrested twice for drug possession (no convictions, praise Jesus), and four DUIs, which got his license revoked, Mama was tired of bailing the boy out. But she couldn't blame him. He was feeble-minded and completely unfocused, not in any way mean-spirited or harmful. He was a failure, *her* failure, she felt. At some point, she had stopped hoping that Alonzo would turn over a new leaf and focus on something besides partying and gambling. He was still running off all the time to Vegas or the nearest casino—he thought she didn't know?—but she just thanked Jesus Christ her Lord and Savior that he wasn't dead or in jail.

Now Alonzo was married to this hot tamale who ran through his money as quickly as a woman walking barefoot over hot coals. Not a shocker that they had eloped. Mama would have been there to raise her hand when it was time for objections to be made known. But Vanessa had trapped him. Mama hadn't even believed the girl was pregnant until she'd started showing. To Mama's great annoyance,

Vanessa looked ravishing even in her ninth month. No swollen feet or face, just a perfect little bulge at the center of her perfect little body.

Mama hadn't liked Vanessa from the word go. It was clear that Vanessa didn't care for regular black people, just the really good-looking, rich, or famous members of the race. Lamont and Alonzo passed muster but get her around some *folks* and she looked as if she were about to break out in hives. In Mama's 'hood, blacks and Latinos were two peacefully coexisting tribes. Apparently things went down differently in Venezuela.

But it was after showing newborn Pedro off at the hospital, saying over and over, with obvious relief, "He's so light, he's so light," that Vanessa had zoomed to the top of Mama's sh** list. A creamy dark-chocolate woman, Vernetta Lee Jackson never let anyone run that light-skinned/dark-skinned nonsense on her. A Mama Jackson truism: *Let one person make you feel like less and that's how the next person will treat you.*

Vernetta was never a truly beautiful woman but she'd always carried herself as if she were. The truth was she looked better now than she ever had. Pilates had toned her full figure and regular oxygen facials kept her skin supple and nearly unlined. It was a point of pride with her that she'd never had plastic surgery, so she freely owned up to her real age of sixty-four and always reminded folks, "Black don't crack" when they commented on her youthful appearance.

Her appearance was something she'd always kept up, even when she'd had only a few dollars to spare. She'd bought discount at Loehman's, painted her own nails and toes, and had her hair pressed every week at Buckshot Shorty's on Gates Avenue. That was back in the day. It had taken her a minute to get into the groove of spending serious money and "living triple large" as she liked to joke, but she'd found her footing. Now she shopped at Galeries Lafayette in Paris and Bergdorf's when she was in New York, had a standing Monday appointment at Georgette Klinger for a full day of beauty treatments, and had her wigs custom-made. All thanks to her darling Lamont.

Mama checked the time again. Now Vanessa was fifty minutes late. The unmitigated gall! She wanted to wring that girl's neck sometimes—no, most of the time—but...she sighed.

As much as she disliked the uppity little hussy, Mama had to count her blessings because Vanessa had turned her into a grandmama. Mama called her grandson PJ—as in Pedro Jackson—just to spite Vanessa and remind her that Jackson might not be *her* last name but it was the name of her half-black son and it would be the surname of Ms. de la Cruz's grandkids one day, too.

And Mama had to admit that marriage had had a calming effect on Alonzo. He still wasn't doing much at the company but he'd stopped carousing and getting into bar brawls. He loved being a father and was much better at parenting that Vanessa ever cared to be. But he let his *mujer* punk his ass on the regular. Whatever Vanessa wanted, Vanessa got.

Women. That was a weak spot for both of her sons. Alonzo had already made his bed but she could still keep Lamont from getting pickpocketed. Although he was a prime target for all these money-hungry harlots, Lamont wasn't a sucker for a pretty face like Alonzo. *Atta boy,* Mama would think whenever he dumped some dime-a-dozen bimbo who was trying to muscle in on the massive bank account that was supporting the Jackson family.

Among all the "here today, gone tomorrow" women Lamont had

taken up with, Kendra Truesdale had been a real contender. A well-mannered girl from a middle-class family in Florida, Kendra was the ideal mate for her darling son. Lots of women knew how to make pleasant conversation, but the true gift was knowing when to shut up. Kendra was gifted that way. And, unlike so many of these gals today, she wasn't so obsessed with her career as to lose sight of what was truly important: Lamont's happiness.

Most important, Kendra paid Mama the respect she felt was her due as the matriarch of the Jackson empire. Plus she was black. Mocha-skinned. And very shapely.

Her parents had come to visit a few times when Lamont and Kendra were an item. Boring small-town people, but they were decent and Mama liked them. She felt a bit sorry for Harold and Pat Truesdale because they seemed to have the false impression that Kendra was a bigtime model-actress when Mama had never seen her in a damn thing except for some rap videos. But she was trying.

Mama really thought Lamont had found The One...until he unceremoniously dumped the poor girl. When Mama asked why, he'd cryptically responded, "Never can tell."

Kendra came to Mama for advice on getting him back soon afterward. She broke down in tortured sobs and Mama's heart went out to her. Lamont was such a stellar catch that the pain of having him slip through her fingers must have been unbearable. Mama told her, "Absence makes the heart grow fonder, sweetheart. Don't call him. Let him miss you." Sound advice, or so Mama thought, but after eight months Lamont didn't seem to be missing Kendra at all.

She'd decided to ask Kendra to lunch. They were meeting today at Cipriani, Mama's favorite restaurant. She took a last sip of tea, carefully placed her Limoges teacup back on its saucer, and rose from her chair.

As for no-show Vanessa? When that money-vacuuming drug fiend crawled out of her hole, she was going to get the tongue-lashing of a lifetime. And Vernetta Lee Jackson was going to love every minute of it.

◆

CHAPTER 15

Funky Fresh Dressed

LIKE SHE HAD JUST RUNG UP A BOTTLE OF SHAMPOO at Rite-Aid, the woman behind the register at Scoop said matter-of-factly, "That will be seven thousand two hundred and seventy-five dollars."

Mimi gasped audibly. Vanessa didn't blink. She slapped Lamont's black Amex onto the counter with authority.

You had to be a big spender to get an Amex Centurion card. It was invitation only, a leap up from platinum. For Mimi's style makeover, the ladies had carte blanche for one day only. Vanessa had been acting like a contestant on *Supermarket Sweep,* racking up as much as she could for Mimi—and herself—in the allotted time.

Per Imani's instructions, Mimi had shown up at Vanessa's SoHo apartment at eleven this morning. She was shown in by a meek, broken-English-speaking woman who was holding the hand of the most adorable boy she'd ever seen. "Miss Vanessa come soon," the woman told her.

Mimi had assumed Lamont's sister-in-law would be black. From the looks of her son, probably not. The boy, whom the nanny called Pedro, grabbed at Mimi's hand as if he were desperate for a playmate and led her to his room. There was a floor-to-ceiling *Lion King* mural painted around all four walls. Mimi didn't mind the wait because she and cute little Pedro crawled all over the rug, playing with his truckload of toys.

Over an hour later, Vanessa slunk into the room in an oddly glamorous look that answered the question that the average woman asked herself when flipping through *Vogue*: who would buy these outrageously priced clothes and put them together in this way and where would they go looking like that? Vanessa de la Cruz would, to go on a wild shopping spree with her rich brother-in-law's credit card, that's who.

It was a mild March day, so Mimi, wearing jeans and Pumas, was perplexed as to why Vanessa was rocking her fall look. On her feet were what looked like Timberland work boots but they had skinny wooden heels and pointy toes. And they were pink. Brown corduroys hung low from her narrow waist and the shrunken hot pink turtleneck exposed her supple stomach. She had a Gucci bucket hat sitting high on her head like she didn't want to mess up her hair and dark tinted, goggle-sized glasses covering half her face.

"I'm ready" was Vanessa's greeting.

Pedro ran up to her for a hug but she just patted him on the head instead. Mimi couldn't really get a good look at her with the glasses and the hat but there was something familiar about her. As they headed down to the Ford Expedition Imani had ordered for them, Vanessa grabbed a short olive-green bomber jacket with fur trim and an enormous apple-green purse.

After settling in, Vanessa removed her shades and hat. Mimi recognized her instantly. It was Vanessa de la Cruz! The model. Mimi had seen her in so many magazines. *She* was Lamont's sister-in-law?

"Wow," she gushed. "I...I didn't recognize you at first. Everyone just said Vanessa, Lamont's sister-in-law. I didn't know they meant *you!*"

"Lamont's sister-in-law?" Vanessa repeated, offended at the secondary billing.

"I always thought you were so gorgeous," Mimi said unabashedly.

"Thought?" Vanessa begged her pardon. "Or think?"

"Oh yeah, I think you're gorgeous," Mimi corrected herself seriously. "This is so exciting."

"Isn't it?" Vanessa agreed, taking a liking to Lamont's new artist instantly.

Mimi wasn't sure she could emulate Vanessa's casual chic style but she wanted to. When Mimi asked where she'd gotten all the things she was wearing, Vanessa was happy to oblige with a rundown.

"Manolo," she said pointing to the boots. "Almost impossible to get but I'll see what I can do. Pants are Katayone. Jacket by Marc Jacobs. Sunglasses, Christian Dior. This sweater I got...where? Oh, someone sent me this. I forget who. The bag," she said stroking it more affectionately than she had Pedro, "is an Hermès Birkin. And the hat is..."

"Gucci," Mimi answered. It had logos all over it. She had never heard of any of those other designers, except for Christian Dior, and she didn't know he made sunglasses. "I love your look. I want to get stuff like that," Mimi bubbled, without any real understanding of how much "stuff like that" cost.

Vanessa smiled appreciatively. "De nada, sweetie. Lamont said to hook you up from head to toe."

Mimi had wondered if the saleswoman at Barneys, where they had gone first, was going to accept a credit card from a Spanish woman who was probably not named Lamont Jackson. But it hadn't been a problem. Not at Barneys (where they had lunch at Fred's, nor at Bergdorf's, Prada, Hermès, Manolo Blahnik, Jimmy Choo, Chanel, Roberto Cavalli, the Nike superstore, the Levi's store, Jeffrey, Intermix, or Calypso). Vanessa had coordinated their route so they could work their way downtown.

Many of the salespeople knew Vanessa and appeared to be almost salivating when they saw her coming. They were helpful and she was snippy but they all seemed to be thrilled just to be in her presence.

Vanessa hadn't once looked at a price tag. Mimi had tried on a suede coat at Prada and couldn't find the price tag so she asked Vanessa (in a whisper so the snooty hovering saleswoman wouldn't hear), "How much is this?" Vanessa very loudly replied, "We can afford it." At the other stores, she had puttered around looking at things while Vanessa settled the bills. She hadn't realized just how much they were spending until this shocking revelation at Scoop. She felt like putting some of the things back. God, that was a lot of money!

Mimi was kicking herself for spending some of her *own* advance money at Urban Outfitters. But how was she to know Lamont was going to buy her everything she could ever want—jeans, coats, boots, sneakers, underwear, bags, head scarves, sunglasses, skirts, casual dresses, dressy dresses, socks. Some of the stuff was way sexy. Other things she just didn't consider her style. But Vanessa kept saying, "It's a must-have." Lamont was buying her all this stuff and Vanessa approved so who was she to argue?

They walked out of Scoop and Vanessa bumped into a friend heading in.

"Hey Nessa," the pretty woman said sweetly and Vanessa greeted her in an equally pleasant tone.

"Kendra, this is Mimi," Vanessa said, proudly showing off her beautiful young charge. "She's just been signed by Lamont."

Kendra was pushing thirty and looked it. She was the kind of woman everyone considered pretty until an exceptionally beautiful woman—someone like Vanessa de la Cruz—walked into the room and made her pale in comparison. Needless to say, running into Kendra made Vanessa feel just fabulous.

"*You're* a rapper?" Kendra asked, looking Mimi up and down.

"No, I sing," Mimi said politely, ignoring the woman's head-to-toe evaluation.

"Really," Kendra said, processing this information. "Lamont is handling singers now?"

"She's the first," Vanessa confided. "Branching out and all that."

"I just had lunch with Mama Jackson," Kendra volunteered, letting Vanessa know she was still somewhat in the mix. "Were you supposed to meet her today?" She knew the answer to that. Mama had bitched about it extensively.

"Was I?" Vanessa asked without concern. She had completely forgotten.

"I see you two really went crazy today," Kendra noted anxiously, watching the salesman carrying bag after bag out to the car.

"Yes," Vanessa sighed. "We've been everywhere. So tired. Must

dash." She air-kissed Kendra and hopped into the car. Mimi obediently followed, forcing a smile at Kendra, who didn't return the favor.

KENDRA TRUESDALE absentmindedly pushed clothes along the
racks, annoyed by this unexpected encounter. Lamont's new singer
looked very young. She had to be at least ten years younger than
Kendra. Eighteen? And she was pretty. Beautiful really. Just the kind
of girl Lamont would like. Kendra hated her already.

Kendra had once thought Vanessa might be her sister-in-law.
Now Vanessa couldn't spare more than a minute to talk to her. How
'bout a "Hey, Kendra, what have you been up to?" That would've
been nice. But she'd learned not to expect too much from Vanessa.
That one was so self-involved. Maybe it was for the best that she
hadn't asked. Other than the audition she'd gone on this morning for
a Kaopectate commercial where she had to say the word "diarrhea"
twice in six lines of copy and which she probably wouldn't get anyway because she never booked anything, she hadn't been up to much
more than talking nasty to anonymous men on the Hot Calls phone
sex line.

Since her career—if you could call it that—as an actress was
going exactly nowhere, she'd been doing the phone sex thing. A
friend of hers, another out of work actress, turned her on to it and
though she hated it, the money was decent. It paid for acting classes
and whatnot. This inadvisable shopping jaunt fell under the category
of "whatnot."

Before pursuing acting in earnest, Kendra had been featured in
many high-profile rap music videos. Her shapely body—full natural

breasts, voluptuous hips attached to an inexplicably tiny waist, and an ass that looked like an African sculpture—thick shoulder-length black hair, and dark bronze skin that seemed to glow even in the winter kept her in high demand on the hip-hop video circuit. She was not the stereotypical video ho, mind you. Those girls' jiggling body parts only made the final cut. Kendra was featured, face and all, as the sexy love interest of Jay-Z, L. L. Cool J, Puff Daddy, Snoop Dogg, and Flo$$ to name but a few. She was the main chick next to the biggest names in hip-hop. They all tried to run the same lines on her but she kept it strictly professional.... Okay, she'd fucked Nelly *once* but that was all!

An appearance in a Flo$$ video was what put her on Lamont's radar. She wasn't clear on why his assistant had summoned her to his office but it didn't take long to figure it out. He asked her where she was from (Naples, Florida) and what her dreams were (to be a serious film actress) and what her favorite movie was (*Pretty Woman*). He told her he was "intrigued" by her. He said she had something special. He told her she could do a lot more than sit next to some rap star and look pretty. Then he suggested they have dinner sometime and took her home number.

She waited for him to call for over three weeks. She thought about calling his office (she hadn't gotten his personal numbers) but decided against it. When he rang, it made her happier than she had been in a long time, even though she didn't think he was all that cute. But he had a way about him that made her palms sweaty. It was definitely the power thing.

After they'd slept together once, he asked her to take an HIV test at his doctor's office because he hated rubbers. It offended her—did he think because she slept with him after only three dates and she had appeared in rap videos that she was some kind of slut? But then he said, all cool and collected, "Hey, if you don't want to, don't," and she sensed an implied threat, like he had another girl on speed dial who'd run right over with her test results in hand if she didn't. She had the test the next day. When it came back negative (Lamont gave her his verbal assurance that he was "clean") they started doing all kinds of freaky things in bed.

Two weeks into the relationship, he told her the video thing was tacky and said she'd have to move on from that. (Lamont almost never made suggestions, he made commands.) He got her an agent to set her up for commercial and film auditions, which Kendra felt was a great big step toward her goal of becoming the next Vivica A. Fox.

She and Lamont were together for two years, the longest relationship Kendra had ever had. He laced her with money and the hottest clothes. They went on trips to Maui, St. Bart's, Saint-Tropez. They took weekend trips to Miami or Atlanta for A-list industry parties. Everything first class. Being Lamont's official honey gave her status. When she ran into the rappers whose videos she'd appeared in, they treated her with more respect. She'd even had her picture on *New York* magazine's party page, taken at a charity benefit she'd gone to with Lamont, although they didn't list her name in the caption. They called her "a friend."

Everything seemed to be moving along perfectly. Before Lamont, she was always hustling to get her next job to pay the bills, dating guys she liked but didn't love, and prone to bouts of depression. During the Lamont phase, she still wasn't working much but at least was getting better auditions. She just loved that man to death. And the lifestyle wasn't too hard to love either. It was the happiest she had ever been in her entire life.

Then he dumped her. Wham bam and that was it. She never saw it coming.

"SO KENDRA'S A FRIEND OF YOURS?" Mimi asked as the driver made his way to the Malia Mills store.

"Not really," Vanessa said lightly. When Vanessa opened her mouth it was hard to tell if she was going to speak or yawn.

"You don't like her?"

"She's Lamont's ex," Vanessa reluctantly revealed. One day Lamont was all into Kendra and the next day she was gone. Vanessa had never gotten the full story nor did she particularly care. She'd learned to keep out of Lamont's business. Staying on his good side meant she got little treats like today.

"She wasn't very friendly," Mimi pressed.

"She was nice enough," Vanessa said cautiously.

"To *you.*"

"Everyone is. To my face," Vanessa said bluntly. She had no close girlfriends. They all became catty sooner or later. "Sweetie, you have to understand that everyone wants Lamont's attention. Now that you're his pet project, you're getting more attention than anyone."

"Pet project?" Mimi did not like the sound of that.

"You know what I mean," Vanessa said, tiring of the conversation. "He's putting a lot of energy into launching your career. People can get jealous."

"So Kendra is jealous of *me* just because I'm signed to the label?" Mimi asked, trying to understand. "He's, like, my boss."

"Yes, but you're pretty and you're female and she's jealous of that, I'm sure. I heard she was devastated when he dumped her. She wouldn't even leave her apartment for weeks." Vanessa pushed a lock of hair behind her ear. "If I were as fat as her, I'd be depressed, too."

After a beat, during which Mimi wondered if they were still talking about the same person, she said, "She's not fat!"

"She has fat *aura*," Vanessa said. "It's only a matter of time."

Mimi caught herself staring at Vanessa and she was about to turn away because it was rude but Vanessa just sat there comfortably, looking straight ahead. She was obviously a person who had grown accustomed to being stared at and enjoyed it. All day Mimi had marveled at how perfect Vanessa's skin was. Did she have to go to a dermatologist and get those peels like Mimi had been getting? Vanessa's hair was so shiny and bouncy and every time they went into a different store, the lighting would pick up all the different shades of brown woven in the long strands. Was that natural? In profile, Vanessa's nose had the perfect slope and Mimi could see how far her eyelashes fanned out. And whenever Vanessa walked by, she'd get a sweet whiff of her perfume. After being out all day, she could still smell the scent—it never faded.

Now, sitting ten inches away from Vanessa, Mimi felt like she was looking at an airbrushed picture of her in a magazine and, somewhere within the magazine, a perfume strip was open. But Vanessa was so bitchy to everyone she had encountered that Mimi wondered if maybe she had PMS or something. Mimi assumed the only reason she had been spared was because she had come with Lamont's stamp of approval—or maybe Vanessa actually did like her?

Vanessa was gorgeous, rich, and she had everything anyone could ask for, including an adorable, healthy baby. *What on earth does she have to be so cranky about?* Mimi wondered. Like that mean comment about Kendra. Was that her way of being funny?

But then Mimi smiled, having a delayed reaction to the fact that Vanessa had called her pretty. Lamont thought she had star quality and Vanessa de la Cruz, Miss Perfection, thought she was pretty. Life wasn't so bad.

"So why'd Lamont dump Kendra?" Mimi asked.

"Who knows," Vanessa replied as the car pulled up to the Malia Mills shop.

This was going to be their last stop. Mimi didn't know what kind of store it was until they walked in and she saw it was filled with bathing suits.

What a sweetheart Lamont is turning out to be, she thought. *Hooking me up with Lena, having me styled by Vanessa de la Cruz, buying me all this stuff!*

Vanessa held up a brightly striped bikini and noted her approval. "Cute."

Picking up on Vanessa's mantra of the day, Mimi jokingly agreed, "It's a must-have."

◆

CHAPTER 16

Killing Me Softly

MIMI HAD NEVER BEEN A BIG FAN OF HIP-HOP. That was the funny part. She knew the bigger names, had heard songs on the radio and seen videos on MTV, of course. The music was inescapable. But she wasn't totally up on it.

Hanging out with Lena changed all that. Hip-hop was played at all the parties they'd been going to and Lena religiously listened to the Funkmaster Flex radio mix show. On the rare occasions that Lena drove her Range Rover she cranked whatever rap CD she'd purchased that week or a mixed CD of hip-hop favorites that she'd burned. Usually they took car services, in which case Lena would make the driver tune to Blazin' 104, which played mostly hip-hop and R&B songs that had hip-hop remixes. The music was the bass-heavy, expletive-filled soundtrack of Lena's life but Mimi didn't mind the overload. She was turning into a hip-hop head, though unlike Lena, she didn't know every single word to every single song.

Now here she was at Grove Street Studios about to sing the hook on a record with Supa Phat E. Lena had had her listening to various rap-sung collabos all week like she was in training for a prizefight. Phat E was one of Lena's favorites. "You're lucky to get down with him," Lena had gushed. "Everything he touches turns platinum. His flow is just...bananas!"

Ivan, the studio engineer, poked his head into Studio A. "You still in here?" Ivan waved for her to follow him and she did. He opened the door to Studio B and there was Daryl, sitting at the mixing board with a song playing at an ear-shattering level.

"Phat E said he'd be here by nine," Ivan said and disappeared.

"'Sup girl," Daryl said, lowering the volume a smidgen.

"You've been in here all this time? I've been waiting for an hour in the other room."

"Yeah," he said, not looking up from the mixing board. "I was just about to slide up in there. Just finishin' up this other song." He handed her a yellow piece of lined paper with some words scribbled on it. "Your lyrics."

Mimi looked at the chorus. It was five lines.

The first: *Gucci, Prada, Dolce Gabbana.*

The last: *I wanna be your flyass bitch.*

She couldn't make out the other three lines, Daryl's handwriting was so bad. It didn't matter what they said because she didn't like that last line at all. "I wanna be your flyass bitch? You actually want me to say that?"

"I guess so," Daryl answered crisply. "I wrote it." He snatched the page back, saying, "We might change it depending on Phat E's part."

The ink was barely dry on her contract but Daryl had already cultivated a strong dislike for her. His reasons were threefold. For one, she was a performer who'd eventually enjoy more attention than he ever would as a behind-the-scenes producer. Secondly, she was poised to become Lamont's newest darling. And lastly and most gravely, Mimi was tall and pretty. Too tall and too pretty. He couldn't front, she was a true dimepiece. Just the kind of hottie who would never give him any pussy under any circumstances.

All together, these observations made Daryl so mad he felt like karate chopping a wooden block in one forceful blow. *Hiii-ya!* But in the studio *he* was the boss. On that point, they needed to be clear.

Following Daryl into Studio A, Mimi wondered why everything he said sounded like a threat. These lyrics were awful but trying to press the issue would only anger him further. If Lena were here she'd no doubt be saying how hot these lyrics were. The other songs they'd listened to had lines like that. She'd just have to cooperate and do her best. Anyway, it wasn't her song, it was Supa Phat E's. And it wasn't going on her album, it was for this soundtrack. *Her* album was going to be completely different.

As soon as Daryl settled in, she nervously pulled out her song book and showed it to him.

"You wrote all this?" Daryl asked, noticing that all the pages were filled.

"Yeah," Mimi said, teetering on the edge of the couch. "I have five other books but I re-copied my favorites into this one."

Swiveling back and forth in the chair in front of the mixing board, Daryl skimmed the lyrics of the first song "Like a Dream." Corny. He turned to the next page and checked out "Soul Cry." Cornier. He read the chorus of "On the Inside" and, without looking at another page, decided it was the corniest of all the songs she'd written.

"You tryin' to be the black Celine Dion or sumpin'?"

"No," Mimi snapped, wanting to grab the book back.

"Are these songs you wanna record for your album?" Daryl asked, using his long pinkie nail to satisfy an itch between his cornrows. "Or you just showin' me these 'cause you want me to know you write?"

"A little of both," Mimi said hesitantly. He obviously didn't like the songs. "I don't have to record those but I definitely want to be part of the writing process, you know? I want to be sort of like Lauryn Hill. Or Erykah Badu."

"Reeeeally," Daryl said contemplatively, trying not to let his face register surprise at this ridiculous bit of information.

If he were a real asshole he would have given voice to his first reaction, which was *Bitch, you ain't no Lauryn Hill and you ain't never gonna be! Not on this label.* If he were committed to his A&R job, he would have done his duty and diplomatically explained that the label had some slightly different ideas about what kind of artist she should be. Which was more radio-ready, supremely cross-marketable J.Lo and less soul-searching, average-selling Erykah Badu. He thought Lamont had gone over that with her. But what would Daryl know? Lamont never told him anything.

Instead, he gave her a vague "We'll see" and turned his back on her and got back into his music.

Around nine, Ivan walked in and jovially announced, "Supa Phat E in the house!"

As Supa Phat E bounded through the narrow studio doors, the literal meaning of his name became instantly clear. Super fatty!

Mimi realized her mouth was hanging open, so she quickly shut it. She knew he was on the big side but *damn,* in person he was stupendously large. He had to be over three hundred pounds. *Well* over.

He was wearing a plain white cotton undershirt that could have been used as a hammock for newborn triplets. Yellow sweatpants with white piping hung below his insanely bloated belly and his plump, dimpled fist clutched a matching yellow jacket. Bouncing off his midsection, at the end of a thick platinum chain, was an enormous diamond *E* designed in such jagged script it looked like the work of Zorro. The combination of the yellow sweatsuit (Phat Farm, naturally), the jeweled initial bigger than the head of an average young child, and his crackling kinetic energy made him seem like a cross between Big Bird and Superman. The only small things on Phat E were his feet.

"What's poppin' y'all" was Phat E's exultant greeting. It felt like a whoosh of pure oxygen followed him into the room.

"Phat E," crowed Daryl, standing up from the board to give him the customary b-boy salute. They clasped hands, curled their bodies toward each other, and tapped shoulders, using their free hands to tap the other's back. Daryl was so small and Phat E so large it looked like Daryl might disappear into Phat E's embrace never to be seen again.

"Country D," Phat E said. "How you?"

"Hyped, playboy," Daryl said. "Ready to blaze this record."

Mimi couldn't stop staring as he and Daryl ribbed each other. She stood up and waited to be introduced. Daryl started up the music, obviously with no intention of introducing them, so Phat E took it upon himself.

"Ernesto Moore," he said gallantly. He took her hand and theatrically kissed it. "You must be Mimi. Nice to meetcha." He sank and sank and sank into the sofa and patted the small remaining space next to him. Mimi took a seat and Phat E immediately swooped his arm around her. "So this your first record?"

"Yeah," she said. "And I'm really excited because I hear everything you touch turns platinum."

"Believe what ya heard!"

"I love your flow," Mimi added. "It's bananas."

"Awww," Phat E swooned, soaking up the compliments. "That's right. Just stick with me, baby."

"Can I see your rap part of the song?"

"Sure," Phat E said. "Soon as I write it."

He looked up as Ivan strolled back into the room carrying a plastic folder. A wiry, shaggy-haired white guy, Ivan considered hip-hop a creative and powerful art form and, after working with all the big-name hip-hop artists, he no longer got a headache from breathing in marijuana fumes. He tossed the folder onto Phat E's lap.

Phat E thanked Ivan, then turned to Mimi and said, "Now that we're all cozy and shit, let's order."

Mimi looked over at the folder. Inside its transparent cover was a white sheet of paper that read: MENUS FOR SUPA PHAT E. PLEASE DO NOT TOUCH! Ivan had done that. People were always misplacing the menus and a good selection of varying cuisines that could be delivered in a timely fashion was the only real request Phat E had when he came to the studio.

After mulling over several types of food, Phat E decided it was a seafood night and had the receptionist put in an order for two since Daryl and Ivan declined to join them for dinner.

After close inspection, Mimi decided Ernesto was rather cute. He had smooth, clear skin the color of wet sand, short tightly curled brown hair and a sparse, elegantly sculpted goatee. She hoped he hadn't noticed her recoil slightly at his girth when he entered the room.

"Hey, Ivan," Phat E said. "Throw me the pad."

"Make magic, baby," Ivan said as he tossed Phat E "his tools," a fresh yellow legal pad and a No. 2 pencil. Brand-new, just sharpened.

"Like Copperfield," Phat E replied.

His first top-ten hit had been written this way and ever since he superstitiously followed the same routine to the letter. Within minutes, Phat E was completely lost in his rhyme-writing. He was well-respected by music critics as a true poet who wove intricate rhymes about the plight of the young urban male. "Only God Can Judge," on which he ruminated about growing up as a fat kid, from his second album, *Food Is Love,* was considered to be his finest work to date. But like most hip-hop artists, he found a way for art and commerce to profitably coexist. He was concerned with selling records and he knew people, especially the young kids who were his core audience, wanted to party more than they wanted to ponder. "Gotta pay the bills," he'd chirp when he came into a studio as a hired gun to guest star on another artist's album.

That's what he was doing tonight. Triple Large was releasing the *Good Lookin'* soundtrack and they were paying the Hitz, Inc. superstar his going rate of $150,000 per song to take part. Even if almost no one saw the movie, a soundtrack would sell briskly if it featured hot songs from a variety of well-known rappers. And Phat E was the biggest. In every sense.

An hour later, the receptionist buzzed over the intercom. "Dinnertime," she trilled.

The food had an intoxicating effect on Phat E. The more he devoured—he moved from lobster to crab legs to a baked potato dripping with sour cream with the dexterity of a DJ—the giddier and more talkative he became.

Even though he rapped about his slick girl-getting abilities and his sexual prowess with such "tricks," he admitted the ladies' man status was just part of his rap-star image. His devoted wife, Renee, "his angel," was the only woman he ever went home to. She'd loved him before the fame and riches. At Benjamin Franklin High she was proud to walk the halls with her overweight Ernesto even though he had ballooned to 280 pounds by the senior prom.

"She wants to have a baby," he said. "But I can't even knock her up! Something wrong with my sperm." He shrugged. "We're going to a fertility doctor and everything."

"Keep trying, Phat," Mimi said supportively.

"She thinks it has to do with my weight. The doctor said it doesn't," he insisted. "But she wants me to go on a diet anyway. She's worried about me getting so big. She tries to feed me all this low-calorie food. You know what she taped on the fridge?" He paused and cocked his head. "This article with a big headline that says 'OBESITY KILLS.' How fucked-up is that!"

Mimi smiled sympathetically. He sighed.

"I know she's probably right," he conceded, wiping his greasy palms with a paper towel. "But goddamn, I'm Supa Phat E! How'm I gonna get all skinny and still represent, yaknowahumsayin'?"

"Yeah, I hear you," Mimi said, feeling very comfortable with Phat E. "But she only did that because she really cares. She's got your back."

"And that's why I love her," Phat E said. He slouched down in his chair and exhaled, having finished his seafood workout. "So what about you?"

"What about me?"

"You got a man?"

"Me? Nah."

"Yeah, well, I don't know if there are many suitable fellas in this crowd you're running with, little lady," Phat E mock-lectured.

"Why?"

"'Cause niggas in this industry is all about gaming. I ain't about games. I got my lady. She's been down with a nigga since times was rough, ya heard?"

Mimi smiled, thinking, *Why can't I find a guy like Ernesto?*

"But you wouldn't believe how many women throw themselves at this here swole-up nigga," Phat E said, thoroughly amused. "Even though they know I'm married, *happily* married. I don't understand females sometimes. I mean, why chase the nigga that every other chick wants? Why sign up for that kinda stress? I'm not saying you have to be with a lazy, broke mo'fucker. But what's wrong with the average hard-working brother who'll take care of you and love ya right?"

"Your wife got both," Mimi quipped. But he'd posed a good question. Jamal had been a star quarterback in Toledo and wasn't that what made him so attractive? That all the other girls had wanted him and she'd had him—for a while?

"Ya heard!" Phat E exclaimed, jumping up from his chair.

Mimi was so startled that she almost slipped off hers.

He scooped her up in his arms like he was about to do curls and she was the barbell. "But I'm one of a kind, baby!" As she giggled, he carried her back to the studio singing "Back to work we go" to the beat of "Chapel of Love."

After laying down his lyrics, Phat E was beyond tired and wanted to jet but he stayed to encourage Mimi as she supplied her vocal con-tribution. On her ninth take, after singing the lines Daryl had written, Mimi warbled some of her own creation. She'd been listening to Phat E rapping all night and she had some complementary lyrics rattling around in her head.

As soon as Daryl heard the unfamiliar words, he cut the music. "What was that?"

His voice sounded loud and disapproving in her headphones. "I don't know," Mimi said in her most apologetic voice. "It just came out that way."

"Get out here," Daryl shouted and Mimi removed the headphones and walked out of the recording booth into the main studio room. Before Daryl could yell, she said, "I just thought we could try it."

"Don't think, *sing*," Daryl snapped as Phat E wheezed, half asleep, on the couch. "Hey, Ivan, maybe you should print that up on one of your signs and put it in the booth," Daryl snickered to Ivan. "'Don't think, sing!' You know, just as a reminder."

"I don't like it your way," Mimi said boldly. This wasn't *her* song so she probably shouldn't be trying to rewrite the lyrics. But this wasn't about the song. Daryl was trying to humiliate her. Lena's "kill him with kindness" strategy hadn't gotten Mimi anywhere and she was just about sick of his jacked-up attitude.

"Nobody asked you," Daryl said. He sat back in the chair and folded his arms, taking pleasure in reprimanding her.

Mimi looked at Ivan. His expression seemed to be saying, *Leave it alone.* But she didn't want to leave it alone. For years, she'd been singing the stupid songs Kenny wrote for them when she had a book full of her own songs. Now Daryl had hardly even looked at the songs in her book before deeming them crap. And he had barely heard the lyrics she was trying out tonight before pulling his power play.

"Maybe we should ask Lamont," Mimi said without thinking. When she saw the immediate look of panic on Ivan's face, she wished she could have inhaled the words. Ivan knew that threatening to go to Lamont with any complaint about Daryl was akin to a guy telling his girlfriend, "Yes, those jeans do make you look fat." It was the ultimate no-no.

Daryl suddenly got up and walked toward the couch where Phat E was fidgeting in his sleep. Mimi and Ivan didn't know what he was about to do. They watched him grab the phone.

"Wanna take it straight to the top, huh?" Daryl said, his usual sarcasm now sounding sinister. "Good idea. You ain't never written a real song in your life but why don't you call the boss and tell him you wanna start today." He stabbed at the buttons. "It's only four in the morning. He never sleeps. And he calls me all the time at this hour. I'm sure he'd love to chat."

Mimi didn't think he was really calling Lamont. Was he? *Right now?* She'd only said that because she couldn't think of anything else to say!

Daryl held out the receiver. "It's ringing."

Mimi rushed over to take the phone. She hung it up and turned to walk back to the booth and do whatever Daryl wanted.

Then Phat E sprang up on the couch. "What's poppin'," he yelped, pawing at his face and looking around like he didn't know where he was. That broke the tension in the room and everyone, including Daryl, laughed.

"Mimi wants to rewrite the hook of your song," Daryl blurted, assuming Phat E would blow her off as a novice just as he'd done.

Mimi was expecting Phat E to object as well but, to her pleasant surprise, he said, "Great, let's hear what you got, baby!"

When she went back into the booth and sang her lyrics, Phat E, now wide awake and taking up much of Daryl's former terrain at the mixing board, complimented her through her headphones. "I likes, I likes," he said. They played around with the hook for hours, and wound up using a combination of Daryl's lines and hers.

When they left at eight AM, Phat E put his arm around her and, even though she told him her apartment was within walking distance, he insisted on giving her a ride home. "It's great that you can write," he told her as they strolled out to the street. "That's how you make real paper. Rule number one in this biz: Write your own songs and own your publishing."

Daryl followed them out, keeping quiet. He hadn't said much since Phat E went into command mode. Phat E was a hip-hop god, one that Daryl was not prepared to challenge. Mimi climbed into Phat E's black Hummer H2 and watched the guys jovially embrace each other in farewell. But as Phat E went around to the driver's side, Daryl didn't seem to have any warm feelings left for her.

"Later," was all Daryl said and she saw a look in his eyes that told her there would be hell to pay for what had happened tonight. And she'd be the one footing the bill.

◆

CHAPTER 17

Thug Passion

"I FEEL WEIRD," Mimi said, shifting uncomfortably in the booth at Swirl.

"You haven't even had a drink yet," Vanessa replied, wondering where Lena was.

"No, down *there*," Mimi mumbled.

"Oh, your *pussy* feels weird."

Mimi's face contorted into an expression of embarrassment.

"So, what do you call it?" Vanessa asked, amused.

"Not *that*," Mimi said quietly.

"Sweetie, how can you love your pussy if you can't even say the word?" Vanessa sighed, thinking this little chica had a lot to learn. "*My* pussy is my best friend."

"I'm sure it is," Mimi said dryly. She had never thought about hers as something she should love or not love. It was just there.

"What do you think I should call it? *Va-gi-na?*" Vanessa said, precisely enunciating each syllable.

Mimi tried not to smile but couldn't help it.

"I want you to say it," Vanessa insisted.

"What?"

"You know what," Vanessa urged. It was fun to make Mimi squirm. And so easy.

"My...pussyfeelsweird," Mimi said very quickly and very quietly, sorry she had ever brought it up.

"It was your first time," Vanessa said easily, looking around to see which bold-faced names were in attendance that night. "You'll get used to it."

After their first meeting, when she'd noticed unsightly whiskers sprouting out of the bikini Mimi was trying on, Vanessa had dragged her to J Sisters for a bikini wax. Not a Brazilian, for which the J Sisters had become famous. (There was even an autographed photo of Gwyneth Paltrow in their salon, on which the star had written, "Thanks for changing my life.") Vanessa said she was getting a modified Brazilian—a "down below baldy"—which left a strip of hair visible up top. She let Mimi come into the small room to watch her getting all prettied up, after which Mimi was so aghast, she refused to go next. But Vanessa browbeat her little follower into submission. Mimi screamed with pain when hair was ripped, she was flipped over, and her legs were twisted like a pretzel. She felt like she was in the throes of childbirth. Vanessa held her hand, acting like her bikini-wax Lamaze coach. "Now that you've gone bare, you'll never go back," Vanessa had reassured her afterward. "Guys love it!" Now all Mimi had to do was find a guy.

"Please don't tell me you're a virgin," Vanessa said, thinking it was a definite possibility.

"Not at all," Mimi exclaimed defensively.

"High school boys, huh," Vanessa sniffed. Vanessa sniffed a lot. It was like an open carton of rancid milk followed her everywhere.

"Some," Mimi said, her voice full of false confidence. "My last boyfriend is a quarterback at Georgia State," she added, though "last" implied there had been others, and really Jamal was her first and only boyfriend. "He got a football scholarship."

"Really?" Vanessa was intrigued by celebrity, even at the collegiate level. "You think he'll go pro?"

"I don't care," Mimi sniffed like Vanessa was always doing. "It's over with us." She was relieved to see Lena heading toward their table because she did not want to get into a discussion about that jackass Jamal.

With her frayed 7 for All Mankind denim mini, Lena had on a fitted gray T-shirt with a color photo of a very young Grandmaster Flash bending over a turntable with the words "yes yes y'all" written underneath in bubble letters. Her red-and-white 1988 high-top Air Jordans were purchased at Premium Goods in Brooklyn, a store that trafficked in hard-to-find classic kicks. The price for such footwear began at $300. While she was out in BK she'd had a four-finger gold ring that spelled L-E-N-A made.

A picture or column mention of Lena's having this old skool moment would no doubt wind up in some magazine and she would no doubt whine about how annoying it was that everyone else would then bite her style but, truth was, that was the very reason she'd gone through all the trouble.

From her shoulder, she pulled down a late eighties ghettoblaster (she'd gotten it on eBay), put it on the table, and turned around. "Look what Crazy got me!"

It looked like she had Vaseline smeared all over her lower back. Mimi leaned in and Vanessa picked up the votive candle on the table for illumination. Underneath the ointment, they could make out the word "CRAZY" a few inches above Lena's ass, in inch-high gothic letters.

Mimi and Vanessa exchanged horrified glances.

"Oh, girl, you're trippin'!" Mimi whooped.

"*Loca* is right!" Vanessa cried (about the tattoo and the outfit). She would never consider getting a tattoo anywhere on her body. Why tamper with perfection?

"Hush," Lena said gaily. "You know it's hot!"

"So it's official, I guess," Mimi murmured disapprovingly. She hadn't seen Lena in a week because Crazy G was in town. Mimi was concerned because Lena told her she'd "flown him in," which Mimi took to mean she'd paid for his plane ticket. And since she couldn't have guys stay at her huge place or Henrietta, the housekeeper, would report it back to her father, they'd been holed up in the W Hotel on Union Square. Doing the nasty nonstop. Mimi was sure Lena had paid for the room.

"Yes," Lena swooned, in too much of a tizzy to catch Mimi's disapproving tone. "We're in love."

"Did he get a tattoo of your name?" Vanessa ventured.

"No, but I got him a necklace from Jacob's!" Lena said, as if accepting an expensive gift from *her* was somehow an expression of *his* love. Though she was still trying to cut down on the boozing, she ordered a shot of tequila. She was so happy she had to celebrate. She'd just have one. Or two.

"Oh, from Jacob's! You're really ballin' now," Vanessa droned sarcastically. She thought the trinkets that all the rappers bought from the Diamond District gem merchant known as "Jacob the Jeweler" were ridiculously tacky. Alonzo had explicit instructions never to buy her anything there.

"Ballin' fo' real," Lena carped back, reveling in the fun of offending Vanessa. "Fifteen Gs."

Mimi was lost. Who was Jacob?

"You spent fifteen thousand dollars on that nobody!" Vanessa wailed, truly concerned now.

Lena felt like she'd been slapped. Vanessa was calling her nigga a nobody? He was on the verge of being signed by a major label! And she was going to be right there by his side when it happened.

"He's a great lyricist, Nessa," Lena explained, pulling on her gold doorknocker earrings, which she could tell were already infecting her holes. "He's about to blow up. Kaboom! And you can't get much for fifteen Gs. It was tiny."

The waitress brought the tequila shot and Lena took it from her hand and knocked it back without ever letting the glass touch the table.

"Wait, wait. Back it up," Mimi interjected. "You spent fifteen thousand dollars on a necklace for Crazy G?"

Lena shrugged as if it were nothing.

"What's your father gonna say?" Mimi said in a grave whisper. Vanessa had told her that Lena's father was some big-time lawyer and he despised rap, rappers, and purveyors of rap music like Lamont. Most of all, he hated that his Park Avenue–reared daughter was so obsessed with all three. Mimi wondered what he'd think if he learned Lena was dating a thuggish rapper named Crazy G who practically had a bottle of Hennessy glued to his hand.

"He won't know," Lena said in her best I-can-do-whatever-the-fuck-I-want voice. "Daddy's accountant will notice but I'll just tell him Jacob's is a clothing store."

Mimi smelled the distinct odor of trouble but she decided to leave it alone. Mustafa returned to the table from the bar, where he had been chatting up a friend. He sat next to Vanessa, who immediately announced, "Lena's gone *loca*!"

Mustafa wasn't sure why this was news. Wasn't she always?

Lena hefted her butt onto the table and peeled back the waist of her mini so he could get a good look. "It's still healing."

He leaned close, inspected the tattoo, and threw his hands in the air ecstatically. "Oh, ba-bee," he squealed. "It's so hot!"

Lena scooted off the table, turned on her boombox, which started blasting LL Cool J's "Rock the Bells," pulled her fuzzy red Kangol down low, and busted out doing the wop until everyone lapsed into hysterics.

◆

CHAPTER 18

Don't Believe the Hype

LAMONT LAY IN BED CONGRATULATING HIMSELF.

It was a personal coup to have caught the attention of the woman (barely a woman at twenty-one) every man desired and every woman envied. And tonight he'd done more than just catch her attention. Much more.

She was Emma White. Übermodel of the moment. You couldn't go anywhere without seeing her sun-kissed visage or her impossibly perfect body. In the window of Victoria's Secret wearing only a Miracle Bra, on the sides of buses in Calvin Klein ads, on the cover of *Vogue* every other month, in commercials, swinging her luscious golden tresses in slow motion and blowing kisses for Cover Girl. Everywhere you looked, there was the gloriously beautiful Emma White.

Vanessa hated her with a passion.

He'd had models, he'd had a supermodel or two, but Emma was the super of all supes, in her prime, and caught up in the euphoric throes of sticking it to her, he did the unthinkable: banged her without a doctor's go-ahead. Or a condom. She seemed so fresh-faced, so "clean."

Now Lamont rolled over and cursed himself for going bareback. He'd pulled out but damn it had felt good. It had been so long since he'd felt the sweet warmth of a pussy. If he knew a woman wasn't relationship material (not many were) and he'd soon be rid of her, he wouldn't send her to get tested, which meant, stuck between a rock and a hard dick, he had to use rubbers. Aside from the threat of disease, you never knew when one of these gold diggers would "accidentally" wind up pregnant after they told you they were on the Pill. His last real girlfriend, Kendra, had been sent to his doctor for Depo-Provera shots every three months so there would be no slip-ups!

So many stupid guys got trapped like that. Flo$$ had just caught his third paternity case. All that meant was a permanent headache and a lot of money spent supporting a woman you'd never loved and may not have even liked all that much, or else the general consensus was that you were a deadbeat. He'd heard that if a chick had your baby she had legal rights to 17 percent of your income. Seventeen percent of his annual salary would make a bitch a millionaire. It had taken him a long time to make his first million. Longer than nine months. Seventeen percent just for fucking a guy who's doing all the work? It was a shell game.

He'd be a fool to take that big a risk just to dip into some hole for a few minutes. Lamont shuddered dramatically at the possibility. He couldn't stand children. He often had trouble sleeping and everything needed to be just so for him to clock some deep REM time. The temperature had to be exactly 65 degrees, the sheets had to be at least 300 thread count, the room had to be completely dark, and he could not be touched at all or he'd wake right up. The mere thought of a screaming baby within fifty feet was more than he could bear. He had never held his two-year-old nephew, though he had Imani buy the kid the most extravagant birthday gifts she could find.

But the ravishing Emma White wasn't the trapping type. She probably had more paper than he did. He'd heard that she'd cleared fifteen million dollars last year alone. Realizing that was more than he'd made last year, for a moment he felt inadequate. His ego recovered as he reminded himself that models were like athletes. They had maybe a five-year window during which they could make the bulk of their money before they fell off into oblivion. He, on the other hand, would be around for a long, long time.

And if he took over Irv's spot as chairman and sold Triple Large to Augusta, he would soon be a very wealthy man indeed. He rewound that thought and replaced the "if" with "when." *When* he took over Irv's spot. *When* he sold Triple Large. The power of positive thinking could do wonders.

He looked at the bathroom door through which the angelic supermodel had disappeared. He'd always been able to get women but there were some, the real super-fly girls who thought their shit didn't stink (and those were the ones he wanted the worst), who'd treat him like a roach before his pockets got fat. Now he was worthy of the baddest bitch in the world! He wanted to call Nate and Witchy immediately to gloat. They'd been with him earlier when he ran into her.

"Monty," Emma had addressed Lamont familiarly, though they'd only met briefly on a few occasions. "I hear you signed a singer."

"Sure did," he'd said.

"I thought you only worked with the *homeboys*."

"I'm branching out."

"Did you know it's *my* dream to be a singer?" she'd said in her Texas drawl.

It happened to be karaoke night at Curb. "Why don't you go up and sing something, Emma," Lamont had encouraged. "Show us whatcha got, baby."

"I couldn't! I just sing in the shower. I'm not ready for so much exposure," she'd said. It might have been a funny remark considering how far and wide her modeling gigs had exposed her, but the irony was lost on Emma.

"Well, maybe you could audition for me privately," Lamont had suggested.

He was shocked when she actually took him up on his subsequent offer to come back to his place for a nightcap. And he'd gotten her singing all right, hitting all the high notes between his Pratesi sheets!

But he couldn't call his boys yet. That would have to wait until she was out of earshot. And he wouldn't dare ask her to leave in the middle of the night. He was so lost in his reverie, thirty minutes had gone by before he realized she was still in the bathroom. Probably doing her model shit.

He tapped at the door. "Emma," he said softly. "Emma, baby, you taking a bubble bath or something?"

No answer. He hesitantly pushed the door but it opened only a few inches. He pushed harder and saw a pale foot with perfectly manicured red toes pointing toward the ceiling.

What the hell... He squeezed into the bathroom. "Emma!" he screamed in horror.

She lay on the hard tile, naked and seemingly unconscious. He couldn't help marveling at how hot she was. She had full, perfectly round, natural breasts and neatly trimmed blond pubic hair. Had she passed out? She had been drinking, but not enough to lead to this.

Lamont bent down and gently slapped her once-rosy cheeks. "Emma, baby," he wailed. "Wake up. Emma!" Lamont tried lifting her taut torso and noticed something on the floor by her waist. A syringe.

He leaned back against the marble bathtub with Emma's golden locks splayed across his thick thighs. Raising two clenched fists skyward, he howled, "Fuuuuuck!"

This fetching, flaxen-haired Southern belle who had beguiled him with stories of how close her family had been growing up in a "lil' town outsida Dallas" could not be a fucking junkie! There wasn't a mark on her exquisite body. Lamont rocked back and forth, stroking her face feverishly. Then he dropped her like a stone, her head knocking on the floor as he raced to the phone.

"Oh this is a damn shame," unflappable Nate said ten minutes later as he bent down on Lamont's bathroom floor to check Emma for a pulse. He'd sped right over after calling Mustafa "the non-performing performance artist," a known drug abuser.

The ten minutes had seemed like an eternity to Lamont. "Wake up, Emma! Wake up!" he'd pleaded as if she were just in a really deep slumber. Lamont held her head in his lap and gazed at her perfectly symmetrical features until he saw something else. Tomorrow's likely headline in the *New York Tribune*:

SUPERMODEL OD'S IN RAP MOGUL'S PENTHOUSE

"Fuuuuuck!"

He hadn't even done anything to her! But those media vultures would make it seem that he was the villain. That he had somehow defiled her. It would somehow come off like he'd killed her! Just because he was a hip-hop nigga who'd had the nerve to rise from the Marcy projects and she was the whitest woman in America.

That's why calling an ambulance was not an option. Nate was his personal 911 in delicate situations. Nate would help him move her so if she died, she'd die elsewhere.

"Damn, she's hot," Nate commented as Mustafa rummaged through his black doctor's bag.

Lamont stood looking over Nate's shoulder. It was good thinking that Nate had called Mustafa. Only a druggie knows how to treat a druggie. Lamont hadn't even thought of that. He'd been so panicked.

"Heroin," Mustafa diagnosed.

"But she doesn't have track marks," Lamont said.

Lamont felt himself trembling and he hoped that Nate and Mustafa wouldn't notice. He often instilled fear in others but letting his own fear show was unacceptable. He couldn't remember the last time he'd felt this scared. Usually a crisis invigorated him, shifted him into battle mode. Business maneuvers often felt like life-or-death situations to him, but this really was. He'd spent almost ten years building a name and a burgeoning empire. If this incident turned out badly, it could change everything.

But, he suddenly thought, *would it be all bad?*

Scandal boosted careers all the time. It helped minor celebs break out onto the national radar. And he hadn't done anything to Emma. She had gotten into this all by her damn self.

The reasoning was Machiavellian, but so what? Nate's uptight, overeducated girlfriend, Jordan, had given him a book called *What*

Would Machiavelli Do? a few years back. He never read anything that didn't affect him professionally. Jordan was always reading some five-hundred-page novel "for fun" by the pool in the Hamptons or when they all went on vacation together. What a bore! He read video treatments for his artists. He read magazine articles in which he was mentioned, and even then just skimmed until he saw his own name. He had no time to read for pleasure. *If it don't make dollars, it don't make sense.* If he wanted information, he watched CNN.

Machiavelli? Never heard of the guy. But he'd gobbled that book up flying home from St. Bart's. He sensed that Jordan was subtly trying to tell him something, teach him some lesson. The book was her Christmas gift to him and he saw on the back cover that it cost $11.95. *Don't put yourself out, Jordy baby.* She couldn't even splurge on a hardcover? And that year Imani had sent the cheap bitch a pair of Jimmy Choos.

But it had turned out to be a good read. He still wasn't sure what point Jordy was trying to make (she was always working an angle) but he had Imani send her a thank-you note that said, "Loved the book. This nigga's got it all figured out."

Ends justified the means. Said it all, didn't it? A dead supermodel in his apartment (through no fault of his own!) would get him into *Vanity Fair* for sure.

"Look between her toes," Mustafa said calmly. Lamont spread her toes apart and noticed tiny scars between them.

"Damn, she even has nice feet," Nate said. "They soft?"

"No, they're cold," Lamont shouted, regarding Nate with a scornful look, "because she's DYING in my fuckin' crib, money!"

Why would Emma do this to herself? She had everything. And to think he used to drool over the glamour girls, believing them way beyond his reach. Then he made a name for himself and a little money and they began coming on to him. But it didn't take long to realize they weren't all that special. Sometimes they smelled bad, some of them were average pretty when the makeup came off or their tits sagged when the bra came undone, and all of them were more insecure that you'd think any woman of their good looks and fortune would be.

Lamont looked at poor Emma, sprawled out on the marble floor, lips turning blue, and felt sorry—for himself. *Another fantasy bites the dust,* he thought. Maybe he should find a normal girl with a normal career. Someone who brought less drama. Beautiful though.

No, he told himself after a moment's contemplation, *that'd probably be boring.*

Mustafa plunged a shot of Narcan into Emma's breastbone with the precision of a surgeon and they all leaned over her, waiting for signs of life.

Emma finally let out a strangled gasp of breath and moaned quietly. Her dainty hand went to the throbbing at the back of her head. Her eyelids fluttered. Then her baby blues focused curiously on the three black men staring down at her perfect, naked body.

◆

CHAPTER 19

Gossip Folks

"FUCK TRAVIS PETERS," Lena shouted as she barged into Mimi's apartment, shrouded in an oversized Triple 5 Soul hoodie. She flung a folded copy of the *New York Tribune* at Mimi's chest. "What an irrelevant little prick!"

As Mimi bobbled the unexpected pass, the toothbrush that was hanging from her mouth fell to the floor along with a foamy string of Crest Ultra White.

"Who is Travis Peters?" Mimi mumbled, wiping her mouth.

"A gossip columnist and professional fuckin' playa-hater!" Lena took a seat on the black leather couch in the living room. It made noise when you sat on it and she made a mental note to tell Mimi to ask for a furniture allowance so she could feminize the apartment. She put her Starbucks cup down on the table and started tapping a fresh box of Marlboro Lights. "Can't a bitch have a little fun without it being all over town?"

Mimi went to the kitchen and placed the newspaper on the

counter. After rinsing her mouth and setting aside her pink tooth-brush, she grabbed an ashtray and returned to the couch.

"Mimi," Lena said impatiently. "You've gotta read it!"

"Read what?" Mimi said, rubbing her eyes. "I don't know what you're talking about. It's ten in the morning." Mimi did a morning stretch and slumped back on the arm of the couch. "I swear, girl, you are the only person I know who can be having a bad day before the day even begins."

Mimi had slept most of the day yesterday after another all-nighter in the studio and her body clock was still off. She had sup-plied the hook on another song that was going on the Triple Large tenth-anniversary album featuring all the artists on the label. She wasn't even really singing. It was more like moaning. Daryl had said, "Pretend I'm fuckin' you and you're about to come." What a grotesque image! She couldn't even look the studio engineer in the eye after that. And she really did have to pretend. She'd never had an orgasm. At least, not with someone else in the room.

Lena flicked her lighter. "Travis Peters has ruined my whole day and for what?" she said. "Because I had a few drinks?" She cut on the television. "And panties give me yeast infections! Just get the paper and read it. Page eight."

Mimi huffed and lifted herself from the sofa. She stood at the kitchen counter and opened to the page. She quickly scanned the gossip column, taking in the headlines. Then her eyes locked on a picture that was actually on the adjacent page, page nine. A picture of herself. Her heart fluttered. The second thing she noticed was her name in bold. She read:

Hip-hop heavyweight **Lamont Jackson** is branching out. He recently signed a songstress named **Mimi Jean** (above) to a deal with his Triple Large Entertainment. The Toledo native has been in town for only a few weeks but she seems to have gotten into the swing of New York nightlife. The statuesque 20-year-old stunner has been hitting all the hot spots with **Lena** "Make It a Double" **Whitaker**, wild child daughter of powerhouse entertainment lawyer turned Oscar-winning movie producer **Marlin Whitaker**, and model **Vanessa de la Cruz**, Jackson's sister-in-law, who also took Jean on a whirlwind shopping spree last week with Jackson's Amex Centurion card. The trio were spotted late Saturday night downing tequila shots at Swirl. Later at Lint, Whitaker, inexplicably dressed like an extra from Krush Groove, spent an hour crawling around on all fours trying to locate her rhinestone-encrusted cell phone, giving a few appreciative men an X-rated peek up her denim miniskirt. Jean's album will be released next spring but she will soon make her debut singing the hook on a song with rap superstar **Supa Phat E.** The rap-sung collabo will be included on the Triple Large–produced soundtrack for the upcoming romantic comedy *Good Lookin'* starring **Morris Chestnut**, **Sanaa Lathan**, and **Taye Diggs**. "She's going to be the next J.Lo," Jackson told me before adding, "but Mimi can really sing." (Watch out, Lamont. J.Lo holds grudges.) Hopefully, Jean won't follow the lead of Miss Whitaker, who many believe has a rehab stay in her future. Bottoms up!

"I'm no lush," Lena was yelling from the living room, puffing hard on her cigarette. "And that's the last time I wear a skirt! You came off sounding good, though."

Mimi rushed over with the paper and spread it out on the coffee table. "It says that I was doing tequila shots," she cried. "I wasn't! I only had soda."

Lena slowly cocked her head and cut her eyes at Mimi. "Bitch, do you think these motherfuckers care if the shit they print is accurate?"

Mimi slowly read the paragraph again. "Well, it's not like he made all this up," she said. "The stuff in here about you *is* accurate." She sent a smirk Lena's way.

Lena looked away. "Yeah, Travis has spies everywhere." She glanced back and noticed Mimi, wide-eyed, reading the words for a third time. "But it says you're gonna be a big star. Focus on the positive!"

"But how did they get this picture?"

"They have people all over," Lena said disinterestedly.

A guy had snapped a few pictures of Mimi and Vanessa that night before Lena showed up. She'd thought he wanted a picture of Vanessa because she was a famous model. Vanessa made her switch places in the booth so he could get her "good side." Mimi had no idea who the man was. She'd just smiled.

"You got an item in record time," Lena said, still pouting. "Are you excited?"

Mimi stared at the picture until a smile crept across her face. It *was* a nice picture. She just couldn't believe it was staring back at her from the newspaper. "Well, yeah, I guess I am," she said softly. It sounded more like a question than a declarative statement.

Then she suddenly felt a rush of excitement. "I'm going to send this to my mom," she chirped, beginning to tear the page. "And Toya and Keesha. Everybody in Toledo!"

Lena swung her leg over the table and planted her brand-new Nikes on top of the paper. "Don't send it to your mother."

Mimi furrowed her brow and tried to smooth the page that was now ripped down the middle. "She'll be so excited to see my picture," she said. "In the newspaper! And it says that I have talent."

Lena shot her a pitying sidelong glance, thinking *Oh God, Dorothy, don't start clicking your heels because Kansas or whatever ain't nowhere for you to be.* "She'll think you're here boozing it up every night."

"That's what it says about you," Mimi said, folding the page up. "Not me."

Sometimes it annoyed her that Lena wanted to call all the shots. "Don't wear that, it's corny," Lena had told her the other night when they were getting ready to go out. "Stop talking to that guy, he's a buster," she'd whispered when a cute guy started chatting Mimi up at the club. And, an hour later, "We're leaving, I'm over this place!"

But, mostly, Lena was a barrel of laughs and Mimi couldn't imagine what she would have done here if she hadn't had Lena to take her around and show her the ropes. And sometimes Mimi wondered what Lena ever did without *her.* Lena didn't seem to have many other friends. And, of course, she had no job and she wasn't in school. For the first time, Mimi really understood what the term "life of leisure" meant.

"My father's gonna have a coronary over this," Lena said, sulking. "He's reamed my ass for a lot less than what it says in here."

I would too if I were him, Mimi thought. What father wanted to read in the newspaper that his daughter was getting slammed on tequila and crawling around in public with her coochie all hanging out?

"Thank God he's in L.A. so maybe he won't hear about it," Lena said, the possibility making her perk up briefly. "But he's got a lot of friends here and those people just love to point a fuckin' finger." She slunk back down, placed her hand on her stomach inside her sweats, and sighed. "But you got your picture in there with your first item," Lena said encouragingly, her mood fluctuating by the second. "It took me at least five or six mentions before I got a picture. Shit, ten before I had a *good* picture."

Mimi wasn't really sure why Lena was mentioned in the column at all. Vanessa was a model. And now Mimi was a recording artist. But Lena didn't do anything but hang out with people who were well known. She could tell that Lena actually liked the press attention even if it made her sound like a 12-step reject.

The phone rang. It was Vanessa. She asked Mimi, "Did you see the paper?"

"Yeah," Mimi said, excited all over again.

"I can't believe this!" Vanessa snarled. "I should fire Ally C. She doesn't deserve to be called a publicist."

"Believe what?" Mimi said.

"They called me a model."

"You *are* a model, aren't you?"

There was an ominous pause. "I'm a *super*model! Big difference," she shrieked and slammed the phone down.

"Yeah, she hates that," Lena said sympathetically when Mimi relayed the brief phone conversation, upset that Vanessa had hung up on her.

Lena stubbed out her third cigarette in fifteen minutes. "Okay, get dressed," she said. "We're going to lunch. Then we'll go shopping so we'll have some cute stuff to wear out tonight. We have to celebrate."

"Celebrate what?"

"Chile, you got your first item," she said. "In this town that's like having your cherry popped. And I deserve some fun after waking up to *this*. I'm not gonna let Travis Peters fuck with my flow."

Mimi grabbed the newspaper and scurried away to change.

"We'll just have to go someplace low-key so we can kick it in peace," Lena called behind her.

In the privacy of her new bedroom, Mimi stared at her first bit of publicity. She skimmed both pages and came across another item that made her heart jump. Oh my God! How could Lena not have mentioned that one? She must not have seen it. Mimi had to tell her before someone else did. She crept nervously back to the living room.

Lena looked up. "What?" she said, perplexed by Mimi's distraught expression.

"Um, Lena, there's something in here about Crazy G," Mimi said anxiously. "Didn't you see it?"

"I missed it," Lena said, grabbing the paper. "I just read the part about us." Why was Mimi acting so weird? A mention about Crazy G meant he was moving up in the world. He'd just signed with Def Jam. It was probably a mention about that. Lena scanned the bold-faced names and didn't see anything about Crazy G. "Where?"

Mimi sat down next to Lena on the couch and pointed to the section that was headlined "Sightings." Crazy G's name wasn't in bold because he wasn't the famous person being mentioned. Paulina, the *P* in the girl group PYT, was. Lena read the item that was buried amid the other celebrity sightings about town: "**Paulina Rivera**, the fetching lead singer of the platinum-selling R&B trio PYT, canoodling at Lint with rapper Crazy G, a new signing to the Def Jam roster. Her rep says, 'They're just friends.' Sure, maybe he was just examining her for cavities."

Lena gasped for air as if she'd been punched in the gut and then burst into violent sobs. Without a word, Mimi wrapped her arms around Lena and let her cry. Mimi wanted to find the right words to console her but what could she say? Her girl had been played and after broadcasting her love of Crazy G all over town, everyone would know it.

CHAPTER 20

◆

Magic Stick

BY THE TIME KENDRA TRUESDALE ARRIVED at Dylan's Candy Bar, Pedro Miguel Antonio de la Cruz Jackson's third birthday party was in full swing. The cornucopia of colorful confections on display in the huge store made her feel like she was stepping into a gumball machine.

"Who invited her?" Vanessa muttered to Alonzo. They watched Kendra walk directly over to Mama Jackson. "Why is your mother inviting people to *my* son's party without asking me?" Vanessa whined.

"Because it's her *grand*son's party and she can invite anybody she wants," Alonzo snapped back. "She organized the whole thing anyway."

Alonzo kept a close eye on Pedro, who, in keeping with the party's Western theme, was running around in a little cowboy hat and vest, waving a toy gun. Vanessa didn't feel the need to stand watch since his three nannies were present. Also running around the party was a video crew from The E! channel, a reporter and photographer from *Parents* magazine, a photographer from *Us Weekly*, and the Jackson family's personal lensman. Ally C., with the help of an assistant named Kerri D., was in high gear making sure the press corps were getting everything they needed.

Pedro ran up to his parents. "What's doin', pardner," Alonzo said easily.

Over Pedro's head, Vanessa whispered to her husband, "Maybe you can lasso me later, cowboy." Alonzo's eyes lit up and he forgave his wife every caustic comment she'd made that day about his mother and all the "ugly kids and their ugly parents" at the party.

The ultimate in cowgirl chic in her tan suede, fringed Ralph Lauren pants, a gingham top tied at her waist, and two long, loose pigtails, Vanessa took her son's hand and walked toward the camera lights.

WHILE MAMA WAS STRAIGHTENING the faux ponytail sprouting from the top of her head, she urged Kendra to go over and talk to Lamont.

"Do I look all right?" Kendra asked, blotting her lips and fidgeting with her snug sweater.

Mama looked her up and down. "Are you wearing a bra?" she asked bluntly.

"Um, no," Kendra faltered, completely caught out there.

"You gotta do what you gotta do," Mama allowed, giving her an encouraging pat on the back.

Mama studied Lamont's reaction when he saw his ex approaching. Mama could always tell a fake smile from a real one on her boys. Lamont was definitely pleased to see Kendra. And that pleased Mama immensely.

When they'd had lunch last week, Mama hadn't breathed a word to

Kendra about the new developments at Augusta. Lamont had told her to keep it on the low and she respected his wishes. Anyway, her agenda for their lunch had been personal, not professional. She'd given her formal support for Kendra's campaign to win back Lamont. A man of Lamont's stature needed a wife to handle his social affairs. More so now than ever with this new high-profile position on the horizon. Lamont was approaching forty and it was high time he settled down.

Mama had decided Kendra Truesdale was just the woman for the job. Lamont didn't seem to recognize that yet but...Mama always knew best.

THE CORNER OF THE PARTY where Lamont was situated looked to be operating like a makeshift office. Since he could not fit on any of the child-sized stools or benches, he was hunkered down in a leather armchair that belonged to the owner (who happened to be Ralph Lauren's daughter, Dylan). Imani and her assistant, Vicki, were standing guard and Lamont was speaking heatedly to Witchy, who was nodding in agreement. It was a scene Kendra had seen many times before. It didn't matter that this was a child's birthday party and the rest of the room was an uncontrolled storm of activity. Lamont was his own movable office and his shop was always open for business.

Kendra approached cautiously because he seemed to be deep in conversation and she didn't want to risk the embarrassment of having Imani turn her away. But then Lamont spotted her and smiled. Her stomach did a little flip as he dismissed Witchy and beckoned her through his personal velvet rope of assistants.

"Sit," he invited, pulling up a kiddie stool. He turned and pumped some Sour Patch Kids out of the candy dispenser to his right.

Kendra positioned herself on the orange stool and had a flashback of the last time she'd run into Lamont, three months ago. She'd been coming out of her facialist's office and she'd looked a fright. Her face was glistening with post-treatment salve, her hair was haphazardly clipped up, and she had on her oldest sweats and a North Face parka. Lamont, looking as dapper as ever, was exiting a restaurant on Prince Street. He invited her to hop into his car to get out of the cold and, despite her unsightly appearance, it was an offer she couldn't refuse. They caught up with each other on the trip uptown. He told her he was just back from spending the holidays in St. Bart's. The previous year she'd gone with him on the trip. She wondered who he'd taken this year. She decided not to mention that she'd spent an unglamorous Christmas in Florida with her family, traveling on a bargain basement coach class ticket.

When they reached his office, it seemed for a moment like he might kiss her good-bye. Just an affectionate peck on the cheek, but it would have made her day. He leaned in, hesitated, then pulled back and *blew* her a kiss. She knew it was because her face was all lubed up and she cursed her rotten timing. He instructed his driver to take her home and told her he'd call so they could have dinner sometime. She'd just been starting to get over him, but after that encounter she found she missed him more than ever. And then he'd never called.

Today she was prepared. Her thick black hair was loose and wavy the way Lamont always liked it. The outlines of her nipples were visible through her thin, pink cashmere sweater. The color nicely complemented her bronze skin and she knew the Levi's superlows flattered her undeniably magnificent ass.

"I ran into your mother last week," Kendra said, feeling the need to explain her presence. "She invited me."

"That's cool," Lamont said agreeably. "I don't even know half these people."

"You must really like this place," Kendra said, feeling awkward because it had been so long since they'd had any real interaction. "I know you love your sweets."

Lamont shook the candies in his hand and smirked. "I'm trying to cut this shit out." He ruefully rubbed his potbelly, hidden under a black Sean John velour sweatsuit.

"You look like you've *lost* weight," Kendra said, trying her damnedest to sell the line.

"Thank you for that," Lamont said, appreciating the white lie. "Unfortunately, my suits are telling a different story. I've decided I'll have everything custom-made before I ever set foot into Rochester Big and Tall."

Kendra laughed as Lamont refilled his empty hand with some Swedish fish.

Vanessa and Ally C. suddenly appeared in front of them, followed by a trail of eager photographers. Vanessa dumped Pedro into Lamont's lap while Ally C. plopped an adult-sized cowboy hat on Lamont's head. Uncle Lamont beamed and Vanessa leaned over them, effectively blocking Kendra from view. After the photographers took their shots, Ally C. grabbed Pedro and the small army of people hurried off. Not a word had been spoken.

"So you seeing anybody?" Lamont continued, as if there had been no interruption.

"No," Kendra said, feeling a rush that he'd asked. She wanted to seem available but at the same time she didn't want to seem undesirable. "I was dating somebody," she added vaguely, wishing it were true.

"Really," Lamont remarked neutrally. "What happened?"

Kendra decided to go for broke. "He didn't *excite* me." She cocked a provocative eyebrow.

Lamont noticed Kendra's erect nipples straining against the soft fabric of her sweater. "Sorry to hear that," he purred.

"What about you?" Kendra said, reaching behind him to grab some sweets, brushing her breasts against him in the process.

"No one special," Lamont admitted, feeling the beginnings of a hard-on as he recalled the many delicious feasts he'd had on Kendra's immense brown nipples.

"Sorry to hear that," Kendra remarked coyly, sucking on a sugary cherry ball.

Lamont allowed his eyes to openly linger on her sticky red lips. Kendra had always liked to play games. They'd had a lot of fun playing some of them together. He felt like taking her hand and putting it down his pants. She had the softest hands. Or better yet, pushing her sticky sweet mouth into his lap. He tensed with frustration as he looked out at the chaotic room teeming with hopped-up kids, wild-eyed parents, and a myriad of party performers—including one very scary-looking clown on stilts. Not exactly the ideal place to have a visible erection. And yet the inappropriateness of the situation excited him that much more.

Lamont shoved Kendra's hand down into his sweatpants and

directed her hand into a full Schwarzenegger grope. "I've missed you," he whispered hoarsely, his bulge expanding at Kendra's touch.

"You should've called me," Kendra said, keeping her tone flirtatious while trying to pull her hand away.

"I did," Lamont said, his rap going on automatic pilot. "Your machine didn't pick up." He kept Kendra's hand pressed inside his pants.

"Try calling back next time," Kendra said. She wrestled her hand away. She knew Lamont was into "public exhibitions" but this was going too far.

"I feel like I could hit a homer with this," he said, quickly glancing down at his wood.

"You could," she whispered seductively. She held his gaze and smoothly ran her hand down the back of his neck, feeling a shiver of arousal just from being near him, from touching him again. Fondly recalling the wild nights they'd had, she lifted her mouth to his ear and breathed, "You always knew how to hit the right spot."

Lamont puffed out his chest and enjoyed a hearty laugh. He uncrossed his legs and grabbed the crotch of his pants, rearranging the fabric to conceal his excitement before some photographer came rushing back over.

Kendra sat up very straight, giving him a moment to reminisce about their good old days. Then, using the tip of her pink tongue to lap up the stickiness from her lips, she spread her legs slightly and tilted her voluptuous sweater-straining chest toward him. She was all ready to propose a get-together in the very near future until she realized that Lamont was peering intently at something behind her.

Kendra glanced over her shoulder and saw the little singer girl bouncing toward them, a Rapunzel-like cascade of wheat-colored locks billowing behind her. As Mimi was ushered right through the guards women, a huge smile formed on Lamont's face.

Then Mimi came to a full stop and emphatically shook out her hair like she was in some kind of Herbal Essences commercial. Kendra, a pacifist by nature, felt like bitch-slapping her.

Lamont thumped his hand on his chest and pretended to choke on his candy. "Daaamn," he said more enthusiastically than Kendra thought necessary. "It looks *really* good."

As Lamont began to introduce the two women, Kendra moved herself from the stool to the arm of Lamont's chair, leaned over, and murmured, "We've met."

"Yes, the other day," Mimi said, wondering if she could make a graceful exit. Kendra had made her feel that she was not welcome. "I wanted to talk to you about something, but . . ."

Lamont searched out Mimi's eyes from underneath Kendra's smothering cleavage. "Talk to me," he said. "Now's a great time. Kendra was just leaving."

Kendra sat upright, her hurt and anger plain.

"Good to see you, baby," Lamont said. He practically shooed Kendra away, as Imani kept a watchful eye on the situation, gauging whether she'd have to step in to get rid of his ex.

Kendra bent over, nipples deflated and gave Lamont a dispassionate kiss on the cheek. "Nice to see you, too," she remarked coolly. For Mimi and Lamont's assistants she had only bitter smiles as she stormed off.

She heard Lamont say, "I'll call you!"

Yeah, right. She'd heard that one before.

◆

CHAPTER 21

Patiently Waiting

"SHE'S GOT A SERIOUS ATTITUDE PROBLEM," Mimi said.

In the ten seconds since Kendra had departed, Lamont had already forgotten about her. "Who?" he asked, gawking at Mimi's long, silken hair.

Mimi decided not to say anything more because whatever was going on between Kendra and Lamont was none of her business. She began petting her hair like it was a horse's mane. Since she'd had it done, she couldn't stop playing with it. She felt as glamorous as Beyoncé on a good weave day. "So you really like it?" she asked.

"Hell yeah!" Lamont said, still examining it. "I can't believe that's your hair. It looks completely different. Beautiful. How do they even do that?"

"I had it flat-ironed," Mimi reported. "By Rod, Lena's stylist."

"And it's lighter, too," Lamont said.

"Rod and Lena decided I should get a little color," Mimi explained.

"Sit down," Lamont commanded and she did.

He poked her chest. "That's cute, too," he said, pleased that her imaging was coming together.

She looked down at the red script letters that spelled Mimi on the left side of her navy blue hoodie. "Vanessa had it done," she said.

The day before, ten personalized Juicy Couture sweatsuits in a rainbow of colors had arrived by FedEx at Mimi's apartment. They were from Fred Segal and Mimi hadn't known who he was. Later, Vanessa told her she'd ordered them from *the store* called Fred Segal in L.A. (Scoop, where they had gone shopping, sold Juicy but they didn't monogram and that, according to Vanessa, was a must.) Mimi liked the suit fine but she'd really worn the outfit today because Vanessa said it had to become her casual uniform and Mimi was afraid of what Vanessa might do if one of her fashion edicts was ignored.

"Thanks again for all the stuff," Mimi gushed.

"You're welcome again," Lamont replied. He noticed a lot of people staring at him from the middle of the room, where gifts were now being opened.

"They just brought out your gift," Imani called out. "Smile and wave."

He smiled and waved. "What'd I get him?"

"A child-sized Hummer."

He stood to get a peek. Pedro was sitting in the pint-sized SUV, smiling, surrounded by press. "That shit is dope!" he said. "It looks just like the real one."

Lamont spied Daryl across the room and frowned. Lost in a mountain of gifts, he was stuffing all the crinkled wrapping paper into garbage bags. He had a tiny cowboy hat tilted over his cornrows with a rubber band under his chin and, over his extra large Vokál tee, a black leather holster that did *not* look like it had come from Toys "R" Us.

As an afterthought, Lamont said, "I thought throwing this party was my gift."

"Yes, you paid for the party," Imani informed him. "But Mama wanted you to give a present people could really see."

"Ah." He nodded. "Chocolate," he requested as he found himself surrounded by only jelly candies.

"Any preference?" Imani asked. "White, dark, milk..."

"An assortment please," Lamont replied.

Imani's assistant, Vicki, rushed off.

"I tried to get in to see you this week," Mimi said, jumping in before his attention wandered again. "We haven't really talked about the direction of my album."

"Yeah," he said, while waving to someone on the other side of the room. "It was a busy week for me."

"But Imani said I could talk to you today. So..." she said, pulling out her trusty songbook, "you know I write my own songs."

"What is Lena doing?" Lamont wondered aloud, watching Lena, loaded down with camera equipment, flitting around the party like a butterfly on crack.

"She thinks she wants to become a photographer," Mimi said. "She's trying to get candid shots or something."

Lena had spent a ton of money on camera equipment because she'd randomly decided that being a celebrity photographer would be a cool profession for her. In the six weeks Mimi had known her, it was the third vocation Lena had considered. She especially needed something now to take her mind off the Crazy G debacle.

"Anyway, like I was saying, you know I write."

Vicki reappeared with a huge orange bowl filled with assorted chocolate candies and handed it to Imani, who then wordlessly set it on Lamont's lap.

"Sorry," he said. "What are we talking about?"

"My songs," Mimi said. "You know I write songs."

"No," he said, picking through the bowl. "As a matter of fact, I didn't."

"I do." She opened the book, since his hands were occupied. "These are songs I've written. I play piano, too, you know."

"Wonderful," he said and glanced at the page she held open. He flinched at the song title, "Soul Cry," as if the words were rising up to slap him. He read the first line. Corny. He went back to his chocolate. "Great," he said blankly. "You write. Now I know."

"Well, don't you want to read some of my lyrics?" she suggested.

"I don't think that will be necessary."

"But...but..." Mimi stopped and composed herself. Daryl had shot her down but she thought he had a personal grudge against her. So she'd decided she would approach Lamont. Anyone could see that Lamont's opinion was the only one that mattered around here. She thought if she could get Lamont on her side, if she could prove herself to him, she'd have a chance to be more involved creatively on her album. But now he was giving her the same brush-off as Daryl! "We haven't really discussed the direction of my album," she said again. "I want to start writing new stuff but I'm not sure what you want."

"We have proven, award-winning songwriters who are already submitting material," he said, "so don't you worry about it."

Daryl hadn't mentioned that. "So who are they? Like who have they worked with."

"All the big people."

"Like who?"

"Christina Aguilera, Usher, Aaliyah," he rattled off impassively, put out that he was being questioned. "Faith Evans, Destiny's Child, J.Lo…"

She liked most of the people he was naming but then she interjected sourly, "J.Lo?"

"What's wrong with J.Lo?" Lamont questioned. "Don't you like her?"

"I like *her*," Mimi admitted. "I guess I don't really like her music. I don't think she's a good singer."

"Same could be said of a lot of people," Lamont remarked, nibbling on a white chocolate–covered pretzel. "You don't need to be. It's the age of technology."

"But, I mean, she's all about image."

"So? A strong image sells records," he countered. "More than a strong voice a lot of times." He put on a sarcastic grin. "Triple Large Entertainment ain't a not-for-profit organization, kiddo."

Kiddo? Mimi thought and tried to repress her scowl. That was what her mother's sleazy boyfriend had sometimes called her. She didn't appreciate it.

"Well, I want to sell records but I don't want to be some flashy J.Lo type," Mimi grumbled. She was confused. What exactly was he saying? That she couldn't write her own songs? That she should be like J.Lo? What? She just wanted a straight answer.

Lamont signaled to Imani that he needed water. "Right, you

want to *touch* people," he said, remembering the first conversation they'd had at his apartment. He thought she'd gotten over that. "So, my dear, what exactly do you want to be?"

"I want to be like Lauryn Hill or Erykah Badu," Mimi announced proudly.

What the hell is she talking about, Lamont thought, getting agitated. "The songs on your demo were not up that alley," he growled. "And the songs you sang at the audition weren't either."

"I know," Mimi acknowledged quickly. "But I was in a group. Kenny was writing the songs and I was going along with what we had to do." She caught her breath. "But now I'm on my own," she stated firmly. "I can do my own thing. And I want to be more of a neo-soul singer."

"Why would you want to be a neo-soul singer?" Lamont groaned. He'd known they were going to have to shape her up but he hadn't realized she was so far off from where they were heading. "You're not fat. You're not ugly."

"Lamont!" Mimi stuck her notebook back in her bag. She obviously didn't need it anymore.

"What next?" he snorted. "Wrap your head in a kente cloth and start rocking dashikis?" He shook his head disapprovingly. "Ain't gonna happen, my *half*-Nubian sista."

"Erykah Badu is not fat or ugly," Mimi objected strenuously, putting a little neck movement into it because she was truly offended. She used to wear head wraps and they looked totally cute!

"She ain't *sexy*," he huffed, waving a chocolate-covered pecan cluster.

"I'm sure a lot of guys think she is!"

"Trust me," he said. "They don't."

"Why does she have to be sexy? She's a talented artist."

"I like Lauryn Hill," he confided, deciding to take the conversation another way.

Daryl approached and shoved a cold bottle of Dasani into Lamont's hand. There was only Evian on the premises so Imani had sent him to the store. Even Vicki, who two months ago was an unpaid intern, was not subjected to store runs.

"Great," Mimi said hopefully. "Why can't I be like her?"

"Lauryn Hill isn't a neo-soul singer," he pointed out, gulping the water while keeping an eye on her. "She's hip-hop. She started out in the Fugees and broadened her audience with her solo, but fundamentally she was still hip-hop. She's not neo-soul."

"Meaning what?" Mimi said, now feeling like she was on the losing end of this battle and not sure how she had wound up there.

"Meaning hip-hop sells!" he said triumphantly. "And you're signed to the hottest hip-hop label in the game, so it's a good start for you, I'd say. And we're gonna put together a dope album for you with the best producers and the best songwriters and it's going to be a motherfuckin' smash." He winked at her. "I know a little bit about making hits, kiddo. So just listen to me."

He stood up and stretched.

Mimi sat there, dazed.

"What's in the little bags?" Lamont asked Imani, noticing gifts being doled out.

"Candy," Imani reported. "I had two put in your car."

"I paid for them," Lamont grunted. "Get me three more."

He put his hand on the back of Mimi's head, ruffling her soft, fragrant hair, and kissed her on the forehead. Then he marched toward the front door.

Lena made a beeline for him, waving and shouting his name like a veteran paparazzo. She jumped in his path, hustling backward and knocking several small children aside as she fired off a succession of quick shots.

Lamont played the part of hounded celebrity to perfection. He gave her his best smile and never broke stride.

◆

Living Triple Large

CHAPTER 22

◆

The Way You Move

THREE MONTHS LATER, Mimi sat in Lamont's office gleefully watching the rough cut of her video with Supa Phat E for their song, "Flyass Bitch," which was already getting major play on the radio.

The first time Mimi had heard it on Blazin' 104, she'd been shopping with Lena for kicks at Dr. Jay's on 125th Street. They both started singing and dancing around the store and almost ran out without paying for the sneakers they were trying on. "It's so hot, it's so hot," Lena kept saying about the song. Impressing Lena was the feat of the year, as far as Mimi was concerned.

Shooting the video had seemed to take forever. Really, it was two fourteen-hour days. Mimi was happy she'd had Phat E right there next to her most of the time to tell her what to do and to keep her relaxed. Lamont had been there, too, but he'd done the opposite: told her what to do and made her nervous. The director, Josh "White Boy" Goldstein, hadn't seemed to appreciate so much unsolicited input from Lamont.

Mostly they shot on a soundstage in Queens that was set up to look like a nightclub. Mimi hung in her trailer with Lena and Vanessa when she wasn't needed on set. In the video, Lena appeared next to her during the club scenes and driving around the city in a maroon Lexus SUV. Vanessa refused to be an extra in a music video, declaring it was beneath her. But she styled Mimi head to toe, from her wraparound Gucci shades to her quilted Chanel boots. Lena brought an entire Louis Vuitton trunk full of her own gear.

Watching the video now, Lamont didn't seem too excited. He was just tapping the remote control on his thigh until one image made his eyebrows shoot up. It was the scene where Mimi had to press her entire body against Phat E and put her lips very close to his face as he rapped directly to the camera. Lamont had left the set during that part because he wasn't getting good cell phone reception.

Shooting this scene on the first day had been awkward for Mimi. "Get closer," Josh kept directing her. "Move in more. He's supposed to be your man. Act like you adore him. Let's try it again."

After the fourth take, before Josh could try his gentle approach again, Phat E swooped his ham hock of an arm around her and said, "Aaalll right, girl, I need to break for lunch. If you don't get all up on me, I'mma put you on my lap and you might find eight inches of dick up your skirt!" The entire crew of thirty roared with laughter. Mimi blushed red and nailed the part of seductress on the fifth take.

Seeing it now, Lamont didn't think she needed to look quite that cozy with Phat E (he wasn't even on the label!) but he let it go. He swiveled around in his chair to face Mimi on the sofa.

"Very good, nice job," Lamont said enthusiastically when the reel ended. "The song is doing so well that this will go right into rotation on MTV."

Mimi radiated with happiness as he buzzed Imani and told her to get someone named Fatima on the line.

"Now, sweetheart, how's the media training going?" he asked her.

"Good," Mimi answered.

She had been seeing a woman who was teaching her how to handle herself during interviews. The sessions were helpful but it was a pain to have to go during the day when she'd rather be sleeping. She had been in various studios for the last three months recording, usually at night. She'd been working in Atlanta and Miami as well as New York with several different producers. When she got a day off, all she wanted to do was sleep!

But there was no time to rest. Besides the media sessions, she had appointments with the latest addition to the Mimi makeover team—a personal trainer. Mark Jenkins was a military man–turned–celebrity fitness guru and his claim to fame was that he had made some of the biggest names in the music industry puke from overexertion. For their first workout, he had Mimi jogging around the Central Park reservoir with a parachute harnessed to her back. Afterward, Mimi told Imani she didn't think she could handle any more sessions with Sergeant Mark. Imani had said, "Don't give up. He'll have your thighs firmed up in no time!" *Now her thighs were a problem?* Mimi played sick to get out of the next session and then Imani scolded her because the label had to pay Mark his $1,500 per session fee anyway. Now, all Mimi could think while running was, *This is a rip-off!*

"I wanted to talk to you today about something that goes hand-in-hand with the media training," Lamont said.

Mimi sat at attention.

After a long pause, he said, "You're black."

"Uh, yeah, I know." What was he talking about? "My dad was black." Mimi heard herself talking about her father in the past tense and stiffened.

Lamont waved his hand impatiently. "That's what I mean," he said. "You can't just say your dad is black. *You are black.* We can't have you doing that 'I'm a little this, a little that' thing." He saw confusion on her face. "So you're black, understand?"

"No," Mimi said snippily. "I don't. My mom is Italian and my mom raised me." She couldn't believe what he was asking her to do. "You want me to lie," she said, her voice rising, "and say my mom is black?"

"No, I don't want you to say that," he said, looking at her fair complexion and long, highlighted locks. "People probably wouldn't buy that anyway. But you have to come across as black-*identified.* Be mindful of that. When you're asked what music you grew up listening to, mention black artists."

Well, I can do that, Mimi thought, *because it's true.* She grew up listening to her mother's favorite soul singers and now she favored popular R&B. But she also listened to Avril Lavigne, No Doubt, and Evanescence. What about Nelly Furtado? She was on the brown side. Could she be mentioned?

"You can say that your mother is white," Lamont allowed, "but say that you consider yourself black. Okay?"

Mimi didn't like the sound of that. Her mother might be hurt. "Why does it matter?"

"Listen to me," Lamont said sharply. "It matters. Image is everything and we can't have you being all wishy-washy on that point. We need you to *read* black."

It didn't really matter that much to Mimi. She did consider herself black. But she also considered herself Italian. Why was he making it such a big deal? "Well, Alicia Keys is biracial," she pointed out. Mimi loved Alicia.

"Exactly," Lamont said, stabbing his finger in the air. He'd been about to take the conversation there. "Alicia's mom is white but that girl reps the black side to the fullest," he said admiringly. "That's what you need to do. Be like Alicia."

Well, when he put it that way, Mimi thought she could do as he wished. Not that she had any choice. No one ever second-guessed or disobeyed Lamont. He never raised his voice with her but he had a no-nonsense way about him that made her feel on edge every time she was around him. The other day she realized that he'd sent her to six "improvement specialists" (vocal coach, dermatologist, hairstylist, cosmetic dentist, personal trainer, media coach) even though he'd initially told her she was so gorgeous and talented. It made her feel like once he'd gotten a closer look at her he'd come to the conclusion that she looked a whole lot better from a distance. She was constantly trying to prove to him that she was worth all the trouble. But the more money and effort the label poured into her album and imaging, the more pressure she felt to be successful. To be perfect.

It didn't help that whenever she was around Lamont, he seemed to be charting her progress. He'd give her a subtle once-over and say things that let her know he was aware of every little thing that she was doing, even though she might not see him for weeks. The other day he'd offhandedly told her, "Your skin's looking a lot better." It was a backhanded compliment, if it was a compliment at all, but she'd become so desperate for his approval that she blurted, "Omigod...thanks!"

Now he was telling her that she was not black enough. And she found herself saying obediently, "Sure, Lamont, I can do that. I can read black. I can be like Alicia. Maybe I should wear some cornrows!"

Lamont smiled. "I might let you rock some cornrows," he said, thinking how damn adorable Mimi could be sometimes. "But I'm not speaking quite that literally." He could see that he really needed to spell it out for her. "You see, honey, white record buyers today don't care about race," he explained slowly, as if speaking to a second grader. "Not the young audience, anyway. They want what's cool. Alicia is cool. And so are you."

Mimi smiled.

"Flo$$ is cool, Radickulys is cool. White kids buy into coolness as defined by black artists. They want to be down. I mean, look at all these pop stars who are trying to flip it and align themselves with hip-hop. Christina Aguilera has a soulful voice and she's Spanish, but imagewise she was as white as she wanted to be on that first album, wasn't she? But listen to her now."

He began mimicking Christina's voice: "'Yeah, you know, I'm workin' wit Rocwilder and Redman on my new album. Yeeeah, it's gonna be on fo' real.'"

Mimi cracked up at his dead-on impersonation.

"Last week for the first time in history, all of the top ten singles on the Billboard chart were by black artists. Did you know that?"

"No," Mimi said, and let him continue. She'd learned that Lamont wanted to hear himself talk, not hear what anyone else had to say.

"That blows my mind!" he said. "This is the mainstream top

forty chart! And *nine* of those ten records featured a hip-hop artist."
He sat for a minute, nodding to himself. "Then last night, I see
Aaron Carter on MTV *Cribs*. And I'm watching this blond, blue-eyed
kid, who's got a squeaky clean image and I'm asking myself, 'Why is
this kid a teen heartthrob? Why does he have three platinum albums
at sixteen?' Because he's just like any other kid. So what makes him
special? And the answer is...nothing. That's his selling point—his
ordinariness. Other kids can identify with him because he *is* them.
And you know what this average, white suburban kid who just happens to be a pop star is wearing as he gives a tour of his Florida mansion? A diamond stud in each ear, a bandanna under a backwards-
turned baseball cap, and a white T-shirt with a huge portrait of Tupac
spray-painted on the front." He laughed. "Hip-hop is not just part of
black culture anymore. It's the predominant force in youth culture,
in popular culture. It sets the trends, the lingo. It leads the way." He
paused to let his words sink in, then he gave himself a verbal pat on
the back. "You could say I'm a big part of that."

"Yes," Mimi said seriously, bowing her head slightly as if he were
the Dalai Lama. "I know."

"And look at that kid, Trey, from that group Chi-town," Lamont
continued. "That cat sold eight million albums with his boy band
and now his solo album is coming out and motherfuckas say it's
gonna be the R&B joint of the year. He doesn't have one white producer on there. The *R&B* album of the year," he repeated, eyes
bulging as if to say, *Can you believe that?* "And I guarantee it's going
to do pop numbers."

Mimi nodded vigorously. "Yes," she said. "I see what you're saying."

"So, white folks want to get a little taste of what we got, our flavor," he said, suppressing a smile because Mimi looked like she was about to take out a spiral notebook and start scribbling notes. "If you're cool and your material is right—which it will be—they'll come around to you. But you know what our real problem is?"

"No," Mimi said.

"Black women," he told her.

"Black women?"

"Black women will hate you if you try to half-step on the race thing."

Mimi thought back to those girls who'd hate on her in high school and felt a twinge of anxiety.

"You're already the pretty light-skinned chick with the long flowing hair," Lamont continued. "Remember when Mariah first came out and she tried to play that 'I'm Irish and Venezuelan and whatever else' bullshit?"

Mimi knew all about Mariah's mixed-race heritage. It was one of the reasons she idolized Mariah. Mariah also wrote most of her songs and Mimi felt she didn't get enough credit for that. She'd even dragged Toya and Keesha to see *Glitter* just to support her songwriting, biracial sister. "But she *is* black and Irish and Venezuelan so why shouldn't—"

"Bitches *hated* her for that," Lamont continued as if Mimi hadn't spoken. "I mean, black folks still bought her album because she has an amazing voice and she got such a big marketing push that she was hard to ignore. But there was an underlying resentment in the community that she wouldn't just say straight out that she was black. It kind of made it seem like she was trying to sell out, though I know Mariah and she's cool as hell. It took her a while to get past that and it wasn't until she got with some hip-hop niggas that she finally did.

She may have gone too far with *that,* which made her lose some of her core audience, but that's another conversation."

Lamont took a breath and folded his hands on his lap. "Remember that your fans will only know you through magazine articles or quick sound bites on television, so we have to be careful about the image we present. Now somebody like Halle Berry did it right." He smiled as he said her name. He'd always wanted to nail that fine ass Halle Berry. "Halle always *read* black and the streets loved her for it from day one. But she still had tons of crossover appeal and won herself a goddamn Oscar! So be like Halle."

"I thought I was supposed to be like Alicia," Mimi said with a teasing smile.

"You know what I'm saying," he said, grinning back. "Embrace who you are. Be proud of it."

"Okay, I get it," she said. She couldn't believe they had had this discussion at all, much less for so long. "I'm black and I'm proud."

He narrowed his eyes at her. Was she being cutesy? He couldn't tell. "Don't ever say that in an interview," he instructed.

"What?"

"'I'm black and I'm proud.' Sounds like an Afrocentric greeting card. Sounds forced."

"I'm not going to say that in an interview, Monty," she said. "But I get the point. I'm going to *read* black."

Okay, that's done, Lamont thought. *She's more of a fixer-upper than I expected, but she's shaping up.*

Imani buzzed. "Fatima on line two."

"Fatima," Lamont said into the speakerphone. "How you doin', baby?"

"Good, Monty. Working my ass off."

"I know you are, you always stay busy. And you're about to get even busier. I have a client for you. You've heard of my new singer, Mimi?"

"Yeah," Fatima responded. "I heard the song she did with Phat E. It's bangin'."

"Thank you," Lamont said, accepting the compliment as if he had sung the track. "I've got her right here in my office. Say hi, Mimi."

"Hi," Mimi said, wondering who she was talking to.

"Hey girl, love the song," Fatima called out. "How's your album coming along?"

"Great," Mimi replied.

"So, Fatima, I want you to work with Mimi. She needs a lot of help. You got the time? Can we start this week?"

"I'm in L.A. right now, but I'll be back next week. We can start then. Cool?"

"Cool," Lamont said. "Hold on and I'm going to have Imani pick up and schedule with you."

"Great. Bye Mimi. Can't wait to meet you," Fatima said sweetly, and Mimi replied, "Yeah, me too."

After Lamont buzzed Imani and told her what to do, he hung up.

Immediately Mimi wanted to know, "Who is Fatima?"

"She's the best choreographer in the game," Lamont said. "She works with everybody. Watching that video, I realized something."

"What?"

"You can't dance."

CHAPTER 23

◆

Girls, Girls, Girls

"SO YOU A MODEL?"

"No," the pretty young black woman replied. "I'm a booker at the agency."

Daryl was slightly disappointed by that answer. He'd come to Lint tonight for the IMG agency's model party hoping to hook up with a cover girl, not a booker.

"A booker?" Daryl said slyly. "You should be a model." He looked around at all the statuesque women littering the room. "You as hot as any of them."

"I know," the woman answered matter-of-factly, offended because she'd never said she wasn't. She was only sitting next to Daryl because there was nowhere else to chill. Daryl had intentionally gotten there early to lock down prime seating on the velvet couch in the corner.

"I'm a record producer," he said, offering a hand, which she took reluctantly. "They call me Country D."

"That's nice," she said, supremely aloof.

"I work at Triple Large," he offered proudly. "A&R. I groom talent."

"Triple Large," she said, getting interested now. "What's Flo$$ like?"

Daryl felt his cell vibrating in the pocket of his jeans. He prayed it was not Lamont. Every time Lamont had a half-baked idea, a minor errand, an outrageous demand, or a completely random thought, Daryl's phone rang. Or his pager trilled. Or the intercom in his office buzzed. You couldn't just work for Lamont. You had to live for him. Even when Daryl was asleep, Lamont was there. In his dreams. At least in those scenarios Daryl could come out on top.

He looked at the name glowing on the screen and breathed a sigh of relief. It was his boy Cordell, a producer who'd done some hot tracks for Nelly. He answered and Cordell said he was going to roll over to Lint with his people. Great, because Daryl had come with only two of his boys, both of whom had seemed to disappear amid the sea of lovelies. He needed a real *posse,* one that was going to surround him at all times. It would make him look a lot better.

Bad enough that he'd gotten on the list for the party only by using Lamont's name. If Lamont had been here, Daryl knew his boss would have had his pick of women, even though there was nothing attractive about that slick hustler other than his phat wallet. Those hot chicks Lamont got? Money-hungry hookers, every last one of 'em.

Daryl tapped the pretty booker on the shoulder. She was trying to act like she was in deep conversation with her equally attractive friend next to her. "Flo$$ got a fake leg," he said when she turned around, looking at him like he was a Jehovah's Witness on her doorstep. "Didja know that? More than one. He got a whole bunch in different skin tones so if he got a tan he can be one color all over."

Finally, she smiled. "That's so funny. I read somewhere that he lost his leg in a car accident. I think it's cool that he deals with it so well."

"Cool?" Daryl sneered, annoyed that she wasn't put off by his tidbit of inside info. "That shit is nasty!" He almost added, "if you ask me," until he realized she hadn't.

IT'D BEEN A LONG TIME since Lamont had found himself home alone before midnight on a Saturday night. But here he was. He, Nate, and Alonzo had gone to see the new Al Pacino movie. Afterward, they couldn't remember where that model party was being held tonight. Imani, always on duty, for once hadn't picked up her cell to give them the location, so they'd called it a night.

Bored, he opened a bag of chocolate chip cookies in the kitchen. His bingeing was getting out of control. And the way he'd taken to standing and evaluating his body from every angle in the full-length mirror, he was becoming positively girlish! It was awful and he had to cut it out.

"Only one," he told himself before eating the first cookie and "last one" before eating the next *ten* until there really was only one left and his binge was forced to come to an end. He dusted cookie crumbs from his hands over the kitchen sink and washed the snack down with a glass of two-percent milk. He was thoroughly disgusted with himself.

When he flicked on the light in his bedroom, he jumped back so quickly, he banged his elbow on the wall. Kendra, clad in a lacy black negligee, lay atop his comforter. "Surprise," she whispered seductively.

"Are you out of your mind? How did you get in here?" he cried.

"Trevor let me up. Your door was open like always."

"Trevor who?"

"Your doorman, sweetie pie."

Lamont unbuttoned his Burberry shirt. That doorman was obviously too susceptible to sweet talk. What if she had been stalking him? "Well, you're lucky that I rolled in alone or you would have been really embarrassed." He shook his finger at her.

Kendra positioned herself into a most flattering pose. "So you want me to go?" she said coyly.

Lamont just smirked and sauntered into his palatial master bathroom. He thought of a saying that had made him roar with laughter when he'd first heard it years ago: Show me a beautiful woman and I'll show you a man who's tired of fucking her. Were truer words ever spoken? But after years of hitting it with some of the most beautiful women, it had come to seem more tragic than funny.

Years ago he would have been thrilled to find a creature as sexy as Kendra lying in his bed. Now it barely caused a ripple in his pants. He'd had her. Countless times. He had to find some new way to ratchet up the excitement these days. He could shoot his wad no problem but it wasn't *fun*. It wasn't a rush. What was left? He'd done it all, tried every position with beautiful women of every shape, size, and creed. Worse yet, he couldn't be as sexually uninhibited as he once was. After a woman he'd once been with later tested HIV-positive, he realized he'd dodged a bullet and become more careful.

"You can stay," he graciously called out as he took a piss. "Since you've already made yourself so comfortable."

After their brief, titillating encounter at his nephew's birthday party, he'd lived up to his word and called her. A week later they'd had dinner and wound up sleeping together. It was a nice feeling, familiar but new at the same time. He'd realized over dinner that he had missed her. He'd never really given himself a chance to consider it. Kendra was a good listener. And, unlike other women he'd dated who always seemed to be mentally tallying up what they could buy with his money, she made him feel like she genuinely cared for him. They slept together a few more times after their reunion (she'd been re-tested at his request) and he felt himself easing back into an old groove with her.

Then he met Paola, a Brazilian model whom he just had to have. Kendra was placed on the back burner while he wooed the Brazilian. With the intention of sealing the deal, he invited her to Miami one weekend when Diddy was hosting a party there. He wound up slip-ping it to sexy Paola at three o'clock in the morning on the beach at The Shore Club. Then they came back to New York and she started acting like she owned him. Four weeks later, Paola was out and Kendra was back in.

Not *officially* back in. She'd spent the night last weekend. He'd meant to call her sometime during the week but never did. He'd got-ten two blow jobs in the last week. One in the wine cellar at Lint and another in the bathroom at Villa 4. Then he'd run into Paola the other night on his way out of Heaven and her sad brown eyes had seemed to plead, "Monty, baby, what happened to us?" So he had no choice but to usher the poor thing into his car and let her come home with him. *Sorry, Kendra, all booked up this week.*

Lamont waltzed out of the bathroom and jumped in surprise again. A platinum-blond Amazon whose obviously enlarged breasts were spilling out of her demi-cup was climbing into the bed with Kendra. Where had this one been hiding?

"Happy Birthday, honey," Kendra cooed.

"My birthday isn't for another two months."

"It's a belated birthday present," Kendra said cheekily. "I didn't get you anything last year."

Lamont beamed. *Fuck the model party!* He was having his own model party right here.

Three-ways were always a welcome departure from routine but they were hard to come by. Setting one in motion usually required some spur-of-the-moment coaxing and, for him, full-on bacchanalian hedonism didn't happen that way. Only blow jobs did. There was no way to get two tipsy girls tested on the way home from a club. And, honestly, where was the fun if you had to use rubbers?

"Her paperwork is on the table," Kendra announced as she strolled into the bathroom to get the toys she had stashed under the sink earlier. Lubricant and a lavender-colored Jack Rabbit vibrator.

One thing about Kendra, she was thorough. When he and Kendra had been together, they had managed to ménage on occasion. Kendra found the girls—she knew exactly what type he liked—and had the tests done by Lamont's doctor.

Lamont instantly became rock hard. He hurried toward the bed, barely glancing at the test results. He trusted Kendra. And that was a comforting feeling because after that fiasco with Emma the junkie model, he'd been so worried that he'd caught something that he couldn't get it up for anyone for three days. The doctor said he was all clean but to check back in six months. Models…couldn't fuck with them, couldn't fuck without them!

Good old Kendra was obviously trying to get back with him and, boy oh boy, she was doing a fine job of it! He hadn't had a threesome since they'd broken up. His reason for dumping her: simple boredom. Whatever he wanted to do, she was down. But after a while that got tired. When were women going to learn that unpredictability was what kept a nigga's dick hard?

She had never pressed him to take their relationship further. Not in any overt way. But she was running up fast to thirty, a dangerous marker for a single woman. Right after her twenty-eighth birthday, when they'd been together almost two years, she'd started giving off unmistakable where-is-this-going vibes. One morning he rolled over, looked at her, and wished she weren't there. Two days later, he gave her the "it's not you, it's me" speech (version six) and then she wasn't.

But Kendra wasn't boring him tonight! Lamont undressed down to his silk boxers and flung the covers off the blonde. Without saying a word to her, he peeled back the bit of black lace that was barely covering her pink nipple and hungrily took to it like a baby calf to an udder. Out of the corner of his eye, he saw Kendra pulling her negligee over her head and reaching for the light switch.

"Lights stay on!" he barked.

To start, there was an impressive exhibition of girl-on-girl foreplay followed by some Lamont-in-Kendra thrusting accompanied by a little simultaneous vibrator action on Blondie. Then a positional switcheroo afforded some Lamont-in-Blondie action during which Kendra had a forceful, squirting clitoral explosion courtesy of Blondie's tongue. While Kendra took a break and went to the kitchen to get Lamont his sugar fix, Blondie was allowed to pleasure him with an I-don't-really-care-for-them-but-be-my-guest rim job. After Kendra served Lamont some chocolate cake from atop her sturdy rack, a wild free-for-all ensued. The night came to a rewarding close with a feverish round of dual sucking on Lamont, which was, of course, mandatory.

After three hours of sexual athletics, Kendra was exhausted, the blonde was gone, and, alas, Lamont found himself feeling bored once again.

Kendra hopped in the shower and Lamont flicked on the plasma television hanging on the wall opposite his king-size bed. He idly surfed the hundreds of channels until he saw a little boy in a too-big suit singing a gospel song. *Showtime at the Apollo.* The kiddie acts.

Kendra came back smelling fruity fresh and prepared for more, if necessary. Lamont's mind was elsewhere. He grabbed the phone and hit the speed dial.

"I want a kid," Lamont said wistfully, forgoing any introductory pleasantries like "Hello."

Kendra looked up from lotioning her elbows.

"What did you say?" Daryl yelled into the phone from his booth at Lint, where he'd answered Lamont's call.

"I want a kid," Lamont repeated.

Kendra immediately dropped her lotion and began to rub his back. Lamont turned and looked at her strangely.

"WHAT?" Daryl shouted, walking toward the club's bathroom. He huddled in a corner with a finger in his free ear.

Lamont heard a lot of background noise. "Where are you?"

"The IMG model party at Lint," Daryl was happy to report. "Bitches up in here is sick."

"Elite has hotter chicks," Lamont commented.

"A kid?" Daryl said.

"Yeah, everyone else has kids!"

Kendra tried to climb on top of him. She'd been thinking of putting some ice on her privates, but she was a trooper. If Lamont wanted a baby, they could make one right now. Who was he talking to? Some other girl right in front of her?

Lamont gave her a *quit it* look and pushed her aside.

"Well, can't really help you with that, playa," Daryl said, wondering what Lamont was talking about. He hated kids.

Now Lamont had a quizzical look for the phone. Then he started cackling, his mouth open so wide he looked like he was in the dentist's office. It was a mad-scientist laugh, which meant he was truly tickled.

"I mean, I want a kid rapper, you stupid motherfucka! Find me a kid rapper! A Lil' somebody."

Massively disappointed, Kendra went back to her moisturizing, moving on to her feet. And she remembered she'd had the Depo-Provera shots and couldn't get pregnant anyway.

"In that case," Daryl said, "I might already have somebody."

"A kid, you thought I wanted to have a kid," Lamont cackled into the phone, amused at the implausible idea.

"Hey, who knows? Even a money-stackin', pussy-chasin', pimp muthafucka like Lamont L. Jackson might need some unconditional love one day."

That made Lamont smile. He was surprised Daryl knew what the word "unconditional" meant.

Lamont hung up the phone and took a long, hot shower and then, though clean, vigorously washed his hands with antibacterial hand soap like he was prepping for surgery. He climbed into bed, pulled up the covers, and picked up the medical paper still sitting on the nightstand.

"That bitch's name was Svetlana?" He chortled. Lamont's chortle was a step down from his full-on cackle. It was reserved for mildly amusing surprises. Lamont tossed the paper aside and kissed Kendra on the cheek in one swift movement. "Good night, baby."

He rolled over on his side, facing away from her, and snuggled up to the pillow. He usually didn't like to be touched in his sleep and the California king gave him a wide berth but tonight, when Kendra nuzzled up against his wide back and slid her supple, sweet-smelling arm around his ample waist, he took her hand and rubbed it tenderly.

Kendra was thrilled to have such warmth shining down upon her. She'd done the right thing by sneaking in. Anything to keep Lamont interested and happy.

Lamont was asleep within ten minutes. He dreamed that Mimi was straddling him, naked, swishing her long, honey-colored locks all over his big fat belly.

◆

Party and Bullshit

"YOU DIDN'T TELL ME MARY J. BLIGE was going to be here!" Mimi said, looking up through the huddle of girls.

Lamont shrugged. "I didn't know she was coming." He'd seen Imani and Lena running around, whispering to each other, before running back to the guest bedroom of his rented Hamptons summer home that was now functioning as Mimi's dressing room. Something was up and they were trying to keep it from him. He didn't like that. "So what's going on?"

"Nothing," Imani answered before Mimi could. "She's just a little nervous. But we're all good. Nothing to worry about." She made fanning motions with her hands, trying to get rid of him. Vanessa, Lena, and Kiko, Lena's makeup-artist friend, were willing him out as well. Mimi was already nervous, and they all knew Lamont's presence would only add to the problem.

"Good," Lamont said, backing out. "You've got ten minutes." He gave Mimi a "get it together" look and left. He was not about to coax a singer into singing!

"Look up," Kiko said, brandishing a mascara wand.

Sitting on the edge of the bed in a slinky pink-and-white Diane von Furstenberg dress that Vanessa had chosen for her, Mimi looked up. "But 'Love No Limit' is her song! If it were something else, I wouldn't be as worried."

When she had sung in front of people before, she had always gotten jitters. Once she had gotten out there, though, the nervousness usually faded. But she'd never sung for an audience like this. Lamont had a stage with a band set up in his backyard by the pool and he'd decided on the song she should sing. At first, Mimi had suggested Alanis Morissette's "You Oughta Know." Lamont had said, "You're not white and you're not a rock chick. Why would you even say that? You're buggin'!" After that she kept her mouth shut as Lamont and Witchy had a confab about what she should sing. They decided on Mary J. Blige's "Love No Limit." Mimi loved that song and they'd had her rehearsing all week with the band and the vocal coach—but no one told her she was going to have to sing it in front of Mary! And then earlier Lena pointed out Andre Harrell, the music mogul who'd discovered Mary J. Blige. And everyone was buzzing that Puffy was going to show up.

After the girls checked out Mimi to make sure everything was in place, Imani led them all out to the living room.

"Take a deep breath," Imani counseled.

Lamont was on the stage, making some introductory remarks to his guests. He and Nate had rented this four-bedroom East Hampton home two summers in a row (cost from Memorial Day to

Labor Day: $350,000). They lived south of the highway, near the beach, unlike earlier years when they hadn't known the lay of the land. Location, location, location was everything in the Hamptons if you were trying to impress and Lamont always was.

Usually he didn't send out invites to his annual July Fourth bash; it was strictly word of mouth. But this year there had been formal invitations because tonight, before the spectacular fireworks, he'd show off his new discovery, the first princess of Triple Large. All in attendance appeared eager to get a look at the new young singer Lamont had been crowing about to anyone who'd listen.

"We're going to stand over to the right," Imani reassured Mimi as Lamont told some ribald joke that got plenty of laughs. "Just look at us, okay?"

Mimi shook her head and tried to breathe.

"Do not look at Mary J. Blige," Imani said because she could see Mimi was staring at her. Imani used her index finger to turn Mimi's face away. "I repeat, do not look at Mary. Look at us. Sing to us and you'll be fine."

And that is what Mimi did. She didn't make any chitchat as Lamont did so easily with the hundred or more people sitting on white folding chairs in his backyard. She just went right into the song and looked only at Imani and Lena and Kiko for the first verse. Then she eased into it, relaxed some, and she could see the people behind her girls were getting into it, mouthing the words. Then she finally snuck a glance over at Mary J. Blige, though she was telling herself, *Don't do it!* Mary smiled at her and it was probably the best moment of her whole life. As soon as she ended the song, the fireworks began. Lamont had timed it perfectly.

Afterward, everyone was coming up to tell her how great she sounded. "Mimi," they'd say rushing across the grass, and she'd think they were people she'd met before, and then she'd realize they weren't. "You were great," they'd say, or "Lamont was right about you." And then they'd just trail away, never introducing themselves. It was weird. Since the girls had dispersed, she wandered around the property feeling like she didn't know what to do with herself, being accosted every so often by some random admirer.

After changing out of her performance dress, she peeked into the second guest room and found Vanessa, alone, snorting some coke. Uncharacteristically generous, Vanessa held out the powder-covered mirror, but Mimi declined and walked out.

By the pool, where DJ Samantha Ronson was spinning, Lena was putting her mack down on Trey, the white, cornrow-wearing least-known member of the multiplatinum-selling boy band Chi-town. Wearing a powder-blue Rocawear short set, Lena dangled her legs in the heated water and sipped a glass of champagne, and she had another full glass sitting next to her. Mimi tried to join them but Lena's body language was saying she wanted privacy with Trey so Mimi just stole Lena's extra drink and went to look for someone else she could hang with.

She was relieved to see Jordan Grant, Nate's longtime girlfriend, heading in her direction. Jordan was what brothers would call red-boned. She had fair skin with a rosy underglow and the tips of her wild curly afro sported a natural reddish tint. A health food and yoga nut, she had a toned, athletic body to rival Madonna's.

Mimi checked out Jordan as she strode across the grass, her gauzy aquamarine strapless dress billowing over skinny jeans and piles of beaded bangles and jangling necklaces. Jordan was the managing editor of a cool women's magazine, *Sistah Girl,* one of Mimi's favorite reads.

"Hon, you are being summoned by Lamont," Jordan said, grabbing Mimi's hand and leading her inside.

"Where's Imani?" Mimi asked. "And Kiko?"

"They left an hour ago," Jordan said. "Went back to the city. Are you the designated driver tonight? I'm sure Lena has already knocked back a few too many."

"I don't know how to get back to Lena's place," Mimi said. They'd driven out to Lena's father's Hamptons house last night after midnight in Lena's Range Rover, Lena doing eighty-five most of the way. Lena had driven them over here tonight from her dad's place.

"If you have to," Jordan said, "you can stay here. The second guest room is empty until tomorrow."

They found Lamont holding court in the living room, telling tales out of school. "He gave her the shot and then she started groaning and shit. It was like that scene in *Pulp Fiction.*"

A tipsy blond woman slumped on the sofa next to him begged, "Names, we want names."

Lamont threw up his arms. "I can't!"

All the people around him groaned with bemused frustration and the blond trilled, "Of course you can."

Even though he had just asked Jordan to find Mimi, he now asked, "Where's *Grimy?*"

Jordan made a face as if to say "who cares" and trailed away.

"Mimi, this is Jake Queenan from MTV," Lamont said. "Be nice to him." Jake smiled. Lamont gave Mimi his seat and confiscated her half-empty glass of champagne. He didn't want her following Lena's alcohol-soaked lead.

"Be right back," he said.

Mimi wanted to follow him because she didn't know what to say to this MTV guy or to the other people to whom Lamont had not introduced her. He set her drink down on a nearby end table and Mimi reclaimed it as soon as he was out of sight.

"Where's Grimy?" Lamont growled at Daryl, who was standing in the kitchen picking at a plate of leftover barbecue.

Daryl wiped his greasy mouth with a napkin. "Shit, I dunno."

MC Grimy had shown up at ten with his pitbull, Lil' Dirty, chained in the hatchback of his Escalade. Daryl had invited him to the party—without getting Lamont's permission. "Grimy doesn't know how to move in this crowd," Lamont had complained to Nate. "And I always have to roll out my pimp routine with him," he'd sighed, seemingly exhausted at the thought.

Lamont had welcomed his thug genius with open arms but gave Daryl strict instructions to keep an eye on the crazy motherfucker. But following orders was not Daryl's strong suit—to put it mildly.

Lamont saw Nate coming down the back staircase and asked if he'd seen Grimy up there.

"No," Nate replied. "But somebody is getting their freak on in the empty guest room."

Lamont set off, Nate close on his heels. Without knocking, he pushed the door open and laid eyes on Grimy and Anne Brown, wife of Bradley Brown III, whose company managed the substantial assets of the black elite. Because she never said a bad word about anyone and her only goal in life was to be the perfect, agreeable wife to Bradley, Lena had taken to calling her "Prissanne"—like Joanne or Roseanne—behind her back.

Anne was the most proper black woman Lamont had ever met in his life so he was stupefied to find her alone in a bedroom with Grimy, sprawled across the bed wearing nothing but an ivory lace bra and matching panties!

"Grimy," Lamont yelled, turning to Triple Large's rap superstar, who was standing beside the bed in long black shorts and a plain black T-shirt that hung to his knees. He looked like he was about to pounce. "What the fuck are you doing!"

"Just kickin' it," Grimy said.

Excuse me? Lamont thought, feeling like he had opened the door to *The Twilight Zone.* Grimy was the type of nigga Anne would ordinarily cross the street to get away from, albeit discreetly so as not to offend. Lamont looked at Anne, wishing she'd cover up, and didn't know what to say. Was she drunk?

"Oh, Monty," she blathered. "We're just having some fun. Grimy is the most beautiful person. He's so lyrical."

"Anne, you're drunk," Nate said. He pushed Monty inside the room and closed the door behind them. This was obviously a "situation" and he didn't want anyone else to see what was going on.

Grimy was about ready to leave now that Lamont had busted the party up. But Lamont was just getting started with him.

"Grimy, she's drunk and she's married. To my money manager. Do you know who Bradley Brown is?" Lamont immediately knew how stupid that sounded because Grimy definitely did not subscribe to *Black Enterprise* and probably managed his money by stashing it in shoeboxes under the floorboards of his house in the Bronx. "What are you doing, nigga? This is not cool!"

Grimy looked confused. "*You* the one told me to fuck a white bitch."

Dumbfounded, Nate and Lamont looked at each other, silently trying to translate Grimy-speak, then whipped back around and chorused vehemently, "She's not white!"

Anne lay on the bed rubbing her chest so vigorously that it looked like she might snap her pearl choker.

Grimy looked at her. "Close enough."

That was almost funny but Lamont was trying to keep from exploding right now. Then it occurred to him that Anne was more than drunk. She still hadn't put her clothes on and none of this was anything she'd ever have thought about doing even in her most perverse fantasy.

"Grimy, did you give her something?" Lamont asked.

"I put a few treats in the drinks," Grimy said nonchalantly.

"What?" Lamont demanded breathlessly, losing his trademark cool. "What did you give her?"

"Just some X," Grimy said.

Lamont grabbed Grimy's shirt and freaked. "You gave her Ecstasy!"

"C'mon, it's a party drug!" Grimy said, shaking Lamont off. Grimy had never done X—he was strictly a weed man, hallucinogens were not his thing—but he'd heard it could make women crazy so he wanted to check out its effects.

Lamont went over to Anne and quickly handed her the white dress she'd discarded at the foot of the bed. "Here, Priss...I mean, Anne."

"Thank you," Anne said deliriously as the dress slipped through her fingers. "Such a lovely party, Monty. Really. *Really.* Thank you for having me."

Even drugged up on X without her consent, with an ex-con trying to maul her while her husband's clients looked at her in her La Perla lingerie, Anne was still unfailingly polite.

Lamont was trying to hustle Grimy out but Nate caught what Grimy had really said. *In the drinks.* Plural. "How many drinks did you put it in?" Nate asked, sounding very lawyerly.

"I don't know," Grimy said, shrugging.

Lamont almost strangled him. He pushed Grimy outside to his truck and said, "Good-bye Grimy. Never come back."

Lamont slammed the door of the truck and told Grimy's barking dog to shut the fuck up. "Grimy, do you realize I could get sued behind this shit?" Lamont snapped. Small chance of that since most of the people at the party were already well acquainted with drugs, but he had to make Grimy see the severity of his actions.

Lamont stared at Grimy fumbling with his keys and wondered how he was able to produce such stellar work in the studio. Grimy had an unparalleled work ethic and his lyrics were dark, socially political, insightful, comical, *and* they could always get a party jumping.

Outside the studio, Grimy was just dark.

Lamont shuddered to think where Grimy would be if he'd never given him a record deal. It was becoming painfully clear that Grimes was no thug genius. More like an idiot savant. But that tag would not look so good on the cover of *Rolling Stone.*

Lamont decided not to waste time going off further on his star rapper because it would make no difference anyway. Grimy was

Grimy. And whatever Lamont thought of him personally, he sold records. Lots and lots of records. And that was the name of the game.

Daryl was in the guest house, about to cop a feel off some cute partycrasher when Lamont stormed in and, as usual, pissed all over his parade. "Where is Mimi?" Lamont shouted, as if Mimi was a toddler Daryl had lost at the mall.

"Around," Daryl said offhandedly, annoyed that Lamont expected him to baby-sit every artist on the label all the damn time and was now embarrassing him in front of this cutie, who, up until ten seconds ago, had thought Daryl was a nigga with real clout.

Lamont grabbed Daryl's arm and pulled him outside.

"Grimy put X in the drinks," he shouted. "And I'm holding you responsible, you little bitch."

"Me!" Daryl yelped. "Why it always gotta be my fault?"

"I told you to watch over him," Lamont fumed. "So he wouldn't do shit like this. Now no one can find Mimi." Lamont pushed Daryl hard in the chest, causing him to tumble across the lawn. "Where the fuck is she?" Lamont screamed. "*Where?*"

"I don't know," Daryl yelled back, his palms skidding on the dewy grass.

A few of the remaining guests who were outside looked over toward the commotion.

"Find her!" Lamont shouted.

Daryl glanced up, saw the cute partycrasher peering through the window of the guest house, and thought about rushing Lamont. Just taking his legs out and beating him senseless. He'd get fired, he'd be banished from Lamont's camp forever, Lamont would ruin his name in the industry...but at least he'd have his dignity. But before he could get to his feet, Lamont had stormed back to the main house.

Daryl searched the property for half an hour to no avail. He flicked on the light in the pool house, got a quick glimpse of Lena and that loser Trey fooling around on the couch, turned the light back off and retreated, even more annoyed at Lamont's verbal and physical assault. Lena never gave him any play but she'd give it up to that boy-band wigger? Forget Lena, anyway, she was a user. Those two probably deserved each other.

Daryl stood on the far side of the pool, wondering where to look next. He hoped the partycrasher was long gone and he'd never have to face her again. Then, with a mixture of relief and concern, he saw Mimi stumble out from between the tall stalks of the neighboring cornfield. She was barefoot with dirt all over her face, hair, and white Lacoste polo dress.

He ran up to her. "Mimi, where'd you go?" he said urgently. "You aiight?"

"Country D," she gurgled. She placed her hands on his face, caressed his blotchy skin. "You are sooooo pretty."

He was pretty? Oh yeah, Lamont's little princess was definitely drugged way the hell up. *Great*, Daryl thought. *He's really gonna have my ass now.*

◆

CHAPTER 25

Under the Influence

LAMONT HAD BEEN SITTING on his bed for over two hours, listening to Mimi talk and talk and talk.

"Monty, do you really think I'm beautiful? Do you really think I have *It*? Do you really think..."

Jordan had driven Anne Brown home in Anne's Mercedes, with Nate following in his car to bring Jordan back. Lamont planned on calling Anne tomorrow to apologize profusely and convince her it was best not to tell Bradley what had happened. He'd already asked Imani to figure out what kind of gift to send.

"Yes, Mimi," Lamont cut her off, fearing she might go on with this "do you really think" thing for hours. Witnessing her behavior on X convinced him to never do it. He cringed at the idea of vomiting personal information the way Mimi was right now.

But it *was* illuminating. Everything he might want to know about her was coming to the surface.

"I love Phat E," she swooned. "He's the best. He let me write my whole part of our song even though Daryl said it sucked. I've written a lot of songs, you know, I have a notebook..."

Yes, yes, he'd seen the notebook. But what was she saying about the Phat E song? "Wait a second. *You* wrote the chorus?" Daryl had not mentioned that. Lamont thought he should give some X to Daryl as a truth serum so he could find out what else that dwarf was doing behind his back.

"I just did it over and over again until Daryl said it was okay. Was it okay? Was it..."

"Yes, Mimi," Lamont interrupted. "It's a big hit. You should be very proud." He put his face in his hands. He was never going to get to bed.

Mimi told him about her ex-boyfriend, Jamal, who had gone to Georgia State on a football scholarship and immediately started dating someone else.

No surprise there, Lamont thought.

She'd gotten pregnant when he came home on a college break. "When I called and told him, he told me to have an abortion," she said.

Again, not a surprise.

"And I told him we were both responsible," she said. "And you know what he said to me?"

Lamont had a feeling the word "What?" would open the floodgates of emotion but he couldn't help asking.

"Jamal said, 'If that's how you see it'!"

Then she started sobbing, which confused Lamont because wasn't Ecstasy supposed to keep you blissfully happy for the duration of the trip? He hated it when women cried. He massaged his temples.

"He told me he loved me....I didn't even want to have the

baby... but how could he have said that to me.... I had the abortion but I only told Toya.... He wouldn't even pay for it.... He didn't even care.... He said he had another girlfriend.... Well then, why did he sleep with me when he came home?"

Lamont was forced to console her, thinking the whole time, *This is not how I planned to spend my holiday.*

Now she was admitting to sleeping with another guy. "I didn't even like Floyd. He was a real player. Everyone called him 'Fuck 'Em and Flee Floyd.'"

Ha! Lamont thought upon hearing the name. *That was a good one!*

Mimi pouted and slapped him on the arm when she caught him laughing under his breath.

"Floyd told everyone, but I denied it," she said shamefully. "I never let on to anyone it was true."

"So this was after that cat Jamal dumped you?" Lamont said, oblivious to his insensitivity.

"No," she said defensively. "It was when Jamal first went away to Georgia State."

Lamont frowned. "So you cheated on him first?"

She leaned over and started slapping him on the back. "I was drunk! It didn't count! I was drunk! It didn't count!"

"Get off me," he said while thinking, *If you were my girlfriend and I found out, it would've counted. Being drunk doesn't excuse everything, girl. Know your limit and keep your fucking legs closed.*

"Do you think I'm awful?" Mimi whimpered, falling back against the pillows.

"Of course not. That guy took advantage of you," Lamont said, feeling very put-upon. "You've only slept with two people?" The intimacy of this situation was making him uncomfortable. To lighten the mood he cracked, "Lena probably fucked two guys last week!"

"So you think Lena's a slut?"

"No," he responded quickly. "I didn't say that." See, this conversation was getting him in trouble. She was the one on drugs but he was still getting caught out there. "What Lena does is her business. I'm just saying... don't worry about it."

"So, you don't think I'm a bad girl," she purred. Jordan had cleaned her up after her romp in the cornfield and Mimi was now wearing Jordan's long white nightgown. It was damn near sheer.

Ooh, why don't you show me how bad you can be, little mama, Lamont thought. She was turning him on—he could see those tiny but inviting breasts through the nightie—but he couldn't do anything with her. She worked for him. He rubbed the crotch of his sweatpants, hoping she didn't notice his growing hard-on. The way she was acting, she might grab it, and he never liked to start anything he couldn't finish.

But, no, he wasn't going to touch her. She was on drugs, she'd be screaming rape tomorrow, and he wouldn't blame her if she did. Nailing her now would make him no different from "Fuck 'Em and Flee Floyd." As much as he'd love to give it to her, it would be wrong any which way you looked at it. She was an artist on his label and he never liked to mix business with sex. He wouldn't just be able to get rid of her afterward like other women. If he wasn't going to have a relationship with her, it would turn into a pain once she started catching feelings. Which he was certain she would do if he put it on her as only he could.

And, surprisingly, he had a protective feeling toward her. He would try to get her to go to sleep and that was all. But with all this bad girl talk, it was going to be difficult.

He went down to the kitchen to take a breather for a minute and to get another bottle of Dasani. Nate had said to keep her hydrated and Mimi was gulping water down like a marathon runner.

When he returned she was standing in front of the toilet in his bathroom with the door wide open, nightgown up and panties down, wiping herself. He involuntarily turned his head. Christ, she was rocking a down-below baldy! He wouldn't have pegged her for that. He rubbed his crotch again and walked back to the bed.

When Mimi came out, she looked down at his frantically tapping foot and said, "What's wrong with your feet?"

Indignantly, "Nothing!"

"One of your toenails is black."

"I jammed it playing basketball."

She bent down and started stroking his foot. "Your feet are so . . . *ugly*," she squealed.

Lamont pulled his foot away. "No, they're not!"

"Yeah, they are." She wrinkled her nose. "They're crusty!"

"Shut up!" He went to the drawer to get some socks.

Mimi rolled all over the bed, laughing hysterically. "Those are the ugliest feet I have ever seen," she screamed into the pillow.

He came back and sat on the bed. "Leave my feet alone!"

She tried to stifle her laughter. "Do you get manicures?" Vanessa told her he did. His hands were beautiful, well-moisturized, and his nails always had a clear sheen.

"Yeah," he said sheepishly.

"So why don't you get pedicures too instead of walking around with those nasty feet!" She rolled around on the bed and howled.

"Everyone sees your hands," he said sharply. "I'm not going to put a Bulgari ring on an ungroomed hand!"

"But you'll put those ugly-ass feet into your four-hundred-dollar shoes?"

"Pedicures are gay!" he retorted.

"And manicures aren't?"

"It's a fine line."

That really set her off. She was howling so loud he thought the neighbors a cornfield over might come knocking.

"Ha...ha...ha," Lamont drawled sarcastically. He knew she wasn't in her right state of mind but an insult was still an insult. Were his feet *that* bad?

All of a sudden, she was right behind him, her arms around his neck. "I'm sorry," she baby-talked. "Did I hurt your feelings?"

He tried to shake her off. "My feelings don't get hurt."

"I don't care if your feet are crusty and ugly," she said. "You're still a beautiful person on the inside."

"You think so," he said, wondering if she'd say that tomorrow when she wasn't feeling so damn ecstatic.

She slipped her arms around his waist and rubbed herself against his back. On the bare spot between his T-shirt and his drooping sweatpants, right above the crack of his ass, he could feel the wet spot seeping through her thong. Was she aroused? By him?

"Yes, Lamont," she hummed. "You're the best."

Lamont found himself in a compromising—and arousing— position. To fuck or not to fuck. That was the question. Hey, maybe she really did like him. He glanced around and saw that her eyes were closed and her face was smashed up into his shoulder. So he pushed down the elastic waist of his sweats—he had no underwear on—and began to openly stroke himself.

"You want me to kiss..." And she mumbled something unintelligible into his neck. Then she sucked.

Oh shit. That was his spot! He felt a tingle of arousal surge from the soles of his ugly feet to the tips of his graying hair.

"Do you want me to...," she whispered again, lapping on his spot.

He thought she'd mumbled kiss "it" and he wanted to say, YES! He hunched over and stroked faster.

"Do you?" she said, between nibbles.

"What?"

"Want me to kiss them."

Them? If she was talking balls now, it was over! "Kiss what?"

"Your feet!"

Not what he had in mind but he snapped his sweats back up and said, "Sure."

She scrambled around and plopped down on his lap. She grabbed his pudgy cheeks and gushed, "Monty, I love you."

"Do you?" he found himself cooing back as he hugged her. He wasn't drunk or high but it was like the effects of the X were seeping into him through osmosis. "How much do you love me, baby?"

"So much," she purred, all loopy. She crushed herself into his chest. "Please don't ever leave me."

"Never, baby," he whispered back, taking great pleasure in being the temporary object of her affection. He couldn't resist pressing his boner up between her legs. It took every ounce of self-control he had to not push that thong a little to one side, slip himself out of his sweats, and go in for the kill. "I'm always here for you, precious."

"Everyone leaves me," she breathed directly into his ear. "My father, Jamal..."

Just give it to her, Lamont told himself. *She wants it. She needs it. Stop being so selfish, man!*

"Monty," she purred, detecting Lamont's stiffness between her legs and wiggling on it.

"Yeah," Lamont moaned softly.

She pressed her hand on top of his bulging sweats and chirped, "Oh...you love me, too."

A hard dick does not equal love, he thought. *But right now, honey, I sure like you a helluva lot.*

"Do you like it when girls get that half-Brazilian?"

"Um-hmm," he hummed enthusiastically.

"Vanessa said guys love it. You don't think it looks weird?" She stood up, took two steps back and yanked her nightgown up. "Give me your honest opinion, okay?"

Before she could expose herself, Lamont closed his eyes, frantically waved his hands, and screamed, "No!" Like he was a vampire and her Brazilian-waxed pussy was a cross.

With her thumb inside the top of her thong, ready to flash, she said, "I just want you to tell me if you think it's sexy."

"I do," he wailed thinking, *I just saw it and it's sexy as hell.* "I do! I know what it looks like."

She bent over and kissed him softly on his closed eyelids, then on his forehead and both sides of his face. Lamont opened his eyes and looked up at her as she batted her long eyelashes. "Show me how much you love me," she pleaded tenderly.

Lamont was ready to throw in the towel and give her what she wanted. *How long does it take to get blue balls?* he wondered. He wouldn't know. He'd never been denied sex.

"What happened to you kissing my feet, hon," he said to distract her. He didn't know how much longer he could keep her at bay.

She dropped to the floor and slipped off one of his socks. She kissed the top of his right foot. She looked up at him. "I didn't mean to hurt your feelings. Saying you had nasty feet and all."

He shook his left foot. "Don't forget the other one."

Kneeling on the floor, she pulled off his other sock and kissed his left foot.

He slipped his hand inside his sweats and stroked. He was just about to say, "Come here, sweetheart, lemme show you something," when there was a soft knock at the door.

He swiftly kicked Mimi back and barked, "Come in."

Jordan stuck her head in. She'd heard the screaming while she was sexing Nate in their room so she'd pushed him off to come down here and investigate. Not that she hadn't heard women screaming in Lamont's bedroom before. The best thing about this summer house was that the second largest bedroom was all the way at the other end of the floor, far from Lamont's. She had no desire to be kept awake all night listening to Lamont slap some girl's ass. (She couldn't speak for Nate.)

Jordan saw Mimi crouched down on the floor, laughing hysterically, with the nightgown bunched up around her waist and her thong barely covering what needed to be covered. "What's going on in here?"

"Look at her," Lamont said. "She's a mess. She won't stop laughing."

Mimi crawled over and scaled Jordan's athletic body. Lamont was glad she had Jordan's full attention. If Jordan saw his dick tenting up his sweats, she would jump to conclusions. He smoothly pulled the duvet over himself.

"Jordan, Jordan," Mimi wheezed, kissing her on the cheek. "Where have you been? I missed you! Come in! Let's talk! You know *Sistah Girl* is my favorite magazine!"

As she tried to pry Mimi's arms from around her neck, Jordan looked at Lamont and they both shook their heads.

"Great," she said. She walked Mimi back to the bed. It was already past four AM and she wanted everyone in the house, mostly herself, to go to sleep. But she knew that letting Mimi go to sleep in a bed with Lamont was trouble waiting to happen.

"Are we okay in here?" Jordan questioned, looking directly at Lamont.

"Yes, we are," he declared, staring her down.

"Why don't you go sleep in the extra room downstairs?"

"This is my room," Lamont fumed. "You trying to kick me out of my own room? I pay the bills up in here."

That was so like Jordan *not* to give him the benefit of the doubt. Lamont saw her as one of those irritating feminist types, always trying to make everything seem like the man's fault. They'd found a way to get along for Nate's sake and now that Jordan had, at twenty-eight, moved up to second in command at *Sistah Girl* and become a more influential member of the media, Lamont had more reason to be friendly with her.

As Jordan gave him her patented "I'm on to you" look, Lamont wondered for the hundredth time. *How can Nate think he's in love with her?* Here he was, alone and erect, with this twenty-year-old hottie who wanted to fuck his brains out and all he was doing was keeping her hydrated! Well, he was making a valiant effort and for that alone he should be applauded.

"What kind of person do you think I am?" he said, almost hurt. He silently added "bitch" but he could only imagine what Jordan might do if he called her out like that. She was a graduate of Brown University and had a graduate degree in journalism from some other uppity school but she wasn't above slapping a nigga. Even him.

"Tell me. What kind of person *are* you?" she challenged.

"Wait, are you guys getting into a fight?" Mimi murmured, grabbing both of their hands. "Let's just all be friends, okay?"

That broke the tension. Lamont and Jordan both laughed.

"Come on, Mimi," Jordan ordered. "I'm going to put you to bed. Downstairs."

"Are there even sheets on that bed?" Lamont asked, suddenly feeling a little upset that she was taking Mimi away. He remembered Anne lying on just a mattress cover.

"We have sheets in the closet," Jordan said, pulling Mimi toward the door. "I know you don't stoop so low as to make your own bed, LL Cool J," she smirked, knowing he hated being called that, "but I can handle it."

Lamont pulled Mimi's arm back toward him. This was none of Jordan's business. She hadn't even known Mimi until tonight and now she was getting all Mother Teresa and treating him like he was some kind of child molester.

"Jordy," he said, knowing she hated that childish nickname, "go to bed. She's not about to go to sleep yet and she'll wind up right back in that cornfield." He softened a bit, knowing that was the only way to get rid of Nate's ball and chain. "I'll stay up with her." He forced a smile.

Jordan gave him a final warning look, said good night to Mimi, and left, wondering what had gotten into Lamont. Was he turning into a decent person in his old age?

As soon as the coast was clear, Lamont went down to the kitchen with his cell to make two calls. The first was to Carlos. When Lamont went to the Hamptons, he liked to drive himself out. He had all these cars but he never got to drive them! He usually came out around three in the morning on Thursday when there was no traffic and took business calls by the pool on Friday. This weekend he'd tooled out in his 2004 Ferrari 360 Modena Spider—titanium, with a blue leather interior. But now he called Carlos to inform the driver that his weekend off was over.

The second call was to Kendra. Lamont told her about Grimy's stunt, exaggerated about how stressful it had all been on him, and told her Carlos was on his way to her apartment to pick her up.

Until daybreak, Mimi begged him to give it to her. Or, as she kept saying, "Show me how much you love me." Her bizarre phraseology gave him the creeps. He hoped it was the X that was making her so mushy because if that was how she thought of sex in her normal state, she had some serious issues. He finally told her he couldn't "love her" because he didn't have his Viagra. A joke, obviously. She began to let out a piercing howl and he put a pillow over her face until she promised to keep quiet.

As they lay next to each other on the bed, she writhed against his back and told him what a fabulous, handsome, and all around swell guy he was. He stayed erect the entire time and almost came as much from the praise as her constant rubbing. When she finally fell asleep, he turned over and stared at her for a while, wondering if she had meant any of the sweet things she'd said to him. Probably not. He cuddled up to her until a quarter to nine when the sound of wheels crunching gravel outside alerted him to the arrival of Carlos and Kendra. He made sure Mimi was all covered and went down to let them in.

Carlos quickly passed out on the sofa and, without delay, Lamont dragged Kendra up to his bathroom and, after about thirty seconds of foreplay (on him), roughly fucked her on the edge of the bathtub while Mimi snored in his bed.

All things considered, Kendra could not have been happier.

◆

CHAPTER 26

Aftermath

QUIET AS A COUPLE OF CHURCH MICE, Lamont and Nate entered the guest house. Since it had become Daryl's domain, they referred to it as the slave quarters. They climbed the stairs to the loft area and looked at Daryl sleeping, a puddle of drool collecting on the pillow beneath his head. Lamont walked around the bed and deposited himself in the overstuffed chair. Nate stood next to him.

Lamont stuck his leg out and rattled the bed with his pristine white sneaker. Daryl jerked awake, pulling at the bedsheet and blinking rapidly. His eyes began to focus and he scooted up toward the headboard.

"Wassup?" he croaked. "What time is it?" Even half-asleep, he knew that Lamont wasn't coming in to invite him to the beach. "You need bagels? Lox?"

"So you're a thief now," Lamont said. It was not a question.

"Huh?" Daryl was just beginning to remember everything that had happened last night.

"You stole Mimi's publishing," Lamont said, his voice grumbling like clouds before the storm.

"No, I didn't," Daryl responded reflexively.

"Mimi told me everything," Lamont said, deliberately vague.

"Told you what?" Daryl replied, vaguer. He knew by now not to volunteer any unnecessary information.

"That you stole her publishing."

Daryl wanted to shout, *Mimi don't even know what publishing is!* He looked at Nate, Lamont's consigliere. Another asshole. But not as bad as Lamont, that was for sure. "She said that?"

"She said she wrote the chorus to the Phat E song," Lamont divulged. "That means you stole her publishing fees."

"But," Daryl managed, "we both..."

Lamont threw his hand up in an aggressive gesture. "Mimi said she wrote the *entire* chorus." Who knew if that was true or not? She was so out of it last night. But there was some funny business going on and Daryl had to be watched at all times.

"She didn't," Daryl insisted. "She changed one tiny part but I wrote most of it."

"So what are you saying, Country D?" Lamont said, a serrated edge to his voice.

"Um, I..." Daryl trailed off, trying to think.

"You should've shared the credit?"

"Yeah," Daryl said, cobbling his story together on the spot. "That's what I put down on the credit sheet I handed in." He swung his legs over the edge of the bed. He didn't want to be lying down for this. It was bad enough that he was in his drawers.

"You did?" Lamont pulled his cell out from his shorts. He hit a button, waited for it to ring, and then said, "Imani, did you happen to see the original credit sheet for the Supa Phat E song?" Pause. "Was Mimi listed as one of the writers?" Another pause. "Thank you, my darling."

"Hey, I don't know what to tell you, money," Daryl said before Lamont pulled the phone from his ear. Imani was such a bitch. She was probably laughing her ass off right now. "I handed in the right credits. If there was a mix-up, don't blame me."

"Ah," Lamont said, "but I do."

"It was a mistake then," Daryl claimed. "Shit happens."

Lamont looked at Daryl's nasty blotchy skin and thought about firing his ass right then and there. But he wanted him to finish Mimi's album as well as the tenth-anniversary album. In truth, Daryl was proving himself to be a great producer. That's the only reason he'd lasted this long. Daryl was beginning to create an identifiable sound that spelled commercial hit. Lamont wanted to squeeze every last drop of creativity out of him before sending him on his way.

Daryl rubbed the crust from his eyes and Lamont threatened, "Don't cry, nigga!" He leaned up from the chair, pointing a thick finger. "Shed a tear and you're over!"

Incredulously, Daryl blinked his *dry* eyes. He wanted to swing, not cry. He squelched a violent urge to scream, *Don't you have a better way to get your kicks than tryin' to punk me before breakfast, you fat muthafuckaaaaaaaa!*

"Daryl," Lamont said, eyes narrowing to slits. "There's only one thing I hate more than a thief."

Daryl shivered as a cool morning breeze swept through the room.

"And that's a liar." Lamont glowered at him, waiting for a full confession.

Daryl wasn't about to offer one.

Lamont could wait. Their silent face-off lasted two minutes—during which Lamont pictured Mimi on her knees kissing his feet and Daryl pictured his hands around Lamont's neck, choking the life out of him.

Finally, Daryl surrendered. "I stole her publishin'," he confessed, flinging his arms up in defeat. He could never win with Lamont. "There. I said it. I stole her fuckin' publishin'. I'm a thief!" He walked over to the window, thrust his fuzzy cornrowed head out, and yelled into the early morning quiet, "I'm a thief! I AM A THIEF!"

Inside the main house, Mimi, still passed out in Lamont's bed, and Kendra, in the guest room directly beneath, simultaneously stirred but didn't wake up.

"Don't forget a liar!" Nate prompted as he watched Daryl losing it.

"I'M A LIAR!" Daryl screeched out the window, giving in completely.

Nate had advised Lamont several times to fire Daryl for insubordination. Daryl was reckless, lawless, and disrespectful in countless ways. Yes, he was a good producer, but Nate was afraid that one day Daryl would do something that would seriously damage Lamont and the entire company. To Nate, Daryl was nothing more than a succubus with a good ear.

Daryl flopped back onto the bed and snarled at his tyrannical boss, "Happy now?"

No one enjoyed seeing Daryl teetering on the emotional brink more than Lamont Jackson. "It's a start."

Nate and Lamont tramped down the stairs and walked back

toward the house. Knowing Daryl might be watching from the window, they didn't start laughing until they got inside.

Lamont felt like he had done his good deed for the day. He went to rouse Kendra so they could head to the beach. Maybe he could get some sleep there.

Daryl *was* watching from the window. Looking at their backs, he pulled down his boxers, exposing himself, put his middle fingers in the air, and mouthed, "Suck...my...dick."

SEVERAL HOURS LATER, at the Whitakers' Hamptons property, another interrogation was about to begin.

Marlin Whitaker had begun calling his daughter's cell phone at seven that morning when he awoke, after finding the door to her bedroom wide open and the bed still made. At noon he had called Anne Brown to get the number of Lamont's place and had been informed that Anne was still in bed.

Lena finally called at one and returned to their Sag Harbor home an hour later, looking like she'd had a spectacularly hard night. Mimi, too, looked beat.

"What happened?" Marlin demanded immediately.

"Daddy, we had some drinks and I didn't want to drive home," Lena answered, trying to sound like the responsible daughter he wanted her to be.

"You should have called."

"It was late. I didn't want to wake you."

Yesterday, Mimi had noticed that Lena acted very differently around her father. Lena didn't say "I ain't" or "I gotta." She said "I am not" or "I have to." And she didn't curse. The first time someone called her "Marlena," Mimi looked around like, *Who's that?* Lena shot her a look and Mimi managed not to laugh.

"Well, that was a smart decision," Marlin relented, quite aware of his daughter's habits. "I don't want you to drink and drive. But call next time."

"Okay, Daddy," Lena said, relieved. She tried to head up to her room with Mimi but Marlin reminded her that they were scheduled to have "a talk." Mimi went upstairs without her, thinking how handsome and fit Marlin was for such an old guy. He actually looked a little like Denzel Washington, but with gray hair.

Lena followed her father into the kitchen and steeled herself.

"So your year off is up," he said. Lena folded her arms on the table and set her head down. He sat down and peered at her. "What are your plans?"

Though Marlin loved Lena fiercely, his paternal devotion was tested constantly by her party-girl nonsense and general delinquency. He had quietly donated money to four private schools in New York, in apologia, after she'd gotten bounced again and again for skipping classes, buying a term paper, accusing (falsely) a male teacher of making sexual advances, posting caustic remarks on one school's Web site about another female student, and probably a dozen other minor infractions that Lena had managed to keep from him.

Marlin frequently lectured her about the added social responsibility an African-American girl from her background had to bear. He often told her that rich white girls could "act a fool" without being branded with a lifelong stigma but white folks would be all too happy to hold her up as an example that all their money could never buy class.

Lena always snickered when he said things like "act a fool" because he enunciated everything so properly he sounded like Mr. Belvedere. He had once bragged to her that he knew all the words to Alicia Keys' CD *Songs in A Minor,* citing it as empirical evidence that he could, in fact, "get funky with it." Lena laughed in his face. *At* him, not with him. Sometimes she just felt plain sorry for the man. He was so square he was practically round. She hadn't known him to have a real relationship since her mother died, though he always had dates for social functions. He probably wasn't getting any from *them.* The ones Lena had met all seemed to be manufactured by Frigidaire. What he really needed was one steamy night with a high-class hooker. That might loosen him up, but pigs would fly before he'd get involved in something so *unseemly.*

Lena let out a heavy sigh. Why had she even come back? "Well," she said, trying to get her brain to work despite the X hangover. Her mind drifted to Trey. What a night they'd had! They'd both drunk from the same laced champagne glass and she'd had the best sex of her life.

"Marlena," Marlin demanded, startling her back to reality. "I'm waiting. Let's hear it."

"Well," she repeated, knowing it was put up or shut up time. Daddy was easily manipulated but even he could be pushed only so far. What could she say? She had no plans. Then she thought about a sign she'd seen on the subway the other day. She took the subway three stops to Barneys occasionally when she felt like keeping it really real. "I was thinking of going to Parsons." She glanced up to see his reaction.

"Parsons School of Design," Marlin said approvingly. "Interesting. When did you decide on that?"

"I've been thinking about it for a while," she said, picturing the ad she'd seen on the subway three days ago. She sat up and adopted her best "I'm focused" voice. "I love clothes and I was thinking of starting my own label—like Rocawear or Baby Phat."

"Hmm," was all Marlin said. Lena hadn't even applied yet but already she was thinking about starting her own company. Just like her. And she'd be coming to him for the start-up capital no doubt. But it was a plan. She'd always been a clotheshorse.

"You don't think it's a good idea?"

"Oh yes, I do," Marlin responded, careful not to extinguish the first spark of ambition she'd ever had. "Do you have a sketchbook?"

She blanked. *A what?*

"A sketchbook, Marlena. You can't just show up there. You know Graham Thompson's daughter went there," he said, warming to the idea. "She really liked it. But there is a rigorous admissions process."

There is? Lena thought. She had heard of the school but she didn't know anyone who'd ever gone there. She figured any school that had to advertise on the subway would take anyone as long as the check cleared.

"Well, I don't have a book, per se. But I've been doodling. I can put everything together. Where can I buy a really nice book?"

"You'll have to do some research on that," Marlin said, wondering if his daughter was serious about this. She was a good starter, a terrible closer. "But I'm very proud of you. This is a promising step."

It felt wonderful that Marlin was offering her some encouragement. She was relieved that she had talked her way out of this grilling, though concerned that she had never sketched anything in her entire life. She began to head to her room, tugging at the back of her short jacket to cover the awful tattoo.

But Daddy wasn't finished. "Marlena, who is Jacob?"

Fuck, Lena thought, *I almost made a clean getaway.* Thinking about the necklace she'd purchased for Crazy G made her stomach churn. After reading about his budding affair with that girl-group ho, she'd paged the two-timing thug eight times, each message she left angrier than the last. He'd never responded. "It's a clothing store," she said innocently.

"Where you spent fifteen thousand dollars?" Marlin pressed, his voice tight as a coil.

"It was research for my clothing designs," she fibbed, impressed with herself for making that up on the spot. "They carry a lot of young, avant-garde designers and I was looking at how the pieces were made. I know it's more than I should have spent and I'm sorry," she said preemptively.

Marlin's body got stiffer as she spoke. "Funny. My accountant called Jacob's and they told him they sell jewelry exclusively. They told him to come on by if he was in the market for something *icy*...which, they explained, means a piece of diamond-encrusted jewelry."

Lena shuddered. *Shit!* She knew that lousy accountant would notice it on the bill but she didn't think he'd go the extra yard and call!

"Okay, okay, fall back," Lena sputtered. "I bought a necklace there. But I said I was sorry!"

Marlin wasn't in the mood to forgive. "Well, you have to show it to me," he said disgustedly. He knew that Lena had no idea what it took to *earn* fifteen thousand dollars—or even five for that matter. She tossed bills around like they were Monopoly money. He was at his wits' end trying to get her to understand that life was not an endless cocktail party. "I'd like to see what this fifteen-thousand-dollar necklace looks like. Do you wear it with your sweats? That must be quite a look."

"No, I don't wear it," she said quickly.

"Why not?"

"I have it at home in the safe."

"Oh, so it's too expensive to wear but not too expensive to buy. With my money. Thank you for the clarification."

Lena was on the verge of tears. Real ones, not the crocodile tears she often employed at moments like these. It had been so stupid, buying the necklace for Crazy G. And for five minutes her father had looked at her the way he only ever looked at her sister, Alexandra. And now she had messed it all up. Again. She slithered back down to the table, lips quivering.

Marlin was a sucker for tears. "Look, Marlena, I really think going to Parsons will be a positive experience for you," he said gently, but his anger could not be entirely quelled. Lena had been given second, third, fourth, fifth chances...and she'd blown them all. This was the end of the road. He wasn't going to cave. Not this time. "You cannot continue to go from one party to the next," he said, his tone beginning to calcify, "drinking and hanging out with gangster rappers. Without the benefit of undergarments! You are a complete embarrassment to this entire goddamned family!"

Marlin immediately regretted the words that flew out of his mouth. More so when Lena's tears sprung forth with the force of a busted water main.

"Honey," he said lightly, putting a hand on her back as her body convulsed with sobs. "I want you to focus on getting your sketchbook together for the rest of the summer. And call Parsons about their admissions process."

He watched her closely, bent over at the table, and wondered where he had gone wrong. After his beloved wife's death, he'd known Lena had needed him more than ever, but his career was peaking. The guilt he felt about not being able to give her his full attention only exacerbated the problem. He gave her gobs of money instead of his time and forgave her every indiscretion when what she really needed was an old-fashioned ass-whupping. But keeping her out of trouble was a full-time job for which he didn't have time. Her older sister, Alexandra, was doing the family proud, getting her MBA from the Wharton School of Business. He hoped Lena would soon tire of this teenage rebellion—especially since she wasn't even a teenager anymore—and chart her own course.

"I'm going back to L.A. this week," Marlin said. "Do you want to come with? Let's spend some time together. I miss you, honey."

Lena wiped her drenched eyes, looked up at him, and managed a small smile. He missed her? He was making time for her? "Okay," she said, thankful that talk of the necklace had come to an end without any punishment. "I'll come out for a few days."

"Great," he agreed. "But you know your credit card limit is five thousand a month—maximum." He cringed that he gave her that much. He'd grown up in an upper-middle-class family but he'd had to work every summer and chip in for his first car! "So your charging privileges are suspended for three months."

Lena gulped. "What! How am I going to *live?*" she wailed, dead serious.

"Well, let's see," Marlin said bitterly. "We have an account at the supermarket, we have an account with Grand Transportation, which you use far too much considering you have a car, you have a Mobil card, and you get a two thousand-dollar *cash* allowance every month. To my knowledge, all your basic needs are being met. And then some."

Lena opened her mouth to say something, but Marlin beat her to the punch. "Cut your losses," he snapped. And *that* was the end of that.

◆

CHAPTER 27

Children's Story

IN A RARE MOMENT OF STILLNESS, Lamont reclined in his ergonomic office chair, facing the wall-to-wall windows behind his desk, and watched people balancing cellophane-wrapped sandwiches on their laps with cans of soda set beside them on the concrete steps of the public library. *Imagine how many people have stomped up and down those steps,* he thought as the soothing sounds of Jill Scott wafted through his office. *So dirty.*

He heard someone enter the room. Without looking he knew who it was. Even his own employees had to schedule time with Imani before meeting with him.

"I got someone here to see you," Daryl said. He hadn't been near Lamont in a week. A good thing. He'd been grinding in the studio nonstop. He was dog tired but refused to let it show. Lamont had once told him that sleep was for "low-wage earners."

Daryl called out to the hallway. "Yo!"

As Lamont swiveled around, in scampered an adorable dark-skinned boy sporting a three-inch-high Afro. He was neatly attired in a yellow polo shirt, pleated khaki shorts, and Stan Smith sneakers.

"Meet Billy tha Kid," Daryl said expansively.

Daryl gave the cue and Billy tha Kid confidently busted a rhyme about girls, school, and sports. It ended like a public-service announcement when he said something about staying away from drugs. He smiled broadly when he finished and looked at Daryl.

Lamont betrayed no sign that he was either impressed or displeased by the performance. "How old are you?" he asked.

"Twelve."

"Where you from?"

"Harlem."

"Is that how they dress in Harlem?"

"No, but..." Billy tha Kid shifted his body awkwardly and looked at Daryl.

"But we worked on his presentation a little bit," Daryl said. "Cleaned him up for the mass-market audience. This cat I know from uptown introduced me to Tha Kid and I been working on his image an' shit."

"I see," Lamont said flatly.

"I know he gotta be acceptable for parents to wanna buy his record for *their* kids, ya feel me? 'Cause Billy's a badass kid, his mom's just got out of rehab—"

"I ain't no badass kid," the little boy piped up. "And leave my mama outta this, nigga."

Lamont cracked up. Now he was interested! He decided to talk to the kid in a way that would make him feel comfortable. Lamont could adjust his vernacular and flip it to cozy up to anyone from any walk of life. "That's right, shorty, don't let nobody talk about yo' mama!" A beat. "So what is the deal with Moms anyway?"

"You know," Tha Kid said, looking down at his sneakers, "she's cleanin' up."

"That's good," Lamont said. "It takes courage to be able to do that."

Tha Kid glanced up.

"And she got you, right?" Lamont said gently. "You get a deal, make some dough, help her out. Take care of her."

Daryl was not happy with the turn the meeting had taken. Lamont hated kids and now he had this hoodrat eating out of the palm of his hand!

"Yeah, but he was way too gully a month ago," Daryl interjected. "I cleaned him up. Whipped his ass into shape."

Tha Kid looked like he was about to whip Daryl's ass and he probably could have. They were about the same size.

"I'd like to have seen that," Lamont said. "What you were like a month ago. Come on, kid. Break me off a lil' sumpin'."

Tha Kid looked at Lamont, then Daryl. Confused. Daryl had been coaching him for this audition for a month. Telling him to drop the cursing, stop talking about all the "asses he tapped." And he was a good student because he desperately wanted to be down. He just wanted to be a rapper like his idol, MC Grimy.

Now Lamont was telling him to do the complete opposite and Daryl was looking at him like he'd better not. But Lamont was the boss. Tha Kid read *The Source*. He knew Lamont was the nigga to impress.

Tha Kid pulled off his polo shirt to reveal a white tank top, pulled his shorts down low, and hopped up on a chair in front of

Lamont's desk. He kicked the dirty version of "Baby Gangsta," his best rhyme, throwing his arms around for emphasis.

When Tha Kid finished with a menacing (for a twelve-year-old) snarl, Lamont stood and clapped his hands together in wild applause. "Now that's the shit!" Lamont boomed. "See how much better that was. You gotta be you!" Tha Kid took a seat and Lamont bent over him and poked his tiny chest. "Do what you know. That's what people respond to."

"I came up with the name," Daryl interjected proudly, standing proudly at his full 5 foot 5¾ inches.

"Yeah, Billy tha Kid," Lamont said, liking the sound of that. He looked at Tha Kid. "What's your real name?"

"William," Tha Kid answered. "William Bridges."

Lamont turned to Daryl. "So his real name is Billy and he's a kid. Very clever of you." He turned back to Tha Kid. "I like that name. You like it?"

"Yeah, I think that shit is hot," Tha Kid replied and gave Lamont a pound. "Billy tha Kid was a gangsta."

"An outlaw, yes," Lamont corrected. "Is your Moms here with you?"

"No, Country D brought me down."

"You mean Daryl," Lamont said, not even throwing him a glance. "Okay, well, go wait outside for a minute. Tell the girl out there, Imani, to give you some cookies or something."

"So you gonna put me on or what?" Tha Kid asked boldly.

"We'll see," Lamont chuckled. He liked his attitude. It was all a rapper had. "But you got skills, yo."

"Mos def," Tha Kid said. He kicked Daryl in the shin as he ran out the door, griping, "And you made me take my braids out!"

"Dope, right?" Daryl said, waiting, as always, for enormous praise.

"Yep, I want him," Lamont said. "Grimy's going to oversee his album."

"Grimy! I don't need no over-fuckin'-seer. I found him! I groomed him!"

Lamont enjoyed it when Daryl got confrontational. Gave him more reason to belittle him. And that was always fun. "You groomed him to be some prep school nerd when he had all the right shit naturally."

"Yeah, but you think..." Daryl said hesitantly.

"What?"

"You think people are gonna accept that from a kid? It could be controversial."

"Controversy sells records," Lamont said calmly. "And we'll tone it down some. We won't have him talking about gunning people down. Everything ain't *The Cosby Show*. That kid deserves a voice. His Moms is on drugs? Think of how much he could mine from that." *And if she's a dopehead, we can get him real cheap,* Lamont thought.

"I guess," Daryl agreed halfheartedly.

"He has a valuable story to tell," Lamont said, pulling out the standard line he used whenever anyone questioned the violent, sexually suggestive, misogynistic, homophobic, or just pointlessly offensive lyrics of any of his artists. "That's what will set him apart from these other kiddie rappers."

"I'm feelin' it," Daryl said, fully on board. "His Moms is dyin' to get him signed up."

"You'll produce," Lamont decreed. "But Grimy will work with him on lyrics and help him with his image. Grimes should take him under his wing." Lamont thought on it for a minute. "Hmm, maybe we should say Grimy found him. He could be Grimy's little protégé."

Lamont hadn't even said it to irritate Daryl. He was just thinking out loud. He was staring off and when he brought his focus back, Daryl looked ready to explode. He targeted Daryl with steely eyes, silently daring him to challenge.

"Cool," Daryl seethed.

He rightfully deserved the credit for this discovery—and he would find a way to get it—but he was too worn out to put up a fight. Wouldn't matter anyway. With Lamont, he could never win.

◆

CHAPTER 28

California Love

LENA HAD SAID she was going to L.A. for a week. That had been three weeks earlier and she still had not returned. Her new man, Trey, was out there working on his album so why would she leave? Vanessa had gone to Palm Springs for a cover shoot for *Vogue* that was going to feature all the premier models from the seventies to the present day. She had already called Mimi complaining that if she got stuck on the gatefold of the elongated shot—and not on the actual cover that people could see on newsstands as they walked by—there was going to be hell to pay. Mimi was getting lonely. And spending every night in Daryl's company only made her feel lonelier.

Mustafa, Vanessa's best buddy, had called Mimi three nights ago at Vanessa's behest. Though he was African and looked it—tall, whippet-thin with flawless, glistening ebony skin so penetratingly dark you'd think he bled black—he'd been educated in Europe so he had an amusing Senegal-by-way-of-Paris accent, and having a conversation with him was like piecing together a puzzle without having any idea what the final picture might look like.

"So waaassuup?" he'd said when he rang. Apparently it was a rhetorical greeting because he went on before Mimi could respond. "I went to Miami last week. I was on vacation."

Vacation from what? Mimi wondered.

"I stayed at Loews. It was nice. A good rate. One twenty-two. Very good. Excellent, you know." Pause. "Then I stayed at The Loft. You know they have a kitchen there. You can cook if you want." Pause. "I went to see Youssou N'Dour last night. At Manhattan Center. That place on Thirty-fourth Street, you know."

You-who? Mimi wondered.

"It was good. Someone just called me and said they had pass so I go just like that. It was good, you know." Longer pause. "So waaassuup?"

"Nothing much," Mimi finally said. "I haven't been out or anything since Lena went to L.A. I've just been working on my album."

"Aww, poor baby," he said earnestly. "Work so hard. You wanna go out tonight for some heep-hop? At Halo. Tonight is heep-hop."

"Halo?"

"Yeah, they play good music. Or Apartment. You want to go there? It's in the district packing meat." Mimi giggled. "Why you laugh?"

"It's called the meat-packing district."

"Oh yes, the meat-packing district." Pause. "Yeah, I just like to go out, watch people. Last week I went to Apartment and I meet this guy. He tell me he is investment banker. And we talk to the girls. And at the end of the night he give me a card. It say pharmacist, you know. You have to be very careful about people." Long pause. "So waasssuuup?"

Mimi agreed to go out. Daryl was working on the tenth-anniversary album and a new one for a cute little boy named Billy tha Kid so she had a couple of nights off. Mustafa arrived at her apartment two hours later wearing faded Rogan jeans, a starched white shirt with an ascot fluffing out at the neck, and, atop his gleaming bald head, a banded fedora pimped to one side. They breezed right into Halo, where they ran into some of Mustafa's friends. They swilled apple martinis, danced all night, and had a grand old time. Still, a night out with the girls it was not.

So Mimi called Lamont to see if she could get approval to take a short vacation to L.A. Luckily, Lamont said he was going to the West Coast for a few meetings about some movie soundtracks Triple Large was trying to secure. And there were some producers and songwriters he wanted her to meet in Los Angeles, so it all worked out perfectly. Imani took care of all their reservations.

Now they were sitting in first class on an early-morning nonstop American Airlines flight to LAX.

"So, Mimi, let me ask you something," Lamont said, getting all chummy midflight. He was glad she'd asked to go to L.A. He knew people there—he knew all the major people in all the major cities—but he didn't have a crew there. And he felt naked without his entourage. "Do you think I'm fat?"

She crinkled her eyes. Was he joking? Did Lamont care if he was fat or not? He was...kind of. But what was she supposed to say? Yes?

"Forget it," he clucked after an interminable pause.

"No, no," she said, touching his arm. "I thought you were kidding."

She still didn't answer the question. She didn't want to. If she said yes, he'd be mad. If she said no, she knew he'd say she was lying.

"I only ask," he said, turning back to her, "because that night when you were all drugged up..."

Oh God, Mimi thought, cringing at her hazy recollections of that night. Sometimes out of nowhere she'd get flashbacks of her begging Lamont to make love to her and a shiver of mortification would run up her spine. After that night, she didn't think she'd ever be able to face him again. But it was sweet how Lamont had taken such good care of her. Imani said Lamont had been furious with Grimy, who Mimi thought was a complete psycho for doing what he did and whom she avoided like the plague afterward. Though Lamont had never said a peep about her Ecstasy trip, something intimate had transpired between them. Now it was like they shared a little secret that neither of them would ever speak of. She'd thought he was being a gentleman by not mentioning it, knowing that it would make her uncomfortable. So why was he bringing up the incident now? She felt a wave of humiliation rolling toward her.

"You said, and I quote, 'Monty, you're really packing on the pounds!'"

"I did not!" she shrieked, so loudly that the people across the aisle looked over.

"Yes," he said seriously, "you did."

"Well, I didn't mean it!"

"Yes," he said seriously, "you did."

"It was the"—she lowered her voice to a confidential whisper— "it was the X talking."

"No, it was you being truthful because of the X."

"What else did I say?" She could remember only bits and pieces. She wished she could forget the whole thing.

"You said you should be the president of the itty bitty titty committee."

Mimi blushed. "Now *that* I remember," she said. She looked down at her chest. "But I guess that's not really a secret."

"I think little titties are sexy," he lied.

She scrunched up her nose because when he said "titties" it sounded vulgar, but then she realized he'd complimented her and she brightened. "You do?"

"Yeah." He smiled at her. "They suit you."

They sat quietly for a minute until he said, "You know, it's my birthday next month. I'm having a party at Jo Jo, Jean-Georges's place. Intimate. Exclusive. *InStyle* is covering it."

In truth, Ally C. was working on the coverage. *InStyle* told her that since Lamont was not a mainstream celebrity, all his artists and celebrity friends would have to be in attendance for them to consider it. At that very moment she was corralling every famous person Lamont had ever brushed up against.

"Really? It's my birthday next month, too!"

"Wonderful," he said, thinking he could get some press for her out of that. "We'll have a joint party."

"That sounds cool," she said cheerily. "Toya will be here then. She's going to come from Toledo to work on the album. It'll be fun to see her again."

She was so excited that Toya was coming. Though Keesha was still harboring some resentment about her leaving the group and rarely called, Mimi had kept in touch with Toya. A few months ago

Mimi had decided to get Toya an iMac and a digital camera for her birthday and to get one for herself too so they could e-mail. She asked Imani where she could go for computers and Imani called the PR person for Mac and got them wholesale. Flo$$ had appeared in a commercial for the company so it was all love. Mimi would come home from a wild night with Lena and Vanessa, during which she'd snap candid shots, and then send her digital images straight to Toya.

Lamont's brow furrowed. "Toya who?"

"You know. My friend Toya. She was in the group with me. She's coming up to do the background vocals."

"Daryl said that was okay?" Lamont said hesitantly.

"No," Mimi said. "I just invited her. You said she could do background vocals on my album."

"When did I say that?"

"That first day when I came to your apartment," Mimi responded nervously. She sensed she was in trouble.

If I said that, Lamont thought irritably, *I didn't mean it!* "Sweetheart, you need to get approval from me before you start making moves like that."

"Sorry," Mimi huffed. Then a polite, "Well, is it okay?"

"I don't think so," Lamont said, measuring his words carefully. He didn't want to be trapped at thirty thousand feet with a weepy girl. "We already have some experienced people to do backup." Could that chick even sing? He wanted Mimi working with only top-notch people, not amateurs. Not high school buddies.

"But I already told her!" she said hotly.

"Well, *un*tell her," Lamont snapped then caught himself. Mimi was too trusting. This small-town girl was probably planning to hitch her wagon to Mimi's star and never go home. Mimi had friends. Lena, Vanessa, people he had hand-picked. People he trusted. He hated hangers-on who tried to penetrate his inner circle.

Mimi fumed, wondering how she was going to break it to Toya. Lamont got up and went to the bathroom as soon as he registered the bad vibes emanating from Mimi's direction.

When he returned, Mimi was still angry, but had composed herself. "So how old are you going to be?"

"Thirty-nine," he answered dispassionately.

"Really," she chirped, sounding surprised. She could hear the discomfort in his voice so she decided a little dig was in order. "I thought you were *much* older."

That was for Toya, she thought, pleased with herself.

Lamont just turned and looked out the window.

AT THE FRONT DESK of the Four Seasons in Beverly Hills, Lamont stood barking into his cell at Imani because his bag was in Cleveland. Mimi was a few steps away talking on her phone to Lena, who was bubbling over with plans. Just as he ended the call, Lamont heard a husky voice call out his name.

He turned around and found himself at eyelevel with a man's chest. He looked up and saw the face of six-foot-six-inch L.A. Clippers star Rayshaun Atkins.

"Rayshaun," Lamont greeted him. "What up, kid?"

"Enjoying the off-season," Rayshaun answered. All limbs, he was clad in baggy denim shorts, a throw back Dr. J basketball jersey, and size sixteen red-and-white Air Prestos fresh out of the box. A walnut-sized diamond stud gleamed in each ear. "I damn near wore that Radickulys CD out in my truck. Been blastin' that shit for months."

Lamont glowed with pride. "Yeah, and what about Grimy's album? You still listening to that?"

"No doubt. It's his best yet. When's his next joint droppin'?"

"Soon, soon," Lamont said, ever the salesman. "I heard you just re-signed with the Clips. What was it? Eighty-five million over six years?"

There were two things Lamont was always in the mood to talk about: the success of his artists and how much money other rich people were making.

"Trying to get filthy like you, nigga," Rayshaun replied modestly, meaning filthy *rich*.

Lamont truly appreciated the compliment because, unlike Rayshaun, he didn't have a guaranteed contract and he wasn't twenty-three—which made him feel a bit vulnerable and he didn't like that feeling in the least.

Mimi ended her call, spun around and immediately recognized Rayshaun. He had been featured in a series of Nike commercials and one for McDonald's. He was the only basketball player that she knew by sight other than household names like Shaquille O'Neal. Her heart fluttered. She'd always thought he was so cute! And Lamont was talking to him!

Mimi stepped up, interrupting the impromptu meeting of the RBMMAS (Rich Black Men's Mutual Admiration Society).

"Rayshaun, this is my new singer," Lamont introduced her. "Mimi Jean."

Rayshaun looked her over. "You did that song with Phat E?"

"Yeah," she said quietly.

"I recognize you from the video. It's my favorite song."

She blushed. It was? Where was Lena to witness this?

"And the remix is off the hizz-ook," Rayshaun said.

"They been spinning it at the clubs out here?" Lamont asked with great interest. The remix featuring Radickulys had just gone out to club DJs. It wouldn't be added to radio playlists until the following week.

"Playing it all the time."

"Get the crowd jumping?" Lamont pressed.

"Hell yeah," Rayshaun enthused. He looked at Mimi. "Me included."

Forget the record and the video, Mimi was thinking. She was more interested in Rayshaun's superhero-like arms. She studied a tattoo on his sculpted upper arm but the dark green ink on his mahogany skin was difficult to make out. Then she realized it was a basketball falling into a net with his name—RAYSHAUN—arching over the top. It took up almost the entire expanse between his elbow and shoulder.

Her admiration wasn't very subtle and Rayshaun winked at her before turning back to Lamont. "You know I can spit," he announced confidently.

Oh Christ, Lamont groaned inwardly. This often happened to him. Kids who recognized him from some magazine article were constantly handing him demos. At the airport, at clubs, on the street. Did these people walk around every day loaded down with their wack-ass CDs just in case they ran into someone like him? And some of them had tapes! Who listened to cassette tapes anymore? Now Rayshaun thinks he can spit? *Negro, puh-leeze! Another baller who wants to be a rapper is exactly what I don't need.* Didn't these niggas know that all people wanted to hear from them was a howl after a slam dunk?

"Yeah?" Lamont said, trying to sound interested but hoping Rayshaun didn't whip a demo out from his pocket. "I'll be here for a couple of days. Hit me off with your shit."

"Cool," Rayshaun said agreeably. "A friend of mine is in town, staying here. I'm having a little party for him Friday night at The Lounge. Why don't y'all swing by. Around eleven."

Rayshaun glanced at his wrist to consult his frostbitten time-piece. "Gotta run," he said and smiled broadly at Mimi before departing.

Struck dumb, she just smiled back.

"Come on, Mimi," Lamont commanded, heading for the eleva-tors. When he realized she was still standing in the same spot, mouth half-open, watching Rayshaun walk all the way to the front door, he had to double back. "Let's go," he snapped and dragged her away before her vapors could fog up the entire lobby.

◆

CHAPTER 29

Bring Your Whole Crew

MIMI SAT AT THE TABLE, trying to pick out the perfect penis.

"Don't be shy, ladies," said Lou Paget, the instructor. An attractive, fortyish, natural blonde who had the soothing demeanor of a yoga teacher, she was not what Mimi had been expecting. But on second thought, she realized she'd had no idea what to expect.

Last night, she'd gone to a burlesque show at the club Forty Deuce with Lena and Trey while Lamont wined and dined some movie people. She'd excitedly told Lena all about her run-in with Rayshaun and the conversation had inevitably led to the question: If he's 6′ 6″, how big is his dick?

"You'd probably choke on it," Lena had said.

"I don't do that," Mimi had replied.

"I used to be scared of the dick but now I throw lips to the shit," Lena had said, quoting Lil' Kim. Lena could pull a rap quote out to suit any occasion.

"I'm not scared," Mimi had said hesitantly, feeling once again like a nun in the company of Lena, who had done everything—sexually and otherwise—and been everywhere. "It's just that…"

"What?" Lena had said.

"I don't know how!"

Lena had said she'd fix that. Since Lena was still on credit card suspension, Mimi had to pay the $250 fee for both of them to attend a popular sex seminar which drew women from all walks of life who had the desire to learn how to blow properly. Lena said you usually had to book far in advance but, as with most things, Lena had "connects."

"Six-inch, eight-inch, black, white, mulatto, or the ever-popular five-inch executive model, also known as the Porsche driver," the teacher trilled. "Take your pick."

Lena had already grabbed the eight-incher in jet black. Just to represent, Mimi went for the mulatto. Six inches.

The ten stylish women (and two obviously gay men) were gathered around a conference table in the Beverly Hills center with their "instructional products," as Lou called them. Mimi flipped through the pamphlet. You got a lot for $250.

"The Ladies' seminars—developed by a woman for women, are designed to empower women," the pamphlet read. "They are not simply about sexual intercourse, although that is covered. They concentrate on oral and manual stimulation as a means to mutual, safe sexual satisfaction."

There were also lubricants, sex toys, and books available for purchase. Mimi was definitely buying *The Big O: Orgasms: How to Have Them, Give Them, and Keep Them Coming.* And at $16.95, *How to Be a Great Lover: Girlfriend-to-Girlfriend Time-Tested Techniques That Will Blow His Mind* looked like a must-have, too.

"Our sexuality is where we all come from," Lou began. "It's also our most powerful form of communication. It creates life and it creates love."

She then gave a demonstration of how to put a condom on a man using only one's mouth. "Men complain that they lose their erections when they put on condoms," she said. "Believe me, that doesn't happen when you do it this way."

Watching her deft abilities, Lena leaned over and cracked, "You go girl."

"Now, ladies," Lou said. The two gay men seemingly took no offense. "Your turn."

THE NEXT DAY AROUND NOON, on his way out to a meeting, Lamont knocked on Mimi's door. They were staying on the same floor of the hotel but she had a room and Lamont had a suite. She appeared surprised to see him and just stood in the doorway. After brushing past her and coming inside, it was Lamont's turn to be surprised—by the sight of Rayshaun relaxing in a chair by the window.

"Rayshaun just stopped by. He's picking up his friend at the hotel," Mimi quickly volunteered. Rayshaun smiled at Lamont.

"Did Imani call you about the schedule today?" Lamont asked Mimi, knowing that the ever-efficient Imani surely had.

"Yes," Mimi said dutifully. They were supposed to go to a studio to meet with some producers who might be working on her album. Imani had given her the info and ordered a car to pick her up.

"I'll meet you there at three," Lamont said, and bid them a hasty farewell. He was slightly annoyed. Rayshaun was a decent kid as far as he knew, but Lamont didn't like anything involving Mimi going on without his approval.

Lamont did all the talking at their afternoon meeting, but on the way back to the hotel, Mimi tried once again to discuss her album's direction with Lamont.

"So those guys we just met have worked with Britney and Jessica Simpson," she said, trying to ease into the conversation gently. Her attempts to give creative input on her album had not been met with anything but impatience from Lamont. And he'd been in a snippy mood today so Mimi was treading with extra caution.

"Yes," Lamont said, staring out the window.

"I thought we were going for a more hip-hop, R&B feel?" Mimi's ideas about her sound fell more toward live instruments and soulful vocals but she'd resigned herself to the "hip-hop-R&B" image that Lamont was pushing. She'd rather be that than bubblegum pop.

"We are," Lamont said tersely. "But these guys might give you a big radio single."

"I think the album is sounding a little schizo."

Lamont looked at her, his hand wearily cradling his face. "Your complaints have been noted," he said blankly.

They rode for a few minutes, an awkward tension filling the town car.

"You know Rayshaun has a couple of kids, don't you?" Lamont said after a while.

"He does?" Mimi asked, wondering why Lamont was even mentioning that to her.

"Just thought you should know."

"Why would I care?"

"You're the one who invited him up to your room," Lamont quipped.

"I didn't invite him," she protested. Lamont sounded almost... jealous. Was that why he'd been so short with her since then? No, it couldn't be. "He was there to see his friend, not me."

"Sure," Lamont said, knowing how many times he had run similar games on women. He patted Mimi on the knee. "Just want you to know that he comes with a lot of *baggage* that you might not want to carry."

"Well, I don't even like him," she said, not very convincingly.

"Of course not," Lamont responded dryly as the car pulled around to the front of the hotel. "It was just an FYI."

Later that evening, Alonzo and Vanessa checked into the hotel. Lamont had ordered Nessa and Alonzo to come out because Lena and Mimi did not constitute enough of an entourage.

Alonzo had flown in from Vegas. Gambling was his favorite pastime. If he couldn't get away for a long trip, an overnight in Atlantic City would do. Sometimes he won big, sometimes he lost big. Sometimes he played the slots, sometimes he played at the big-money craps tables. He usually told Lamont and Vanessa that he was going off to scout some rapper. Lamont was always so preoccupied, it never occurred to him that the artists Alonzo was supposedly scouting never materialized. Lamont didn't really expect Alonzo to discover anyone—he didn't have the ear for that. But he was undeniably loyal to Lamont and that was all Lamont required.

Alonzo's frequent trips were also a means to get away from Vanessa. Another kind of wife might have been suspicious of a husband who traveled so much, but whenever Alonzo told Vanessa he was going on another trip all she said was "Bye-bye."

Mimi swung by Vanessa and Alonzo's room at eight to pick them up for dinner. As Vanessa finished dressing and prattled on about how bitchy the other models had been during the photo shoot in Palm Springs (as if Vanessa were a paragon of sweetness), Alonzo hugged Mimi as if she were family.

Every time Mimi was around him, she wondered how this man could be a blood relation of Lamont's—that's how gorgeous Alonzo was! He was always dressed very cool, like tonight in his baggy jeans, black silk T-shirt, sizable diamond cross hanging from his neck—not formal like Lamont.

What does Vanessa have to fight about with him? Mimi wondered. He seemed like a sweetheart. He probably regretted ever going through the pain and trouble of having Vanessa's name tattooed on the side of his neck.

The four of them went to Georgia's, a soul food restaurant that Lamont said was owned by Denzel Washington. Mimi hoped they'd see Denzel there mingling with the diners but Lamont had said, "It doesn't work that way, hon." So when Eddie Murphy unexpectedly appeared at their table, Mimi almost blacked out. One of the deals Lamont was hatching was to provide the soundtrack for an upcoming action comedy starring Eddie, so Lamont made a big push to have him join them for a minute. But once he did Lamont and Alonzo just chatted with him about sports and music and family stuff as if Eddie were a regular guy, not a Hollywood superstar.

"How many kids you have now?" Lamont said, glancing toward Eddie's supernaturally gorgeous wife, who was sitting with a few friends across the room. When Eddie proudly said five, Lamont joked, "If I could have a guarantee that my wife was going to look that fine after pushing out five babies, *sheeit,* I'd get married tomorrow. No pre-nup!"

The guys all roared, Eddie hiccuping his trademark laugh.

Vanessa was enthralled to be in the presence of a truly A-list movie star but seemed nonplussed when talk turned to another woman's beauty. She refused to turn and peek at Mrs. Murphy. Maybe she was beautiful, but so fucking what.

When Eddie had moved on, Mimi breathlessly asked Lamont how he knew him. Pleased that the box-office star had accorded him such respect (in public), Lamont said smugly, "That was the first time I ever met him."

Lamont and crew made their entrance at The Lounge at half past eleven. Rayshaun cleared room for them in the VIP area with his posse. He made sure Mimi sat next to him. Lena and Trey showed up a little while later, wearing matching FUBU track suits.

Trey went around and jubilantly slapped hands with everyone, but when he said, "Wassup, my niggas," almost the entire party turned at once and looked at him like, *Who you callin' 'nigga'?* Except Vanessa, who had become immune to hearing the n-word and didn't see the problem. Trey paled whiter than he naturally was and his flustered reaction made Lamont, Alonzo, and Rayshaun's entire crew flop all over each other with laughter. Lena looked like she wanted to curl up and die.

Rayshaun had the DJ spin Mimi's "Flyass Bitch" remix four times over the course of the night. No one at the party seemed to mind hearing it so much. Mimi was thrilled, Lamont equally so.

When Rayshaun offered to drive Mimi back to the hotel, Lamont said, "Don't worry, we're all going back together," gave Rayshaun a pound, and dragged her toward the waiting car. Rayshaun trailed behind and told Mimi he'd holla tomorrow.

Before she could respond, Lamont answered for her, as if Rayshaun was trying to make a date with *him*. "We're leaving early. Catch you on the rebound, playa!"

CHAPTER 30

◆

My Name Is...

"IS LAMONT BACK FROM L.A.?" Kendra asked.

"Yes," Mama said, and then moved on to the topic *she* wanted to discuss. "Have you ever thought about getting a real job, dear?"

"A real job?" Kendra repeated, flustered.

Mama Jackson noticed raindrops starting to fall. Seat-belted in the back of her chauffeur-driven Mercedes sedan, she pushed the button to raise the side window. "Yes, you know. A job that actually pays money at regular intervals. You don't seem to have had many of those. *None* that I know of." Mama's tough love was the gift that kept on giving.

"I just got a job on *Law and Order* as a matter of fact," Kendra countered, hoping Mama didn't watch the show.

"Wonderful," Mama cried. "And you didn't tell me? I love that show. What kind of role?"

"Just a small part. But pivotal. A nonspeaking role," Kendra said. She didn't dare reveal she was playing a hooker who gets killed in the opening sequence. Hopefully, Mama would miss it. If she blinked, she probably would.

"Well," Mama said, her enthusiasm evaporating, "you'll have to tell me when it will be on."

"Won't forget," Kendra said, not meaning it. "Where are we going?"

"It's a surprise," Mama said. She wasn't finished with giving advice and Kendra was obviously trying to divert her attention. "It's just that I worry about you, Kendra," she said honestly. "How do you support yourself?"

"I manage," Kendra said tightly.

I get paid plenty for my hot calls, Kendra thought. Although she could have done without the third degree, she was glad someone cared about her well-being. Sometimes it seemed like no one did. The first thing people asked you in New York was, "What do you do?" When Kendra said she was an actress they perked up. When they found out she had never done anything of note, the conversation quickly went downhill.

"And you're always turned out in the latest fashions," Mama continued. "How do you pay for all your beautiful clothes?"

Mama liked that about Kendra. She dressed with style, never slutty. But Mama was beginning to wonder if Kendra had a sugar daddy stashed away somewhere who paid for her designer labels. That could become an embarrassment for Lamont. If Kendra was creeping with someone else, Mama would not be able to continue to support her efforts to win Lamont back.

"I have friends in the fashion industry," Kendra explained. "I go to a lot of sample sales. And I get little jobs here and there. Enough to keep me afloat."

Mama was satisfied with that answer. She enjoyed spending time with Kendra—she was the closest thing Mama had ever had to a daughter. After Lamont was born, Mama had suffered a late-term miscarriage. No one ever talked about how much it hurt to lose a child that you had never held in your arms. To this day, she still thought about her unnamed baby girl. Mama had three nieces and she spoiled them like crazy now that she had the means. When Kendra had been with Lamont, they'd regularly done all the girl things together—visiting spas, going shopping, seeing Broadway shows. Mama had never told Lamont that she and Kendra had continued to do those things. Sometimes she felt like they were having an affair! But soon Kendra and Lamont would be back together again, just as it was meant to be. Kendra would be part of the family. Her daughter-in-law.

"If you ever need money, Kendra, don't hesitate to ask," Mama said. "Don't be too proud. Everyone needs a little help now and then." She took Kendra's hand and squeezed it.

Tears welled in Kendra's eyes. Mama was so sweet. She'd have to quit with the nasty talk for pay. Mama wouldn't be angry if she found out, she'd just be disappointed. Which was worse. She felt closer to Mama Jackson than she did to her own mother, who didn't have a clue how hard it was to make a go of it as an actress in New York. When she got really depressed, Kendra could never tell her own mother how bad things were. She would just tell her to come home to Florida. It was to Mama Jackson that Kendra would turn.

When Mama said things like, "Have you ever thought of getting a real job," Kendra didn't take offense. She'd often asked herself the same thing. But what would that mean? Buying business attire and taking the subway to sit in a cubicle all day, hoping for a 4 percent raise at review time, or worse, folding sweaters at the Gap? She had no college degree and no definable, marketable skills. She wasn't even computer literate. She had temped once, answering phones at an advertising agency. The people there always seemed frazzled and nervous, like they were one wrong move away from getting fired. No thanks. That life wasn't for her.

And phone sex is? a little voice inside her head said mockingly. But she kept telling herself that it was only a temporary way to pay the bills.

The car pulled up in front of a five-story brownstone on East Twenty-second Street. "Here we are," Mama said. "Mama Gena's School of Womanly Arts."

"What is this?" Kendra said, disappointed because she'd hoped they were going to a new spa or something like that.

"I read about it *New York* magazine. I liked that the woman calls herself Mama, you know," Mama Jackson said. "She teaches a class on how to make the most of your womanly wiles. All this sister goddess stuff. I thought it'd be fun."

"Maybe," Kendra said, unbuckling herself. She was game. "Let's see what this Mama Gena has to say."

Mama's uniformed chauffeur opened the door and Kendra put one leg out.

"Be sure to tell me all about it," Mama said, fingers curling in a wave.

Kendra pulled her leg back in. "You're not coming?"

"Heavens no. I have another appointment. With a real estate agent. I'm looking at new apartments. My place is starting to feel a bit small."

Kendra looked wounded. Mama was sending her off to some

flirting school? That was the big surprise? Kendra already knew how to work her damned womanly wiles!

"Dear," Mama said, a bit huffy now that Kendra was holding her up. "I don't need the class. I was married for thirty-two years, honey. And *I* left *him*. Lamont Sr. still calls me every week trying to get me to move down to Florida. He's getting so senile, half the time I can't understand what he's talking about. But the one thing he is very clear on is that he wants me back. But guess what? I raised my children. I took care of him for all those years. And I've nursed enough people in my lifetime. It's time for me to have some fun."

Kendra sat in chastened silence with the car door open, drizzle falling on her lap.

"You, on the other hand, have trouble keeping a man," Mama chastised. The class cost $500 per head! Kendra should be bowing in gratitude. "Now go. Don't be late."

She bent over and gave Kendra a peck. Not an air-kiss, but real mouth-to-cheek contact. Then a gentle push to get her out of the car.

Kendra stepped out to the sidewalk. The chauffeur closed the door and got back into the car.

There was a knock on the back window. Mama put it down halfway and said, "Yes?"

"Thank you for thinking of me," Kendra said, stooping in the rain.

"Not a problem," Mama said, looking straight ahead. Then her chauffeur eased back into traffic.

*　　　*　　　*

FARTHER UPTOWN, Lena was sitting in Lucy's diner with a girl named Maryslesis, the nineteen-year-old cousin of her drug dealer Boogie.

"I like this one," Lena said, pointing to an expertly rendered drawing of a slinky dress on a tall model in Maryslesis's sketchbook. "Looks like an Oscar dress."

"Thanks," Maryslesis responded sincerely. She was a pretty Dominican girl with curly brown hair and a sweet, round face.

"Hmm, this one is nice, too." Lena pointed to another drawing, of a girl wearing satin cargo trousers and a fur-collared bomber jacket. Casual chic. "I like your versatility. You can do high and low. That's important."

"Thanks."

"So how do you know how to draw like this? You never took classes or anything?"

"No," Maryslesis answered. "I can't afford to. And I don't have the time. I have to work."

Work? Lena shuddered. Boogie had told her that his cousin was mean with a charcoal pencil but she worked at a Laundromat in order to help her single mother provide for her younger siblings.

Lena had assumed she'd be able to produce a few sketches for her interview at Parsons. How hard could it be? But what she had come up with looked like shaky Etch A Sketch drawings. Boogie suggested that Maryslesis would be able to teach her to draw. She'd need lessons seven days a week for months to get anywhere near Maryslesis's skills.

"So you just taught yourself?" Lena asked, perplexed.

"Yeah," Maryslesis sighed. "I look at pictures in magazines. I go online at the library and print out information on how to design. I sketch. I try things. I have some free time at the Laundromat, 'cause during the week it's not that busy."

"You go online at the library?" Lena didn't like the sound of that. It sounded like a real hassle—long lines, slow connection, all kinds of nonsense.

"I can't afford a computer, Lena," she said.

How sad, Lena thought. She had a flat-screen iMac but she used it mostly for downloading hip-hop remixes on Kazaa. "I have an old computer. You want it?"

"Of course," Maryslesis gasped. "Yes, yes!"

"Good, because it's taking up space in my downstairs closet. I want to start my sneaker archive in there."

"Thank you so much," Maryslesis began to gush. "This is just—"

"You're welcome," Lena interrupted. "So tell me. What are your future goals?"

As Lena munched her greasy burger and fries, Maryslesis launched into a passionate monologue about her far-fetched dreams of becoming the next Donna Karan. She was touched that Lena was so interested.

When she finished, Lena said, "You have a lot more potential than the other posers I interviewed."

"There were others?"

"Yeah," Lena said. She had not revealed the full plan to the others. None of them ever made it past the first round. "You have a great eye. Your work is really phenomenal, Maryslesis. You just need more formal training."

"But you still want me to tutor you, right?" Maryslesis ventured cautiously.

"Tutor," Lena muttered. "That what Boogie told you?"

"He said you had an interview at Parsons and you need help."

"True. I do have an interview at Parsons. And I do need help. But there's been a slight change of plans." Lena tapped on the sketch-book. "I need this."

Maryslesis's brown eyes grew wide. "You want to *buy* my book?"

"Among other things," Lena said. She opened the book and looked at one of the sketches. "You see here where you signed this one? Can we erase that?" She rubbed at the signature with her finger and it began to smudge.

"So you want to buy the book and take it to the interview?" Maryslesis said, still not sure where this was going.

"Yes, and I want you to tell me all the technical things. Tell me what to say. How to present myself."

"Okay," Maryslesis agreed.

"And then, once I get in and register and all that," Lena contin-ued, "I want you to go to all the classes."

Maryslesis's head jerked up like a sleeping puppy that had just been awakened by a loud noise. "Are you serious?"

"Very."

"You want me to go full-time?"

"As many credits as you can handle," Lena said expansively.

"But how is this going to work? What if people find out?"

"How would that happen?" Lena snapped. "You gonna blow the whistle?"

"No, but I mean, you're going to the interview and then I'm going to the classes. We don't even look alike. You're gonna get busted."

"I doubt it," Lena said easily. "The people who do the interviews aren't the same people who teach the classes. I checked that out. But for the interview and registration you need picture ID and everything. I go in—with your book—then I register and pay and do all the official stuff. Then you go to the classes and win us raves. Using my name. I have it all worked out. Don't worry. You just keep sketching."

"What about graduation? Everyone comes to a graduation," Maryslesis said.

Lena fidgeted. She had not thought that far ahead. But she'd find a way around it. Maybe she'd have them mail the diploma. It could be worked out. "Leave it to me," she said.

"But, Lena, I don't know. People could still find out. And why don't you just use my book to get in and then go yourself? You can afford to go. You might like it."

"I don't have the talent," Lena admitted. "Wish I did. And the schedule is kind of taxing."

"So why are you doing it at all?"

"Don't worry about it, girlfriend," Lena retorted condescendingly, not wanting to get into her drama with Daddy. "And while you won't have the little piece of paper with your name on it, you'll have formal training. I bet you'll be able to get an internship with a designer. Look," she huffed, "I'm offering you a full scholarship!"

Maryslesis glowed. *Dios mio,* this was fantastic! She was going to Parsons! For free! "So you'll pay for all the classes, books, drawing materials, everything I'll need?"

"Not just that," Lena replied grandly, but Maryslesis didn't let her finish.

"But I have a job," Maryslesis hedged, doubting she'd be able to go full-time and work too since the Laundromat closed at seven. And part-time pay wasn't going to put food on the table.

"I know," Lena said, thinking, *Bitch, you'd rather work at the Laundromat? Hear me out!* "In addition to the scholarship, I'll pay *you*. I don't want you to just show up. I need you to excel," she said. Silently adding, *so I can bring those glowing reports back to Daddy.*

Maryslesis was floored. This was the best day of her entire life! "How much?" she asked softly, not wanting to sound pushy.

"Let's see," Lena said. Now that she was on credit card suspension, Lena was tearing through her cash allowance and writing bad checks and I.O.U.s all over town. And she'd had to get creative, like going to the gas station to load up on cigarettes and all manner of sundries on the Mobil card. "Things are a little tight for me right now."

Maryslesis eyed her curiously. Boogie told her Lena lived in a huge apartment and always paid for her weed with hundred-dollar bills.

"But my cash flow should be back on track by the time we get accepted." Lena knew that once she got in, Daddy would be so thrilled he'd let her lean on some serious cash. Shit, she was going to ask for a bump up in her allowance! And he'd gladly pay for any and all of her school expenses, which she would mark up considerably. "So let's say, for you personally, two thousand per class, half up front and the rest payable at the end of each semester."

Maryslesis gulped down her Coke and chewed nervously on a chip of ice. *¡Dios Mio! ¡Dios Mio!*

Lena was having a ball. She felt like a CEO. "And there will be added incentives. I don't know how they grade over there at Parsons, but if you rank in the top tier of your class, I'll throw in something extra. To be determined later."

Lena looked at the overjoyed expression on Maryslesis's face and asked, just as a formality, "So you down?"

Words could not convey Maryslesis's eagerness. She nodded her head vigorously, her curls bouncing. "And your real name is Marlena," Maryslesis bubbled.

Lena pursed her lips. Why'd Boogie have to tell her that?

"And my name is Maryslesis."

"Point being?" Lena said impatiently, signaling for the check. Now this chick was bugging her. She wanted to bounce.

"Our names kind of sound alike," Maryslesis remarked in a breathy gush. "The beginnings at least. And now I'm going to be your double. Isn't that funny?"

"Hysterical," Lena deadpanned. "At least when people call you Marlena at school, it won't come as such a shock." Lena clasped their hands together over the priceless sketchbook as if they were about to pray, and said serenely, "You see, it's a sign from God." She looked up.

The tear welling in the corner of Maryslesis's eye fell as she, too, looked up to the heavens. *Dios Mio.* It surely was.

CHAPTER 31

◆

My Philosophy

THOUGH LAMONT WAS FEELING CRANKY because he'd put himself on the Zone diet, he cheered up when he saw his youngest star-in-the-making. "What up, Kid."

With a gangsta lean, Billy sidled over to the sofa in Studio C of the Hit Factory. He was decked out in his Sean John linens and a diamond necklace that read KID hung around his neck. A gift from Grimy.

"What up, big man!" He gave Lamont a pound.

Lamont was stretched out with his Nikes propped up on the arm of the sofa, wishing he could get his hands on some real food. The Zone people delivered three meals a day—breakfast and lunch at the office and dinner at home. All rabbit food. And they provided low-calorie "treats." Lamont did not consider anything low-cal a treat.

His deprived stomach was making gurgling noises but no one could hear it. They were listening to the final mix of Grimy's album. Grimy was on the other side of the room with one-fourth of his posse, The Dirty Dozen.

Billy looked at Lamont's sneakers. "Yo, what size are you?"

"Thirteen."

"Hold on," Billy said and bopped out the door.

Witchy was leaning against the wall since Lamont wouldn't make room for him on the sofa. "I'm a twelve," Witchy called out, annoyed that he hadn't been asked.

They knew where Billy was going. Everyone in the office had heard the story of how Billy had lifted Daryl's wallet and ordered twenty-five pairs of sneakers from Nike.com with Daryl's credit card. Billy had gotten Daryl's billing address from his driver's license and had the order shipped to the studio. Everyone got sneakers except Daryl. Billy put the wallet back so Daryl didn't even know what had happened since he hadn't yet gotten the credit card bill.

When Lamont heard of Billy's prank, all he said was, "That's one smart kid."

Billy returned and gifted Lamont and Witchy with kicks in their respective sizes.

"Where's Daryl?" Lamont asked.

"Around here somewhere," Billy said, unconcerned. Daryl had been running back and forth between two rooms at the Hit Factory, working on Mimi's album and the TLE anniversary project. He came in occasionally to oversee the progress of Tha Kid's record but Grimy and various producers were running things creatively.

"Find him for me," Lamont ordered and Billy ran off to do as he was told.

Daryl hadn't been to the office for weeks. Witchy had been keeping tabs on him, but Lamont wanted an in-person progress report on the projects Daryl was handling.

But soon after Billy had gone on his hunt for Daryl, Lamont got up to leave. He decided he didn't want to speak to Daryl tonight. It'd just make his stomach growl more.

"So, Grimes," Lamont said to his thug genius, who was disappearing in a cloud of Newport smoke. "You got a name for this one yet?" The record sounded great but Lamont couldn't concentrate. He had to go get some dinner.

"Yeah," Grimy said, blowing smoke rings. "Ghetto Transfusion."

DARYL WAS WALKING INTO A PARTY with Nicole Narain, *Playboy*'s Miss January 2002. Everyone who was anyone was there. They were all looking at him with the gorgeous black playmate on his arm. She was five foot nine. He was ten feet tall.

Passed out on a couch in a small side room at the Hit Factory, his dream was about to turn into a *wet* dream until he felt something brushing his face. He groggily slapped himself into a state of semi-consciousness. The room was completely dark. He hadn't slept for more than four hours a night in weeks.

Then he felt something crawling on his hair. He sat up and started screaming like a girl. What was that? He heard a squeaking sound. A mouse? He had a terrible fear of mice.

He heard muffled laughter. Still half-asleep, he lunged for the light switch on the wall. The sound of the tittering got louder. He knew that laugh.

Billy flipped the switch by the door, flooding the room with light. Daryl jumped as Billy's spotted gerbil raced around his bare feet.

He hopped from one foot to the other, yelping. He looked like he was doing a tribal dance.

"Get that rat away from me!"

Billy ran over and scooped up his pet. "It's not a rat," he said, insulted. "Brownie's a gerbil." Brownie had brown spots all over his white fur. Billy held it up to Daryl's blotchy skin. "You guys could be related."

"Get that thing away from me!" Daryl yelled, shivering with disgust. "And get the fuck out." He was so tired he felt punch drunk.

"Big Man's looking for you," Billy said. "I told him you were sleepin' on the job."

"He's here?"

"Yeah," Billy said. "Hurry up. He's been waiting on you." Billy walked out of the room and slammed the door.

Daryl slipped into his sneakers. Damn, his breath was funky. He hurried to the door, trying to wake himself up. As soon as he got into the hallway, Billy flung Brownie through the air and the jumpy gerbil landed—plop!—right on the back of Daryl's neck.

Daryl squealed and flailed frantically in the hallway, spinning like a top, as two Hit Factory employees looked on from the lounge. "Get it off me! Get it off me!"

Billy almost died laughing.

"RAYSHAUN ATKINS DOESN'T HAVE ANY KIDS," Jordan insisted.

She'd invited Mimi to a Heather Headley concert. Now they were grabbing a late dinner at Odeon.

"Lamont said he did."

"I don't think so," Jordan said.

"How do you know?"

"I don't know. Not for sure. But I know Rayshaun's agent very well and he never mentioned anything like that."

"That's weird," Mimi said. "It doesn't matter, though," Mimi sulked. "He never called me. But then I lost my cell in L.A. and I got a new number. Maybe that's why. You think I should call him?"

"Did you give him your home number?"

"Yes," Mimi said, sensing where this was going.

"Then he still could have called you," Jordan said gently. "Don't call him. A guy like that has enough girls sweating him."

Mimi picked at her food. "Lena said I should call him."

The blind leading the blind, Jordan thought. "I bet he's going to call you," she said, trying to lift Mimi's spirits. "He's just playing it cool. I could see you two together."

"You could?"

"Sure. You're about the same age, he's cute, you're cute, you've got your singing thing going on. You might be the new black power couple."

"But he has all those kids. He must have a girlfriend, too. Or at least a baby mama."

"I told you, I don't think that's true."

"But Lamont said."

"Lamont says a lot of things," Jordan snapped. "Doesn't make it true. He thinks he has the goods on everyone. But he gets things all wrong sometimes."

"You don't like him, do you?"

"Lamont?" Jordan waved her fork. "He's okay. He does his thing. I do mine."

"I think Lamont is really sweet. He bought me all this stuff when I first got here. He always looks out for me."

"And since you're an artist signed to his label, that is by extension a way of looking out for himself. Lamont isn't exactly selfless."

"What's the story with Kendra?"

"They dated. He dumped her."

"But she's been out in the Hamptons with him. Are they getting back together?"

"With Lamont, anything's possible."

"She never talks to me. She acts like I did something awful to her."

"You did. You got Lamont's attention. It doesn't matter that you just work with him. She's very insecure."

"But she's so pretty. What does she have to be insecure about?"

"Honey, a black woman trying to be an actress is a nervous break-down waiting to happen."

"Why did Lamont dump her?"

"He was probably just bored with her," Jordan said, shaking her springy Afro. "I've known Lamont for seven years and in that time I've seen a lot of women come and go. More than I can count."

"That's why you don't like him?" Mimi asked. "Because he's a player?"

"No. He's a single man. Let him do his thing. Ninety-nine per-cent of the men in this world, if they were in his position, would do the same thing. He's living the fantasy for them all. And I *do* like him. He's funny, he can be very nice when he has reason to be and he's the hardest-working person I've ever met. You have to admire that. Honestly, I feel kind of sorry for him."

"Sorry?" Mimi repeated, thinking Lamont was the last person anyone could feel sorry for. "Why?"

"Because I don't think he's happy and I wonder if he ever will be."

"Every time I see Lamont he's smiling, joking around," Mimi said. "He seems pretty happy to me."

"Just because someone's smiling doesn't mean they're happy," Jordan commented. "Now don't get me wrong, I think Lamont is happy. At least, on a surface level. I mean, listen...we all know he's a pussy chaser. But he is, as they say, an eight-figure nigga, and a man like that finds pussy sitting on his doorstep wrapped in a big red bow. So technically, I suppose he's more of a pussy catcher or receiver than a chaser. And the irony is that by becoming so successful he's lost the fun of the chase. For men, that's the best part. And that's probably why he can't ever be happy for any length of time with any woman he dates no matter how beautiful, sexy, fun or"—she raised an eyebrow—"*freaky* she might be. It's like he's always talking about how sexy he thinks Kiko is, right?"

Mimi nodded. He regularly flirted with Kiko but she'd always manage to give him a friendly brush-off.

"And Kiko is a gorgeous, sexy girl but not any more than most of the women Lamont dates," Jordan went on. "If we even want to call the activities Lamont engages in *dating*. But Kiko just isn't interested. She likes real young roughneck types. And that is what keeps her so desirable to him. That he can't have her."

"Right," Mimi said.

"But I guarantee you, if she slept with him just once, she wouldn't be sexy to him anymore. His love life is that same sad song playing over and over again. Getting women isn't a challenge for him and Lamont is a man who lives for challenges. He has money, success, and the women other men can only fantasize about. Yet he's never satisfied. There's always the next mountain to climb." Jordan pushed her plate away, leaned back, and exhaled. "That's sort of sad, don't you think?"

◆

CHAPTER 32

La Di Da Di

"I FEEL LIKE MY BOOBS ARE GONNA FALL OUT," Mimi complained, tugging at her one-button fitted velvet blazer. The lapels met only a few inches above her navel. She was naked underneath. Except for some body bronzing lotion Vanessa had sprayed on.

"Boobs," Vanessa scoffed, pulling a black, calf-hugging boot up to her knee over fishnet stockings. "What boobs?"

"Nessa!" Mimi wailed, wobbling over to the full-length mirror in Vanessa's dressing room. Her feet were killing her. Her shoes had heels like spikes.

"Who cares," replied Vanessa, who had picked out the purple jacket. "You look fabulous." She stood behind Mimi in the mirror, pleased with her styling. "Anyway, it's Tom Ford for Yves Saint Laurent Rive Gauche," Vanessa declared as if that said it all.

"Where did we get these again?" Mimi asked, looking at the faded jeans adorned with floral embroidery. "Robert Cavel?"

Vanessa brushed Mimi aside to get exclusive mirror time. "Roberto Cavalli."

"Roberto Cavalli," Mimi repeated, moving to one of the seven other mirrors in Vanessa's closet. "Yeah, I love them."

Vanessa admired herself in the long antique mirror. The criminally short black leather hot pants and hot pink Dolce & Gabbana satin corset combined with the fishnets and boots made her look like an escapee from the Moulin Rouge. Just the look she was going for. Mustafa was meeting them at the party so she was forced to mentally massage herself: *Perfect, baby... love you... besos.*

"My hair looks kinda poufy," Mimi worried, patting the fluffy cascade of waves falling down her back. There had been hair and makeup house calls earlier in the evening.

"Big hair is in right now," Vanessa decreed, rummaging through drawers and drawers of accessories. She caught Mimi putting a tentative finger to one of her kohl-rimmed eyes. "Don't touch!"

Mimi put her finger down. "Sorry. I like the necklace, too," Mimi said, sliding her index finger over the glittery pendant that spelled MIMI in a vertical dangle from the chain around her neck. She wondered if they were real diamonds. "Where'd you find this?"

"I had it made," Vanessa said, searching for her vial of coke. "That's why the jacket needs to be so open. The necklace is the focal point." She spritzed Mimi with three quick bursts of Agent Provocateur and said, "Let's go."

Outside, Lamont and Alonzo were waiting in their respective luxury vehicles. Vanessa got into the Range with her husband while Mimi stepped into Lamont's vintage black Rolls-Royce limo. It had black velvet curtains on the side windows. She felt a little bit like she was in a hearse.

"You look gorgeous," Lamont gushed, detecting the sweet scent of perfume.

Mimi noticed his jacket was very similar to hers. "We look like we're going to a prom," she cracked.

"Vanessa picked it out," he said, flicking an invisible piece of lint off his deep-purple velvet Armani suit, which was perfectly complemented by a lavender Paul Smith shirt. "We're having a joint party. She thought our looks should be in sync, you know," he explained, experiencing a rare moment of uncertainty.

Mimi heard the doubt in his voice. "You look gorgeous, too," she said obligingly, patting him on the knee.

"And trust me," Lamont said, quickly recovering his bravado. "This party isn't going to be like any prom you've ever been to!"

Jo Jo was in a townhouse on East Sixty-fourth Street. As they came to a stop, Mimi pulled back the curtain. Ally C.'s face was pressed against the window.

"And hey," Lamont said before she could get out. "You're nineteen tonight."

"What?" Mimi said as Ally C., wearing a headset, carrying a clipboard, and looking frazzled as always, swung open the door and helped her out.

The *InStyle* photographer flashed off a series of shots as the two guests of honor sauntered inside arm in arm. "I'm twenty-one," Mimi whispered while holding her smile.

"I know," Lamont said while holding his. "But I decided you should be nineteen. It's a better age to hit the teen market. Just go with it."

Ally C. ushered them through the throng of well-wishers. The elegant restaurant was closed to the public tonight. Two long, beautifully arranged tables of twenty spanned the narrow room, and on each plate sat the evening's menu with the words "A TRIPLE LARGE BIRTHDAY CELEBRATION" engraved on top.

Mama Jackson arrived fashionably late, just before the three-course meal was to be served. She always liked to make an entrance and in tonight's geisha getup she certainly did. She had on her Suzy Wong wig, a jet-black bob with sharply cut bangs, and a blood-red cheongsam with a mandarin collar over red pants.

Lamont pressed his hands together and bowed his head when she approached. "Oooh Mama, me love you long time," he teased, causing a ripple of laughter at the table.

"Don't play with me, Junior," she teased back. She air-kissed him, careful not to muss her immaculate maquillage. "If it weren't for me you wouldn't be having this party."

"You tell him, Mama," Nate said, pulling out her seat between himself and Lamont.

"No, dear," Mama said, picking up the placecard that simply said MAMA. She pointed to the other side of the table where the guests had their backs up against the wall. "I like to face out."

Everyone looked around with confusion because the seating had been carefully planned and impromptu seat-switching would invite the wrath of Ally C. Lamont snapped high in the air and his publicist appeared, quickly resolving the dilemma to Mama's satisfaction.

Ally C. dashed back to the side of the *InStyle* writer, a petite thirtyish white woman wearing fashionable cat-eye glasses. After dinner she went around and got quotes from all the "names" in attendance.

Since she was not familiar with the hip-hop set, Ally C. pointed out who was who.

The reporter couldn't miss Flo$$ (who she recognized from last summer's blockbuster action flick, not his three multiplatinum albums) as he made his usual splashy entrance. Whenever he went out to an event he was preceded by six rent-a-models in designer bikinis and heels (even in winter) that matched his own colorful out-fit. Tonight's color scheme was canary yellow and the bikinis were Versace. One girl was assigned the task of carrying the small boom-box that played Flo$$'s personal anthem, a song called "That Nigga," which outlined just how fly he was.

Irv Greene, not a late-night partier, made a cameo appearance with his wife of forty years, Enid. He took his leave right after the pair of four-tier, almost-too-beautiful-to-eat cakes made by celebrity baker Sylvia Weinstock were brought out and "Happy Birthday" was sung.

Lamont knew the reporter was going to want a quote from Mimi, so while she made her way through the room, he prepped his ingenue.

"The *InStyle* reporter is going to ask you for a quote," he explained, pointing the woman out. The photographer saw them sit-ting together and approached to snap a few shots. Vanessa must have smelled the photo opportunity because she appeared from the other side of the room with supersonic speed and trailed away again as soon as the flashes stopped.

"Say that thing you said in the car," Lamont continued. "About going to the prom. That's funny. It's a good quote."

The reporter was on the other side of the room asking Mama

what she'd gotten Lamont as a gift. "Mine isn't out there," Mama said, nodding toward a table piled high with presents. "I got him a black leather Gucci massage table. Had it delivered yesterday."

Lamont saw the reporter approach Don Gambino next. He wondered what The Don was saying. Gambino had arrived clutching an open bottle of champagne and wearing nothing but a diamond machine gun pendant under the unzipped jacket of his orange velour warm-up suit. He didn't travel with an entourage, he traveled with a mob. (And that's exactly what they called themselves, Gambino's M.O.B. They had a group album scheduled for release.) It wasn't unusual for him to show up at a party with the mob and its peripheral members running thirty deep. Tonight the count had come to a mere sixteen, all guys except for Hitz, Inc.'s lone female rapper, EnVee. Gambino had gotten loud at the door and Ally C. had had to read him the riot act: "You know the rules, Don. Fifteen hot chicks and you're in. All these dudes, *c'mon,* I can't do it! You gotta lighten up!" Her assistant, Kerri D., had been sent inside to consult Lamont, who had sanctioned "a plus-six entry." So Gambino had "lightened up" (hotspot lingo meaning send half your crew home) and stormed in followed by his core six.

The reporter then stopped to speak to Lena and EnVee. This was the first time Lena and EnVee had met but they'd been in deep conversation for over an hour. The royal blue Lady Enyce jumpsuit Lena was rocking (with one leg rolled up, Cool J style) looked like something she'd borrowed from a gas station attendant. But zipped down low, her bursting cleavage made it clear she was all woman.

EnVee's nom de rap came from the initials of her given name, Nadine Villard. Her recently released sophomore LP, *Green With*

Envee, featured just her emerald eyes on its cover. She had a peaches-and-cream complexion but a black girl's attitude and inflection. She claimed her great-great-great-grandmother was black and she repped that one drop of negritude to the fullest. (Coincidentally, Gambino, the head of her label, had an equally milky coloration and everyone knew he had two black parents so that lent credence to her claims.) Her short, spiky, naturally auburn hair was dyed black streaked with magenta stripes this week. She was a rising hip-hop star and the album was charting high so, naturally, Lena was trying to befriend her.

When the reporter finally made it over to the guests of honor, Lamont said, "I decided to do something a little more low-key this year. The big party thing is played. Intimate is in. We're doing elegant for dinner and then we're going to move upstairs and set it off."

When he was done, the reporter turned to Mimi for quotes. "I told Lamont in the car that I felt like we were going to a prom," Mimi giggled into the woman's small tape recorder, Lamont's hand pressing gently on her back.

"And then I told her," Lamont chimed in, " 'Baby, this isn't going to be like any prom or any party you've ever been to!' "

A small smile flickered across the reporter's face, then she asked, very businesslike, "And who are you wearing?"

"What?" Mimi said.

"No. *Who*," the woman stressed. "Which designers." She held the tape recorder up to Mimi's mouth with a seriousness that Melissa Rivers only wished she could convey. This was not a game. "I need to know who made everything you have on."

"The jeans are Roberto Cavalli," Mimi began, feeling like this was a pop quiz. The reporter nodded. "And the jacket is..." Mimi tried to remember. "Tom Ford by..."

"Tom Ford for Yves Saint Laurent Rive Gauche?" the reporter spit out so quickly that Lamont and Mimi both looked at her like she had Tourette's syndrome.

"Yes!" Mimi exclaimed. "And the necklace was a gift from Vanessa de la Cruz. She had it made."

"And the shoes?"

"I don't know who made them," Mimi said wearily. "But they hurt."

The reporter promptly popped Mimi's foot out of the stiletto pump. She noted the label and whispered into her recorder, "Shoe by Christian Louboutin."

Mimi exhaled happily, feeling like she'd passed the test, and Lamont was pleased with the way she'd handled herself.

"You're not leaving yet, are you?" Lamont asked the reporter. She shook her head. "Well come on, sister, party's just getting started." With Mimi on one arm and the reporter on the other, he headed upstairs, where the music was already thumping.

Kendra traipsed behind them, heated that Lamont had barely spoken to her all night and that he'd had her seated at the table where he *wasn't*.

Lena was ensconced in a back corner smoking a blunt with EnVee. Mimi didn't indulge, thinking it a bit outrageous that they were getting high in such a public place. She'd heard Lena playing EnVee's album and she tried to chill with them but EnVee was standoffish. Which Mimi thought was rude because wasn't this *her* party?

When the DJ threw on "Break You Off" by The Roots featuring

Musiq Soulchild, Mimi shouted, "This is my shit!" and stole Lena away from EnVee so they could dance.

At the back of the room, Nate approached Lamont and pulled a velvet box from his coat pocket.

"Look," he said, popping it open to expose a diamond engagement ring. He held it under the table with his back to the room. Jordan was walking around, chatting everyone up, her black leather pants paired with a white T-shirt silk-screened with an image of Tupac giving the middle finger.

"I'm going to propose," Nate confided.

"Again," Lamont crowed skeptically. Nate and Jordan had been engaged briefly three years ago and gone from breakup to make up several times since.

"Yeah, but this time I'm doing it right," Nate said nervously.

"How many rings have you bought?"

"This is only the second one. The other times we talked about it but I never actually had a ring. What do you think?"

Lamont took a look at it. "Pretty nice," he said blandly. He felt like Nate was chumping himself. "She really got you sprung."

"Come on, man, you know Jordan is cool. I love her," he said almost apologetically, slipping the ring back in his pocket.

Lamont looked at Nate's jumpy eyes and thought, *No woman has ever gotten me open like that and no woman ever will.* Lamont held out his hand.

"What?" Nate thought maybe he wanted to get a closer look at the ring.

"Hand in your pimp card, nigga," Lamont thundered. "You're done!"

Nate smirked, refusing to be clowned.

Alonzo sidled over. "What's so funny?"

"Nate's proposing to Jordan," Lamont blurted.

Alonzo gaped at Nate. "Again?"

Nate gave him the finger and drifted away. Lamont and Alonzo cackled together.

Daryl arrived around one, coming straight from the studio. He would have preferred to stay there. He was in a groove mixing some of Mimi's songs. But he was the designated hype man at the frequent parties Lamont threw. The fun of getting up on the mike and pumping the crowd was diminished by Lamont's *insistence* that he do so. Lamont made even the fun stuff feel like work. At least he'd gotten away from Billy tha Brat for the night.

Daryl went right up to the DJ booth that had been set up for tonight's party, grabbed the mike, and got to work.

"IS BROOKLYN IN THE MO'FUCKIN' HOUSE?" Daryl bellowed.

There were some cheers.

"TLE all-star Radickulys up in here. Diiirty South! *Our* album got the charts on lock," Daryl howled, giving himself a little plug that Lamont might not notice. "Go out and cop that."

Dicky jumped on a chair at his table, where he was surrounded by a bevy of beauties. His hair was parted in a zigzag down the middle and his two huge Afro puffs were held in place by white sweatbands.

Daryl spotted him and they pointed at each other, both yelling, "Say whaaat!" DJ Spinbad threw on Dicky's single of the same name.

"Uptown! Uptown!"

Some cheers.

"This is for the ladies," Daryl crooned, as DJ Spinbad segued into Flo$$'s latest hit, "You So Purrrty," a song that complimented females of every stripe.

Flo$$, wearing baggy yellow leather pants and a yellow Angels baseball jersey, pulled Mimi out onto the floor. He began rapping his own lyrics, waving a yellow hand towel that he used to mop his sweaty bald head while his bikini girls hovered nearby, swaying to earn their keep.

Dicky's gaggle of gal pals stared down Flo$$'s model clique because Dicky and Flo$$ had been very publicly feuding for over a year, stemming from the time Dicky had accidentally smudged Flo$$'s brand-new, limited edition S. Carters and refused to apologize. Dicky had recorded the dis record "Pegleg," Flo$$ had responded with "No Dick," and Dicky was about to expose his ghetto-fabulous labelmate's hated real name in the all-bets-are-off rebuke, "Eugene." Though they had quickly let bygones be bygones after the original sneaker skirmish and were on good terms privately, Lamont was encouraging the public feud because it garnered so much press. *MTV News* had even done a half-hour special on it.

"Flo$$ settin' it off on the floor!" Daryl yelled, encouraging other people to get up. Then he commanded, "My fine black women holla back one time!"

Every black woman in the house obviously considered herself fine because they all hollered back.

"Where my white women at?"

Lamont laughed as übermodel Emma threw an ivory arm high in the air. She'd recovered nicely but he and Nate still referred to her as "China White." The freckle-faced twin snack-food heiresses, Tina and Rosie Krohn, were tossing their red hair around while whooping it up surrounded by their equally boisterous rich-white-girl posse. And he spotted the *InStyle* reporter, obviously tipsy, hoist her martini glass.

"We got Vanessa de la Cruz holdin' it down for all my butta pecan rican mamis," Daryl shrieked.

Venezuelan Vanessa hated being called Puerto Rican but she was too fucked up to notice. She flung her arms up on the dance floor and Alonzo held her up. He was glad Mama had already gone home.

"Lena 'Make It a Double' Whitaker gettin' her groove on!"

As the Outkast song "Hey Ya!" came on, Lena, drunk and in her own world, started shimmying and singing the words, "Shake it, shake it, shake it like a Polaroid picture..."

"White Boy Goldstein!" Daryl screeched. "I see you, playa. Pimp that Kangol!"

Josh Goldstein, premier hip-hop video director, was on the floor trying to infiltrate the rich-white-girl posse and dancing like he was having a seizure.

Witchy was dancing nearby, putting Josh to shame. With his Bruce Jenner wings flapping away, he was busting some rhythmic moves that gave new meaning to the phrase "pretty fly for a white guy." Daryl gave his boss no shout-out.

"We got MC Grimy in the house!"

Lamont saw Grimes nod in the corner as the crowd cheered his presence. Next to Grimy's side was a young black woman wearing a cheap shiny dress, heavy makeup, and a shellacked pileup of a hairdo. Lamont waved Imani over.

"Who's that chick Grimy's with?" he almost slurred. He rarely drank alcohol, usually preferring to be the calm eye in a party's storm. But he always indulged at his own birthday party.

"His wife," Imani exclaimed.

He threw her a shocked look. "Somebody married him?" he shouted, then thought, *Of course. He's rich. He's famous. He's Grimy.*

"I think it's a common-law thing," she yelled over Daryl's continued shout-outs. "He calls her 'wifey.' But they've been together a long time. They have three kids. You know what her name is?"

"What?" Lamont said eagerly, sensing a punch line and a hearty laugh coming.

"Her actual, legal name is Beautiful," Imani said. "But people call her Beauty for short."

Lamont tossed back his head, parted his fleshy lips, and felt the laugh rumble all the way up from his gut.

Daryl got giddy as an A-list wave of diamond-laden ballers washed in. "Make way, make way, we got the number-one bad boy comin' through, P. DIDDY IN THE MO'FUCKIN' HOUSE Y'ALL," Daryl announced worshipfully, because Diddy was his idol as a producer and as a human being but every time he ran into the brother, Diddy looked right through him. "Fabolous...Dame Dash...Jigga...The Roc... HOLLA!"

All the rap royals stopped by Lamont's table in the back to pay their respects. Ally C. and Kerri D. started scrambling to have more tables brought up from downstairs so each of the stars and their attendant posses could have comfortable VIP-worthy seating arrangements. Lamont waved the reporter over, hoping she wasn't too far gone to get more quotes.

"We got The Firing Squad up in this piece," Daryl boomed. "Gambino...my nigga Supa Phat E...EnVee...Killa M.C.... Nasdaq...Blinky Blinks...Cool Breezy!"

Gambino jubilantly pumped his bottle of champagne, spraying his surrounding peeps.

Daryl gave Spinbad a nod and the DJ threw on "In Da Club" by 50 Cent. Spinbad started scratching on the first line. *Go shorty... Go shorty... Go shorty, g-g-g-g-go shorty... Go shorty, It's yo' birthday...*

He let it go and everyone continued singing along...

Go shorty, it's yo' birthday
We gon' party like it's yo' birthday
We gon' sip Bacardi like it's yo' birthday
And you know we don' give a fuck 'cuz it's yo' birthday

"A special birthday shout-out to our new Triple Large princess, Mimi Jean," Daryl whooped.

Mimi, Vanessa, and Lena were falling all over each other on the dance floor. Mimi was drunk enough not to notice that her boobs were indeed falling out of her Tom Ford for Yves Saint Laurent Rive Gauche blazer. Lena and Vanessa were too drunk and high to point out that she was now wearing two raccoon eyes of kohl eyeliner.

Spinbad cut the music down to a reverential level so Daryl's final shout-out could take center stage.

"And to the nigga who makes shit happen, the nigga who holds it down, the nigga who taught us all how to trick bank *and* bitches, the check writer, the shot caller, baller supreme, our Daddy mo'fuckin' Warbucks... Monty Jackson."

The whole room cheered. Kendra, playing Lamont extra close, actually stood and applauded. Lamont raised a manicured hand in modest acknowledgment. Lamont never danced.

The music pumped back up....

WE GON' SIP BACARDI LIKE IT'S YO' BIRTHDAY
AND YOU KNOW WE DON' GIVE A FUCK 'CUZ IT'S YO'
BIRTHDAY...

Daryl had done his duty. He hopped down looking to holla at one of the fine black women he'd spied from his perch.

Grimy took the mike and fell into a rapturous state giving an impromptu performance of "This Rap Shit," a big hit from his third album. The crowd helped him out with the chorus, a repetitive chant of "Fuck all y'all."

Half past three with the party still going strong, Spinbad dropped the remix of "Flyass Bitch" that featured Radickulys. Phat E twirled Mimi onto the floor and represented for all the big men by displaying surprising mobility. Much to Lamont's delight, the song re-energized the room. The record had been a hit and the remix would be, too.

Mimi was so tall in her heels he could see her head above everyone else's. Dancing and laughing, honey-blond hair snapping every which way, tiny boobs exposed to all, she forcefully sang along, even rapping Phat E's part, then Dicky's, not tripping on any of the words.

Watching her, Nate leaned over to Jordan and observed, "That girl has changed, hasn't she?"

"Yes," Jordan agreed mildly, wondering if it was for the better. "She's a flyass bitch for real. Who knew Lamont was the Henry Higgins of our time?"

While Kendra massaged his thigh, Lamont downed his tenth glass of champagne, beamed at his new Triple Large princess, and drunkenly thought, *That's my girl.*

◆

CHAPTER 33

Put It on Me

"SURPRISE!" everyone yelled.

Mimi turned to Lamont, embarrassed to the point of tears. "What is this? We had a party last week!"

"That was a press thing," Lamont said. Like their party at Jo Jo hadn't been a total blast. "You did that for me. I'm doing this for you. Lena said you wanted to go bowling."

He frowned over at Lena as if to say, *Did you give me some bad information?* But when Mimi hugged him and gave him a big kiss on the cheek, he started smiling again.

They strolled into the Chelsea Piers bowling alley with Lena, Nate, Jordan, Kiko, Vanessa, Alonzo, and Imani right behind them. Tonight was Mimi's actual birthday and they'd all just come from dinner at Mr. Chow. Now here was Dicky and almost everyone from the Triple Large office waiting for them. Glittering banners proclaimed: HAPPY BIRTHDAY, MIMI!

After dinner, they had piled into cars and Mimi thought they

were going to a club or something. No one would say. Then their caravan of SUVs pulled up at Chelsea Piers, a massive complex on the
West Side Highway. There were some huge yachts moored at the
dock and Mimi thought maybe they were going to get on a boat. She
hadn't expected anything like this!

She *did* want to go bowling. Lena kept promising her they would
but they never got around to it. The Chelsea Piers alley wasn't anything like the one at home. Especially not tonight. Lamont had
rented out one whole side of the place, about twelve lanes. There was
a DJ spinning all night and two TVs hovered above each lane, one for
the computerized scores and one that was playing rap videos on
mute. Waitresses would come to your lane to take orders for drinks
and snacks.

Everything was free. At least for them. A long link-up of velvet
ropes kept people from the other side out—though no one was really
bowling on the other side. It was all kids standing by the ropes trying
to get autographs from Dicky, EnVee, and Phat E. And from her!
People knew her from the video and song she'd done with Phat E.

Since ever-watchful Lamont was ensconced down at the end in
the VVIP lane behind a wall of security—schmoozing, not bowling—
Mimi felt free to indulge in a few Bellinis. He was always warning her
about drinking, saying, "Don't be like Lena." But he'd encouraged
their friendship so who was he to talk?

She took over a lane with a few of the other girls—Lena, Vanessa,
Imani, and Kiko, who was so loud and funny that she made Lena
seem shy. Mimi had a blast watching Lena and Kiko trash talk each
other to death. Every time Kiko would step up to bowl, she'd rub her
hands before touching the ball and say, "Lemme go 'head and get a

strike so I can shut this bitch up." In four games, she never did get a strike and Lena took great joy in that.

Although she loved the surprise, Mimi wished she'd known they were going to go bowling. Then she would have worn pants. All night she was practically doing a curtsy when it was her turn to roll. The girls kept laughing at her. But she was wearing a thong underneath her mini!

At one point during the night, she looked up and caught Lamont staring at her. He waved with an uncomfortable expression on his face. Busted with her fourth Bellini in hand, she waved back and gave him her sweetest don't-be-mad smile. And though Lamont still had her telling everyone she was nineteen, they both knew she was twenty-one now, of legal age, so he couldn't say anything.

At the end of the party, Lamont insisted she ride downtown with him because he had a present for her at his house that he'd forgotten to bring. It was obvious that she was drunk. She turned her ankle three times in her cork wedges on the way to the car. But he just helped her along and didn't chastise her for drinking. Her head was buzzing like crazy and he kept the windows open on the way home so she could get some air. When she let out an intoxicated sigh in the car, he patted her bare knee and said, "Enjoy yourself. It's your birthday."

That's sweet, she thought. But when Mimi's head lolled back on the car seat and she started looking rather queasy, Lamont warned, "If you have to throw up, tell me and we'll stop. Don't you get sick in my car, girl!" Now there was the Lamont she knew and loved.

*   *   *

IT WAS ALL OVER FOR HIM the instant he'd seen her prance into Mr. Chow that night wearing a tiny, pleated black skirt. She'd arrived with Lena and Kiko just as everyone else was getting situated. Kiko had done a really nice job with her makeup. Her juicy lips were glossed to a high shine. And the outfit was some fly designer shit. Vanessa had told him the skirt was Chanel. The little lace-up top, too. It looked great but Christ! A pleated skirt? It was so naughty schoolgirl that he immediately felt the blood flowing inside his shorts. He realized he felt like a horny school*boy* every time he got around Mimi.

The first time she'd come to his apartment, he'd imagined what it'd be like to have her. But then he often had thoughts like that, whenever he encountered an attractive woman. And, more often than not, he got those women. And then the fantasy was over. Ever since the ecstasy incident in the Hamptons, when he'd gotten a peek at her bare little pussy, he'd been thinking about her way too much. Wondering how she'd taste. Having dreams about her. Closing his eyes and picturing her face when anonymous women blew him in public places. Thinking about her every time he was inside Kendra.

And then they'd gone to L.A. and she'd gotten all starry-eyed over Rayshaun. She was playing herself, hanging all over that ignorant overgrown boy who'd made his loot the easy way—by being born with giant genes. FUCK RAYSHAUN! So what if he'd told her Rayshaun had a few kids. He didn't know that to be true, but with those ballplayers it was a good bet. She didn't need to mess with him. Rayshaun would use her and toss her aside like all those NBA guys did with women. They were all dumb as fucking bricks and they wore disgustingly tacky suits. Mimi deserved better.

He knew that Rayshaun had gotten her phone number and he knew Rayshaun would call. So he had no choice but to confiscate her cell and tell Imani to get her a new one with a new number. And he was forced to start checking the voicemail at his old apartment. Though Imani had looked at him oddly when he'd asked for the code, she knew better than to question him.

Rayshaun had called the day after they got back from L.A. That pussy crook could barely wait! The message basically amounted to, "Yo, yo, yo...holla back." But there would be no hollering back since Lamont promptly deleted it. He erased another one two days later and a third a week later. Rayshaun sounded a bit defeated on the last message. *My bad, playa.* He never called again, not any messages that Lamont caught and he'd been checking on the regular. But he wondered if she'd called him.

Mimi needed that level of protection. She was like a fawn grazing in the woods, oblivious to how horrible people could be. Look what had happened with that ex-boyfriend of hers! And the role of her protector was one he was happy to play.

Mimi was not like all the other women who looked at him with the reflection of dollar signs in their eyes. Mimi didn't want anything from him. She just wanted to write her little songs and make her record. She was busy doing her thing, having fun with her friends, not sitting by the phone waiting for him to call like Kendra.

All these other women who wanted to bag him, and become Mrs. Jackson, made *him* feel like the hunted animal. When *Ebony* had put him on their list of most eligible bachelors, hundreds of letters and headshots flooded the office. What did all those desperate bitches know about him except his net worth?

Trouble was, he was actually *feeling* something for Mimi that he had never felt before. He never obsessed over women. *Ever.* He chased them, lusted after them, fucked them every which way, and maybe even told himself he loved a few of them. But he always decided when it would end and once they were gone, there was always someone new to keep him from missing the old someone. How did he wind up in this position over some kid?

Like tonight. That skirt. She was wearing it just to be cute. Kendra wore short skirts and tight sweaters for the sole purpose of titillation. Kendra had an agenda. Mimi didn't. At the bowling spot earlier, he'd come back from the rest room and glimpsed precious Mimi bending over in that little skirt, accidentally flashing a thin string of black thong and exposing her tight bare ass. He wanted to dash over and impale her standing up right there on the shiny alley floor.

Then Lena and the rest of them started laughing and Mimi turned around, looking adorably red-faced. She didn't notice him watching. But she caught him staring later and he felt embarrassed. He was a grown-ass man. A grown-ass rich man with a slew of employees who said "how high" if he told them to jump. And he had a schoolboy crush. When she caught him staring, he waved at her. It meant too much to him when she smiled and waved back.

He had planned to give her his gift after dinner. But then he'd realized that he'd left it at home so he had the perfect excuse to get her to come back with him. He'd decided that tonight was going to be the night. He'd held back before because she was on the label and it could turn into a major headache. But his feelings weren't subsiding. They were getting stronger every day. He wanted to be with her.

He wanted to take care of her, spoil her. The mere thought of anyone else's being with her made him crazy with jealousy.

He felt like they'd been having months of foreplay and she didn't even know it. Or did she? Sometimes he thought she was flirting with him. Other times he worried she was only being nice for the same reason that everyone else felt they had to be nice to him. Because he was the boss.

◆

CHAPTER 34

Ill Na Na

MIMI STAGGERED UP THE STAIRS in Lamont's apartment, feeling unbalanced from the alcohol and hoping he wasn't peeking up her little black skirt.

"You have really nice legs," she heard him say from behind her. She went straight to his fridge and got some water.

"Your present's in here," he said, sauntering into his bedroom.

She followed, looking through the window at the city lights, whose glitter illuminated the room, and sat on the edge of his huge bed. Lamont was in the bathroom. She could hear him peeing. Then she heard the sink running for what seemed like a long time.

He came out and picked up a tiny white envelope from his bedside table.

It was the kind of envelope that would come attached to a bouquet of flowers. But there were no flowers, just the envelope. It had her name on it.

She set the bottle of water on the table. "This is my present?"

"Yeah," he said, standing in front of her. "Open it."

She pulled out a business card. It read:

Victor I. Rosenberg, M.D., F.A.C.S.

Plastic and Reconstructive Surgery

She looked up at Lamont. "You want me to get my nose done?" She felt like she was going to throw up, then, as quickly as the feeling descended upon her, it passed. "There's nothing wrong with my nose!"

He smiled down at her. "Of course not. Your nose is beautiful."

She looked at the card again.

"It's not for your nose," he said quietly.

"Well then?"

"It's so you don't have to be part of the itty bitty titty committee anymore."

She was momentarily lost then, aghast, she shrieked, "You want me to get fake tits!"

"I don't want you to," he insisted. "*You* want to."

"I never said that," she said, thinking this was beyond weird.

"You said you hated having no boobs."

That was true. She hated her flat chest, although she wished she hadn't shared that information with Lamont. And she wouldn't have if Grimy hadn't drugged her with ecstasy.

"Just go for a consultation," he suggested. "Kiko went to him."

"Kiko has fake boobs?" she cried, shocked. Kiko's breasts were perfect, very natural. She never would have guessed.

"Yeah," Lamont said enthusiastically. "He did a good job on her. So think about it. Nobody's forcing you. But if it's something that really bothers you, why not do it?"

She stared down at the card in her hand. She didn't know whether to be appalled or thrilled. "And you're going to pay for it?"

"Happy birthday," he said, bending over to kiss her lightly on the forehead.

She thought about it for a second. Would it hurt? How big should she get 'em? Would they look as good as Kiko's? Then, helped along by her continuing buzz, she threw her arms around Lamont's thick waist and sang, "I'm gonna have boobs!"

He rubbed his hand over the top of her head, laughing heartily. She could feel his belly jiggling. She stayed in that position for a while, warm and comfortable, while he stroked her hair.

Then she felt something. Something firm pressing under her chin. She pulled back and nervously looked up at him.

"Sorry," he almost coughed, sitting down next to her on the bed.

"I should be getting home," she sputtered, suddenly utterly embarrassed that she was in Lamont's apartment in the middle of the night, in his bedroom with the lights off, talking to him about her breasts, or lack thereof, while he had an erection. It was definitely time to go.

"It's so late," he said, brushing a lock of hair from her face. "Stay here. I have two guest rooms."

"I can get a cab," she said nervously, and not because she felt pressured by him. She realized that, in spite of her better instincts, she *wanted* to stay. Here. With him.

What's WRONG with you? she screamed at herself. *He's old! He's fat! He's, like, your boss!* It was wrong on so many different levels. So why wasn't she moving off the bed?

He was staring at her and she felt like he could read her indecision on her face. "Did I thank you for the party tonight?" she started babbling. "That was so sweet. It was so much fun. I was completely surprised..."

He silenced her with a kiss. She didn't protest. It felt nice. She kept waiting for his tongue to dart out. Jamal used to be all about the tongue. It was like wrestling with him. But Lamont's tongue stayed in. It was just their lips, nibbling and kissing. Until she couldn't stand it anymore and stuck *her* tongue in his mouth. He'd obviously just brushed. They kissed for a long time and she was thinking, *What am I doing? I shouldn't be here.* But she didn't stop.

She kept waiting for him to grab her or do something but he didn't do anything except put his hands on the side of her face and kiss her. She hadn't realized what a bad kisser Jamal was until she had this to compare him to. Finally, Lamont scooped her up and put her on his lap, facing him. Her wedge sandals slipped right off and she wrapped her legs around his back. She cupped his face like he had hers and suffocated him with a flurry of quick kisses.

It surprised her when he began to moan. Real quiet. She couldn't believe the big strong guy who used to make her so scared was producing these mushy sounds. For her. Realizing that she could make him moan like that made her feel excited. And powerful. For the first time since she'd met him, she felt like she was in control.

Between her legs, she could feel the bulge inside his jeans. She wanted him to take it out. She started rocking back and forth on him, kissing him, and he began moaning louder. He had a hand on her back and she didn't know where the other one was until she felt a thick finger come up through her legs from behind. His finger slipped into her thong and her moans drowned out his. The finger slid back and forth in her slick crease. Then he began to rub a spot she didn't know she had.

"Look at me," he whispered hoarsely, and pulled back from kissing her while his hand stayed busy. He tried to look directly into her eyes. "I want you to look at me."

Feverish with embarrassment, she did just the opposite. She tucked her face into his thick neck. She heard him laugh a little, his minty breath hot against her earlobe. Look at him? She shouldn't even *be* here! She shouldn't be doing this! But she was. The more she thought about how wrong it was, the more she wanted it. And not just his finger. God, she was dripping all over his hand! She wanted to close her mouth and just silently enjoy it. But she couldn't choke back her yelps and moans and high-pitched squeals. She buried her face deeper into his neck to quiet herself. There was a faint smell of his cologne. She breathed it in.

"Mimi," he whispered insistently. "Mimi."

"Lamont," she whispered back, eyes shut, still rocking.

"No, Mimi," he said, but not in a whisper. She felt his hand slide away. Where was that finger running off to? She wanted it to come back. Now.

"Mimi," he said in a serious voice. "Stop."

She leaned back to look at him. Still feeling tipsy, her snug black top clinging to her damp skin, she vaguely heard him say something. They were the last words she expected to hear coming out of his mouth. She looked at him uncomprehendingly.

"This was a bad idea," he repeated.

"What!" she cried, flushed with embarrassment and disbelief. She had been thinking the same thing the whole time but he'd started it! Now she was all hot and bothered. She didn't want to go home and she didn't want to sleep in his damn guest room. She wanted him to get all up under her skirt and get it going!

"This isn't right," he said, shaking his head. "This will just confuse and complicate everything. And you're a sweetheart, baby, you really are. I don't want your feelings to get hurt. And if we do this, believe me, they will."

It sounded downright scary, what he'd just said. Like he was making her a promise or something. She hadn't thought about anything other than right here, right now. The last man she'd been with was Jamal, and that had been almost a year and a half ago.

She looked at Lamont as he stared off into the distance, pulling at a strand of her hair. She couldn't believe how sweet and shy he was acting. She didn't think he *could* be this way. He was normally so loud and bossy.

They sat quietly for a moment until she locked her arms around his neck. As soon as she tried to squeeze, he abruptly grabbed her around the waist with both hands and swung her off his lap, like some Olympic figure skating move.

"Yeah, you should go home," he said. "I'll take you down to get a cab."

He started to get up but she swung her leg back over him and said firmly, "I don't want to go home." She knew she could make him moan again.

"We're not playing anymore," he warned, sounding like his usual gruff self. "You have to leave. Let's go!"

"You don't really want to throw me out," she challenged him. She squeezed her thighs around him. "Anyway, it's my birthday," she whispered. "So you can't."

She smiled down at him, expecting him to smile back.

Lamont stared down at the carpet, having an unprecedented attack of conscience. God, if Nate or Alonzo could see him now they'd be laughing their asses off. Here she was, practically begging him for it! Had she been thinking about him all this time, too? His heart was beating so fast. He couldn't believe she wanted him as much as he wanted her! No, she couldn't want him that much but, shit, her pussy was soaked in anticipation. God, he wanted to taste it. He'd been fantasizing about her for months. Here was his chance and he was chumping out?

When she'd let out those babyish squeals…Lord! He'd practically come on himself! She was so sweet, innocent. She trusted him. But she didn't know what he was really like. If he started something with Mimi, it was going to end badly. For her. She didn't deserve that. Not that Kendra did either. Kendra was sweet, too, though not innocent. He and Kendra were adults. They both knew the score. Mimi was just a child. She didn't get it. He couldn't be with her the way she would eventually want him to be. And her album was important for the company, more important than satisfying this immature fantasy. He couldn't be weak and give in to it. It wasn't worth it.

He looked up and she was smiling at him. "I gave you a present and a party," he said, quiet but firm. "You've had a great birthday. It's time to go."

"No," she said, and, shockingly, reached over and unzipped his jeans. His fully erect dick popped right out of his boxers. Her eyes grew wide at his thickness. With that gesture, he unreservedly gave in to his desire for her. Who was he kidding?

She delighted him by confidently grabbing his engorged penis and smoothly lowering herself on top of it. She was most definitely not going home tonight. Shit, he might *never* let her go home because it *was* worth it. He couldn't remember the last time he'd been this excited. Sliding up and down, her little pleated black skirt looked like an umbrella opening and closing over his lap. He put one hand firmly on her upper back and held her around the waist with the other.

With her knees pressed against the edge of the bed, she was gliding on him smooth as silk and her fluttery squeals were driving him berserk. On the fifth upswing, his breathing quickened to the point of hyperventilation. By the time her ass plopped down onto his thick thighs, he exploded. He couldn't control himself. He was frantically tapping her on the back and tapping his foot on the carpet, grunting, "Oh fuck! Oh fuck!" She urgently tried to dismount but he clutched her in a crushing embrace. He didn't want her to move an inch.

He was still quivering and gasping when a breathy exhale of words that sounded a lot like "I love you" flew out of his mouth, at once thrilling and terrifying him. This had to be a bad dream. He'd said those words to many women—when he'd felt they'd earned it. A deliberate, strategically timed "I love you" was one thing. But involuntarily? No. That wasn't in the script for tonight and neither was this one-minute showing.

He quickly filled the horrific silence with a breathless apology for his abbreviated performance. "Sorry, baby," he whispered anxiously, still gulping for air. "Sorry. You really got me going. I haven't come that fast since..."

She pulled herself off him and stood up, looking terribly upset.

"Since I was your age!" he cracked and had a cheerless laugh.

He'd finally gotten her, the one girl he cared to impress, and he'd humiliated himself. He sat there with his deflating dick hanging out of his falling-down jeans. He felt worthless.

"Very funny," she said, slipping into her sandals. "You came inside me!"

"I'm sorry," he said glumly, still reeling with an ill feeling of inadequacy. He grabbed a tissue from the drawer and wiped himself.

"Well, I bet I'm *more* sorry," she said, tramping into the bathroom. She was furious at herself. How could she have sex with him without a condom? Or at all! What was she thinking? God, she was hornier than she'd realized.

"Baby," he pleaded, zipping up and following her. "Don't be upset. I mean, what are the chances?"

"I don't want to take *any* chance," she said, sitting on the toilet. "Could you please close the door?"

Lamont stepped inside and closed the door behind him, trying to think of how he could save face.

"Lamont," she said, laughing a little to herself. "I meant can I have some privacy please."

"Oh right," he mumbled and left. He sat on his bed and sulked. Jesus, could it have gone worse? That was the most embarrassing sexual experience he'd ever had. And if she got pregnant, that would be a disaster of epic proportions. She'd already had an abortion and would probably want to keep it. But that was out of the question when she had a record to promote!

In the bathroom, Mimi dampened a hand towel and started rubbing herself vigorously between her legs like she was trying to get a stain out of a skirt. *I'm so stupid,* she told herself. What if he had some kind of disease, like that guy Lena had been with? What if he'd given her something? Ugh, now she felt gross. She stripped and jumped into the stall shower.

The next thing she knew, Lamont was back. "I'm sorry," he called over the loud jets of water.

"I know," she said. "It's all right. It was my fault."

"No, it was my fault," he said.

"Okay, it *was* your fault," she said.

He leaned up against the sink. "So you want to watch a movie?"

Mimi turned off the water. A movie? It was almost three in the morning and all she wanted to do was go home and forget this ever happened. They'd just had sex but she realized he hadn't even seen her naked. And she didn't particularly want him to now. She cracked the glass door and peeked her head around. She nodded toward the stack of towels on the edge of his sunken tub.

"I think I should just go home," she said as he handed her a towel. "So . . . I'll be out in a second, okay?" She forced a smile at him.

Lamont got the hint. They'd just had unprotected sex so he thought they were on pretty intimate terms but apparently not. He walked out, miffed.

She came out of the bathroom with drops of water sparkling in her hair, clutching a towel around her body. "Lamont," she said hesitantly. "Do you have anything?"

"To wear? Sure," he said, getting up. "I'll give you some sweats."

"No," she said. "Do you have any . . . diseases?"

Lamont stopped midrise and looked at her incredulously. "Are you fucking serious?"

She retreated a step, biting her lip.

"Diseases?" he shrieked. How dare she!

"Sorry, Lamont," she said. "But you get around, you know? And Lena told me this story and it scared me."

Through gritted teeth, Lamont seethed, "I am completely clean, sweetheart. I can assure you of that." But his anger drained away as he watched her blink back tears. She couldn't even look at him. She was really upset and Lamont felt like an ass.

Awkwardly, he tried to take her hand but she pulled away. "It'll be okay," he said. "If anything happened... if you got, you know, pregnant," he mumbled, hating even to say the word, "I'd be there for you. To take care of you."

"Would you?" she snapped, fingers tightening around the towel. Jamal had turned his back on her like she was damaged goods. The way Lamont ran through women, he was probably no better. "Or would you be off somewhere fucking Kendra?"

"Wow," Lamont said, completely blindsided by her unexpected verbal jab. He took her hand and held on tight when Mimi tried to pull it away. "I apologize for letting it happen," he said sincerely. "But I'm not like your ex-boyfriend and I'm definitely not like any of these niggas Lena fucks with." Mimi had to laugh at that. "No matter what happens, I'll be there for you."

She quickly wiped her eyes and looked at him. She really *looked* at him, wondering if she could trust this man. "Okay," she said, realizing she was probably venting the anger she still had for Jamal at him. "So I could use those sweats," she said, anxious to get going.

"You can't go now."

"Why not?"

"Because you're still upset," he said. "I can tell. I can't let you be upset on your birthday." He gave her a quick hug and peck on the cheek. "And I can't let you leave here unsatisfied, thinking *that* was the best I have to offer."

He pulled her toward the bed and she went willingly. He laid her down, set a long lingering kiss on her lips, and then, hovering over her, he carefully unwrapped her towel. He lightly sprinkled kisses all over her moist skin until her entire body shivered. Then he tugged her down to the edge of the bed, planted his knees on the carpet, threw her legs over his shoulders and made sure his sweet girl had the best birthday ever.

◆

Baby Love

◆

CHAPTER 35

Dead Presidents

"HEY, EUGENE!"

Pimp-walking down the hallway, Flo$$ stopped, lifted his rose-tinted shades, and leaned back to see Mimi sitting in Helena's office. He was wearing pastel pink baggy jeans, a soft leather bomber jacket custom-designed by hip-hop couturier 5001 Flavors, also in pink, and a white T-shirt that said "JESUS IS MY HOMEBOY" in large pink letters. And setting it all off lovely were two dollar signs made of pink diamonds hanging from his earlobes.

"Don't be calling me by my government!" he joked.

"After Dicky's song," Mimi said, laughing, "secret's out."

"I know! But my moms don't even call me by my given name and she gave it to me! She'll be like 'Euge... Gene... oh sorry F-L-O double dollar sign.'"

Mimi and Flo$$ both cracked up. They had become fast friends since recording "Me & My Bitch '03" for the TLE group album. It

323

was a cover of the 1993 Biggie song and Lamont thought it would be cool as one of the tracks on the tenth-anniversary album.

"That your Benz truck out front?" he asked. It had to be. The license plate read: MIMI TLPI.

"Bouncing on twenty-twos," Mimi crowed, referring to her customized rims, a hip-hop "must-have," as Vanessa would say. "C'mon, pimp, you know how I roll."

Helena rolled her eyes. Since she handled corporate budgets and was the clearinghouse for advances and royalty payments, Helena knew what remained of Mimi's advance would barely cover a cab ride to JFK and back. Apparently, Flo$$, who was usually in L.A. recording or filming movies, was out of the loop on the direction Mimi's love life had taken in the last three months.

"Hello Eugene," Helena said, taking off her reading glasses and letting them hang by the chain around her neck. What was she? Invisible?

"Hey, didn't I just say..." He chuckled and hustled over to give her a hug.

Helena called all the guys by their first names. She was official like that. Grimy was Felix, Radickulys was Richard, and Flo$$ was Eugene. She'd been surprised to learn that Billy tha Kid's name really was Billy.

The guys called her The Loot Lady.

"Your album ain't even out yet," Eugene said to Mimi. "You must've got a real nice advance to afford a whip like that."

"Don't worry," Mimi said. "My paper's straight."

"I'm out," Flo$$ said. "Lamont's waiting on me."

"Peace, black man," Mimi said. "Be prosperous!"

"So I'm definitely moving out," Helena said, picking up her interrupted conversation with Mimi.

"That's what you told me last month," Mimi said. "And the month before."

"I'm serious this time."

"If that's what you say, girl. Do you."

Helena scrolled through a document on her computer. "How are things with you and your man?"

Flo$$'s ignorance notwithstanding, Lamont and Mimi's relationship was the worst-kept secret in the history of the TLE organization. Mimi had been getting a big push from Lamont since day one because this was the label's first R&B release and he wanted it done right. But many staffers felt Mimi was getting preferential treatment now because she was sleeping with the boss. Most new artists didn't get to fly first class or stay at the best hotels when they traveled. Mimi got that and more but only because Lamont wanted it that way. Mimi was so new to the industry that she didn't even realize she was getting special treatment. So Helena didn't think it was fair that some of the staff had given their Triple Large princess an in-house nickname: "Me me me."

"Things are good," Mimi said, blushing. "Great actually."

She stayed over at Lamont's almost every night, and always the entire weekend. Even if she was working in the studio late he'd swing by to get her. He treated her like a real-life princess. Her carriage, the $75,000 sky blue Benz G500 truck, had been his latest gift. No special occasion. He surprised her. He was always doing stuff like that.

Their relationship was supposed to be on the low. "For niggas to want to buy your album, they need to believe you're single," he'd told her. "They want to fantasize about you. If they know you're giving it up to a rich, old cat like me, fantasy's dead. Got it?"

But she'd confided in Helena. Imani knew, of course, but then Imani knew when Lamont took a shit. Mimi suspected a lot of other people in the office knew, too. They'd always been nice but since she'd gotten with Lamont they were a lot nicer. Some seemed almost nervous around her.

But she didn't care if people knew. Why be ashamed? She was in love.

"Are things so good that you might move in with him?" Helena ventured.

"I don't know about all that."

"Why not? You stay over at his place all the time."

"He hasn't asked me," Mimi said. "And I can't ask him." Lamont made the decisions. She liked that. He anticipated her every need. "Anyway, I like my place."

Helena pulled her reading glasses up off her heavy bosom and opened a document on her computer. "I wish I could find a place as big as yours for only two thousand a month," she murmured, looking at the screen. "And in that neighborhood, rents are steep!"

The receptionist buzzed. "Get out here, Helena. Flower delivery."

Helena's boyfriend had cheated on her five times this year, but all it took was an extravagant arrangement of flowers to get back in her good graces. She almost tripped running out of her office.

Mimi sat there thinking, *What?*

She went over to the computer and looked at the Excel spreadsheet. The document was titled "Recoupables." She scrolled down. Each line was numbered.

1	Hermès	$9,500.00
2	Prada	$6,400.00
3	Niketown	$750.00
4	Scoop NYC	$7,275.00
5	Pottery Barn	$ 58.13

Scrolling...

| 14 | Yolanda Davis | $8,500.00 |

The vocal coach. There were six more entries for her. Was that per month?

Scrolling...

| 57 | Dr. Lipsky | $250.00 |

There were twelve more $250 entries for Dr. Lipsky, her dermatologist.

| 98 | Dr. Gobel | $14,375.00 |

Dr. Gobel was the dentist Imani had said was going to bleach her teeth. He'd decided she needed porcelain veneers instead.

| 135 | V. de la Cruz | $10,000.00 |

Four more entries to Vanessa at $10,000 per.

| 138 | Unique Auto Sports | $19,450.00 |

That's where she'd gotten her new rims.

Scrolling...

Scrolling...

Scrolling...

The document was 425 lines long. She hit print.

*   *   *

"IS YOUR ALBUM going to be in on time?" Lamont demanded.

"Yeah," Flo$$ said unconvincingly.

"You're booking all this studio time and then not showing up."

"I'm on the set doing the movie. Sometimes things run over. Other days they got me waiting, waiting, waiting then it's 'Hurry up, get to the set now!'"

Flo$$ laughed. Lamont didn't see the humor.

"Making movies is your secondary job," Lamont said. "Am I going to have to send Alonzo out there to crack the whip on you?"

"If you want," Flo$$ said. Alonzo was mad chill. He'd just hang out at the studio with a brew in hand. And Alonzo always got good Lakers tickets.

"So how's that going anyway? The movie?"

"Crazy," Flo$$ enthused. "They got me driving all these hot cars, surrounded by hotter women. Lysa really knows how to rev a nigga up." He grinned.

"Really?" Lamont said, always interested in pussy talk. Lysa Richards was the twenty-three-year-old doe-eyed beauty costarring in this action movie Flo$$ was shooting. "You twist that?"

"What the hell does recoupable mean?" Mimi yelled, barging into Lamont's office with the freshly printed document in hand.

"Catch y'all later," Flo$$ said, seizing the opportunity to get out of this conversation with Lamont. As he passed Mimi he gave her a peck on the cheek. "I'm in town all week. Holla at your boy!"

"Later," Mimi said.

"Since when do you roll up into my office, yelling at me?" Lamont demanded. And why was Flo$$ being so friendly with her? "I was in a meeting."

Mimi threw the document on his desk. After glancing at it, Lamont said, "Where'd you get this?"

"Helena," Mimi said, then quickly added, "She didn't show it to me. I happened to see it up on her computer when she was out of her office."

Calmly reclining in his chair, Lamont said, "Recoupables are things that the label spends money on that have to be recouped, or paid back, by the artist."

"How am I going to pay all this back!"

"You don't have to write a check for it, honey," he chuckled. "It comes out of your future earnings."

"But it lists all those things that I bought at Hermès, Prada, that day with Vanessa! Those were gifts. From you."

"Did I say that?"

Well, no, come to think of it, he hadn't. "But why is Vanessa on here?"

"She's your style consultant."

"Says who?"

"Me," Lamont said, unruffled.

"And it cost fifteen thousand to have my teeth done? I liked my old teeth!"

"They weren't camera-ready."

"Why do I have to keep going to Yolanda? My voice is good."

"Always room for improvement."

"You can't charge me rent on the apartment!" she wailed. "You own that place!" Now she had him.

"I have to pay maintenance on it. Everyone who stays there pays."

"Two thousand dollars a month?"

"I could get four."

She couldn't think of a quick comeback so she grabbed the document and scanned for further evidence. "My car is on here!" she screeched. "And the rims! You bought me that as a present!"

"Listen to me, sweetheart," Lamont said, unwilling to be yelled at for long.

Mimi simmered, standing in front of his desk with her arms crossed. He was always saying that. *Listen to me.* Like everyone didn't already? She doubted he realized he was saying it. It was like a verbal tic. And she didn't want to listen to him right now.

"This is standard procedure," Lamont said. "Label lays out money. Artist pays it back. Stop stressing yourself. When your album comes out, you'll pay back what you owe and there'll be plenty left over."

"Forget standard procedure," Mimi snapped. She had the nerve to stamp her foot. "I'm your fucking girlfriend!"

"Don't curse, honey."

"Why not? You curse all the time. 'Fuck this, motherfucker that'!"

"I'm a man."

Her neck swiveled. "I'm a *wo*-man."

"I don't want to hear you cursing. It doesn't become you."

"Monty, I recorded a song called 'Flyass Bitch.' Bitch is a curse. A million people have heard me cursing."

"A curse is a four-letter word. 'Bitch' has five."

"But I'm your girlfriend!" she said again.

"Oh, so *now* you're my girlfriend?"

Just last night she'd told him, "I'm not your girlfriend, you know," like she was playing the field or something. He'd said, "Yes, you are" and that had ended the conversation.

"What I said last night...I was just kidding." Last night she'd tried playing hard to get. She was always running over to his place. Always following his orders. She didn't want him to start thinking he owned her. But she still wanted to be treated special!

"I know," Lamont said, secretly entertained by her tantrum. She was so cute when she was mad. "But when you said that, it hurt my feelings, baby." He melodramatically clutched his chest and bounced back in his chair. "And did I get mad?" He smiled.

"Wait a second," Mimi said, back to scanning the pages. "Lena is on here!"

"I know," Lamont said.

"Five hundred dollars, five hundred dollars," she said, flipping the pages and looking at all the entries. "What are you paying her for?"

"Image consultant."

"Her *and* Vanessa?"

"Vanessa is style, Lena is image. She took you to get your hair done, she's gotten you acquainted with the hip-hop scene. You know, all that stuff."

"You're paying her to be my friend," Mimi said almost inaudibly, biting her lip.

"No I'm not," Lamont said. He rushed over to soothe her. "Don't get upset, baby," he said, massaging her hunched back. "Lena adores you. She's your girl. But you know how she is, always with her hand out."

"She asked for the money?"

"Forever crying poor that one," Lamont mumbled. "And don't tell her how much Vanessa is getting or she'll be on the phone in no time screaming bloody murder. If Lena sees a way to make a quick buck she does it. But it has nothing to do with how she feels about you."

"I want to move in with you," Mimi announced. Why shouldn't she? She was always over there. And she *was* his girlfriend. She had to start speaking up for herself. Plus, she worried sometimes that he might be with someone else. Kendra maybe. One night, when she was in Atlanta recording, he hadn't answered any of his phones all night. If she moved in it would send a signal to Kendra—and everyone else—that their days with Lamont were permanently over.

"Great, princess," Lamont said, leading her to the sofa. "How 'bout tonight?"

"You mean it?" She hadn't expected him to go for it just like that.

He pushed her back against the arm of the sofa and straddled her. He unzipped her Baby Phat jacket, and kissed the tops of her perfect 34C breasts. After the augmentation, they'd needed to be massaged. Lamont had put himself on that job. She was wearing a bra but she didn't need it. Those puppies held up pretty nicely on their own.

"Of course, I mean it," he cooed. He made loud smooching sounds on her chest. *Love you, Dr. Rosenberg!* "I was thinking about asking you anyway."

"Really?"

"Really."

"My advance money is almost gone."

"Don't worry. I got you."

He nibbled at her neck. She even smelled sweet. "And hey," he said, pulling back to meet her gaze. "The tits? Not recoupable. Those were a gift outright." He laughed.

She wanted to stay mad at him but, in spite of herself, she laughed, too.

◆

CHAPTER 36

Like My Style

"SO WHAT'S THE DEAL WITH GEMINI?"

"He's all booked up for months," Witchy said, sitting on the sofa in Lamont's office. "We can't get him."

"Anyone can be got," Lamont said. A manicurist was working each of his hands and his barber, a distinguished-looking older black man named Wilson, was shaping up his hair.

Gemini was the in-demand producer of the moment. At the tender age of twenty-five, he'd scored big hits for artists in every genre. Grimy, Britney Spears, Limp Bizkit, Shakira, Diddy, Busta Rhymes, and so on. He had an innovative sound and a rep as a true eccentric. A borderline recluse, he stayed holed up in his home studio in Gainesville, Georgia, sixty miles north of Atlanta, working nonstop. Word was he showered less than he slept. He had a ten-thousand-square-foot house on three acres of lakefront property. The studio in the basement was state-of-the-art, but the house looked like a huge, rundown log cabin. It was known as The Funk Shack.

Lamont wanted Gemini to do a few songs on Mimi's album. The album was almost done, but he wanted guaranteed hits. Gemini could deliver them.

"You know I went down to The Funk Shack once with this artist when I was working at um another label," Witchy said. At Triple Large, one didn't mention other record labels by name unless it was in a negative sense or for the purpose of corporate espionage. It was like working at Coke and fondly reminiscing about your days at Pepsi. It just wasn't done, especially not in front of Lamont. "And Gemini had this stripper staying there."

"Yeah?" Lamont said, already interested in the story.

"So I figured he was fucking her."

"Was she hot?" Lamont said, perfectly comfortable having this conversation in the presence of sixty-two-year-old Wilson and three Asian women he barely knew.

"Four-alarm blaze!" Witchy gushed. "Ass for days. Titties like"— he cupped his hands under imaginary melons— *"pow!"*

Lamont laughed. So did Wilson.

"So I assume she's Gem's girl, right?"

"Right," Lamont said.

"And I'm there. She's there. We talk a few times in passing. She's real sweet. She said she wasn't dancing anymore. And I'm thinking, you know, good for her. She hooked up with Gemini, he got her out of the business...."

"Get to the point," Lamont said.

"And," Witchy related incredulously, "I found out Gem wasn't even hitting it!"

Almost offended, Lamont snapped, "Why the hell not?"

"I don't know," Witchy said, clearly bewildered. "He said he met her through one of his boys. He was trying to help her out. She had nowhere to live so she was staying with him. She wanted to be a singer or something."

"Please tell me you slid in there," Lamont said.

"No doubt," Witchy confirmed quickly. "I told her I was gonna get her a deal and she was all over it. She still calls me every so often." He and Lamont tittered.

After a moment's consideration, Lamont speculated, "Maybe he's *gay.*"

"Gem?" Witchy shook his head. "I doubt it. Just a weirdo."

"That's what Grimy used to say. He said Gem had to light all these scented candles in his studio before they could work. But I heard the songs they did and then Gem had the charts on lock and I was like, 'I don't care if that nigga wants to pour hot wax all over himself and sit on your lap in his funky little studio butt ass naked, let him do his thing!'"

Witchy chuckled while squirming inwardly at the image. "I've called him twice already about working with Mimi. He says he's doing two projects now and he's got two more lined up right after."

"Offer him double his usual fee," Lamont instructed just as Daryl strolled in.

"Offer who double his fee?" Daryl said.

A petite woman rose from behind Lamont's desk and, for a second, Daryl thought he was getting a blow job. "All done," she said.

"Great, hon," Lamont said, examining his beautiful feet. She'd just given them a paraffin wax and applied clear polish.

Wilson got out a pair of tiny clippers.

"Gemini," Lamont answered as the nail patrol packed up and left.

"Gemini ain't worth double his fee," Daryl scoffed.

"I think he is," Lamont countered. "We need guaranteed hits for Mimi."

Daryl had produced six of her songs. Insulted again. "What about the R?"

Lamont huffed, "Kelly?"

"Yeah," Daryl said. "He's a guaranteed hitmaker." He walked over to Lamont's sound system. "And you know he works well with young girls."

With his back to Lamont, Daryl smiled. *Why don't you send your little princess to hang with him? Maybe she'll let him piss all over her new titties.*

Lamont leaned his head back for Wilson. He knew exactly what Daryl was getting at but he would not dignify the comment with a response.

Daryl inserted the CD he was carrying into the player. "This is the 'Baby Love' remix," he said. "It's just the first mix."

"Baby Love" was going to be Mimi's first single. The remix, featuring Flo$$, would be a bonus track on the album.

Lamont listened as Wilson clipped his nose hairs.

The rap verse came in and Wilson almost cut him as Lamont jerked his head up. "Who is that?"

"That's not Flo$$," Witchy said.

"Someone new," Daryl said. "I found him. Just listen. This kid can spit." The song ended and Daryl said, "Whaddaya think?"

"It's pretty good," Lamont admitted and Witchy nodded in agreement. "But it's not Flo$$."

"But this cat is hot," Daryl insisted. "I listened to his demo. It's real good. I think we should sign him."

"Really," Lamont responded mildly. That was not a decision for Daryl to make. "Who is it?"

Daryl stood as tall as he could, steeling himself. "Me."

"No, it's not," Witchy snapped. The song *did* sound pretty good. It didn't sound like Daryl's voice at all. Daryl was always talking in a high-pitched rush of words that tripped all over themselves. This rapper's flow was slow, almost like he was drugged. And the voice was deep. Somehow it sounded just right.

Daryl played it again while Lamont and Witchy listened more intently.

"Since when have you wanted to be a rapper?" Lamont asked, refusing to comment further on the song. He'd already admitted it was pretty good and now he felt Daryl had tricked him into doing that.

Wilson was all finished in Lamont's nose but he lingered to watch this scene unfold. In the three years he'd been coming here to shape up Mr. Jackson, he'd seen Daryl catch a lot of heat.

"All my life," Daryl said, his chest puffed out.

Witchy looked at Lamont to see how he'd respond. Witchy considered Daryl a pain in the ass, as was the general consensus, but he was turning into a great producer.

"So you've recorded a demo?" Lamont asked.

"Yeah," Daryl said, all smiles.

"With whose money?"

"My...my...my own," Daryl stuttered. "Just a few songs."

"Well, hit us off with it," Lamont said.

Wilson removed the smock from around Lamont's neck and dusted away the stray hairs.

Daryl whipped another CD out of his Phat Farm denim jacket. "Got it right here."

"Not now," Lamont said. "I have another appointment."

That took the wind out of Daryl's sails. "So what about this remix?" he said, still hopeful.

"Nah," Lamont sniffed. He was the boss here. He had not sanctioned the recording of this remix and everything had to go through him first. Everything. If Daryl had gone through the proper channels to get signed as an artist like everyone else, maybe Lamont would have given him a shot. But Daryl thought he was above corporate rules. So now he'd have to get to the back of the line and wait his turn.

"We need Flo$$. We need *guaranteed* hits," Lamont said. "Flo$$ is a name. You're not." Lamont stuck out his beautiful toes and admired them, as he dismissed Daryl from his office with, "Get on that, will you?"

◆

CHAPTER 37

Big Poppa

NOW SHE KNEW why Lamont was so eager to have her move in. Every morning they had a quickie. *Every* morning. But, since their very first time, Lamont was never that quick. He'd slip her panties down and poke her from behind. "My sweet baby," he'd moan while fondling her perky new tits and covering her neck and shoulder blades with wet kisses. She'd never even open her eyes. Her closing line: "Daddy, Daddy, I love you."

She enjoyed it more for the closeness than the sexual stimulation. And Lamont wasn't packing a five-inch executive model either! More like the eight-inch CEO double-wide! But sometimes she was tired and she'd wish he'd just finish up and head off to work so she could go back to sleep. She'd learned a breathless squeal of "Daddy, Daddy, I love you" always did the trick. He'd grunt, squirt, and release her with a satisfied sigh.

At first she thought the Daddy thing was funny. He'd say things like, "Don't worry, Daddy will take care of it." Or, if they were going out and she was dressed extra cute, he'd say, all misty-eyed, "Look at Daddy's girl."

Then one night he whispered, "Tell Daddy you love him." She just moaned but he wouldn't let it go. "Tell Daddy you love him," he ordered, thrusting slowly. So she did. And he came. Then he kissed her and said in a husky whisper, "Daddy loves his baby more."

Hey, if that was what it took, she'd do it. Lamont did everything and anything he could to make her blissfully happy. It was the least she could do in return. And that's what she told herself because it made her uncomfortable to believe it satisfied some deep need in her, too. So she kept telling herself, *That's Lamont's thing. It's his game.*

But then he started getting crazy with it. One night, he presented her with a big beautifully gift-wrapped box. He was always giving her presents. (And now she made sure they weren't recoupable!) The gift was a Catholic schoolgirl's outfit. Plaid miniskirt, saddle shoes, bobby socks, the whole shebang. He put on Britney Spears's "... Baby One More Time" and made her dance for him. She was really getting into it but before she could finish he ripped the little white shirt, popping the buttons, and ravaged her.

Lots of Daddy talk that night.

Afterward, she'd said, "You actually own that Britney Spears CD?"

"No," he'd said. "Imani thought it would be a nice touch. She got the whole outfit and everything." Like it was perfectly all right that Imani knew!

At first, *she* didn't want to tell anyone that they were sleeping together. She felt like it was wrong, and somehow that excited the hell out of her. Three weeks into their sexcapades, she blurted it out to Jordan over dinner. Jordan had said, in a disapproving tone, "Oh really? Be careful with that, honey," and changed the subject.

After that, she didn't want to say anything but then Vanessa told *her*. "You're sleeping with Lamont!" Alonzo had spilled the beans. Lena, almost drooling, had said, "Tell us *every*thing."

Hanging out with Vanessa and Lena was like being in a boys' locker room—only with very well-groomed girls. Vanessa would go on and on about her pussy and sometimes she'd have faint marks around her wrists from where Alonzo had tied her up. Then that would get Lena started on how she had to find a nigga like Alonzo to give her a "mad gangsta fuck."

Sometimes it could be too much.

And it wasn't only talk about their own sexual proclivities. They were all up in everyone else's sexual business. Lamont's especially. All the time when they went out Lena and Vanessa would smile and small-talk with some woman and then as soon as the chick's back was turned, the catty remarks would come out. "That's just some bitch Lamont used to fuck," Lena would say. Often. The first time it happened, Mimi had said, "She's Lamont's ex-girlfriend?" Lena had repeated, "No. That's just some bitch Lamont used to fuck."

The women in question were usually white, which prompted Lena to muse, "It's weird though, because Lamont dates only black women publicly. Or should we say women of color, because some of these chicks are brown but you can't tell where they're from. But almost all the women he fucks around with on the low are white. Blondes usually. Blondes with big tits. So does that mean he respects black women so much that he won't just dick 'em down and dismiss 'em like he does these white sluts? Or does he really want to be with a white woman but because he's Mr. Hip-Hop he's afraid it will ruin his street cred?"

Mimi, Vanessa, and Lena had sat quietly for a moment, pondering that one. *Hmmm.* Then Vanessa had chirped, "But with you, Mimi, I guess he got both!"

Mimi touched her highlighted hair, glanced down at her tight new cleavage, and thought, *More like all four... black, white, blond, and big boobs.*

Sometimes they'd all be out with Lamont and every time he spoke to a woman Mimi wondered, *Is that one of the old fuck buddies?* She'd give Lena a look and Lena would subtly nod yes or shake her head no. Then later Mimi would ask him how he knew the woman and he'd invariably say, "From around."

Now that she was with Lamont she didn't like that his personal affairs were so openly discussed. He was her man! And she was in love with him. Shouldn't their love life be private?

But Lena and Vanessa had no shame in their games. One night Vanessa ran into a friend, a gorgeous girl, and chatted with her for a long time. She was being very friendly, which was not Vanessa's usual way.

When the gorgeous friend took off, Mimi had asked who she was.

Without missing a beat, Vanessa had said, "Just some girl who ate my pussy once. I need to give her a call."

"Oh right," Mimi had said, trying to roll with the punches. "That was before you were with Alonzo."

Vanessa had looked at her like she was brain-dead and said, "Alonzo was there."

Lena kept drinking and made no comment.

So Mimi started doling out little tidbits to Lena and Vanessa when they pressed her for info. Everyone thought she was some inexperienced small-town girl. Not after being with Lamont she wasn't! But the Daddy talk she kept to herself. That was too weird. Just because Lamont was almost twice her age, Lena had once remarked, "You're on some Daddy shit!" Mimi had thought, *You don't know the half of it, girlfriend!*

But she decided to throw them a bone. She told them he was always going down on her. That got their attention. Finally she had something of interest to add to the conversation!

"Kendra told me he didn't do that," Vanessa said, shocked. "He did it only on special occasions, like it was a gift. Her birthday and Valentine's were the only times she ever got any tongue action."

"But I bet she had to suck his dick every night," Lena remarked.

Mimi told them that the tricks she'd picked up at the blow job class were making Lamont a very happy man. It'd taken her a while to get up the courage to go there, but once she had Lamont had been very impressed. Too impressed.

"I thought you'd only been with two guys," he'd said, and she bristled that he included that asshole Floyd. She didn't think that should count.

"I have," she'd said.

"Then how do you know how to do that? You're almost *too* good." She felt complimented and insulted at the same time. He was implying that she was some kind of professional blow job artist so she admitted that she'd gone to the class with Lena.

"That's the sweetest thing anyone has ever done for me!" he'd said.

It would've broken his heart if he'd known that she'd gone in L.A.

after meeting Rayshaun. The next day he bought her a beautiful diamond tennis bracelet. Was that all it took? After that she was like,
Whip it out, Big Daddy! But there were no more gifts. At least, not for
blow jobs. So there was no more swallowing like she'd done the first
time. If he wasn't going to go all the way, neither was she!

But the girls couldn't get over the fact that he was giving *her* so
much oral attention. She informed them that, post-Kendra, things
done changed. Lamont ate her out with the ferocity of a famine vic-
tim presented with a steaming bowl of rice. On the counters of all
three bathrooms in his apartment. Kitchen, too. In his new drop-top
coupe, with the top dropped, pulled over on the side of the Long
Island Expressway late one night coming back from the Hamptons.
On the chaise longue on the deck of the penthouse. In the bathroom
at the Hit Factory. In the first-class bathroom on a flight to Miami.

"Anywhere, anytime," she'd told the girls, impressing them
beyond belief. "Begging me for it! Who am I to deny him?"

"Is that why he looks like he's lost some weight?" Lena had
cracked. "Because he's on a pussy diet!"

Ooooh they *screamed!*

But truth was he hadn't lost a pound. Now that she was living
with him, she'd bake cookies, brownies, cupcakes. He'd come home
and see the baked goodies and whine, "What are you doing to me?"
Then he'd inhale the whole plate.

He was getting touchy about his weight but she didn't much care.
He was her sweetie and he knew how to work it in bed so it was no big
deal. But his touchiness about it sometimes worked to her advantage.

One night they got into a spat when they went out and he spent a
long time talking, very cozily, to Emma White, the übermodel. Some

photographer even took a picture of Lamont and Emma all hugged up on each other. Mimi thought it was completely disrespectful to their relationship. They argued all the way home.

Lamont's defense: "If reporters happen to think I'm with Emma, so be it. At least they won't think I'm with *you*. We're trying to keep our relationship out of the press, remember?"

"Bullshit," was all Mimi had to say.

"Look, if I wanted to fuck Emma, I would," he'd snapped. "But I don't. I'm with you, okay? Stop being so insecure."

That night she climbed into bed stark naked with a fresh bag of his favorite Dean & Deluca chocolate chip cookies. As soon as he reached over for some, she slapped his hand away. "Don't," she said. "You're starting to look like Supa Phat E."

He looked like he wanted to cry. "Fuck you!"

"Bet you'd like to," she'd said, continuing to munch. "But you ain't getting any tonight, playboy!"

Then she'd put a wall of pillows between them to let him know she was serious. No cookies and no pussy. His two favorite things. He was furious.

The next morning, he tried for a quickie and got a cool reception. Next thing Mimi knew, music was playing. It was "They Don't Know," a song by white soul singer Jon B., that they'd decided would be their song after they heard it late one night on the WBLS quiet storm.

Lamont started singing, sounding like a cat in heat.

Heard about my past
things I used to do
the games I used to play
the girls that didn't last

Mimi watched him standing over her on the bed, belting his heart out.

> *Girl, let's talk about*
> *what your friends told you*
> *that I'm a selfish man*
> *want my cake and eat it too*
> *maybe in my past*
> *but you've changed me now*

And how could she stay mad at him...

> *Don't listen to what people say*
> *they don't know*
> *bout you and me*
> *put it out your mind*
> *cause it's jealousy*
> *they don't know about this here*

...when he could be silly and romantic like that at six in the morning?

Anyway, they had so much sex, she didn't think he'd have the stamina to cheat on her. But when she'd gone away a few times to record in other cities, Vanessa kept close tabs on him and she'd heard things, whisperings. Just that he'd been seen hanging out with different girls. He hung out all the time, always with a group, so who knew for sure? But he had such a ladies' man rep, it worried Mimi.

Whenever she'd confront him about the rumors, just fishing for any signs of guilt, it was always the same drill. "Who said that?" he'd demand heatedly. She'd never reveal that her main source was actually his own sister-in-law. He'd then try to discredit the unidentified rumormonger by saying, "Whoever it was, they're not your friend, you hear me? They're a fucking hater! Probably some dumb bitch who doesn't have a man and doesn't want you to have one either! Stop listening to that shit!" And the conversation would end. Soon after, an expensive piece of jewelry would materialize under her pillow.

Daryl wasn't helping matters. He had become surlier than ever, even though he was making a name for himself as a producer. He'd become a tyrant in the studio and his head was swelling to more blimplike proportions every day. He insisted everyone call him "Country D." Most people didn't bother to comply, certainly not Lamont, but if she called him Daryl when they were in the studio he wouldn't respond. She had to repeat herself, referring to him as "Country D," and then his ears would start working.

One night at the studio when she'd been trying to reach Lamont, Daryl had said, "Leave the man alone. He's probably busy. With Kendra maybe." He knew Kendra was a sore spot for her.

"Lamont is in love with *me*," she confidently informed Daryl.

"That's what they all think," he snorted.

"You think he'd cheat on me?"

"I don't think. I *know*," he said. "Can't teach an old dog new tricks."

Asshole! "You don't know anything," she snapped.

"I know I got three months in the office pool."

"Office pool?"

"Yeah. I give it three more months 'til your love spell wears off. Some folks are rollin' the dice on six. Odds for a year are a real long-shot."

She went straight back and told Lamont. "I'll handle it," he seethed. She didn't know what he had said to Daryl or the people at the office but subsequently Daryl would only growl at her and the reception she got at the office became downright frosty.

There was no way he'd cheat on her. No way. He was so obviously in love. He told her all the time. Almost obsessively. And he made her tell him.

Every morning after their quickie, he'd shower, dress, and then come back to the bed, smelling of Bulgari cologne, and kiss her lightly on the forehead. "Call you later, angel," he'd coo. "I love you."

One day he must have been preoccupied because he rushed out without his usual mushy farewell. When she heard the front door slam downstairs, she picked up the phone and called his cell. "You forgot something."

He came back up, looking tickled. "Sorry, princess," he'd gushed, hustling over to the bed in his Armani suit, and smacked her with an extra wet one.

Later that day, she swung by the office around lunchtime and told him she wanted to go to a movie. He took off the rest of the day and they went. They held hands, munched popcorn, and enjoyed a chick flick during office hours.

Yes, Lamont was definitely in love. With her. His princess. Let the haters hate.

◆

CHAPTER 38

So Fresh, So Clean

DRESSED TO KILL, Lamont walked out of the bathroom in his office.

On the sofa sat Jay Alvarez, a twenty-six-year-old senior editor at *Vibe*. He was doing a feature on Lamont for *Vibe*'s annual juice issue. This was their third time hanging out together.

"So you graduated from City College," Jay asked. "You majored in business?"

"Yes," Lamont said. "My mother was really pushing that. I was the first in our family to go on to higher education. But I don't know how much I got out of it. I was interning at a label at the same time. I feel like I learned more from that experience."

Lamont pulled out his black Gucci loafers, sat on the sofa next to Jay, and slipped them on with a shoehorn.

"What I never understood about school was why the economics teacher wasn't practicing economics personally for his own welfare. How can you be an expert on something if you're not doing it? No disrespect to teachers. It's an honorable profession if you're, like, a kindergarten teacher. And if you're a woman. But there are a few sub-jects—like business—where it's, like, why aren't you using that wealth of knowledge to benefit yourself? Why are you teaching it in college instead of running your own business? They say those who can't do, teach. But I can do, so I do. You know?"

They walked out. They were going to a Boys & Girls Club bene-fit at Tavern on the Green. Imani was two steps behind, carrying a large black umbrella.

In the elevator, Lamont said, "So how many pages is this story, Jay?"

"Three pages of text and one full-page picture."

"And what is everyone else getting?"

"Some people are getting two pages of text. Some are getting three."

"Who else is getting three?"

"Damon Dash, Don Gambi…"

"Whoa," Lamont said. "Isn't it a little early in the game for Gambino to be getting three pages of text?"

"Not with the numbers he's putting up on *Billboard*."

"Why not four text, one for the picture?" Lamont suggested. "Five pages total."

"For Gambino?" Jay said, just to fuck with him.

"For me," Lamont said evenly, not giving this boy the pleasure of a reaction.

"No one is getting five pages."

"Are you a senior editor at *Vibe*?"

"Yeah."

"Then you can get me five pages total."

"No one is getting five."

"Am I going to have to speak with someone?" Lamont said, the "someone" being the editor-in-chief of *Vibe,* of course, but keeping the threat vague so if it ever came up in the future, he could deny it.

"Speak to whoever you want," Jay said as the elevator doors opened. "But no one is getting five."

"Fine," Lamont said as they walked through the lobby. When they got to the door, Imani opened the umbrella and ran out in the steady rain to the waiting Maybach and opened the door.

Lamont stood in the lobby, humming to himself.

Imani came back and walked them to the car, holding the extra-large umbrella over them for cover, slammed the car door, and went back into the building.

"Running a label is nothing more than a hustle," Lamont said. "The drive to win, surrounding yourself with the best people, the best talent, people who want it as bad as you, and putting your all into it. I have a lot of integrity, soul, and love for what I do. I think people pick up on that. I think authenticity is a big thing."

"So what do you do for fun?" Jay asked. "What do you do when you want to relax?"

"Relax…" Lamont repeated slowly, as if he weren't familiar with the word. He idly picked up the white envelope that Imani had placed on the backseat. He fiddled with it for a second and slipped out the card inside. He squinted at it, pulling it very close to his eyes and then holding it out at arm's length in front of him.

Seconds later he was seemingly talking into the air but, after hanging out with him several times, Jay knew he was talking into the cell phone piece that dangled from his ear. "What font is this!"

Lamont boomed. "Twelve? *Jesus,* Imani, are you kidding me? You know I need fourteen!" He huffed loudly then said, "Yes, please do."

Jay tried to read the words that were printed on the heavy stock card.

"I have to give a little speech tonight," Lamont said, picking it up. "Just an introduction really. My eyes are getting bad, you know?"

"Right," Jay said.

"I have a hard time relaxing," Lamont continued, getting back on track. "My mind is always going. I get a massage twice a week. Olga. She has magic fingers. I have to schedule that time to wind down."

"But you go out a lot. You're very social. You vacation. You do the St. Bart's thing."

"Yes," Lamont said. "But even in St. Bart's you hang out with people you work with. You talk shop. That is fun for me. My fun is all business-based."

"And you hang out with a lot of beautiful women," Jay said. "That must be fun."

"Chasing beautiful women feels like work," Lamont said. He smiled. "Isn't that right, Carlos?"

A man of few words, Carlos came back with his standard reply: "You right."

"I wanted you to come to this benefit, Jay, because I'm concerned that you're not getting my human side."

"Your human side?"

"It's crucial that you get that. Make sure you talk to my mother." Lamont gave Jay his mother's numbers. "I don't want any arrogance in this piece," Lamont continued. "That's crucial. I've been coming to this Boys & Girls Club benefit for four years." Lamont put his hand on Jay's shoulder and leaned in to make a *crucial* point. "But this year I decided to get more involved. So for the past month I've been raising money for this event. I raised two hundred thousand. I got on the phone and shook motherfuckas down, you understand? Because our children are important. *That* is my human side."

"Right," Jay said, fiddling with his tape recorder. "I already spoke to most of your artists for secondaries."

"What'd they say?"

Radickulys's secondary quote about Lamont: "He's up early, always thinking about the next two or three moves down the line. He's a savage about staying on top. You gotta respect that. He's got a lot of haters in this industry, but he shrugs it off and keeps it moving."

Flo$$'s secondary quote about Lamont: "When I first started out he would tell me, 'You don't see what I see.' Because I'm a regular nigga from the streets so you know how it is. You're just living your life and doing you. But he'd be like, 'You don't even see who you are.' He really shows you there's a bigger place you can take yourself in the world with class and all that shit. Because Lamont is a real classy nigga. Check out his suits! And he taught me how to be one, too."

Grimy's secondary quote about Lamont: "When I first got on, I had all these wack-ass niggas around me. They all wanted deals, wanted to ride on my coattails. Big Man saw they wasn't about nothin', and when I was fucked up he'd get at me on the real like, 'These niggas don't give two fucks about you, Grimes. You ain't on the corner no more, kid. This shit is major. You out here, you got a big heart, showing these niggas love, and they don't give a fuck. They're using you and spitting you out. Fuck that, nigga, go get yours.' Those niggas was making my whole situation cloudy, y'know? But after that it was like I felt the sun on my back for the first time."

"They all said great things," Jay reported. He was still waiting to hear back from Sum Wun. "But I need to get Mimi."

"You must speak to Verne DeLuca," Lamont said, naming the advertising guru. "I have a partnership with him. We work on positioning artists, reaching the urban market. It's crucial that you speak to Verne. And Irv Greene definitely. He's like a second father to me. That one's really crucial."

"What about your real father?" Jay suggested.

"No," Lamont said and continued with his list. "Puff. L. A. Andre Harrell. Tommy Mottola. Russell. All crucial. Get direct numbers from Imani and I'll make the calls to let them know you're gonna holla at them."

Still looking directly at Jay, he chirped, "Hey, princess." And with that greeting, Jay knew immediately that he was on yet another phone call. "On my way," said Lamont, using a saccharine voice Jay had not yet encountered. "There's traffic though. . . . Are you wearing a pretty dress? . . . See you soon. . . . Me too."

"Who was that?" Jay said.

"A friend," Lamont said.

"Your girlfriend?"

"No."

Jay sighed. "Come on, Lamont!" Lamont was turning out to be one of his most difficult interviews. He was trying to orchestrate everything. Jay was waiting for Lamont to offer to write the piece himself.

Lamont looked over, irritated. "I get a phone call, I have to take it. What do I have to do, ask you to stick your head out the window so I can take a phone call?"

Jay sighed. "But that is a human side. Your personal life."

"Who I'm fucking is not a human side. It's gossip. You work for *Vibe,* Jay, not the *National Enquirer.*"

"So that *was* someone you're . . ."

Lamont gave him a challenging stare that said, *Go on, son.*

". . . someone you're, you know, dating."

Lamont loudly cleared his throat and looked out of the window.

Jay tried another tack. "So *are* you seeing anyone currently?"

"What have you heard?"

"I heard you were dating Mimi. I actually read that in the paper."

"Rumors," Lamont scoffed. "Falsehoods. I'm not her type. I think she was dating that kid Trey. From Chi-town."

"Really," Jay said, unconvinced. He hadn't heard a peep about that but he'd heard plenty about her dating Lamont.

"I think she dumped him."

"Not her type either, I guess," Jay said.

"Guess not," Lamont replied. "Did you hear what she said about me on Wendy Williams' Show?"

"No, what'd she say?"

"Wendy asked her about the rumors that we were dating and she denied them by saying, 'I'm looking for man who's young, fine, and in shape!' "

Jay cracked up.

Lamont snapped, "What's so funny?"

"That!"

"She didn't have to dis me like that. I yelled at her for that, told her she was a bad girl. There are plenty of fine women who'd love to get all up on a fat old nigga like myself. Carlos, can I get a witness?"

Involuntarily, Carlos said, "You right."

"So that's something that bothers you then," Jay said tentatively. "Being fat?"

"Excuse me," Lamont snorted. "Are you calling me fat?"

"You just called yourself fat!"

"I was being descriptive, not derogatory."

"So was I," Jay snapped. "But that's something you struggle with. Your weight?"

Lamont grabbed Jay's tape recorder and turned it off. "Off the record, yes."

They spent a long lull listening to nothing but raindrops pounding the car. But Jay had perfected the art of waiting out the pregnant pause. If you could resist the urge to fill the silence long enough, subjects would usually rush in with a vital piece of information they were on the fence about divulging. It was always the money quote.

"I look in the mirror," Lamont continued hesitantly, "and I see a man nearing forty with his top going gray and his middle going soft. And that upsets me deeply. I don't know why really. But that is the reality of the situation. I exercise and I try to eat healthy but it's difficult. And you asked me how I relax. Truth is, when I'm stressed, I eat...and when I'm happy, I eat...and when I'm bored, I eat." He sighed. "A lot of sweets. It calms me. I have a wicked sweet tooth. That's the boy in me. It might be a biochemical thing." He handed the tape recorder back.

"But, Lamont, why does that have to be off the record? You just said you want this piece to show your human side. That's it. You're very successful in business and with the ladies but you still care about your weight. I think that's an interesting tidbit. It says a lot about you. It humanizes you."

"It makes me sound vain. I am not vain. I just care about my appearance as any man with any self-respect should. It's off the record."

"Okay," Jay reluctantly agreed. "But I need Mimi for a secondary quote. I haven't been able to reach her."

"She'll be here tonight," Lamont said. "You can talk to her."

The Maybach pulled up to Tavern on the Green. Dressed in a gorgeous Narciso Rodriguez dress, Mimi was outside under the awning. Ally C. rushed over to the car holding a large black umbrella in one hand and Lamont's speech, printed in fourteen-point font, in the other. Imani had e-mailed it to someone at the restaurant and instructed them to give it to Ally C.

Jay and Lamont got out.

"Hey princess," Lamont chirped and kissed Mimi on the cheek. "This is my boy Jay from *Vibe*. The one who's doing that huge, five-page feature on me for the juice issue."

Mimi shook Jay's hand. "It's nice to meet you."

"I was just telling Lamont that I wanted to get a quote from you for the piece."

She took one look at Jay's rumpled brown suit, the sweat glistening on his forehead, and realized Lamont had him shook. "Then you can sit next to me," she said, playfully looking back at Lamont. "I'll give you all the dirt."

Lamont smiled, shot his cuffs, and followed.

◆

CHAPTER 39

Moment of Clarity

"YOU EVER THOUGHT about fixing this place up?" Mimi asked Gem as they walked down to the dock of his lakefront property.

"I like my place the way it is," Gemini said, making his way through the trees with a paper plate of barbecue in his hand.

Mimi followed him down to Lake Lanier, with her new dog, Bezel, nipping at her heels. The black Pomeranian had been Lamont's latest "that's just a rumor, I don't even know that girl" gift. Lamont was probably glad they'd be away for a few days because Bezel needed housebreaking and Lamont's workout area had become the pup's favorite dumping ground.

Mimi, Alonzo, and Bezel had arrived at The Funk Shack this morning. A pale, scraggly-looking guy had opened the door and Mimi thought he was the backwoods version of a manservant. But Alonzo had greeted the man with, "What up, Gem!" Checking out his lumpy Afro, the nappy tuft of hair on his chin, and his bony shoulders jutting out of his white tank top, Mimi thought, *This is Gemini, the hot to death producer?*

"Do you know that toilet upstairs is broken?" Mimi said as they neared the lake.

"There are four other bathrooms," Gemini pointed out.

"And they're all dirty." She and Alonzo were staying at the house in which Gem's considerable all-male posse roamed free. There were bedrooms enough for everyone, but housekeeping was apparently not high on the boys' list. None of the sheets matched and they felt itchy to the touch, the towels were faded and frayed and the bathrooms looked like they were crawling with bacteria!

"Sorry, princess," Gemini said, in a dry tone that didn't sound at all apologetic. "I know you're used to the penthouse, first class and all that."

"How would you know anything about my life?" she said, sitting down at the dock. "I heard you never leave this place."

"Everyone comes to me," he said. "But I hear things. And I have a DSL hookup. I check everything online. The New York papers, Hollywood trades."

"The papers," she teased. "You mean the gossip columns."

Her initial walk-on in Travis Peters's column had turned into a recurring role. Since she had three songs out already—collabos—and the songs and videos had all done extremely well, she was getting some serious attention even though her solo wasn't released yet.

The TLE publicity machine was gearing up in a big way for that release. The label had decided that she'd be known professionally as just Mimi. No last name. If asked in interviews, she was to say her full name was Mimi Jean. Lamont said Castiglione was too ethnic, it sounded like a brand of pasta. (Apparently it was the wrong kind of "ethnic," because they were playing up her Haitian heritage big-time.) And they were pushing the "Triple Large's first princess" angle. That was how Travis Peters always referred to her in his column— "Mimi, Triple Large's first princess." At first she thought the tag was cute but now it just sounded pretentious.

Usually she was mentioned for being somewhere in the company of Lena, Vanessa, or Lamont. They all were featured players in the gossip universe. Recently, sightings had been reported of her and Lamont "canoodling" all over town. (She didn't even know what that word meant. Was it even a word?) Ally C., quoted as her "spokeswoman," had denied every last one of the reports. "They're just friends," she would swear, even though they'd been spotted making out at Nobu. And Curb. And Swirl. Lamont told her people couldn't know they were dating because it was bad for her sexy, young, single girl image. So then why was he always trying to tongue her down in public?

One day, Ally C. asked Mimi to meet at Da Silvano for lunch. When Mimi showed up, Ally C. wasn't there. But Trey, the singer Lena was dating, was. Ally C., who was also Trey's flack, called and said she couldn't make it so they had lunch together. When the meal was over, they'd hugged and gone their separate ways. The following week, there was an item in the sightings section of *Us Weekly's* "Love Buzz" column. "TREY ELFMAN, 23, seen dining a deux with hot new R&B songbird MIMI JEAN, 21, at Da Silvano in New York."

Needless to say, Lena was fit to be tied. Mimi had to get Ally C. to confirm that nothing was going on. Still, Lena wasn't entirely convinced and she kept making snide jokes about Mimi being "after her man."

Lamont was mad because it had gotten out that she was really twenty-one, not nineteen.

"Don't believe everything you read," Mimi told Gem.

"Alonzo told me that you live with Lamont," Gem said, scratching his armpit. "Pretty reliable source."

"I guess so," she admitted. "We're a couple, if you must know."

"You're twenty-one?"

"Yes," she said, watching for Bezel as she roamed in the woods nearby.

"And Lamont's, what...forty-one?"

"Thirty-nine!" she exclaimed, as if two years made all the difference.

"Sorry, princess."

"How old are *you?*" Mimi asked. "And would you stop calling me princess?"

"That's what they call you in the papers."

"I know. But I don't like it."

"Sorry," he said. "And I'm twenty-five."

"How did you become a superproducer by twenty-five?"

"Started young and stayed focused."

"So how did you get your start?"

"I would DJ in Atlanta when I was in high school. I made a name for myself and I got hired for all the proms and parties. And my boy was doing some production work. He brought me in and showed me the ropes. Then I did that song 'Take it Home' for Papa Pimp. You remember that one?"

"Yeah," Mimi said. She'd heard it plenty. It was on one of Lena's homemade rap classics CDs.

"That was my first song. I was only nineteen and since then I've worked with everybody from DMX to ... well, lots of people," he said modestly.

"And you had *Britney Spears* up in *this* piece?" Mimi questioned, turning back to look at the house with its chipping brown paint.

"She worked here but she stayed at The Swiss in Atlanta. She's a pop *princess*," he said, giving Mimi a sidelong glance, "so it was only right."

"Why are you making fun of me, Gem? What have I ever done to you?"

"You show up here with your Louis Vuitton luggage, dripping in ice," he said, visually cataloging all her jewels, "complaining about everything and anything, and you expect me *not* to make fun?"

Mimi looked down at all her icy trinkets and she had to laugh at herself. The two little *M* barrettes holding her hair back, the MIMI necklace, the tennis bracelet, her frosty watch by Chris "The Iceman" Aire, the diamond toe ring ... it was a bit much with her Juicy terry halter dress and Chanel slides. At home, this overdone look had become de rigeur. She was expected to be ghetto-fabulous glam at all times. "Your fans want to see you looking your best," Lamont would say. "Don't disappoint them."

"Okay, it's too much for The Funk Shack," Mimi admitted. "But in New York this is the look! Anyway, Lamont likes me this way. He likes me to dress up and do my hair and nails and get the whole Brazilian bikini wax thing ..."

Gem glanced at her like, *Too much information.*

"... and so I do that. I like it. Is that so wrong?"

"Man," Gem said, looking at her with some amusement. "Britney's not as high-maintenance as you!"

She pointed a charred chicken wing at him. "But let us keep in mind that Britney didn't have to put her bare feet in that mildewed shower!"

"Okay," Gem said, laughing. "You're right. It is getting a little gutter around here. We've had a lot of guests lately and my cleaning lady went on vacation. I'll call and see if we can get her back here tomorrow. I'll tell her, 'It's an emergency!'"

"Thank you," Mimi said, trying not to laugh. "And speaking of ice, those are some big nuggets you've got in your ears."

"They're cubic zirconia," Gem said. "I'm being ironic."

She just stared at him. Ironic? "And those are some pretty fancy cars you have in your driveway."

"Only one of those is mine."

"Which one?"

"The white Denali truck."

"It's not exactly a hooptie."

"I bought it used off Busta."

"So you're cheap and proud of it."

"I'm wise with my dough," he rephrased.

"But don't you ever want to just buy something nice for yourself?" She slapped him on the arm. "Damn, treat yourself, Gem! You're worth it."

"I know," he said drolly. "And I do. I buy equipment. And I buy video games."

"That's it?"

"Those video games aren't cheap."

Suddenly, Alonzo's voice came booming through the trees: "Yo, Mimi, your fuckin' dog pissed all over the rug in the game room. You really need to train this bitch."

Bezel raced out of the trees, jumped on Mimi's lap, and joyously licked her face.

Wearing nothing but a long pair of boardshorts, Alonzo trotted toward them. He picked up speed as he neared the end of the dock and did a cannonball into the lake. Seconds later, his head bobbed up and he climbed up the dock's wooden ladder.

"We're about to play poker," he told Gem as he walked past, dripping. "You in?"

"Nah," Gem said, and Alonzo kept ambling toward the house.

Mimi stroked Bezel's glossy black fur and adjusted her plaid Burberry collar. "Gem," she said wistfully, "do you ever wish that you had gone to college?"

"Not really," Gem said. "Most people go to college to get a job. At eighteen, I already knew what I wanted to do so I skipped that step. And you don't need to go to college to learn stuff. You're always learning in different ways. Life is a lesson every day."

"Oh gosh, what a wise man you are," she gushed sarcastically, getting back at him for his high-maintenance comments. "When do you have time to read all the books you have lying around?"

"I find time. I read a lot of books on finance because I don't just want my business manager to know what's going on with my money. I want to know. And I've read some interesting books about the different ways people relate to money. How you spend and what you buy says a lot about you. It's deep."

"If that's supposed to be another insult about my jewelry," she quipped, "I didn't buy this stuff so stop reading so much into it."

"Ooh, heel, girl," he said to Mimi, not Bezel, and they both laughed. "But, seriously, it's important when you're dealing with this type of money to be educated in what you're doing. People in this business don't care about you, they care what you can do for them." He nodded at Mimi, suspecting that that applied to her as well. "You can borrow some of the books if you want."

"No thanks," she retorted quickly. "Lamont's got me covered. I have everything I need and then some."

"No doubt," Gem said, "but you may still want to take a look at some of those books. I got some by Suze Orman somewhere. You might like her."

"I *said* I'm straight," Mimi assured him. "But I wonder what it would be like to go to college, not just for the education but for the experience. I went out with my friend Jordan and her college room-mate a few weeks ago. And they had so many funny stories about things they did in school. It sounded like so much fun. And it made me think, I'll never have that."

"But you're going to have other experiences that most girls would kill to have. You're going to have an album, and make videos, and go on tour. And you're doing what you love, right?"

"Yeah," she said, very tentatively. "But it's like this was my dream and I'm so grateful that I'm getting to do this. *So grateful*," she stressed because she was afraid he was going to say she was complaining again. "But sometimes it feels like I'm showing up just to do a job more than I'm fulfilling my dream."

"Well, at the end of the day, it is a job. But it's your *dream* job, try and look at it that way."

"Maybe I'd be more in love with the process if I got to write my own songs," she said glumly. "And if I could have more say in what we're doing. But it's all, 'Go here, say this, wear that, smile, sing this song we had written for you and then go sit over there in the corner and be quiet until we need you again.'"

Gem eyed her sympathetically. "Is that how Lamont treats you?"

"No, of course not," she said, regretting her words. She didn't want him to think she was bad-mouthing Lamont. And she wasn't. All Lamont wanted was for her to be successful. "Lamont is amazing, the best. He's so supportive. But you know..." She trailed off.

"Yeah, I know. Your camp is about making hits, not music." He put his hand out, she took it, and he helped her up. "Come on, I want you to hear something."

They went back to the house and settled into the basement studio. It was like Gem's high-tech bat cave. He played her a beautiful, melodic track and explained, "This is a song I did a while ago but I'm trying to work out the lyrics. I need to find the right singer for it."

"You want to use this for my album?" Mimi asked.

"Probably not," Gem said, handing her a piece of paper on which he had scratched out one verse. "I don't think this is what your label wants."

"But what are you going to use it for? Someone else's album? A soundtrack?"

He grabbed hold of her shoulders and shook her. "Loosen up, Mimi. I have no plans to make it commercially available." He smirked. "It's just something I had in my head. You want to write songs, help me write this one."

"Oh, okay," she said, feeling nervous all of a sudden.

Gem walked around, lighting his scented candles, then he pointed at the chair at the far end of the studio. "Now go sit over there and be quiet until I need you again," he commanded, barely able to contain his laughter.

"Gem!" she cried.

"Just kidding," he said, raising the volume of the track. He slid down next to her on the couch. "Songwriting 101. Class is in session. Here we go."

◆

CHAPTER 40

Work It

"SMILE!" Vanessa demanded.

At the Sean John boys shoot, disoriented by the hot lights and the swarms of people running around, Pedro Miguel Antonio del la Cruz Jackson did just the opposite.

"Mama," he wailed, yanking his silky cornrows. "Mama!"

Vanessa watched as the woman her son was calling for swung into action.

"Get out, Vanessa," Mama Jackson commanded, scooping up her crying grandbaby.

So Vanessa did. She grabbed the handles of her alligator Birkin bag and made tracks. She had another appointment anyway. *Something important.*

After being appointed Mimi's "image consultant," Vanessa had made it patently clear to Ally C. that *no one* was *ever* to refer to her as a stylist. Too common. Ally C. had suggested "stylist to the superstars," but Vanessa nixed that title for her new venture since it still contained

the offensive word "stylist." So a press release had gone out trumpet-
ing her work as a "celebrity image consultant," paving the way for the
ultra-glamorous business Vanessa was planning to launch. She'd
decided to handle only the biggest names. Which made it especially
frustrating that her only client, Mimi, wasn't yet a big name.

Lamont had instructed Vanessa to pick out all Mimi's outfits
because he said they needed to build a "fashion profile" for her. He'd
noticed that some female celebrities—the ones who had smart people
behind them—made news just by changing their hair. Having a
defined sense of style ensured tons of free press. Even when they didn't
have a new album or movie out, they showed up at the right places
wearing the right things (or sometimes the wrong things) and—
snap—they were in a magazine.

Vanessa was full of big concepts but she didn't much fancy doing
the detail work required to put an image together. For that, she had
two meagerly paid assistants who borrowed, cataloged, and returned
all manner of designer accoutrement. She could not be bothered running around doing pick-ups and drop-offs.

In Mimi's old living room, she'd set up two rolling racks of complete looks. Vanessa had organized them by category—day, night,
casual, glam, glam casual, etc.—and shoes, jewelry, and accessories
were all bagged to go with each look. They'd been carted over to
Lamont's penthouse after the mogul and his princess had shacked up.
(Vanessa could see the expiration date on that union already.)

When Lamont had taken his new artist/secret girlfriend to a Teen
People event where Radickulys was performing, Vanessa had put her
in custom-made Cavallis with diamond-stud Ms on each back
pocket, a lace-up basketball jersey with MIMI appliqued on the back

in faux bling, and Manolo sneaker boots. Then she'd ghetto-fabulous'd it out by adding tons of real diamond accessories. A hairstylist friend of Vanessa had created Mimi's messy "couture cornrows." A big picture of her at the event ran in the *Tribune* the next day and another appeared in the following issue of *Teen People*.

Lamont felt things were coming along nicely. So did Vanessa. Turning Mimi into a fashion icon would help her image consulting company blast off into the stratosphere!

Then, without warning, she was laid off as Mimi's image consultant. After she'd done all the work of getting Mimi noticed, Lamont announced that he had decided to "pull out the big guns" for her album's release. Vanessa was out, *Vogue*'s style guru was in.

André Leon Talley decreed: Bling bling is dead! They were instead going "boho chic with an edge." Mimi's hair was blond now. Not ash-blond, not honey-blond. Blond-blond. She wore it long and pin straight with a part down the middle.

Vanessa did not give a flying fuck. She was still getting her checks. She'd signed a one-year contract. Less work for her. It was time for Vanessa to concentrate on *Vanessa* for a change.

She ran into P. Diddy at Swirl and tried cozying up to him. She'd heard he was starting a women's line and she wanted to be in the ads. His exclusive contract model. Naomi was posing for Rocawear now. Why shouldn't Vanessa get down with Sean John and give Naomi a run for her money? Their supermodel feud was legendary and long-standing. Neither could remember who or what had started it.

She wasted her whole night caressing the ego of His Diddyness… *Your skin is so dewy, Diddy! What is your skin-care regimen? Have you tried Mario Badescu? Oh, you must! Your rhymes are so magnificent, your empire so vast! Remember when we tripped the light fantastic in Ibiza? It was the best night of my entire life... really! No one has moves like you, baby!* And after she'd had a snort in the unisex bathroom— *Fuck J.Lo. That puta never deserved you!*

In regards to the Sean John campaign, she dropped subtle hints. Maybe the hints were *too* subtle, because he never extended an offer. But the next day he called and said running into her had given him the idea of using Pedro in his boys shoot.

She decided it was for the best that he didn't want her. Going from Karl Lagerfeld couture to hip-hop streetwear was a reversal of fortune she might not be able to bear. Let Naomi slum with the rap trash.

On the heels of the Diddy dis, she'd finagled herself a genuine, indisputable comeback opportunity. It was Fashion Week. She was going to be strutting down the catwalk at the Marc Jacobs show tomorrow morning at nine in the tents at Bryant Park.

But she had to prepare.

"Walk, bitch!" shouted Royale Jenkins, the legendary catwalking coach. A statuesque, jet-black man with pillowy pink lips, relaxed hair pulled into a chic ponytail, and blood-red talons, calling him vicious was an understatement.

From one end of his bare rehearsal space to the other, Vanessa high-stepped back and forth in front of wall-to-wall mirrors.

Right...left...right...left...right...left...dip the hip...position the left hand...dangle the right arm...halt...arch the back...pose...pout...toss the mane and...

The pièce de résistance. Her signature turn at the end of the runway. It was called the "de la Cruz." Royale had helped her craft it many moons ago.

She clenched her toes inside the seven-inch practice stilettos, shifted her weight (125 tonight, but—after a colonic—121 by show-time tomorrow), and then landed in her inimitable twist.

She nailed it!

Royale didn't think so.

He rushed over and grabbed her shoulders. "Look, bitch. You haven't been on a catwalk in six years. A thousand top girls with better gaits than you have died a thousand deaths in that time! You don't have Tyra's sass, you don't have Caroline Murphy's sweetness and light, you don't have Emma White's insanely perfect body…"

Vanessa's eyes glazed over with shame as he named ten other things she didn't have and all the models who did.

"Hear me now," he shouted directly into her face, his hot Altoids breath slapping her hard, his shrill voice echoing in the huge, empty space. "All you have is your walk. That's all you have! You have to work for this! Now walk, bitch!"

He hustled her back to her starting position.

Royale is so wonderful, Vanessa thought. *Where would I be without him?*

And she took it from the top.

Right…left…right…left…

"Stomp, bitch!" Royale screamed from the sidelines.

…right…left…

"Get those feet off the floor!"

…dip the hip…position the left hand…dangle the right arm…halt…

Royale lashed an eight-foot riding crop near her feet. "Full stop!"

…arch the back…pose…pout…toss the mane…

"Easy there!"

...and the "de la Cruz."

"Better."

After six grueling hours, Royale allowed her a three-minute break. She fell down on the stool, spent.

"What's the first rule of catwalking?" Royale demanded.

"It's not about you," Vanessa obediently answered. "It's about the clothes." She'd always hated that rule.

"Yes," Royale said, putting an index finger to his plump pink lips. "But this time, it *is* about you, isn't it?"

Always was, Vanessa thought.

"That's the problem," Royale said. "The rules are being turned on their heads this time. You want everyone to notice you and only you. This is your comeback. This is the defining moment in your pathetic, has-been life."

Vanessa hung on Royale's every word.

"Do you want it, Nessa?"

"Yes, Royale. I want it."

He squirted her in the face with a spray bottle of Evian. "I don't feel your energy."

"I want it!" she shrieked, standing up. *"I want it! I want it! I want it!"*

"Sit," Royale said. "You have another forty-five seconds."

He grabbed a remote control from the windowsill and pointed it at the TV, the only item in the room other than the stool and boombox. A video began to play. It was footage of the infamous tumble Naomi took in '93 while walking the Vivienne Westwood runway in a pair of sky-high platforms. The fifteen-second clip repeated over and over on an endless loop. A catwalking cautionary tale.

"Don't let that be you," Royale warned.

He looked at his stopwatch. "Time's up." He pulled her up. Another Evian spray. He shoved her back to her starting position. "Now stop half-stepping and waaaaaalk, bitch!"

By eight o'clock the next morning, Vanessa was so tired and sore she could barely stand, much less walk. But once she got out there on the Marc Jacobs runway in front of a packed house, music pumping, lights blazing, cameras whirring, she was utterly re-energized. She stepped out in her first look filled with a confidence she hadn't known since she was nineteen.

Sitting front row, a few seats down from Diddy, she spotted Mimi, in head-to-toe Marc Jacobs, squashed between Lamont and André Leon Talley, who looked like they were wearing the same suit. Alonzo was in Vegas.

Right...left...right...left...right...left...dip the hip...position the left hand...dangle the right arm...halt...arch the back... pose...pout...toss the mane and...

Reaching the far end of the runway, the incessant click of the cameras was so intoxicating that she spontaneously decided to hold there for a few extra seconds before going into the "de la Cruz."

Click. Click. Click.

You are beautiful, the cameras were saying.

Click. Click. Click.

You will always be beautiful. You will never age. You will never sag. You are beyond beautiful. You are gorgeous. You are divine.

Click. Click. Click.

You are more gorgeous than Naomi and Gisele and Emma. You are perfection.

Click. Click. Click.

You, mami, are the shit.

She went into her turn and immediately sensed the beginnings of disaster. Her legs got tangled and before she knew what had happened she was off the runway. She opened her eyes and found herself looking up into the horrified face of the most flamboyant man in fashion. She'd fallen off the catwalk and landed right in André Leon Talley's enormous lap.

Mimi leaned over, visibly shaken. "Vanessa! Are you all right?"

Diddy leaned forward, craned his neck, and examined the wreckage, blinking over the top of his shades.

Lamont leaned back, cackling up a storm.

Seated across the runway, Royale looked away.

The show continued uninterrupted.

To everyone's surprise, the next day, Vanessa was on cloud nine. A picture of André Leon Talley, his mouth wide open in horror while he cradled Vanessa in his arms like a toy poodle, appeared on the cover of the *New York Tribune*. In color.

And then in *Women's Wear Daily*.

And in *Us Weekly*.

And as a full page in *People's* Star Tracks!

What the hell did Royale know anyway? The bitch was back.

CHAPTER 41

◆

Lord Knows

TREY DUMPED LENA right before his solo album was released. It
went platinum. She'd just read in *Us Weekly* that he was dating Yvette
Miller. The *Y* in PYT. Last she'd heard, Crazy G was still messing
with the *P*. Lena was convinced it was a conspiracy.

The only bright spot in her life was that her girl Maryslesis was
killing it over at Parsons! Some of her (their) designs were even displayed in an exhibit at the school. Lena had dipped over there to
check them out. Maryslesis was bringing the hotness for real. *You better work, Mami!*

Daddy was over the moon when the first reports rolled in. The
credit card was back in full effect and he'd doubled her cash
allowance. And, best of all, he was bragging about her to everyone.
Now folks knew she was about something!

He was in town and he said he had a surprise for her. *What could it
be?* she wondered, nervously nibbling the end of one of her long microbraids as she turned the corner for Bice, the restaurant where they were

meeting for dinner. New rims for the Range? No, a brand-new ride! That Range Rover was two years old. What should she get? An Escalade? Oooh, maybe her own apartment! She was a little old to be still living at home. If she got her own crib, she could blaze her blunts in peace without his spy Henrietta, that old bat, tracking her scent.

Lena strolled into Bice and looked around. Daddy spotted her, stood, and waved from the back. She'd even worn a dress tonight to make him extra happy. It was an ultrashort, one-shouldered Allen Iverson jersey dress, but it wasn't sweats.

Beaming with paternal pride, Marlin opened his arms wide for a hug. "What a cute dress, honey! Did you make that? Is that one of your designs?"

"Yeah," she lied. She'd actually gotten it at Dr. Jay's. She'd had to go to three stores to find one. They were all the rage, selling like hotcakes.

She pulled out a chair and he said, "Not there. Mrs. Smith is sitting there."

Lena noticed that there was a half-empty glass of water at that place and a few crumbs of bread on the plate. "Mrs. Smith," she repeated, taking another seat at the table for four.

She vaguely recalled Mrs. Smith as the name of one of his uppity friends. He called them all by their first names but she had to refer to them as Mr. or Mrs. Whatever. And they all had a son or a nephew for her to meet. The only benefit of getting written up in the papers as a boozer was that Daddy had stopped playing cupid. The shame was too much for him to bear. Now that he thought she was a star at Parsons, he probably felt she was ready to go back out on the market. The fourth place at the table was probably for Mrs. Smith's "respectable" son. A sneak attack fix-up. She should have known.

"Daddy," she began to whine, "I hope this isn't the surprise."

"Well, yes," he said. "It is. Mrs. Smith went to the ladies' room. But I can fill you in before she comes back."

Oh no, Lena thought, chewing on a bread stick. *Here it comes...Her son is a senior at NYU! He's majoring in film! You'll like him, Marlena. He's cool! He's creative!*

"I'm donating some money so they can start a minority scholarship program at Parsons!" Marlin said, like he was telling her she'd hit the Lotto. "So talented but financially disadvantaged students can have the same opportunity as you." Then giddy as all hell he added, "We're leveling the playing field in the design world, Marlena."

"That's the surprise!" Lena snapped. How was that good news *for her? Fuck a scholarship program*, she thought. *Hook a bitch up with some rims!*

"Yes," Marlin said, almost levitating with joy. "And that's not all."

Never giving up hope, she was expecting him to say something along the lines of, "And you get a brand-new car. Anything you want." *Come on, Daddy*, she thought, leaning forward with anticipation. *Hit me with it!*

"We're thinking of naming the scholarship after you!" he said delightedly.

Lena threw down the bread stick. *I've already got a scholarship program up and running*, she wanted to holler. *And her name is Maryslesis Gonzalez!*

Instead she shouted, "What?"

"Use your indoor voice, Marlena," he urged, looking around.

Lena's mind was racing. She needed to maintain a low profile at the school for this scam to work long-term. Maryslesis's having her designs on display made her a little nervous but she figured it was a good thing. It was Lena's name signed on those sketches. But this scholarship program was going to put a spotlight on her. Why couldn't her stupid father just leave well enough alone!

It dawned on her at that moment that he hadn't said anything about Mrs. Smith or the fix-up. "Daddy," she said, a dampness forming on the back of her neck. "Who is Mrs. Smith?"

"You know her," he murmured.

"That woman who worked on the Fresh Air Fund benefit?" she asked, trembling.

"No," he said and gave her the you-silly-girl look. "*Annette* Smith. From the school." He smiled at someone over her shoulder. "There she is."

Lena began to turn her head. Everything was moving in slow motion. She felt faint. *Lord,* she prayed. *Have a sista's back. Just this one time.*

If Mrs. Smith was someone she'd met during the interview or registration process, she could play it off and decide on her next move later. If Mrs. Smith was one of the teachers who'd met only Maryslesis, she was completely *fucked!*

Lena stood and just as she caught Mrs. Smith in her peripheral sights, she heard Daddy saying, "You two have met." His voice sounded muffled. She felt like she was underwater.

Please, she prayed. *Please let that be true.*

Lena and Mrs. Smith locked eyeballs. She watched Mrs. Smith's smile make a U-turn. For a moment the whole room went black. She couldn't breathe. She was going to pass out. *Oh God, oh God, please forgive me the trespasses I have committed . . .*

"No, um, I don't think we have," said the Dean of Parsons School of Design, confused because she'd gone down to one of the classes yesterday to introduce herself to Marlena Whitaker after Mr. Whitaker had contacted her about his generous offer. This was not the sweet, curly-haired girl she'd met.

Mrs. Smith looked at Marlin.

Marlin looked at Lena.

Lena looked at the door.

Ready, set, go!

Without saying a word, Lena sprinted out of Bice at world-record speed, braids flying like a kite.

◆

CHAPTER 42

You Be Illin'

CRAZY G REALLY GOT AROUND. He'd recently moved on from the *P* in PYT to a new set of letters: EnVee. At Gambino's twenty-ninth birthday bash at Heaven, Lena had been giving her former friend and former *boy*friend the evil eye all night.

Since the debacle at Bice with Daddy, she'd been hiding out at Lamont's vacant West Village apartment. Daddy had called her several times but she never picked up her cell. Unable to reach Lena, he and Mrs. Smith had a talk with the other Marlena Whitaker. Maryslesis confessed all, crying so hard she could barely breathe. Now she was back working at the Laundromat.

Out of respect for Marlin, Travis Peters ran the item blind: "What powerhouse attorney is red-faced after it came to light that his alcohol-swilling, trash-talking party-girl daughter was paying another gal to take all her classes at design school?" It was one of the easier blind items to figure out.

Marlin returned to L.A. and Lena didn't want to imagine how

furious he was. She didn't have to. A few days later her cell stopped working. She tried to go shopping to ease her pain but her credit card was denied. The saleswoman cut it up right there in front of her at the Puma store. Panicked, she went to the Mobil station to load up on cigarettes and whatever she could but it was too late. That card didn't work either.

She slipped back into the apartment late one night, grateful the locks hadn't been changed, and got her stuff. Ever since, she'd been sleeping all day and drinking all night. Mimi kept telling her to apologize to her father. But Lena didn't know what to say to him.

Mimi was now carrying her financially.

"Let's get out of here," Mimi said, thinking, *Poor Lena. Making a fool of herself yet again.*

She didn't know how she was going to tell Lena that she had to get out of Lamont's apartment. He'd finally sold it and he'd told Mimi to kick Lena out. But Lena was in such a bad way she could never bring herself to do it. She just kept urging her to make up with her father so she wouldn't have to say anything. She was thinking of suggesting a stay at a rehab, too. But she knew Lena wouldn't take kindly to that.

"Let's go," Mimi said again, stronger this time. She had to get home. She had a bunch of interviews scheduled tomorrow. Her album was being released next week. Lamont had already taken off, uninterested in celebrating Don Gambino's birth. He'd told her not to stay long because she needed her beauty rest and left Alonzo there to watch over her. But she hadn't seen 'Zo in an hour. Carlos was waiting outside in the Suburban.

"No," Lena slurred, sipping on her fourth Whitaker Whiskey, a potent cocktail that the club had named after her. "I want them to see me. It's ruining their night."

"They make an ugly couple anyway," Vanessa said, crankily coming down from a coke high on the other side of their booth.

They stayed for another half hour, lambasting the Crazy G–EnVee pairing, while hip-hop's new "it" couple whooped it up across the room, noticing Lena's stares but not caring. Eventually Gambino and The Firing Squad urged EnVee to go over and say something to Lena for their amusement.

"How's it going, Lena," EnVee said, sidling up with a confrontational swagger.

That was all it took. Lena stood up in the booth and shouted, "Don't say shit to me!"

"Let's go, honey," Mimi said, trying to grab Lena.

Vanessa sat back to enjoy the floor show.

"You got beef?" EnVee said, unintimidated.

"Bitch, I will crack you in your motherfuckin' forehead," Lena screamed, wobbling on her unsteady feet. She grabbed the edge of the booth for support.

Mimi tried to pull her down.

"You're pathetic, Lena," EnVee snapped and rolled her eyes.

Gambino and crew were standing up to get a better view. They were loving the scene, pumping Cristal and laughing.

Their laughter abruptly stopped when Lena proved to be a woman of her word. As promised, she grabbed her heavy glass of Whitaker Whiskey and smashed it hard into EnVee's motherfucking forehead.

EnVee let out a bloodcurdling scream and hit the floor with a thud, her hands covering her bludgeoned face.

"Alonzo!" Mimi shrieked. "ALONZO!"

Lena tried to jump down on top of EnVee, but Mimi held her back, hysterically screaming, "Alonzooooo!"

Twenty members of The Firing Squad were hopping booths with a quickness, shoving shocked partygoers out of the way to rescue their girl.

Vanessa, still reclining languidly, hadn't batted an eyelash. She'd started plenty of catfights backstage at the shows. She sort of missed them. Vanessa had no interest in EnVee one way or the other because she thought EnVee was ugly and therefore so far beneath her she might as well be in a grave. But when EnVee fell to the floor an inch away from the steel spike of Vanessa's Choo, it was an opportunity Vanessa couldn't resist. She calmly lifted her foot—*slice!*—and left a long red gash on EnVee's cheek.

"*Now* let's leave," Vanessa said.

Security rushed over as Alonzo swooped in and hustled them all outside. Lena was screaming incoherently. Mimi was crying. Vanessa was yawning.

The next day, the cover of the *New York Tribune* was a split shot: Mimi on one side. EnVee on the other. The headline blared:

HIP-HOP GIRLFIGHT!

Page three detailed the ruckus, saying that Lena and Mimi had gotten into an argument with EnVee that had turned physical.

Mimi was horrified that she had been publicly dragged into Lena's mess. She hadn't done anything! Ally C. issued a terse statement saying, "Mimi was not involved in any way in the unfortunate altercation at Heaven last night. She does not condone violence under any circumstances. She wishes EnVee a speedy recovery."

There was no picture of Vanessa and only a cursory mention that she had been present. She finally carried through on her longtime threat to fire Ally C. as her publicist.

Lamont was overjoyed. Mimi's album was scheduled for release in four days and his Triple Large princess was front-page news. Who could ask for anything more?

◆

CHAPTER 43

Top Billin'

MIMI'S DEBUT ALBUM, *The Haitian Mami,* was released on a Tuesday.

That afternoon, she sat in the green room at MTV's Times Square studio and looked at her CD cover for the hundredth time. They'd done three shoots before Lamont gave his final approval. The first pictures were deemed "too slutty." The second attempt was "not sexy enough."

She looked at the cover now and smiled. It was a shot of her from the waist up. She was topless, with her waist-length, straight blond hair (they'd added some extensions) covering her augmented breasts. On her neck was her diamond MIMI necklace.

She flipped it over. The back cover was *her* back. Just her long hair and her henna tattoo that read PRINCESS on the small of her back.

She opened the case and looked at all the track listings printed inside the booklet.

1. Baby Love
Written by B. Casey, B. Casey, D. McHenry
Produced by Country D for Lil' Big Man Productions

2. Yeah, yeah, yeah (Uh-huh)
Written by T. Oliver, S. Barnes, J. Miro, L.Parker, S. Sterling,
D. Styles, K. Johnson, L. Johnson, Q. Johnson, K. Bunkley,
D. Hoarde, D. Mobley
Produced by Troy Oliver for Milk Chocolate Productions, Tone
and Poke for Track Masters Entertainment, Corey Rooney for
Corey Rooney Entertainment

3. Hold Up
Written by D. McHenry
Produced by Country D for Lil' Big Man Productions

4. Did Me Greazy (feat. Supa Phat E)
Written by P. Williams, C. Hugo
Produced by The Neptunes

5. Lord Knows
Written, Produced, and Arranged by R. Kelly

6. Like That
Written by R. Jerkins, Y. Braithwaite
Produced by Rodney Jerkins for Darkchild Productions

7. Lovely
Written by Gemini
Produced by Gemini for Keepin' It Frugal Productions

8. Baby Girl (feat. Ragga Jamz)
Written by A. Elliot and Gemini
Produced by Gemini for Keepin' It Frugal Productions

9. Like the First Time
Written by M. Winans, Sean Combs
Produced by Sean "P. Diddy" Combs for "The Hitmen"/Bad
Boy Entertainment

10. Do That Thang
Written by T. Oliver, L. Lewis, C. Rooney, M. Denny
Produced by Troy Oliver for Milk Chocolate Productions

11. Ten Carats (feat. Lady Di)
Written by A. Carter, G. Mosley, P. Rydell
Produced by Timbaland for Timbaland Productions

12. All Up on You
Written by J. Timberlake, W. Robson
Produced by Justin Timberlake for Tennman Productions

13. Feel Me
Written by Gemini
Produced by Gemini for Keepin' It Frugal Productions

14. What the Deal (feat. MC Grimy)
Written by A. Smith, T. Pitts, F. Leroy
Produced by Swizz Beatz for Ruff Ryders Productions, Inc.

15. Bonus track
Baby Love
(Country D remix feat. Flo$$)
Written by B. Casey, B. Casey, D. McHenry, E. Graves
Additional Production by Country D for Lil' Big Man Productions
Executive Producers: Lamont Jackson, Alonzo Jackson

The only three songs on the album she really loved were the ones she'd done with Gemini. "Feel Me" was a slow groove, really sexy. When she recorded it, Gem had turned the lights down and lit some scented candles. And he had written "Lovely" for her late one night after she'd gone to bed. He'd originally titled it "Princess" but she talked him out of that. She knew if Lamont had seen that song title he would have chosen that over "Lovely" but he never knew about it.

"Baby Girl" was tight to death. Just seeing the name Ragga Jamz in the credits gave her a contact high. Ragga was the Jamaican dance hall king and he'd shown up at The Funk Shack with three friends and an enormous bag of ganja that he'd smuggled into the country. Everyone was thrilled to see him. He'd come to work on his album but Gem decided he and Mimi should do a song together. Gem and Ragga blazed and marinated on the idea one night. Mimi spent much of her time trying to fill in the blanks created by Ragga's patois. It was so thick, she couldn't understand a word he was saying. Not in person nor on the record that they recorded. All she knew was that Ragga really liked her and thought she was a cutie (Gem translated) and that "Baby Girl" was her absolute favorite song on her album.

She wasn't crazy about the track "Like the First Time," but she liked it fine. Everyone said Diddy was a total taskmaster but she'd found him sweet and funny as could be. She just didn't know how he could see anything without taking off his dark shades in the studio.

She *did* love "Lord Knows." That was the only track where she really got to sing. It showed off her voice. She'd never seen the (alleged) infamous video of R. Kelly but she judged Robert solely on how he behaved with her. He was a perfect gentleman and the arrangement he'd done was just beautiful. Still, she understood why

Lamont had sent Alonzo *and* a bodyguard with her to Chicago to record at Robert's studio.

Country D had done six songs, of which only three made the final cut. The first single, "Baby Love" (penned by those cute twins, Brian and Brandon, from the group Jagged Edge), was already in heavy rotation on the radio. Daryl was crowing about it to everyone, taking all the credit, which made its success bittersweet.

She counted thirty-five writers in total. (Did it really take twelve people to write "Yeah, yeah, yeah"?) She hadn't written one song. All thirty-five were men.

Ally C. popped her head in from the hallway. "They're ready for you on the set," she trilled.

Mimi went out and stood in the wings of the TRL set, smoothing her long blond hair, straightening her Joie tank top.

She heard La La, the VJ, introducing her.

Mimi walked out, flashed her $15,000 pearly whites, and waved at the cheering crowd.

◆

CHAPTER 44

No Sleep til Brooklyn

"HOW CAN YOU DO THIS TO ME!" Lena shrieked. She was still in her pajamas even though it was past two in the afternoon.

"I'm sorry," Mimi said. "But Lamont sold the apartment. You need to find somewhere else to crash."

"Can I stay with you guys?"

"No!" It came out stronger than Mimi intended.

"Why not? Lamont has all those extra rooms!"

"It's not possible."

"Why?"

"You just can't."

"Ask Lamont."

"I don't need to ask him."

"He might say yes."

"He won't. Anyway, I'm saying no."

"How can you do this to me?" Lena wailed.

"I'm not doing anything to you. You're doing all this to yourself."

Lena flopped onto the couch and fired up a Marlboro Light. She'd started taking her cornrows out late last night. One half of her head was braided down her back and the other half was a six-inch fan of crimped, dandruff-flecked mess.

"Call your father and apologize," Mimi demanded, standing over her.

"I don't want to."

"Well, you don't have any other options."

"I could come stay with you at Lamont's." Lena took a deep drag and squinted up at Mimi through the smoke. Forlornly, she asked, "How can you do this to me?"

"Why is everything about you?" Mimi snapped.

Lena ashed in a paper cup half-filled with last night's booze. "You're the one who thinks she's all that."

"Don't be mad because I'm about something."

"Yeah, about yourself," Lena said. "That's why they call you Me-me-me!"

Mimi ignored the slight. "Lena, call your father and apologize. Then move back into your huge apartment and get yourself together. Stop acting like you're on the run from the law. It ain't that deep, honey."

Lena didn't appreciate Mimi's lecture or her patronizing tone. She sucked her teeth and dropped her cigarette into the cup.

"Lena," Mimi said, sitting down next to her on top of some discarded braids. "Crazy G is an asshole."

"Who you tellin'?"

"He dicked you down and dismissed you. And walked away with a fifteen-thousand-dollar necklace!"

"I know!"

"Then why the hell do you care if he's with EnVee?" Mimi said sensibly. "Better he's using her than using you!"

Lena muttered, "I know. I know..."

"If you know, why'd you go after EnVee?"

Lena stopped pulling out one of her braids and cut her eyes. "You're taking her side now?"

"Her side?" Mimi shook her head and sighed. Was there no getting through to Lena? "Her side is the only side anyone can take. She had to get twenty stitches!"

"That's fucked up," Lena said, managing to acknowledge the seriousness of the situation without taking any personal responsibility.

"Yes, it is. But are you even sorry? Twenty stitches *in her face*. She's an artist, Lena. That's her livelihood."

"Oh, now that you're Miss Hip-Hop-slash-R&B Princess all you bitches gotta stick together, huh?"

"She's talking about suing you."

"I heard."

Mimi was afraid to say what she needed to say next but she had to. "Your father called me."

"What?" Lena threw a braid on the table. "When?"

"Yesterday."

"What'd he say?"

"He said he'd read EnVee's thinking about suing you. He thinks you need legal representation."

"She ain't gonna sue me. She's just on some shit."

"She has every right to sue you."

"What'd you tell my father?"

"I told him where you were. He's flying in tonight."

"What!" Lena wailed. "How could you do this to me!"

"Grow up," Mimi shouted, at her wits' end. "Your father loves you. He's trying to help you. And you need help." A long silence. "I think you need to go to a rehab."

"Did you tell my father that?" Lena screamed.

Mimi protectively folded her arms against her chest and leaned away on the couch. "Yes."

Lena piled on top of her, yelling nonsensically.

"Your father loves you," Mimi screamed, pushing her off. "I wish I had a father like that! I wish I had a father!"

"You do," Lena said icily, curling into the corner of the sofa. "Lamont."

"Lamont doesn't even like you," Mimi fired back, tired of Lena's never-ending bullshit. "The only reason he hangs out with you is *because* of your father. He likes your father, a man he's never met, a helluva lot more than he likes you."

Lena grabbed the booze and butt-filled cup and tossed its contents into Mimi's lap. "Fuck you!"

Mimi stood up, wiped her Fetish track suit, and gasped, "You... *sloppy drunk bitch!*"

"Poor white trash!" Lena cried, going for a low blow.

"C-list!"

"Daddy dicksucker!"

Mimi responded pithily. "Ho!"

"Fuck you," Lena said, hopping around in a fit. "You... you... you... CUNT!"

After a shocked *ooh-no-you-didn't* hush, Mimi walked quickly to the door before she wound up in the hospital like EnVee. "Your father will be here in a few hours," she shouted, looking over her shoulder. "If you don't want to see him I suggest you get your shit and be out!"

"I will be outta here," Lena screamed from the kitchen, where she was pouring herself a stiff drink. "I don't need you!"

"Good!" Mimi shouted. And before slamming the door, she fired a final dis that she knew would be like a stake through Lena's heart: "You wannabe gangsta bitch!"

LAMONT WAS RIDING UPTOWN in the Suburban with Nate and Alonzo when "Baby Love" came on the radio. He smiled.

"Here's your girl," Nate crowed.

Lamont's smile got bigger.

Then they heard something none of them was expecting. Daryl's voice in the background, whispering, "This is a Country Dizzle pro-duc-shizzle, my nizzle."

It was the "Baby Love" remix Daryl had done with himself on the record. The remix Lamont had expressly warned him could not be released. And he was also shouting out his own name as the producer!

"What the hell is this?" Nate said, an uneasy feeling overtaking him. Had the curse of the succubus finally been unleashed?

If Lamont could have jumped into the radio and cracked the record into a thousand tiny pieces he would have. The remix featuring Flo$$ hadn't been released yet. Daryl must've slipped this one, *his own version*, to the mix-show DJ. Lamont wondered how many other people Daryl had slipped it to.

But this wasn't even the first mix that Lamont had heard. This

was a different mix. And Daryl was ad-libbing all over the record—
"This is the remix," "Country D" this and "Country D" that, "What,"
"Yeah," "Sing that shit," and, in closing, "Yeeeaah, muthafuckas!"

Lamont called Imani. "Where does Daryl live?"

Since Daryl had made some money from his production work
he'd moved from his crummy Bed-Stuy studio to a brownstone
apartment in the cooler Brooklyn neighborhood of Fort Greene. He
could also be seen driving around town in a purple Navigator.

Lamont's Suburban pulled up to the address Imani had provided
them on South Oxford Street at midnight. Alonzo rang the bell but
there was no answer. So they parked down the block and waited.

Just before one, they saw a cab pull up to Daryl's address. But it
wasn't Daryl. It was Lena. She began carting a bunch of Louis
Vuitton bags from the cab's trunk to Daryl's front stoop.

"Is Daryl with her?" Lamont said, peering through the back
window.

The taxi took off, leaving Lena alone with her luggage on the steps.

"What's she doing here?" Nate said.

"Mimi kicked her out of the other apartment," Lamont said.

"Why doesn't she just make up with her father?" Alonzo sighed.

"But, again, what's she doing *here?*" Nate said.

"Let's find out," Lamont said and jumped out. Nate and Alonzo
followed him.

Lamont rolled up. "What's good, Lena?"

She almost jumped out of her skin. "Nothing," she said sourly
when she saw who was behind her. "What are you doing here?"

"We were going to ask you the same thing," Lamont said.

"Well," she said coldly, "I got evicted from my former residence."

"So you're gonna stay with *Daryl?* Don't you have enough problems?"

"Daryl is a real friend," she said, giving Lamont an accusing look. "Unlike some people."

The truth of the matter was that she had never considered Daryl a friend until tonight. Kiko was out of town, as usual, so there was no way to get into her place. And Mimi was her only other real friend. She'd called Daryl as a last resort but as soon as she spoke to him she began to feel better. Daryl couldn't stand Mimi and when Lena told him what had happened, they instantaneously bonded in a "the enemy of my enemy is my friend" kind of way and he'd told her to stop by the studio to get his keys. She was looking forward to staying up all night talking with Daryl, bashing the bitch.

"Sorry about that but those are the breaks, hon," Lamont said and shrugged. "Where's Daryl?"

"I don't know," she said, unlocking the door. "Make yourselves useful and get my bags."

Lamont, Nate, and Alonzo each grabbed one of her duffels and went in.

"Did you try his cell?" Lena said.

"No," Lamont said. He wanted to fire him face-to-face. And he didn't want Daryl to know it was coming. Anyway, if Daryl saw any of their numbers come up on his phone, it was unlikely that he'd answer.

They all entered the apartment. It was spacious but sparsely furnished.

Lena gave Lamont a very obvious once over. "That Zone Diet didn't work out for you, huh?"

"Not at all," he admitted.

"Why are you all looking for Daryl?" Lena asked, lighting a cigarette.

"Just want to have a chat," Lamont said. "Business matters."

Lena raised a skeptical eyebrow. "At midnight in Brooklyn?"

Lamont poked around the place. There were two bedrooms but only one had a bed. The walls of Daryl's room were decorated with eight Tupac posters, a back shot of Lady Di, and a framed *Scarface* movie poster. The living room held just an enormous TV, a black leather couch, and a black lacquer table piled two feet high with rap, car, and porno magazines.

Lamont stretched out on the couch. Alonzo perched on the arm and picked up a copy of *Black Tail.* Nate stood, leaning against the wall.

"Hey, Lena," Lamont said. "Why don't you call Daryl and see when he'll be home?"

"Why should I?"

"Because I'm asking you to."

"What's in it for me?"

Lamont shook his head and pulled out his knot. He peeled off a pair of hundred-dollar bills and slapped them into Lena's hand.

Lena looked at him without any change in expression.

He peeled off two more.

Lena still looked at him.

"That's all," he said and handed her Daryl's cordless.

She pushed in a number. After a brief confab, Lena hung up and reported, "He's on his way."

Ten minutes later, Carlos called Lamont and alerted him to Daryl's arrival. He was parking right outside.

Nate, Alonzo, and Lamont got up and left without a word to

Lena. They darted down the steps and spotted Daryl climbing out of his truck.

"Get over here," Lamont shouted, hustling down the steps flanked by his guys while Carlos was charging up the block.

Seeing the convergence of angry faces, Daryl quickly changed direction, hopped back into his Navigator, and, with a peel of rubber, sped off as Lena watched from the stoop.

THE NEXT DAY, Lamont came to work with the intention of having Daryl's office cleaned out and barring him from the premises. But Daryl's office was already as clean as a whistle. Lamont's office, on the other hand, was a mess.

Snickers bars were smeared all over his desk and a note was stabbed into his beloved office chair with a cheap pocketknife.

In Daryl's messy scrawl, it said: *Fuck you, Fat Man! I quit!*

CHAPTER 45

◆

One Love

IT TOOK ONE MONTH for *The Haitian Mami* to go platinum.
"Baby Love" was well on its way to becoming the most overplayed
song of the year. Daryl's unauthorized remix was playing on all the
mix shows. Then the Flo$$ remix had been released and that was get-
ting big play, too.

A celebration was in order.

When Lamont and Mimi arrived at Tao at ten o'clock for her
platinum party, the place was packed. Daryl hadn't been invited and
neither had Lena. No one had spoken to them since that night in
Brooklyn and no one wanted to.

At midnight, Lamont escorted Mimi to a small stage at the front
of the restaurant. A huge cake decorated with a candy reproduction
of Mimi's CD cover was wheeled out. The music was turned off and
Lamont took the microphone. People were hanging over the balcony
and crowding to the front for a good view.

"First, let's have a round of applause for our girl, Mimi…"

Mimi cringed when he added, "...Triple Large's first princess." She'd told him not to say that!

There was a boisterous explosion of applause and cheering. Mimi smiled awkwardly and waved as everyone gaped at her.

"Tonight is a special night for Mimi. And a special night for me, as well," Lamont said.

All of a sudden the music came back on and Mimi frowned. Lamont was speaking. Someone was about to get yelled at.

But Lamont did not look bothered that the music was interrupting him. Then she realized it was that Jon B. song. Their song.

Lamont got down on one knee in front of seven hundred people. He took her hand and lovingly looked up at her.

She saw Vanessa, Mama, Nate, and Jordan looking down from one of the VIP balconies. What was going on? They all looked as surprised as she did.

"Don't listen to what people say," Lamont whispered, but it sounded pretty loud because he still had the mike. *"They don't know about you and me. They don't know about this here. You should know baby, you're my angel. Nothing's gonna make you fall from heaven. Girl, I just wanna love you."*

All the women in the room simultaneously sighed, "Aaaaw."

He set the microphone down on the floor and took a black velvet box from the pocket of his Armani suit jacket. He popped it open and the *ooohs* from the ladies got even louder.

"Princess, will you marry me?"

Mouth agape, Mimi froze, feeling seven hundred pairs of eyes drill into her.

Mama thought, *My word, what is this?* Then, *Oh no, what about poor Kendra?* Then, *Wedding at the Plaza, dress by Vera Wang, flowers by Preston Bailey. God is good. God is good!*

Imani thought, *Hurry up, Mimi. Say yes. You're embarrassing him! And his trousers are getting dirty!*

Jordan thought, *This poor child doesn't know what she's getting into.*

Nate thought, *Haaaaaaa! Hand in your pimp card, nigga. You're done!*

Vanessa thought, *Yo no puedo creer esto! Casada con el? Yo no puedo creer esto! If that's six carats, I'm getting an upgrade to seven tomorrow!*

Alonzo thought, *I wonder if the Giants covered that spread.*

Mimi looked back at Lamont. He'd lived up to every promise he'd ever made to her. He'd made her a star. She was his princess. He wanted to be with her forever.

She held out her hand. "Yes."

Lamont slipped the seven-carat Fred Leighton on the ring finger of her left hand, then rose and kissed her, prompting wild cheers from the crowd.

Ally C. slipped into the club's office where she had her laptop all set up. She hit send on the mass e-mail she had prepared. It was a press release to all members of the media announcing Lamont and Mimi's engagement and declaring that the wedding would be the social event of the year.

Lamont had approved it yesterday.

◆

What You Wish For

CHAPTER 46

◆

Mo' Money, Mo' Problems

TEN MONTHS after Mimi's engagement was announced, she was on her way to get her nails done when her mother called to break some matrimonial news of her own. Angela was marrying her piece of shit boyfriend, Jerry!

Jerry, the loser who'd borrowed five thousand dollars from Mimi and never paid it back or made a *mention* of repaying her. Jerry, who was all too happy to move into the new house in Toledo that Lamont was paying for without ever chipping in for *anything*. Jerry, who Lamont hated with a passion. Jerry, who Angela said, unbelievably, was looking to retire soon. He was only forty-two! It wasn't like Jerry had an investment portfolio to support him for the rest of his days. Mimi had a pretty good idea who the bum was counting on to support his lazy ass. Marrying Angela was just a way to seal the deal. Well, Jerry had another think coming.

"I should be happy for you?" Mimi cried incredulously into her cell as the town car inched its way through midtown traffic. She rarely drove her Benz truck. Too much traffic and not enough parking. "He's using you! And you better believe I'm not paying a dime for your wedding!"

They got into a long argument during which Angela mainly wailed pathetically, "He wants me. He wants me. Can't you be happy for me?"

"Did he give you a ring?" Mimi asked, expecting the worst.

"No," Angela said, fulfilling Mimi's low expectations. "But he's going to very soon."

When Mimi finally hung up, just as the car pulled up to Regine Nails, she was worked up in a real huff. She liked this nail salon because they catered mainly to upscale and celebrity clientele. There were private rooms downstairs where one could get a spa mani/pedicure done in peace. She wasn't about to get all glammed up just to have her nails done, but since she'd become a "somebody" she couldn't roll up wearing sweats and no makeup at the local nail place like she used to. There was always some nosy bitch who'd stare rudely, obviously recognizing her, no doubt thinking, "She doesn't look so hot in person."

Even though all the manicurists at Regine were Asian, they wore name tags that read Maryann or Linda or Jane or Betty, and that's what they were called, even though everyone knew damn well that their real names were Yung Cho or something. They always accommodated Mimi when she had to switch appointments at the last minute because her schedule had gotten crazy. Whenever she turned up they all greeted her merrily. "Mi-mi! Mi-mi!" they'd sing like a pack of cooing doves. If she had recently been featured in a magazine, Linda or Jane or whoever would pull it out from the salon's extensive collection of glossies and wave it in her face. "Look so pre-teee, Mi-mi!"

They had her *Seventeen* cover framed over the cash register. She had autographed it for them: *To all my girls at Regine Nails, Y'all are the bomb for real! Much love, Mimi.*

There had been other covers—*Teen People, Vibe, Elle Girl, Allure, Maxim, The Source* (styled by Misa Hylton-Brim for their sexy issue). And right after the honeymoon she'd be shooting the most coveted one of all: the cover of *Vogue*. Lamont almost ejaculated on himself when word came down that she'd gotten it. "See," he'd said, enormously proud of himself, "I told you we needed André. He helped us get this!" It was going to be shot by Mario Testino for the couples issue, so Lamont would be featured in the pictures inside. He had already ordered twenty new suits in anticipation.

He had just negotiated her Candie's ad. He was in talks with Pepsi for a spokeswoman deal. "If anyone catches you anywhere near a can of Coke, I'll beat your ass," he'd warned. And a deal with Revlon for a makeup and hair contract was about to go through. She was never allowed to wear her hair curly. Her long, straight blond hair had become her trademark look. It had gotten so damaged and thin it was almost see-through, so they'd had to put in extensions. She wanted to go back to brown but her hair color was a major image change and Lamont wanted to unveil her new look at exactly the right moment. Maybe in the Revlon ad. And he was talking to a garment manufacturer about getting her a clothing line. He was thinking of calling it Mimi Jeans.

All this was great news for her because she hadn't seen a penny from her album, even though it had sold 1.5 million copies. All those recoupables. And they'd discovered at the last minute that Daryl had used a bunch of samples that he hadn't cleared permission for. It was too late to go through the proper channels to get the rights since the album was already done and scheduled for release. So they had no leverage when they tried to settle with the artists whose music Daryl had sampled. It wound up being very expensive. "It's a stick-up!" Lamont had fumed. Witchy got fired over that. Two months later, after sufficient groveling, Lamont hired him back.

The last year felt like a blur of promotional appearances, shows, television interviews, photo shoots. She had gone on a thirty-city tour with all the guys on the TLE label. It was called "Triple Large presents...the Beauty and the Beasts." Billy Tha Kid, whose album *Wanted* had come out just at the end of the tour, did spot dates with his posse, Tha Outlaw Gang. Toya came to do her hair and Kiko was doing her makeup. Then she had her assistant, Gennipha, and Alonzo was there holding everything down. And her bodyguard, Anthony, who went by the oxymoronic nickname Big Ant, followed her everywhere like a 330-pound black cloud.

Some pampering was exactly what Mimi needed right now but she couldn't imagine sitting still for two hours. So she asked the driver to turn around and take her all the way back downtown. She wanted to go home. She needed Lamont.

She called her regular girl, Betty, apologized for canceling, and rescheduled for three days later—with all the wedding plans, it was the first day she thought she'd be able to squeeze in time to get her silk wrap repaired. She tried to call Lamont at the apartment but she kept getting the answering service. When she'd left earlier to meet Ally C. for brunch, Lamont had already gone out to play basketball with the guys. Since it was Sunday, Carlos had the day off, so she couldn't just call the car and get Carlos to find him like she usually did. She tried his cell but it went straight to voicemail. Where was he? She was hoping he could talk some sense into Angela.

She decided to call someone who she knew would share her feelings about her mother's news. "Vanessa," she said as soon as her future sister-in-law answered. "You won't believe this...my mother just told me she's getting married!"

"To that hideous, low-class *slob?*" Vanessa asked in disgust.

"The very one! Can you believe it?" Mimi felt better already.

Vanessa had met Angela and Jerry when they'd been invited to join the whole Jackson clan in the Bahamas for Mother's Day. It was quite a mix.

They stayed at the Atlantis hotel and casino. Mama Jackson didn't seem to mind Angela but she loathed Jerry Morelli on sight. For dinner on the first night with the fashion-conscious family, Jerry showed up sporting a wide-collared, powder blue shirt under a ratty, tan polyester leisure suit. Since Mimi made no secret of her contempt for Jerry, no one else felt the need to befriend him. Only Alonzo, feeling sorry for him, tried to make conversation. After they learned he was a used car salesman, they liked him even less, if that was possible.

After dinner, Angela and Jerry watched in awe as Mama Jackson, sitting at the head of the table swathed in a white linen Donna Karan caftan and palazzo pants that she'd ordered at Berdgorf's trunk show, received her Mother's Day gifts. As if approaching the pope, one by one each family member humbly walked up to confer his or her offering and give Mama "some sugar," though Vanessa only submitted to a drive-by of an air kiss. There were no joint gifts. Vanessa, Alonzo, Pedro, Lamont, Mimi, and, in absentia, Imani—who'd acquired all the gifts and signed the cards with the givers' names—

made separate tributes. After the first gift was unwrapped, Angela and Jerry caught on that they were to applaud like audience members on *The Price Is Right* as everyone else was doing. The last to pay tribute was Pedro, who handed Grandma a picture of the new silver Mercedes that would be waiting for her when she got home. Mama jubilantly exclaimed: "I am so blessed!"

The Atlantis grounds were extensive and everyone ran around for the long weekend doing their own thing, meeting up in the evenings for dinner. Boy, did Alonzo stay in that casino! He was at the high-roller tables almost the entire time. One day he won $75,000 and Vanessa immediately pocketed some of his chips, cashed them in, and bought a bunch of stuff in the Gucci store in the hotel's high-end shopping plaza. She was thoughtful enough to buy Angela a bag with some of Alonzo's winnings. By the end of the trip, all the rest of the chips he'd won were back in the welcoming hands of the Atlantis casino.

Mama tried her luck at the dollar slots—hitting once—but mainly she spent a lot of quality time with her grandbaby. She doted on him, often carrying the four-year-old around on her good hip as if he were a newborn baby. With the whole family there, Mama declared it ridiculous for Vanessa to bring along one of her nanny trio. But since Alonzo, who usually took PJ with him everywhere, went into a trance when he got within ten paces of a gambling spot, Mama's watchful eye was needed. Even when Vanessa was present with her son at the beach or by the pool, Mama had to stay alert so PJ wouldn't turn up drowned.

Two days in, everything was going along swell. Angela wasn't annoying Mimi too much because she was off following Jerry around. They went on some sightseeing tours together and Mimi spotted them one afternoon walking hand-in-hand down the beach. She wanted to vomit. She could tell Jerry thought he'd hit the fucking jackpot. He was being way nicer to Angela than Mimi had *ever* seen but it wasn't genuine. Angela might not see it, but Mimi sure as hell could.

Then when it came time to check out, the jig was up for ol' Jer.

They all assembled in the lobby to go to the airport while Lamont settled the bill. The total was astronomical—which wasn't a shock—but it was a little more than he expected. He scanned the itemizations and thought he found a discrepancy. Lamont quietly pointed it out to the manager, who had been very solicitous all week, giving their group top-notch service. After a long, hushed conference in the corner of the lobby, it came to light that Jerry had, over the course of the four days, charged *twenty thousand dollars* in chips at the casino to Lamont's open line of credit!

Mimi didn't think it possible for Lamont to escalate to such a level of stark raving madness, but he revved up *real* quick. He got right up in Jerry's face, waving the eighty-eight-page hotel bill. "YOU MOTHERFUCKIN' SWINDLER!" he snarled.

Angela was quivering with embarrassment and confusion. Jerry hadn't told her what he'd done.

"When we got here you said, 'Anything you want,'" Jerry sputtered.

Alonzo had to physically restrain Lamont from knocking Jerry the fuck out in the middle of the Atlantis lobby. And restraining his brother was no small feat because Lamont was still fighting the battle of the bulge and losing. (He hadn't even brought his swimming trunks because he would *not* make a spectacle of himself near beach or pool!)

"*Everyone* was charging stuff," Jerry argued, unbowed. "You said it was okay."

That was true. Clothes purchased at the hotel shops, drinks ordered by the hotel pool, meals eaten at one of the eight dining spots on the property, pay-per-view movies watched in the rooms, chips needed to have some fun in the casino were all charged to their rooms and billed back to Lamont's Amex Centurion card. It was the long-standing rule of the Jackson family: Lamont always paid. Trouble was, Jerry wasn't part of the Jackson family.

Lamont tried to chill. People were staring. Alonzo let go of him and Lamont walked over to Jerry. He got very close, put out his hand, and said, "Give me my fucking money."

"Your brother lost seventy-five grand!" Jerry cried, sinking farther into the abyss.

"Hold the baby," Mama yelped, handing Pedro off to Vanessa. Alonzo had to restrain his mother as she tried to slap Jerry with her newly purchased straw hat.

"That was *his* money," Lamont raged. That was one thing Lamont appreciated about 'Zo. Lamont paid his brother's salary and took care of him in a big way, but 'Zo never took advantage. Alonzo never *asked* for anything, never *expected* things, which is why Lamont generously gave to him. "And even if it wasn't, he's my brother!" He lowered his voice. "Now give me my fucking money."

"I don't have it," Jerry said, disturbingly unrepentant. "I lost it in the casino."

"All of it?" Lamont pressed, trying to figure out if this guy had huge balls or was slightly retarded.

Angela started crying.

"Yep," Jerry said, then gave Lamont a hey-no-hard-feelings punch in the arm. "Sorry, big guy."

Jerry Morelli didn't know squat about "rap" or "hip-hop" or whatever they called it. When the local papers would do stories about Mimi, they would always mention Lamont Jackson, describing him as a rap impresario. Impresario? What was that? Made him sound like some kinda wizard or something. Jerry looked the word up in the dictionary. It had two definitions:

1. One who sponsors or produces entertainment, especially the director of an opera company. 2. A manager; a producer.

Opera? That was way off. And the second definition didn't make this guy sound like such a hotshot. All Jerry knew was that Lamont Jackson was one big black dude with one big wad of greenbacks. And the man wasn't afraid to spend it. Mimi was living high off the hog in his big penthouse in New York, wearing a ring that looked like an Elizabeth Taylor castoff, and she'd become famous just like the black dude had promised. And did Mimi really deserve it? Not in Jerry's opinion. Not the way she treated *him*, the only father figure she'd ever known. Lamont wouldn't be hurting for the money and Jerry thought when a man said "anything you want" he should stick by his word.

"You lost it all," Lamont repeated nastily, as Alonzo hustled Mama out to the limo. "Figures. Just like the loser you are." A darkness clouded Lamont's eyes. "I paid for you and your girlfriend to fly down here first class," he whispered ominously. "I put you up in a five-star hotel, fed you, entertained you, and treated you better than anyone else ever will. And you turn around and try to *rape* me?" Lamont squinted at this woefully ignorant man who had burned the bridge that could have taken him to the promised land. "Look," he said, putting a firm hand on Jerry's slender shoulder. "You've had your fun.

Now go back to Toledo and stay there. Do not call my house. Do not even *think* about calling my house. Do not show your face to me again. You have disrespected me and that will happen only once." Lamont shook Angela's hand. "Take care, Angela." Then he gave Jerry's shoulder a quick, sharp pound. "Good-bye."

Lamont turned and walked out to the limo. The hotel manager hurried behind him trying to absolve the hotel of any wrongdoing. The manager returned a few minutes later to find Jerry and Angela, looking disoriented, in the enormous lobby. He told them abruptly that they would have to take the next shuttle bus and ushered them out a side door.

You could have heard a pin drop in the limo. Lamont was obviously fuming and no one wanted to fan that fire. Mama finally broke the tension by exclaiming, "And that's why I stick to the dollar slots, children!" Everyone, including Lamont, laughed.

Mimi felt horrifyingly humiliated but Lamont told her on the plane not to worry about it, it wasn't her fault. And he said he would continue paying the mortgage on Angela's new house because it wasn't Angela's fault either. He didn't think Angela was malicious, just clueless.

Jerry's name never crossed his lips on the whole flight home and no one had mentioned Jerry's existence in Lamont's presence since.

But Mimi was going to have to mention it today. As the car pulled up to the apartment, Mimi couldn't imagine how he would react to Angela's hideous news.

◆

CHAPTER 47

Nuthin' but a "G" Thang

MIMI VAGUELY RECALLED that Lamont was supposed to be getting a massage today. He hated to be disturbed during his twice-weekly rubdowns. He said it was the only time he had to relax. Too bad because he was going to be disturbed today. This nonsense with Jerry was enough to make her pull out what was left of her damaged hair!

As she stomped up to the main floor, she could hear New Age meditation music wafting down from the gym upstairs. Olga gave her a massage occasionally. She had magic fingers for sure but that music was the worst. During her sessions, Mimi picked out the CDs. Something low-key like India Arie or Sade.

Lamont had an extensive collection of soothing, instrumental music upstairs in the gym. The thing Mimi found most surprising about him was that he never listened to hip-hop except when an album needed his approval. Mimi had become a certified hip-hop head. Jay-Z, Biggie, Tupac, Nas, Eminem, all that. She knew every word and pumped her shit nonstop. Lamont didn't like that. He was always turning down the volume in the house or putting in his Jill Scott CDs.

"You listen to too much hip-hop," he'd once said, sounding like an out-of-touch parent speaking to his teenager.

"Who are you to talk!" Mimi scoffed. "You're Mr. Hip-Hop!"

"I know the difference between art and life. You want to live those lyrics."

"Whatever," she'd said. He was just mad because she was always joking that 50 Cent was her "baby daddy."

Then he'd said huffily, "I should let you go live with one of those rappers for a week. Let one of them niggas beat your ass, then you'll coming running back. 'Lamont! Lamont! Save me!' "

For Lamont, hip-hop was a capitalist venture, not an idle pleasure.

Now she climbed the winding staircase, and even though the calming strains of that Muzak were getting louder, she was feeling anything but tranquil. She knew Lamont was going to be furious about this news, too. He hated Jerry as much as she did. She got to the top step and opened her mouth to launch into her tirade about Jerry, not caring at all that she was ruining the mood.

She took in the scene before her and blinked rapidly, her mouth agape. No sounds came out. Lamont was lying on his back on the Gucci massage table. He didn't see her. But Olga did. Stooped over Lamont, her icy blue eyes met Mimi's. Olga's one free hand, the one not busy massaging the shaft of Lamont's erect dick, rushed to her lips and she gasped, "Oops."

Mimi stood frozen on the top step until Lamont craned his neck and looked her way. Then she turned, raced down the steps, and ran into their bedroom. Without thinking, she stepped into the steam shower and crouched down in the corner, pulling her knees up to her chest. She didn't cry. She didn't tremble. A deathly calm swept over her and she just sat there.

She could hear Lamont calling her name. He sounded like he was right outside the bathroom but then the sound of his voice became distant. He must not have seen her and gone away. Good. Let him search every room in this place looking for her. She had nothing to say. She looked down at her left hand. She'd taken her ring off this morning because she was going to get her nails done. Perfect. It was going to stay off. There was no way he could talk his way out of this.

All those rumors she'd heard were true! And she'd been away so much. During The Beauty and the Beasts tour, Lamont flew in only for the fun cities—Miami, L.A., Atlanta. He was always so busy but he called her every night. Now she could only imagine what he'd been doing and with whom. . . . So why'd he make her have all that phone sex?

Well, there was not going to be any wedding! And to think she had almost signed that horrible prenup Lamont had drawn up. It said they would each keep whatever assets they possessed when they entered the marriage. But she had been working and working and still she had no assets! All she had was a triple large debt!

Lamont soon returned wearing just his Nike mesh shorts and stood, confounded, in the middle of the bathroom, until he squinted at the dimpled glass of the steam shower. He pulled the door open.

"Baby, what are you doing?"

Mimi pulled her arms tighter around her bent legs, gazing unseeingly at the tile.

"What are you doing in there?" Lamont repeated.

"What were *you* doing up there?" she said in a faraway voice that sounded like it was coming from an invisible girl on the other side of the palatial bathroom.

"I was getting a massage," he said evenly, stepping inside the shower and letting the door close behind him. "Get up."

She stayed on the ground, gazing at the tile.

"I don't know what you think you saw but..."

Still not looking up, she said in a detached voice, "I saw her bending over your hard dick with her mouth wide open."

"That's not what you saw," Lamont said, hovering over her.

She gazed up at him. "What?"

Lamont held firm. "That's not what you saw."

"Don't tell me I didn't see what I know I fucking saw," she shouted, looking up at his massive, hairy chest. "She was about to suck your dick!"

"No she wasn't," he snapped. "And don't start accusing me of things based on speculation. You have no concrete evidence."

"Oh puh-leeze," she snorted disgustedly. She scrambled to her feet. "Okay, well here's what I do know for sure," she fumed, an inch from his nose. "Your hard dick was in her hand. So maybe it wasn't a blow job *yet* but it was a hand job for sure!"

He stepped back a little until his bare back touched the shower wall. His shoulders fell into a resigned pose. "It wasn't a hand job," he said. "It was a full-body massage!"

When he had the nerve to smile, she violently shrieked, "I HAAAAATE YOU!"

There was a long silence until all the rage and shock and hurt and humiliation she was feeling came rushing out in a torrent of tears.

Lamont tried to wrap his powerful arms around her. She began to frantically swat him away and he felt one of her nails catch him on the cheek. He continued steadily toward her through a flurry of slaps until she was pressed tightly against his chest.

"Don't say that," he breathed anxiously. "Don't *ever* say that. You love me and I love you."

"She's been coming here twice a week the whole time I've known you," she whimpered through her gasping sobs.

"Don't make something out of nothing," he said in a stern voice, holding her in a suffocating embrace. He stroked her long hair while she buried her face in his shoulder. "That Russian bitch is nothing. She's the help. She *was* the help. She's gone and she's never coming back." He kissed her on the back of her head, squeezing her closer. "You mean everything to me. I love *you*, baby. I love you and only you."

Her body went limp and they slid down to the floor with his arms still wrapped around her.

"Daddy's here," he whispered urgently and repeatedly. He scooped her up until she was curled on his lap, sobbing uncontrollably. "Daddy loves you." He gently covered her face with kisses.

And she cried and cried and cried...

CHAPTER 48

◆

It's Like That

"YOU'RE NOT ON MY SCHEDULE," Lamont said, chomping a green apple. "And I have to get to the airport. So I hope this is important."

Sum Wun closed the door to Lamont's office. Twenty-three years old, round-faced with smooth pale skin and a silky black ponytail, women bought his debut album, *I Am...*, because they liked him. He was cute, baby-faced. Guys bought it because they liked his clever lyrics. His album told a complete story from beginning to end, every song another chapter. It had just gone double platinum.

They'd had his party at Mr. Chow. When Sum Wun asked why, Lamont answered: "Because you're Chinese, nigga!" Sum informed him that he was Vietnamese. Lamont said, "Well, same difference." Lamont had been touting him as "the Chinese Eminem," but after that he amended it to "the Asian Eminem" to make him happy and cover all demographics.

"Yeah, it is important," Sum said and took a seat on the sofa. His lyrics were raw and aggressive and he had an angry *persona,* but in person he spoke in a near whisper.

"So, hit me with it," Lamont said impatiently. He was flying to L.A. today. Last-minute trip. There was some problem with a soundtrack they were supposed to be doing. The producers were talking about giving it to Bad Boy. He had to go smooth things over.

"Lamont, I came here to tell you that..." Sum began nervously.

Lamont took a loud chomp of the apple, his mind wandering to thoughts of his wedding, which was less than two weeks away. Six hundred guests at The Plaza. Jesse Jackson was doing the ceremony. Mama was holding everything down so well that he told her she should become a wedding planner. *InStyle* had the exclusive on the star-studded affair but there would be lots of additional press. There better be for all the money he was spending. The tab was close to a million. But with all the press, he was writing a lot of that off as a business expense.

Thank God Mama didn't know that Mimi was barely speaking to him after catching him with Olga. But Lamont was trying his damnedest to patch things up before Mama sensed any tension. This quick trip to L.A. might be the best thing for him and Mimi. It would give them some space. When he was back, it would be full speed ahead to the big day and then happily ever after.

"What did you say?" Lamont asked because he hadn't been paying any attention.

"I want to come out," Sum repeated.

"Of what?" Lamont said. He tossed the apple core at the aluminum trash can under his desk and missed.

"I want to come out publicly."

"I'm not getting you," Lamont said, bending underneath the desk to grab the core.

"Monty, I'm gay."

From behind the desk, Lamont's face slowly became visible again. His hand grabbed at the mahogany edge as he steadied himself and fell back in his chair. He sat for a moment, staring blankly at Sum. Then it looked as if he were doing an improvisational acting exercise and the teacher had just said, "You have just received terrible and shocking news...Go!" In a matter of five seconds, his eyes registered astonishment, horror, disbelief, sadness, confusion. Was he hearing things? He thought Sum Wun, his multiplatinum-selling artist, had just told him that he was... *gay?*

"Monty," Sum repeated, "I'm gay."

Lamont's distant gaze become very direct. "So am I," he seethed, his unforgiving eyes demanding, *Take. It. Back.* "I'm getting married in two weeks and I'm about to take over the head spot at Augusta. I'm happier than a motherfucka."

Sum let out a relieved chuckle. "So you're cool with it?"

"No," Lamont said, stiff as a board. "I was joking because I know *you're* joking."

"I'm not."

"Yes," Lamont told him, "you are."

"Listen, yo," Sum said. "I wanted to tell you first. But I'm thinking of going on Wendy's show and coming out."

This guy wouldn't let it drop! Lamont got up and went around to the front of his desk and sat. "Sum, how are you gay? I know you, money. You are not gay!"

"How do you know?"

"You don't act gay."

"How does a gay person act?"

"You know." Lamont dangled a hand daintily. "Swishy. Effeminate. *Gay*."

"I act like that in private."

"You do?" Then a furious, "No you don't!"

"No," Sum said, smiling. He'd said that only to get a rise out of
Lamont. "I act the same way in private as I act with you. Some guys
are femme, some are as macho and masculine as you."

Lamont cringed at the comparison, which he was disinclined to
believe. "You know how I know you're not gay?" he said, refusing to
move toward acceptance.

"How?"

Lamont hustled over to his CD collection and grabbed *I Am...*
He started waving it. "This!" he boomed. "You got all these songs on
here talking about how you hate faggots!"

"I never said I hated fags."

He hadn't? Lamont had listened to it fully only once but people
had written about it. The homophobic lyrics. There had been controversy about it that had helped Sum get a lot of press. *Is it gonna sell
records?* It did, so it was all good.

"I was just using the word to flip it, you know?"

"No, I don't know!"

"There's a lot of self-hatred in the homie-sexual community,"
Sum said.

"Did you just say *homie*-sexual?" Lamont murmured.

"Yeah. You know, guys who listen to hip-hop, dress hip-hop,
mess around with other dudes but claim they ain't gay. They're on the

down low. They're in denial because they say they hate fags but they *are* fags..."

Lamont turned away as if from the scene of a gory accident. "Look, money," he said, waving a cease-and-desist hand, "I do *not* need a critical analysis of the modern-day homie-sexual. Dead that."

"Did you know that kind of behavior contributes to the spread of HIV infection in the African-American community and..."

"*No*, and I don't *want* to know," Lamont shouted, cringing at the mention of disease. He was being pushed too far. "And you ain't African-American, kid, so don't worry about it!"

"I'm just saying that I used the word 'fag' to flip it. You know how you and your boys say nigga? But it's not a slur when you say it to each other. Then it's like a term of endearment. I wanna do the same thing for the word 'fag.'"

"You thought this all out?" Lamont said, anger charging up to fury. "This is going to be your fucking *cause* now?"

"I feel like I'm living a false self, yo."

"What the fuck are you talking about?!" Lamont screamed. He threw the CD across the room, the plastic case cracking against the television. "WHAT THE FUCK ARE YOU SAYING TO ME?!"

Hearing the commotion, Imani opened the door. "Not now!" Lamont screamed, veins bulging. Imani had barely gotten the door open before she closed it again, wondering what had gotten Lamont so rattled.

"I feel like I need to represent for all the homo-thugs," Sum said, quietly but firmly holding his ground.

Lamont threw himself down on the couch in a big, despairing heap. "The hell you do," he seethed and was *this close* to adding "faggot" before he caught himself. He'd been to many AIDS charity events, a GLAAD event once because Irv Greene had invited him, but he didn't *condone* the shit! It was disgusting! Repulsive! Unnatural! It went against God's word!

Sum looked at Lamont breathing hard and wondered what was really going through his mind. "I didn't say it before because I knew I would catch heat. But now my album is out, people are feelin' me. I've proven myself. I think Wendy's show would be the move."

"Not the move," Lamont countered immediately. "Not at all."

"Why not? Why wait for somebody to out me? I should out myself."

"Who's going to out you?" Lamont asked in a panic. "People know about this?"

"Some," Sum said.

"Like who!"

"My man for one."

"Your man?" Lamont gulped hard and leaned his head back on the sofa. He rubbed his eyes with his right hand and massaged his Buddha belly with his left.

He'd gained ten pounds in the last month. But it wasn't like his normal weight gain. He felt weird, always slightly nauseous. So he'd eat, thinking it would make his stomach feel better but then he'd just feel worse. The food would sit there in his gut. He was constipated. And he was feeling more and more tired. Sluggish. So he didn't work out at all.

Then a week ago he started getting sharp pains in his stomach. It got so bad Mimi wanted him to go to the hospital. He went to sleep, curled up in bed feeling like someone was stabbing him. In the morning he was in so much pain he went straight to his doctor, sure it was an ulcer.

Dr. Linden said it was a stress-related gastrointestinal problem called gastritis. That was why he felt so bloated, like a helium-filled balloon ready for liftoff. Doc told him to put two cement blocks underneath the head of his bed to set it on a slant. That would help him keep food down at night so he could digest it completely. And he couldn't eat anything late at night. Imani got the cement blocks and set it all up perfectly. He could feel himself sliding down the mattress in his sleep and the next morning he and Mimi were halfway off the bed, the tightly tucked topsheet cradling them like a net.

The doctor put him on antibiotics and told him he had to change his eating habits. He had to cut out spicy foods and anything acidic, like orange juice. The most alarming of the doctor's orders was to *quit eating chocolate!* Instead he was supposed to take in lots of roughage, like raw carrots, salad, anything that made a crunching sound. Hence, the apple. His third of the day.

"The antibiotics are going to give you some immediate relief," Dr. Linden had said. "And changing your diet will help a lot. The gastritis could develop into something worse if you don't. But the best advice I can give you is to relax. I know that's hard for you to do, Lamont, but try. Your body is telling you something."

Lamont tried to take that advice now. He took a few deep breaths. "You have a man?" he asked evenly.

"Yeah, I told you I was gay."

"Yes, we've established that," he snapped. So much for calm. "But I thought you meant like in theory. You're a *practicing* homosexual?" Lamont couldn't mask his disgust.

"Yeah. We're in a committed relationship. Our one-year anniversary is next week."

"And you think he might sell you out to the tabloids?"

"No," Sum said defensively. His man was loyal. "But there are people who know about us."

"How many?"

"I don't know. A few."

"Wait a second," Lamont said hopefully, remembering something that gave him hope that this was a prank. "Don't you have a baby with some black chick?"

"Yeah, I do. But that was, you know..." Sum shook his head.

"What!" Lamont yelled.

"That was when I was trying to be something I wasn't. That was before I came out to myself. I was playing a role."

"No, no, no!" Lamont shouted, the full implications of this disaster sinking in. "This is not a good idea, this coming out thing. Stay in!"

"Why? I want to represent for all the..."

"Shut up!" Lamont shouted.

Sum sighed. "Lamont...I came to tell you first out of respect. I could have just gone and done it without telling you."

And I would have had your gay ass killed, Lamont thought. My God! He'd been duped! He would be a laughingstock in the industry! What was he going to do? His stomach had just been starting to feel better after the first few days of antibiotics. Now it was on fire...stab, stab, stab. He had to calm down. He had to convince Sum that this was going to hurt him. He had to talk him out of it. By any means necessary.

"Sum, you really think people are going to accept this? You think you're going to go on Wendy's show, tell the whole world you're a homo-thug and niggas are going to throw pink rice all over you when you walk down the streets?" He shook his head and spat, "Hell no! All the niggas who bought your album, your fans? They're gonna feel duped. This shit is going to ruin your career. Torpedo it. Blow it right the fuck up before your eyes. You're a great lyricist. This is your first album. There could be many more. But not if you do this. Trust me. Some things are better left unsaid."

Sum looked nervous. "You really think so?"

"I'm one hundred percent sure. You want to be gay, then do your thing, kid. But do it in private."

"Thanks," Sum said bitterly.

"Or should I say, faggot?"

Sum flinched and tried to utter an objection but Lamont spoke over him: "Term of endearment, right?" He smirked at Sum. "You're trying to redefine the word? Start with me."

"But..."

"Live your gay life," Lamont continued, "but keep that shit behind closed doors. Shut. Airtight. I'm not going to tell anyone about this conversation. Because I want to see you go on and do big things. Because I care about your career even if you don't."

"I don't know," Sum said warily. "I feel like I'm lying. I really think coming out would be okay."

"What do you want, Sum," Lamont snapped. "Money? You want money? Name your price."

"I don't want money," Sum said. "It's not about that. I want to represent for all the..."

"Stop saying that!"

Lamont got up and started looking around the office for something. He looked under the desk, under the lampshade.

Sum watched him curiously then said, "What are you doing?"

"This is one of those hidden camera shows, isn't it? Am I on that MTV show? What's it called . . . *Punk'd*," Lamont said. "*Punk'd*," he repeated, laughing at his unintended joke. Then he shouted into the air, to the cameras he hoped were hooked up in his office, "That was a good one, Ashton!"

Sum was shocked to see Lamont coming so unglued. He could tell Lamont was really waiting for Ashton Kutcher to race through the door with Imani and a full film crew. "It's not a joke," Sum said cautiously.

"Think about your kid," Lamont said, realizing he had just made a complete fool of himself. He had to get a grip. "You have a little boy, right?"

"Yeah."

"How old?"

"He's two."

"What's gonna happen when he goes to school? Everybody's gonna say, 'Your daddy's a fag!' "

Sum reluctantly agreed. "Yeah, it's going to be hard. I'm not sure how I'm going to handle that. But I have to show him that you've got to be honest about who you are."

"No," Lamont stressed. "You're going to ruin his life! And yours!"

"I'm not so sure about that."

"I am," Lamont said. "This is a terrible idea!"

Imani buzzed on the intercom. "Monty, you have to get going," her voice rang out. "You're going to miss your flight."

"Okay!" Lamont roared back. After he hurriedly threw a few

things into his leather satchel, he flopped down into his chair, out of breath. "Sum, don't say anything yet," he commanded. "We have to talk about this more. I don't think you've really thought it through. Let me strategize on it and I'll get back to you."

"Cool," Sum said and left.

Lamont felt around in the back of his bottom desk drawer for his stash of contraband chocolate. He pulled out a Snickers and tore at the wrapping, then bit it in half.

Sum Wun is a Vietnamese faggot, he thought, savoring the taste of the chocolate and caramel swirling around his tongue. *Jesus H. Christ, what is the world coming to?*

CHAPTER 49

◆

All 'n My Grill

THE NEXT DAY, Mimi walked into Regine Nails in a foul mood. The Olga incident was still weighing heavily on her mind.

The night of "the incident" she was so exhausted and wrecked she'd just fallen asleep with Lamont stroking her hair. She hadn't even told him about her mother getting married. Angela and Jerry would probably never make it to the altar anyway.

Then two nights ago, before Lamont had flown to L.A., they had argued ferociously. She threw the ring at him and told him the wedding was off. He refused to accept that. He swore up and down that nothing had ever happened with Olga. Did he think she was a born-yesterday fool? She made him answer for every rumor she had ever heard and he swore on his father's life that he had never cheated on her and never would. "Why not your mother's life?" she'd asked.

He answered her question with a question. "Mimi, why do people go on all these reality shows?"

He was always trying to change the subject when she caught him

433

doing dirt. But this was so big a departure that it caught her by surprise. She said, "Why?"

"Because they want to be famous," he'd said. "And why do women go on those stupid shows like *The Bachelor*?"

"Because they want to find a man?"

"A *rich* man," he'd said. "With me, you got both."

He always knew how to make her laugh when she didn't want to.

Then he hugged her and started singing their song. He told her he loved her. He told her she didn't even have to sign the prenuptial. *She didn't?* And then he said that it would break his heart if she ever left him. He was close to tears, which she thought was a physical impossibility for Lamont. So she forgave him and told him she loved him, too. She didn't *believe* him but she forgave him. And they both got down on the floor to look for the ring.

Truth was, her feet were turning ice cold. She was only twenty-two. Was that too young to say "I do"? She'd spent her life trying to be responsible. She'd never been able to go to a college dance, or date, or be wild, or do the things Lena, Vanessa, Jordan, and most every other girl she knew had done.

She had to ask herself: Was Lamont really "The One"? Would this be forever? It scared her that Lamont had control over her heart, her career, her finances, her entire life. And, as much as she tried to convince herself that she could trust him, catching him with Olga was like a hard slap in the face that said, *Wake up, girl!*

And she wanted to have kids one day but Lamont acted like he was allergic to children. The question of having a family came up when they went for premarital counseling. Mama made them go see her pastor, Rev. Truffant of Emmanuel Baptist in Brooklyn. The things Rev. Truffant had to say really gave Mimi pause. She could tell Lamont wasn't paying attention. He was probably tallying up how many pages they were going to get in *InStyle*. Now she wanted to go back and see where Rev. Truffant stood on "full-body massages."

She'd told Vanessa, who, not surprisingly, wasn't very sympathetic. "So?" she'd said. "Oral sex is not sex. Don't worry about it."

"Vanessa!" Mimi had wailed. "What if you caught Alonzo getting a blow job from someone else? In your apartment!"

"I'd think 'Oh goody, less work for me,'" Vanessa had said.

Kiko was more understanding. "Oh, girl, I'm sorry," she'd said sadly, like she'd seen it coming all along. Then she'd advised, "Get jewelry, treasury bills, real estate, art, anything that will appreciate in value. Now is the time to strike."

What? Mimi had thought. She didn't want any *art!* She wanted someone to commiserate with her. She wanted someone to say Lamont was an asshole and that she had every right to be filled with rage. But she wasn't going to find that someone within Lamont's circle of friends.

In a desperate bid for sympathy, she'd told her mother about it. "Men cheat sometimes," Angela had rationalized. "He loves you and you're getting married. If he said he was sorry just forgive him. And forget it." She should have known that would be Angela's response.

She had an urge to call Jordan but she was afraid of hearing her say, "I told you so." She found she was really missing Lena. They hadn't spoken in ten months. She saw her once at Swirl but they'd stayed on opposite sides of the room.

Toya said, "If you don't want to marry him, then don't." Like it was the simplest thing in the world.

"But I love him," Mimi had said reflexively.

"That doesn't mean you have to marry him," Toya said.

"But we're having six hundred guests at The Plaza!"

"Tell them it's off," Toya said.

"I can't," Mimi said. "I can't. It will all work out. He's very sorry and he's on his best behavior now."

"Now?" Toya said.

Mimi quickly ended the call because she realized she was sounding like Angela. Toya had really been there for Mimi through thick and thin. Unlike Keesha who, since Mimi's big success, had turned into Hater Numero Uno and was now pregnant with her second kid by her drug-dealing fiancé. Toya had understood when Mimi told her that Lamont had already hired backup singers for her album. Toya had given up on singing entirely, and Mimi paid for her to get her license to do hair. And when Toya came on tour with her, she made sure Toya got paid what all these "celebrity hairstylists" got. It was just like old times—except now they were riding first class all the way!

And Toya didn't make a fuss that she wasn't asked to be an actual bridesmaid in the wedding, just an attendant. Lamont had five groomsmen and there was a group decision—made by Lamont and Mama—about who Mimi's five bridesmaids would be. Vanessa, Ally C., Jordan, Kiko, and Imani made the final cut. Lamont explained there was no room for Toya in the wedding party when Mimi protested. But Mimi knew the real reason was that Toya was a size fourteen, not a four or under like the other girls. Lamont all but said he didn't think she was pretty enough and she'd ruin the wedding photos.

Wasn't the wedding day supposed to be the bride's big moment? In this case, it seemed the groom was excited enough for the both of them. To her, planning the wedding felt like a second job. And a thankless one. Mama had just called and gotten all over her case about another dress fitting. They'd had to have that big white monster altered eight times.

Mimi just wanted to go on a long vacation. Just her and Lamont. They had gone to St. Bart's for the holidays but at least twenty other people had been there, people they saw every night in New York. And Nate and Jordan had stayed in their villa with them. For their honeymoon they were going to Hawaii, but for only five days. Lamont said she had to get back to work on her new album, for which they had already recorded a few tracks.

And she could never go anywhere by herself. Just have time alone. Big Ant was waiting outside right now in the car.

All these things converged like a five-car pile-up and put her into this foul mood. Then before she could dip down to the private room with her manicurist, Anne "Prissanne" Brown was all up in her grill.

"Hello, Mimi," Anne said.

Mimi greeted her coolly. "Hey."

"Excited about the wedding?"

"Uh-huh."

"I heard the *Times* Style section is doing a story on it!"

"Uh-huh."

An awkward silence, then, "You look like you've put on a little weight."

Anne didn't mean it as an insult but as a compliment. Mimi had been working too much and not eating enough. After the tour she'd gone right back into the studio to do her remix album. She had sessions scheduled for the next several nights at the Hit Factory even though the final wedding preparations were going at breakneck speed.

But luckily she'd be working with Gemini, her buddy. Since she couldn't go out of town, what with all the wedding stuff, Gemini had flown to New York for her.

These days she had to remind herself to eat. Her normal weight was 125 but she'd lost almost twenty pounds. And on her 5′ 9″ frame that was not a good look. A month ago there'd been a picture of her on the cover of the *Globe*. It was snapped as she was coming out of a Starbucks in L.A. near where she'd been recording. Vente soy mocha in one hand, cigarette in the other, she looked haggard, bony (except for her boobs, which looked like two grapefruits stuck on her skeletal frame), and basically tore up from the floor in a shredded denim mini, tank top, and flip-flops. The tabloid headline screamed: 103 LBS! MIMI: EAT OR DIE!

Inside, the article quoted "eyewitnesses" and "insiders" who said she barely ate, only drank coffee and chain-smoked cigarettes. All true. (In New York, she had to sneak the cigarettes on the terrace and hide the butts. Lamont said they made the apartment smell, made her smell, and they were bad for her voice.) It was speculated that she had an eating disorder. Not true.

The *Globe* quoted some body image expert saying, "She desperately needs to seek professional help. If she continues to lose weight she's courting death." *Thanks, hon.* But she weighed herself that night and she was 103 pounds. Exactly. How had they known that?

That was so like Prissanne to comment on it but *not* comment on it. She decided to put her on blast. "Reading the *Globe* are we, Anne?"

"The *Globe*?" Anne said primly. "What do you mean?"

"You know what I mean," Mimi whispered aggressively. She wanted to go all Lena on her: *Bitch do you think these motherfuckers care if the shit they print is accurate?* She could picture Prissanne clutching her pearls and falling out in the middle of Regine Nails at the use of obscenities.

Instead, Mimi glared and, as condescendingly as she could, snapped, "Stop reading that trash, Anne. It's beneath you."

"Well," Anne exclaimed, her hand rushing to her chest in a flustered gesture, "I have no idea what you mean." Then as if she were accepting an apology that Mimi had never offered she said, "I know this must be a very stressful time. Good luck with everything."

"Fo' shizzle, my nizzle," Mimi said, intentionally leaving Anne bewildered. Following Betty downstairs, she smiled for the first time in days.

DOUBLE-PARKED in his Range Rover outside Luxe (formerly Heaven) that night, Alonzo beeped his horn. "What up, Nasdaq?" he called out.

Nasdaq, a thuggish and dim-witted rapper signed to Hitz, Inc., stuck his head through the open passenger window. "Hey, where's Big Man?"

"He went to L.A.," Alonzo said. "How are things in the Hitz camp?"

"Yo, I'm ready to jump ship," Nasdaq said, dangling some bait.

"I bet you are," Alonzo said.

"Man, I've known Gambino since he was Donald Jones. I was the first artist he signed."

"Damn, was it that long ago? That's going back like six years."

"Seven! And my album hasn't come out in all that time. He keeps tellin' me I'm gonna get my time to shine. He tells me, 'Just be patient.' How patient can one nigga be? I'm doing all these guest spots but I'm not seein' any real paper. Me and mine need to eat, y'know?"

Alonzo nodded for Nasdaq to move as Vanessa wobbled toward the car on Mustafa's arm. Nasdaq held the door open like he was her footman, his eyes hungrily taking in her ensemble—a microscopic denim miniskirt, stilettos, and a baby tee that read: J'ADORE DIOR. After much cooing and billing, she and Mustafa disentangled themselves for the night.

Alonzo resumed the conversation as soon as Mustafa departed. "Your boy got an album out in record time," he said as Nasdaq reclaimed his position leaning against the passenger window.

"Yo, he is *not* my boy," Nasdaq said, hoping sexy Vanessa might, for once, acknowledge his presence. "Gambino's boy, yeah. Not mine. I wish we could give him back to you."

"We don't want him."

"Who are we talking about?" Vanessa said, flipping down the mirror to check her makeup even though it was two in the morning and she was on her way home. "Let me guess..."

A week after quitting/getting fired from Triple Large, Daryl had inked a recording deal with Gambino's Hitz, Inc. label. His first album, *Country Pimpin'*, released under the name "Da Mack," was out in no time since he had already recorded most of it using studio time that he'd billed to various TLE artists. (All those exorbitant bills that Imani was always on his ass about.) His album had barely cleared platinum status but the way he strutted around you'd think it was certified triple diamond.

Alonzo had run into Gambino inside and graciously congratulated him on the success his label was enjoying. Never far from a bottle of champagne, Gambino raised his Cris in appreciation. "What can I say, nigga? My cup runneth over."

But obviously things were not coming up roses for everyone in the Hitz, Inc. camp. "Your album should have been out a long time ago," Alonzo goaded the disgruntled Nasdaq. "You serious about leaving?"

"Yeah. Dead serious. Can you talk to the Big Man?"

"Sure," Alonzo said. "But why don't you teach your boy Da Mack a lesson first?"

"Like what?" Nasdaq asked, distracted by his close proximity to Vanessa's gorgeous, bronzed legs. "And he's not my boy."

"You think he needs all that ice?" Alonzo rubbed Vanessa's legs. Other men liked to look but only he could touch. "Looks like it weighs more than he does."

Nasdaq chuckled in agreement. The size and weight of Daryl's jewels seemed to grow in direct proportion to his ego.

"And it's all tacky, ugly garbage," Vanessa added, brushing on a fresh coat of lip gloss.

"Why don't you grab some of that? Bet he'd cry like a baby," Alonzo said.

While blotting her lips, Vanessa managed to get out, "I never liked him." As if she ever liked anyone.

"Clown him," Alonzo continued. "Lamont would like that. And you need some ends, right? I know somebody who'd pay for that junk."

"That all?" Nasdaq said. "I'm on it!"

"Okay, then we'll see what we can do for you," Alonzo said.

Since she'd missed the first part of their conversation, Vanessa asked, "See what we can do about what?"

"Nasdaq wants to join the Triple Large family," Alonzo said, turning the key in the ignition.

At last, Vanessa turned her liquid gaze on Nasdaq. He stepped away from the car and smiled hopefully. "We'll see," she said and the corners of her glossy mouth curled up into a faint smile.

CHAPTER 50

◆

Passing Me By

"GEM, IT'S ME."

"Yeah, I know." Mimi's name had come up on his cell. She'd just been sitting next to him in the studio. She'd said she was going to the bathroom. "What's the problem?"

"Meet me downstairs in five minutes. I need to get away from Big Ant."

Five minutes later, Gemini walked out of the Hit Factory and saw Mimi huddled in a doorway down the block, sucking on a cigarette, with her blue Yankees cap pulled down low over her Vuitton headscarf. Her roots were growing out so they had to be covered.

"Is this how it is?" he said. "You have to run away from your watchdog?"

"A damn shame, ain't it?" She stomped out the cigarette and started walking up the block.

"Where are we going?"

"To eat. I need food."

"You walk? I thought you'd have a carriage waiting."

"I want to go to Virgil's for barbecue," she said, continuing to walk up the block. "It's not far."

Reluctantly Gem followed.

"I can't believe you left The Funk Shack," Mimi said thirty minutes later, gnawing ravenously on a plate of ribs.

"You couldn't come to me, so I came to you. As a favor."

"And I happen to know you're getting triple your usual fee."

Gem nodded. "And that."

"I was going to come up for your wedding anyway," Gemini said, shrugging, "so I can kill two birds with one stone."

"And you're staying at The Four Seasons. You're ballin' out of control."

"Your label is paying."

"I don't want to work tonight. Let's go to Foyer!"

"Foyer?"

"It's a club. It's hip-hop night!"

"I don't like clubs. I'd rather go back to the studio. You go. Just come back later."

"Go with who? By myself?"

"You must have a lot of friends here."

"Geeeem," she pleaded. "It'll be fun. We'll listen to some music, have a few drinks..."

"I don't drink."

"You'll have a soda and we'll have a little fun. And then we'll go back to work later."

"Fine," Gem said wearily, as if he'd just agreed to spend the day picking cotton in the hot sun.

Two hours later, Mimi was on the dance floor, feeling lovely after four Caprihanas, shouting...

I don't know what you heard about me
But a bitch can't get a dollar out of me
No Cadillac, no perms, you can't see
That I'm a motherfuckin' P-I-M-P

Gem was in front of her, looking glum, rocking imperceptibly on his heels.

Mustafa showed up with Vanessa, who was looking aggressively fabulous in her diamond DIVA necklace (she'd had it made), a white baby tee that was airbrushed with the slogan "HATED BY MANY, CONFRONTED BY NONE" (a gift from a stylist), and tiny red satin jogging shorts with white piping that said KISS on one cheek and MY on the other (from Patricia Field). Coming and going, she looked like a walking billboard that was advertising bitchiness.

Vanessa gave the unfamiliar man with Mimi the once-over and let her disdain show. Gem was wearing a plain white T-shirt with a fresh barbecue stain, extra baggy gray sweatpants, and plastic Adidas slides over sweatsocks. Vanessa looked like she wanted to make a citizen's arrest for the fashion crimes he was committing. His boxers were visible and they weren't even Calvin or Ralph or Tommy! They looked like Hanes!

When Mimi introduced her companion, Vanessa initially couldn't be bothered to shake his hand. Then Mimi stressed, "Gemini the *superproducer.*" Vanessa spent the next two hours cuddled next to him in a booth like they were best friends. She identified him as a potential client for her yet-to-open image consultancy firm. After an hour, feeling Gemini was sufficiently befriended, Vanessa and Mustafa split to move on to Chromosome.

Gem wanted to leave, too, but Mimi wasn't having it. He finally got her outside, practically carried her.

"Where do you live?" Gem asked her. "You need to go home."

"Downtown," Mimi gurgled as he tried to hold her up. The Foyer doorman hailed them a cab.

"Where downtown?" Gem kept asking her. "What's your address?"

"Downtown," Mimi kept answering. "Downtown."

Gem dug into her purse for her phone as the cab driver waited impatiently for an address.

"What are you doing?" Mimi wheezed.

"I'm calling Ant," Gem said, scrolling through her numbers. "Don't you have his number in here?"

Mimi fell across Gem's lap. "Don't!" She grabbed for the door handle. "I think I'm gonna be sick."

"No sick in my car," the driver yelled, looking over into the back-seat. "Get out!"

Gem opened the door but Mimi only coughed while the Foyer doorman and some random clubgoers watched sympathetically.

When she fell back onto the seat, Gem told the driver, "The Four Seasons please." Twenty minutes later, Mimi was passed out in his bed.

She woke up at eight in the morning. "Gem," she whispered, realizing she was staring at his bony back. "My head hurts."

"That's what you deserve," he said. "Where is Lamont, by the way? I don't think he's going to appreciate your not coming home last night. And don't involve me in your drama!"

"Don't worry," Mimi whispered. "He's in L.A. He's not getting back until tomorrow night."

Gem rolled over. "You better get going," he said, careful to stay on his side of the bed. "I'll see you later. We're working tonight."

He looked over as his cell phone began vibrating on the bed-side table. He answered. "Hi Imani," he said, making a face at Mimi. He listened for a second. "Oh really? Well, we went to dinner last night and then to some club but we couldn't go back to the session." He put his middle finger up to Mimi. "Your princess was too woozy to work so we just called it a night. I'm sure she's at home asleep."

He hung up and said, "Your peoples are looking for you."

"Whatever," Mimi said, crawling back under the covers.

"What are you doing?" Gem said irritably, wanting her to leave. He did a lot of business with Lamont's label and he wished she'd quit with these little girl games that could adversely affect his income!

"I'm hungry," she said. "Order us some breakfast."

Gem leaned over and grabbed the room service menu. "Here," he said, tossing it at her. "Order it yourself."

MAMA JACKSON strolled into the cavernous lobby of the Four Seasons hotel with Jeremy, the wedding planner, trailing close on Mama's Stuart Weitzman heels.

"Remind me why we're having breakfast here?" Jeremy asked.

"Because I hate The Plaza," Mama replied. The Plaza was a fine place to have a bar mitzvah or a wedding, it had old-fashioned prestige that way, but she'd never stay there or dine there. It wasn't her style. The indisputably more chic Four Seasons was.

"So Mimi has her final fitting today?" Jeremy asked once they were seated in the dining area off the lobby.

"Yes," Mama said. "Vera has taken wonderful care of us."

Jeremy looked up and squinted across the lobby. "Hey, there she is now."

"Vera?" Mama exclaimed. But when she turned to look, she didn't see Vera Wang. Instead, there went the bride. Mimi was hurrying through the lobby, looking a fright.

Jeremy threw his arm in the air to attract Mimi's attention but Mama reached over and pulled it back down. "Don't make a scene, Jeremy." She picked up her cell and dialed Mimi's number, thinking, *Why is my future daughter-in-law sneaking out of a hotel at ten in the morning looking so bedraggled?*

When Lamont had called Mama this morning from L.A., he'd said that Mimi had left the studio last night and never returned and then she hadn't answered her phone all night. Now Mama had an awful feeling.

Lamont's fiancée was, sad to say, no Kendra. Mimi was always far too busy to go shopping or to eat lunch with Mama. And she'd become overtly disinterested in the wedding preparations.

"It's a fairy tale any woman would love to star in," Mama had gently scolded her at the last dress fitting. "Appreciate how lucky you are, dear."

Being an understanding woman, Mama allowed Mimi her tantrums here and there. It was just that things had begun to overwhelm her. Lamont was happier than Mama had ever seen him. That was all that mattered.

Mimi had just disappeared from view when Mama heard her answer her cell phone. Mama detected the end of a yawn in her "Hello?"

"Tired, dear?"

"Yes," Mimi said. "I just woke up. I'm...I'm still in bed."

Oh really? Mama thought, wondering what was going on here.

"I know we have the fitting at one," Mimi said. "I won't be late."

"Perfect," Mama said. "See you there."

She looked at Jeremy. He didn't need to be involved in this any further. "Excuse me, Jeremy."

He nodded, thinking she was going to get up. After he'd sat there for thirty seconds, he suddenly realized she wanted *him* to leave, so he did.

"Alonzo," Mama said, after reaching her son at home. "Where is Vanessa?"

"In bed," he said.

"Get her up. Now."

Vanessa got on.

"Were you out with Mimi last night?" Mama questioned.

"Yes," Vanessa answered groggily. "I saw her at Foyer."

"And then where did you go?"

"I left. She stayed there with Gemini."

"With Gemini. Who is that?"

"A producer," Vanessa said, waking up now. Mama never asked to speak to her. "Why?"

Mama wondered if she should reveal anything to Vanessa, then decided Vanessa might be useful for once. "Because Lamont couldn't reach her last night and he was worried. Big Ant said she disappeared on him."

"She wasn't with Ant at Foyer," Vanessa confirmed.

"And now I just spied her leaving The Four Seasons."

Vanessa was completely awake now. "You don't say?" she smiled.

"I'm distressed," Mama said, uncomfortable admitting that to Vanessa. But she could hear in Vanessa's voice that she was holding back information. "What can you tell me?"

Vanessa lay in bed, twirling a strand of hair around her index finger, wondering how she should answer that loaded question. Things she considered: Marc Jacobs was talking about naming a new bag after Lamont's Triple Large princess. *And* Mimi was getting a *Vogue* cover. *And* Revlon was about to sign her to a contract (and not to hawk some disgusting antiaging product). *And* word was that Lamont was forgoing the prenuptial. Lately, all Vanessa heard was bad news.

Mimi kept whining about the Olga incident. Just to shut her up Vanessa had said, "If you're so mad about it, get even." Maybe she had. But with that bum Gemini? Mama thought Mimi was innocent and sweet while the old witch was always on *Vanessa's* case. But had Vanessa ever cheated on Alonzo? No, she had not. Not with another *man*.

"All I know is that Gemini is staying at The Four Seasons," Vanessa said casually.

Mama loudly gulped air.

"But we shouldn't jump to conclusions," Vanessa said.

Mama sat up very straight. "What else are we to think?"

"What was she wearing?" Vanessa asked, looking to seal the deal.

"Jeans, a little pink jacket, and a baseball cap over a long scarf."

"Hmmm," Vanessa remarked, attempting to sound disappointed. "That's the very same thing she had on last night."

Mama hung up, wondering what she should do now.

Vanessa went back to sleep.

CHAPTER 51

◆

Scenario

ALL THE BRIDESMAIDS MET at Mama's place at ten o'clock that night. Attendance was mandatory. Imani, Ally C., Kiko, and Jordan were chatting and nibbling at the cheese plate. Vanessa, arriving fifteen minutes late, went straight for the wine.

Now that everyone was present, Mama took a seat in her chintz armchair and banged a heavy Steuben crystal paperweight on the coffee table like a gavel. "Meeting is called to order."

A hush fell over the living room. They all assumed this was yet another wedding prep meeting. Mama was running a tight ship.

Never one to beat around the bush, Mama announced, "Mimi Jean is cheating on my son!"

Imani gasped, "No way!"

As the other women's jaws dropped, Vanessa sang, "It's true!"

Mama hated to agree with Vanessa on anything but she seconded that statement. "Yes, it *is* true." She told them about seeing Mimi this morning and then Vanessa supplied her supporting evidence.

Annoyed that she had been summoned to be part of this cabal, Jordan said, "You don't know anything for sure. Maybe she has friends or family staying at the hotel for the wedding."

"She has no family," Mama insisted. "Her only family coming to the wedding is her mother. That swindler Jerry is banned."

"She has no other relatives coming to her own wedding?" Jordan said.

"No," Mama replied. "Her father is dead and there's no one on his side." In a casual, matter-of-fact tone, she added, "After Angela hooked up with Mimi's father, her people called her a nigga-lover and never spoke to her again."

Ally C., the only white person in the room, was the only one who looked taken aback at this.

Jordan continued to come to Mimi's defense. "Maybe one of her friends is staying there."

"She has only a few friends coming," Imani admitted, feeling weepy. How could Mimi do this to Lamont? "I should know. We're paying for them all."

"And she lied to me," Mama said. "I called her from The Four Seasons and she said she was still in bed."

At the fitting that afternoon, watching Mimi spin around in her gorgeous tulle princess gown, Mama had felt a heaviness in her heart. Poor Lamont. She wasn't sure if she should tell him. He was so happy and the wedding plans were past the point of no return.

What to do? she'd fretted. *What to do?*

Now she put the question to the room at large. "So the question on the table is . . . do we tell Lamont?"

Imani said, "No. It will break his heart."

Ally C. said, "No. The press is locked in. *InStyle* is covering it for the magazine and the television show, and the *InStyle* wedding issue with Mimi on the cover is hitting newsstands tomorrow! Absolutely not!"

Vanessa disagreed: "Of course you have to tell him. You have no choice!"

Jordan said, "I'm abstaining. It's none of our business."

"My children will always be my business," Mama stated firmly, preparing to cast the deciding vote. Really hers was the only vote. She was pretty sure Lamont had stepped out on Kendra. She was pretty sure he'd stepped out on everyone he'd ever dated. That *was* none of her business. Lamont had never promised those women anything and that was just his independent streak rearing its head. Marriage, however, was a holy sacrament.

Maybe Mimi had gotten her swerve on with this Gemini person. She had obviously been suffering from a hangover today. Lamont was always on her about drinking too much. She couldn't hold her liquor. Perhaps it was a mistake of youth, an itch that had been scratched. Lamont had scratched many an itch, maybe it was karma that she satisfy her own.

Mimi had certainly seemed more excited about the wedding today than she had anytime during the previous few weeks. Mama knew she and Lamont were really in love. Lamont was happy and she wanted him to stay that way. What her boy didn't know wouldn't hurt him. She looked around at the girls and handed down her verdict.

"No," she said. Who did Vanessa think she was, telling Mama she had no choice? "We won't tell him."

But she *would* tell Mimi after the honeymoon that such indiscretions would not be tolerated in the future. She'd let this one slide. But from now on Big Ant was going to be following her everywhere.

Mama banged her makeshift gavel. "Meeting adjourned."

LAMONT RECLINED BACK in his first class seat on the red-eye to New York and smiled. Irv Greene had told him that evening that he had the top spot at Augusta all locked up. The announcement would be made next week. Nate was getting everything arranged for the subsequent buyout of Triple Large. Lamont expected to net roughly ninety million dollars.

And he was getting married in ten days. He'd never thought it would happen. And without a prenuptial! But he had no reservations. No cold feet. Everything in his life felt right.

He fell into a deep, peaceful sleep with the smile still plastered on his face, his stomach as calm as the Caribbean Sea.

It was good to be the king.

◆

CHAPTER 52

Guess Who's Back

ON HIS WAY OUT OF LUXE, Da Mack threw up the hood of his black velvet cape, a prototype from his clothing-line-in-the-works, Mackwear, as his primary security man, Tone Sizzle, cleared a path to his brand-new yellow Hummer H2.

Lena was at the wheel, checking messages on her cell.

Da Mack stopped to sign a few autographs for the clubgoers milling about on the sidewalk. Tone Sizzle stayed close and then pulled him away when too many people started to assemble.

"You still need me tonight?" Tone asked, opening the passenger door to Daryl's car.

"No," Daryl said, "we're just going home."

"Okay, I'll pick you up at your house in the afternoon to go to the photo shoot," Tone said and slammed the door. "Later, Lena."

Lena looked over to respond but Daryl had already put up the tinted window to keep his fans from gawking.

"Where you been?" Daryl said, looking at the time on the dashboard. It was 2 A.M. "You said you was gonna be here by midnight."

"I just got finished," she said, finger-brushing her freshly sewn-in weave. "It took seven hours. And I left you a bunch of messages."

"I left my phone at the Hit Factory," Daryl said. "We gotta swing by there before we go home to pick it up." Daryl ran his bejeweled hand through Lena's long, straight, brown tresses. "It looks real good," he said flirtatiously. "Feels real good. I'm gonna hate to mess it up tonight." He grinned, then turned up the radio to pump Jay-Z's latest, "Change Clothes." "Best believe I sweat out weaves..." he rapped along.

"Give Afro puffs like R-A-G-E!" Lena finished the line. She rolled her eyes playfully. "That's what *you* look like when *your* press and curl shrivels up," she teased as she pulled off.

"Don't worry 'bout me, baby," Daryl said, smoothing his shoulder-length hair. Snoop Dogg didn't have nothing on Da Mack! "My stylist will hook it back up right tomorrow." He began bouncing on the seat, barely able to contain his gleeful energy. "I wish you had been with me tonight," he said. "Gambino was there and they played my new single and the whole place went crazy. Shit was off the hook!"

"I'm sorry I missed it," Lena said. "But I don't need any club crowd to convince me how tight your shit is." At the red light, she leaned over and kissed him.

After years of chasing famous guys, who would have ever guessed that Lena would get what she wanted in the form of one Daryl Cleotus McHenry? When she'd found out that Daryl had quit Triple Large, she told him he was an idiot. But he'd proved himself a good friend to her, letting her stay at his place and all.

A week after she'd moved in (and demanded that Daryl order a top-of-the-line mattress for his second bedroom), he signed with Hitz, Inc. as a solo artist and Country D began to look kinda cute to Lena. Then he let her listen to the album he had recorded and he started looking downright fine! Two nights after signing his deal with Hitz, they slept together. Daryl made up for his shortcomings by being a very enthusiastic and generous lover. He liked to cuddle. She didn't, but she humored him.

But he needed fixing, so she took him to a first-rate dermatologist and got his blotchy skin taken care of. She helped him pick out the right jewels at Jacob's. (She got some, too.) She offered to furnish the apartment and he gave her an unlimited budget to do so. They'd sit on his new furniture listening to his songs while she cornrowed his hair and oiled his scalp. She'd pull out his baby hair and gel it down along his hairline. He liked that. Then she took him to Rod for his press and curl.

When his album came out, she was right by his side, applauding him louder than anyone. They'd moved to a house in Englewood, New Jersey. She furnished it from scratch and covered a wall with all the platinum plaques of albums Daryl had worked on. When he got a platinum plaque for his own album, she hung it right by the front door so everyone would see it first thing as they came in.

No surprise, Daddy was furious about their relationship but it didn't matter. She didn't need Daddy or his money anymore because she had Da Mack. And she didn't need any of her old fair-weather friends. *Fuck Mimi, fuck Vanessa, fuck Alonzo, fuck Kiko, and double fuck that fat fuck Lamont!*

But in her honest moments, Lena had to admit that she missed Mimi. In her brutally honest moments, she had to admit she missed her something awful. And with Mimi's album doing so well, she couldn't escape her old friend. Mimi's voice was on the radio, her face on MTV. Lena couldn't even do her shopping at the A&P in peace. There she was in the checkout line…MIMI: EAT OR DIE. The *Globe* didn't have to play her like that. But, damn, she looked tore up! And since when did Mimi chain-smoke and drink coffee nonstop?

Lena even went to see The Beauty and the Beasts show when it played at Madison Square Garden, taking Daryl's cousin, Monique, who was visiting from South Carolina. They sat in the cheap seats, which Monique had complained about. She begged to go backstage, but Lena didn't want to run into anyone she used to know.

Mimi had Lamont and Lena had Da Mack. Lines had been drawn. The camps did not mix. But Da Mack gave Lena what she needed. They went everywhere together. He kept her busy, sober, and very happy. She was acting as the creative consultant for his clothing line, Mackwear. And he'd taken to calling her his "rich bitch." She loved that.

LYING ON THE COUCH, smoking a cigarette in Studio A of the Hit Factory, Mimi said, "Hey Gem, when we finish tonight let's go to Cheddar!"

"It's already two in the morning."

"Cheddar's an after-hours spot."

"We're working after hours," Gem said tersely.

Big Ant walked in and Mimi sat up at attention on the couch. "Ant, you know what I really need right now?"

He snatched the cigarette, a big no-no per Lamont, and stubbed it out in the ashtray. "Not this," he said.

"An apple pie," Mimi said.

"An apple pie?" Big Ant repeated suspiciously, because that sounded like it was going to take some physical exertion from him.

"Yup," Mimi said. "There's a twenty-four-hour McDonald's on Forty-second Street."

"Okay," Ant said, ripping a piece of paper from a nearby pad to take everyone's order.

"Where's Billy recording?" Mimi asked the engineer.

"I think he's in Studio B," the engineer said.

"Ant, don't leave until I come back," she called out as she headed for the door.

"MAKE IT QUICK," Lena told Daryl as she parked a few doors down from the entrance to the Hit Factory.

But upstairs on the seventh floor, Sheila, the receptionist, had a bone to pick with him before she'd hand over his cell phone. "Just look at this, Daryl," Sheila said. Noting a flicker of disapproval fall over Daryl's face, she corrected herself. "Sorry, Da Mack."

She pulled up her T-shirt an inch or two and revealed a pus-secreting mess around a gold ring in her belly button.

"Damn," Daryl said, stepping back. "What the fuck happened to you?"

"Your girl told me to go to some guy she knew to get a piercing. Said he was gonna hook me up. It cost a hundred and seventy-five dollars and the shit got all infected. And he won't give me my money back." She handed over Daryl's phone.

Daryl walked back to the elevator and pressed the down button. "Well, you wanna tell her, she's downstairs right now."

"I can't leave the desk," Sheila said. "But tell Lena to call me. I'm serious."

Just as the elevator arrived, Billy tha Kid ran out into the reception area with his gerbil in hand. "Country D!" he shouted mockingly upon spotting Daryl. "Country D!"

Daryl stepped into the elevator without responding and quickly closed the door in Billy's face.

Billy took it all in stride. He quickly headed for the stairs.

MIMI WALKED INTO STUDIO B and saw Big Percy, Billy's cousin/legal guardian/bodyguard dozing off on the couch. "Where's Billy?" she asked. "We're ordering from McDonald's."

Big Percy mumbled, "He's running around here somewhere."

Mimi looked in the lounge, which was empty, then went out to the reception area. "Have you seen Billy?" she asked Sheila.

"He ran downstairs to chase after Daryl," Sheila said. "Will you go get him? Last time he ran out of here they found him two hours later playing laser tag over at Bar Code."

"Sure," Mimi said and pressed the button for the elevator.

SEVERAL THINGS HAPPENED ALMOST AT ONCE.

Lena's five-carat diamond stud, a gift from Da Mack, came loose and she bent down, groping for it under the driver's seat.

Daryl walked out of the Hit Factory and headed toward the car.

A masked man stuck a sharp object into Daryl's back, demanding, "Gimme your ice!"

"All of it?" Daryl yelped and the violent jab in his back answered in the affirmative.

Daryl shakily removed his five heavy platinum-and-diamond crucifixes and dropped them into a black laundry bag that was tossed at his feet. Then he slid off his bejeweled Jacob watch, two diamond cuff bracelets, and four diamond rings. They dropped into the bag with a *clank*.

"The belt!" the masked man demanded.

Daryl pulled the enormous diamond buckle off his leather belt and handed it over.

"Empty your grill!"

Daryl popped off his six diamond tooth covers, which spelled out DA MACK.

"Shoelaces!"

Daryl leaned over and pulled the diamond-laced laces out of his Air Force Ones and threw them into the bag.

Bag filled with jewels, the ice-jacker was set to make a break for it when Daryl pushed him back and drew his gun.

Just then Tha Kid burst through the front doors of the Hit Factory aiming to fling Brownie the gerbil on Daryl's head for old times' sake. He had Brownie cupped in his hands ready to send him sailing through the air.

Tha Kid was laughing. Tha Kid was always laughing, always joking around.

But this time the joke was on him. And it wasn't funny. Not in the least.

CHAPTER 53

◆

Let Me Ride

"DRIIIIIVE!"

Lena's freshly retrieved diamond stud fell back under the driver's seat as she threw her hands on the steering wheel and gunned it. "What happened!" she screamed. She'd heard one loud popping noise. A gunshot? "What happened?"

She ran three red lights before Daryl shouted, "What are you doing! Lights, bitch! Lights!"

She stopped right in the middle of the block between Fifty-eighth and Fifty-ninth streets. Daryl climbed down from the Hummer and walked around the front. Lena sat there, shaking, too panicked even to cry.

He hustled around to Lena's door. In the last year since he'd been driving in the city, he'd been pulled over twelve times. Three of those times the cops had found a gun in the car and he'd wound up in jail. His license was suspended, which is why, when it was just the two of them, Lena always drove. But even in this adrenaline-charged moment, he realized running red lights on Eighth Avenue at two in the morning in his brand-new yellow Hummer with DA MACK license plates wasn't the move. And Lena was in no shape to drive.

He opened the driver's side door and Lena scrambled into the passenger seat. "What happened?" she shrieked. The tears were flowing now.

"Somebody jacked me for my jewels."

She was trembling. "And you shot him?"

"No," Daryl said, looking in the side mirror to make sure the coast was clear. "He fired on me." He hit the gas. "But I think he hit Billy."

"Billy!" Lena screeched. "Billy was there?"

"He ran out just as I tried to get away. I think he got shot."

Lena started hyperventilating. "Da Mack," she screamed. She always called him Da Mack out of respect for his newfound success. "We have to call the cops." She pulled out her cell.

If Daryl had learned one thing from Lamont, it was how to keep cool in pressure situations. He slapped the phone out of her hand.

"We have to go back," she said, reveling in the drama of it all. The last six years of her life had been a dress rehearsal for this star turn. "He got Billy! He got Billy!" She saw Daryl's gun on the floor of the Hummer underneath her feet. "We have to call the police!"

"For what?" Daryl said coolly, adding a sarcastic, "You think they gonna get my ice back?"

"You were a witness," Lena said. She shakily lit up a cigarette.

"No, I wasn't," Daryl said persuasively. "I didn't see a nothin'. I came down, got in the car, and we left. We didn't see nothin'. We didn't hear nothin'. So why would we be goin' to the cops? And I don't want nobody knowin' I got jacked."

Lena agreed on that point. It would make Da Mack look bad. But still, what about Billy? "But didn't you see anybody upstairs?" Lena asked.

"Yeah, Sheila," he said. "And by the way, that guy you told her to go to for the belly button thing really fucked her shit up. She got a real bone to pick with you."

"I don't care about that!" Lena shouted, then took a hard drag on her cigarette. "You think Billy got shot? Maybe you can identify the guy."

"He had on a mask," Daryl said as they continued to cruise uptown. "But you're right about Sheila. She's gonna tell the cops I was there. We need to get off the road. We need to figure out what we're gonna do. And we need to dump the gun."

Lena eyed him suspiciously as he worked this all out.

"Nobody's at your father's place, right? He's in L.A.?"

"Yeah," Lena gasped.

"Let's go there," he suggested. "You got your keys?"

She nodded.

"We can dump the gun, get ourselves together, and then call my lawyer."

They parked the car in a garage near the Whitaker residence and went upstairs. Daryl showered. Lena chain-smoked eight cigarettes.

When he came out of the bathroom, Lena gave him one of the many sweatsuits that were still in her bedroom closet. They wore the same size.

"Look," Daryl said. "We'll call my lawyer in a few hours if they say somethin' about it on the news. That's how we heard about it. By then, the cops will probably be lookin' to question us."

"Us?" Lena said.

"I told Sheila you were downstairs in the car. We're in this together," he said pointedly. "We ain't gonna say nothin' about me gettin' jacked, aiight? Nobody needs to know about that. So we'll say I came down, jumped in the car, and left. We didn't see nothin'."

Lena nodded hesitantly. "Maybe we should just tell the truth," she said, blinking at him. She took a drag. "The truth shall set you free, Da Mack," she added dramatically.

"Says who?"

"I don't know. Somebody. And you didn't do anything."

"No, I didn't. Still I don't wanna be involved. But, on the real, I need you to be with me on this." He stroked her long hair weave and kissed her. "You know I love you, right?"

"You do?" He'd never said that to her before. She'd been waiting to hear those words. Now that he was famous she was always on alert, fearing he might dump her to get with the *T* in PYT or something.

"You my heart," he said. "You my rich bitch. So you with me?"

She looked up at him with tears of joy in her eyes. This was the moment she'd been working toward. She was Da Mack's ride or die bitch! "I'm with you," she said.

LAMONT DISEMBARKED from his flight feeling rested and with noticeable pep in his step. He checked his cell for messages. There were forty-eight. His step became less peppy. Forty-eight messages in five hours? And the hours were between three and eight AM. New York time. Something was wrong. As he began to listen to the first one, his phone started ringing. ALLY C. flashed on the caller ID screen. He was approaching the escalator that led to baggage claim when he answered.

"What's wrong?"

"Where are you?" she asked breathlessly.

"At JFK," he said. "What's wrong!"

"We just got here," she breathed. "Stay at the gate. We're coming for you."

He stepped on the escalator. "What's wrong!"

"Gate eight. We're coming. Stay at the gate."

"Ally…" He looked down and saw Ally C. standing right there at the bottom. Imani and Big Ant were next to her. As he descended he could see another security guy they sometimes used, Giant Toby, standing farther back and casting a shadow over them all.

"…I already left the gate. What's wrong!" He could see Ally C.'s mouth moving as he heard her voice on the phone. "Something happened to Billy."

Then she spotted him and it looked like she'd seen a ghost. She started rushing up the down escalator. "Go back," he heard her voice plead through the phone as she rushed toward him.

Ally C. was always dressed in something sleek and black with her blond hair perfectly straight. He looked at her now in jeans and a Hofstra sweatshirt, with no makeup and her frizzy hair sloppily clipped up. If he'd passed her on the street he wouldn't have recognized her.

He put the phone down at his side. "What's wrong," he said to her anguished face. She pushed up against his chest and hissed, "Go back. Go back. *Now.*"

He opened his mouth to say, "Why?" but his question was answered as the mob at the bottom of the escalator came into view.

What...

There was a pack of reporters wielding microphones.

the fuck...

The cameramen turned on their lights.

was happening?

"Lamont!" the reporters yelled. "Lamont!"

Ally C. knew there was no going back now. She grabbed his arm in a viselike grip and, close to his ear, whispered hoarsely, "Make no comment!"

Ant and Toby swooped him up and practically lifted him off his feet, throwing elbows to clear a passage.

"Lamont!"

"Is it a kiddie rap war?"

"Who do you think did it?"

"Lamont!"

"Do you feel responsible?"

In the pandemonium he saw a copy of the *New York Tribune* in the Plexiglas display box at the Hudson News stand. There was a picture of Billy tha Kid. The headline read:

WILD WILD WEST 54TH STREET
"Tha Kid" Rapper Gunned Down Outside
Midtown Recording Studio
In Critical Condition

Lamont made no comment.

They all piled into the Rolls limo and Carlos sped off.

"WHAT THE FUCK HAPPENED!" Lamont screamed.

"Billy got shot," Ally C. said, trying to remain calm.

Imani was crying.

"By who?"

"We don't know," Ally C. said. "It was outside the Hit Factory last night . . . early this morning. Around two."

"At two? What was he doing outside the Hit Factory at two? Where the fuck was Percy?"

"Sleeping upstairs," Ally C. said, as Imani continued crying quietly.

"So how is he?" Lamont said. "Let's go to the hospital."

"Lamont," Ally C. said gently as Ant and Toby looked away. "He's dead."

"Where is Mimi?" Lamont screamed at the top of his lungs. He knew Mimi had been at the Hit Factory last night.

"She's all right," Ally C. reported. "She found Billy downstairs and went with him to the hospital."

"What?" Lamont snapped, his heart and mind racing.

"She was hysterical but the doctor gave her something about an hour ago. She's at home," Ally C. assured him. "She's probably asleep by now. Nate and Jordan are waiting at your place."

Lamont slumped down on the seat. Billy was dead? Murdered? This could not be happening. This could not be happening!

They all rode the rest of the way in silence. Lamont felt the stabbing pain in his stomach return with a vengeance.

◆

CHAPTER 54

They Reminisce Over You

FOR THE FUNERAL, Vanessa wore her black Christian Dior bondage suit with the cut-out back. She waved to the crowd amassed outside the Frank E. Campbell funeral home on the Upper East Side.

She'd dressed Mimi in a shapeless black dress. Mimi had been sleeping a little with the help of sedatives, and crying nonstop when she was awake.

Mama was sheathed in a black Escada, respectable pumps, and a black hat with a brim so wide that Lamont, seated next to her in the front row in a beautiful black Armani suit, had to lean to the side.

Grimy arrived just as the service was starting, with his wife, Beautiful, hurrying behind. He had on an all-black custom-made ensemble with a small diamond cross over his shirt and tie, black wraparound shades, and a black wool skullcap, even though it was summer. As he swept down the aisle, his long black duster coat billowed behind him. He looked like he'd just escaped from *The Matrix*.

Lena and Daryl, who'd been briefly questioned by the cops and released, didn't show.

Irv Greene had called Lamont the morning of Lamont's return from L.A., shouting, "A child has been killed!"

The higher-ups at HMG were not pleased with the media furor that was building. Irv told Lamont to "fix it." The chairman job was in jeopardy.

Under the advice of a damage control expert, Lamont had been busy giving interviews to all comers. People were blaming him, pointing out that Tha Kid's first single was called "Shoot."

Larry King quoted some sample lines:

> *Called you but your moms said you couldn't come to the phone…*
> *Shoot!*
> *Want you in the front of my Range but I gotta get my license…*
> *Shoot!*
> *Thinkin' about goin' pro but I got no hops…Shoot!*

"It was a play on words," Lamont explained on CNN. "Obviously!"

"Hip-hop didn't kill Tha Kid," Lamont told Fox News. "Senseless violence did!"

Mama had suggested postponing the wedding. It wouldn't look right. And Mimi was in a bad state. Lamont refused. Everything was all set.

"We're not going to let this murder go unsolved like Biggie and Tupac," Lamont told *Newsweek*. "An innocent child has been killed. I'm going to see to it that someone pays."

At the funeral, the pastor gave the eulogy and then Grimy got up.

He'd had a third teardrop inked below his left eye. At this rate, his entire face would soon be awash in inky tears.

He mumbled a few words and then rapped a somber, haunting song about promise unfulfilled and laughter being silenced. It had everyone sobbing.

Even Vanessa was on the verge but she choked back her tears. So-called waterproof mascara never was.

Her macho husband was crying enough for the both of them anyway. He knew Nasdaq had been following Daryl that night to grab his jewels. After he'd heard what had happened, Alonzo had tried to contact Nasdaq but he couldn't find him. He hoped that his stupid prank hadn't gone awry and gotten Billy killed. But he wasn't going to tell a soul. Blood relation or not, Lamont would go medieval on his ass if he found out he was in any way involved.

Lamont was openly weeping, a sight so shocking that it cut through Mimi's sedative-induced haze. When he grabbed her hand and squeezed, she put her arm around him. She resolved to pull herself together. He was obviously as broken up about this as she was and they had to be strong for each other. In that moment she realized she truly loved him and she was doing the right thing by committing to him forever. "I love you," she whispered in his ear and he squeezed her hand harder.

The caravan of cars followed the horse-drawn carriage that carried Billy's casket through Harlem as Billy's fans lined the streets to bid their final farewells, waving posters and chanting the words to his songs.

Mimi rode in the Rolls, velvet curtains drawn, with Lamont, Nate, Martin, the damage control expert, and a photographer who seemed to be working for Martin—the only one who'd been allowed inside the service.

Out of his jacket pocket, Lamont pulled a tiny bottle that looked like it would contain eye drops and threw it at Martin. "What is this shit?" Lamont snapped. "It burns!"

"They're glycerin drops," Martin said authoritatively. "It's not *supposed* to burn. I told you only a few drops."

"Glycerin drops?" Mimi said, confused, but they all ignored her, too intent on reviewing the digital images on the camera.

"Well, they worked," Martin said.

"Yes," Nate concurred, looking at one shot. "These are some lovely tears we got going here."

"But that one makes me look fat," Lamont said. "Look at my chins!"

"I could Photoshop it," the photographer said.

The next day Lamont was on the cover of the *New York Tribune*. It was a tight shot of his face, looking stoic (and rather sculpted), a solitary tear streaming down his cheek.

The headline read:

TEARS FOR THA KID.

CHAPTER 55

◆

One More Chance

AFTER WAKING from a two-hour afternoon nap, Mimi showered and wrapped herself in the monogrammed Frette robe that Ally C. had given her for Christmas.

As she walked out of the bathroom, she was slapped in the face by a newspaper of some sort.

"It counts," Lamont shouted. "It counts!"

Dazed, she bent down and picked up the periodical. It was a copy of the *Globe.*

Lamont was sitting on the bed, clutching his stomach.

She sat next to him and looked at the cover. The headline read, "PRINCESS MIMI GOT COLD FEET?"

She flipped to the story inside and saw pictures and a timeline of her drunken night out with Gemini. At 11:15 there was a shot of her dancing wildly at Foyer with Gemini standing in front of her. At 1:45 there was a shot of her outside the club, eyes rolling back in her head, with Gem clearly trying to hold her up. At 2:01 there was a picture of them heading into The Four Seasons. At 10:15 the next morning there was a long lens shot of her jumping into a cab outside the hotel, looking a full-blown mess.

An hour ago, Lamont had come out of his office to find Ally C. in front of his door in a yoga pose with Imani standing over her, exhorting, "Breathe, girl. Breathe!"

They went into his office and Ally C. nervously showed him the advance copy of next week's *Globe*.

"What have I done to deserve this?" he'd raged and grabbed his stomach.

"Nothing," Ally C. had reassured him, rubbing one of his shoulders.

"Nothing at all," Imani had whispered, rubbing the other one.

Now, sitting on the bed, Mimi sighed. "I don't know what you want me to say."

"Tell me you didn't fuck that smelly motherfucka!"

"I didn't," she said, completely offended.

He grabbed the paper and violently ripped it to shreds, letting the scraps fall over them like gray confetti.

"It wasn't me," she said, automatically parroting Lamont's favorite line.

"What are you talking about? There are pictures! My mother saw you there!"

"Your mother?"

"She saw you leaving The Four Seasons and she said you lied to her and told her you were still at home in bed. Imani, Jordan, my fucking mother, all of them knew about this!"

"Oh, I didn't realize...," Mimi said, feeling betrayed. They were all talking about her behind her back? And no one asked for her side of the story?

Lamont looked about ready to go for her throat now that she was hemming and hawing.

"I was there," Mimi admitted. With these pictures, there was no way she could deny it. "I got drunk and Gem didn't know where I lived to take me home. So we went back to The Four Seasons. But nothing happened. I only lied to Mama because I didn't want to tell her I'd gotten so drunk or get into the whole story with her. I swear, nothing happened. Ask Gem."

"And you expect me to believe that! What do you think I am? New?"

"Yes," she snapped. "I do expect you to believe that!"

"I don't believe you," he seethed. "Don't fucking lie to me! Tell me the truth!"

"I just did."

Lamont curled up on the bed, clutching his stomach. It felt like Freddy Krueger was in there working overtime with a butcher's knife. Stab, stab, stab.

"How could you do this to me?" he moaned. "How could you do this to me?" He crushed his face against the pillows. "I want you to admit it!"

"Then admit what you did with Olga."

"I didn't do anything with Olga."

"I didn't do anything with Gem."

"Everyone is gonna see this and think that you did!"

"Not everything in the papers is true. Tabloids especially. You should know that."

Lamont buried his face in the pillows. "I can't believe this is happening," he groaned.

She sat beside him, filled with regrets and questions and conflicting emotions. She felt awful for getting drunk and bringing this embarrassment on Lamont. And she kept replaying that night at the Hit Factory over and over in her mind. If only she'd gone looking for Billy five minutes sooner...She didn't want to think about it—the image of Billy lying out on the sidewalk, all alone in the dead of night, bleeding—but it was all she could think about.

And, still, everyone told her that she should be the happiest girl in the world, and that made her feel ashamed to admit, even to herself, that she wasn't. This was everything that she wanted but not what she wanted at all. They had the wedding rehearsal dinner to get through tonight. But she wasn't sure any more if she wanted to marry Lamont. She wasn't sure if she wanted to get married to anyone.

"You know I had this girlfriend once," Lamont said in a strangled whisper. "I dated her for six months and one day I realized she had never said thank you to me. Not for the dinners, the gifts, the vacations we took. Nothing. And I was mad at myself more than anything. How did I let all that time go by without even noticing? So I took her out that night to the most expensive place in the city. We had a great meal and at the end I said, 'Did you forget something?' She said, 'No, not a thing, I'm full.' And I said, 'No, not food. Did you forget anything else? Is there something you want to say to me?' She just looked at me. A complete fucking blank. I threw some money down and walked out. Left her sitting there. And I never spoke to that bitch again. All the stuff she'd left at my house, I had Imani give to the Salvation Army." He closed his eyes. "I let all these bitches use me," he moaned. "I let all these bitches use me. They don't give a fuck about me. No woman ever gave a fuck about me. Except my mother."

Mimi was not feeling his pain. "And don't you use them?"

"What?"

"They want you for your money and you want them for their looks. As far as I know, you've never dated any average-looking girls with great personalities."

"Just because I like attractive women, doesn't mean I'm using them," he shot back.

"You don't go out with attractive women," she said, pushing it instead of backing down as usual. "You date only gorgeous women and you expect them to look like they just stepped off the cover of a magazine at all times. They're supposed to add to your shine. Maybe they don't give a fuck about you because they know you don't give a fuck about them. Not who they really are."

Lamont stared at Mimi like he was seeing her for the first time, startled by her disrespectful tone. "And you?"

"I never used you," Mimi said. "I love you for you."

He squeezed his massive body into a tight ball. "Then how could you do this to me?"

"I didn't do anything to you," she said. "And I really do love you. If you didn't have any of this stuff I would still love you. You care about the money and all that. That's your thing."

"Is it?" he said, sitting up. He flicked her ring finger. "I don't see you turning down any of the jewelry I give you."

She walked into the bathroom and got her engagement ring off the counter, then she picked up her jewelry box, carried it over to the bed, and emptied all the jewelry into his lap. "Here you go."

"Oh please," Lamont snapped, swatting it all aside. "You're just like the rest of them. Every girlfriend I've ever had says"—he put on a high, whiny voice—"'Why do you work so much? Turn off your phone. Why can't we just be alone? Why can't you just relax?'" He huffed. "But they're happy to accept my expensive gifts and be driven around in my cars and sleep on my Pratesi sheets in my fucking penthouse. You think that shit just falls from the sky? I'm out there from sunup to sundown getting this paper to pay for all of it. And no one appreciates it. No one."

"Lamont," Mimi sighed, "why do you want to marry me?"

"I might not want to now!"

"You want to marry me because I follow orders. I sing the songs that you want me to sing, I say the things you tell me to say, I wear the clothes you have people pick out for me, I have my blond hair touched up every month, and I got fake tits because that's what you wanted. And whenever you say smile, I cheese it up."

"All that's part of your imaging," he snorted. "And you wanted those tits."

"I feel like I'm living a false self," she said.

"False self," he muttered. Where had he heard that before? Someone else had said that. In a flash of recollection, he said, "Have you been talking to Sum?"

"Yes," she said, remembering their conversation and how much she'd related to what he was going through. "He told me he was gay. I think you should let him come out."

"He wasn't supposed to tell anybody!"

"He told me on the down low. Did you call him a faggot?"

"No...yes...he said it was okay...he said it was a term of endearment."

As he stammered to spin the story even for her in the privacy of their home, she looked at him pitifully. "I don't know what you said to him but I think you hurt his feelings. He's very sensitive, you know."

"What do you mean?" Lamont said, feigning ignorance. "I told him it was cool if he was gay. Just not to tell anybody." She shook her head and looked at him with those disappointed eyes that made him feel like a kid with his hand caught in the cookie jar. "What?" he said, shrugging. "You know I love gay people. ALT is my boy! And I'm very active in the fight against AIDS."

"You like André because he can do something for you. Because he helped get me the *Vogue* cover. And you go to those charity things because they're photo ops. But we both know that if you and Carlos caught a fag alone in a dark alley, watch out!"

He tossed off an unconvincing "Not true."

"And there's nothing you'd like more than a pair of lipstick lesbians who're willing to do a tag team on you. That's real sexy, right? But that woman in Ally C.'s office, a no-nonsense *empowered* lesbian, you call her a dyke."

"What are you now?" he demanded, rubbing his stomach. "A gay rights activist? Who the fuck cares!"

"But let somebody *cough* on a nigga, and you're the first one talking about 'Shut 'em down! Boycott!'"

"Look, don't try to change the subject," he snapped, wanting to get back to a discussion of her cheating ways.

She rolled her eyes. As if he wasn't the king of that.

"We're talking about you," he said. "I created a strong image for you. And it worked. I promised you I was going to make you a star and I did."

"What bothers me is that having your picture on the cover of the paper crying fake tears for Billy is part of *your* image," she said, looking him dead in the eye.

"Those were real tears!"

"Don't con me, Lamont. I was there!" she yelled. "I saw you and Martin with your glycerin drops."

"I only used those for backup!"

Sitting on the end of the bed, her shoulders fell and she sighed. "I would call you a liar but I really don't think you know the difference between a lie and the truth. And that's what scares me about you." She shook her head. "Billy is dead," she managed, putting her face in her hands as she tried to choke back the tears. "Billy is dead, Lamont. He was thirteen years old and now he's gone. You had to give that picture to the paper, but I don't see you shedding tears when there aren't any cameras around. Do you even care?"

"What world are you living in?" he raged, slapping her hands down from her face. "While you're in here unconscious like Sleeping fucking Beauty, the national media is trying to crucify me! My new job at Augusta was in jeopardy. When shit goes down, I have to be out there on the front lines. I have to hold it together for everyone. Don't you get that? Crying is a luxury I can't afford."

"You could cry in front of me," she said, wiping at her own eyes. She waited for a reaction but got none. "You talk about 'authenticity' being more important than anything but that's just a good sound bite. You talk the talk but you don't walk the walk. Everything you do is for show. Everything is for money." A mournful silence. "And I don't know if I want to marry someone like that."

"What are you trying to say?" he snapped, as if she hadn't just been pretty direct. If she thought she was going to dump him, she'd better think again. That had never happened to him and it never would. "You're the cheater here, sweetheart."

She was facing away from him but she shot him a sidelong glance. "Did you sleep with Emma?"

Immediately, irately, "NO!" He'd given her the world on a platinum platter and now all she could do was point fingers? Was she so blind that she could not see what a great thing she had? He was everything any woman could want and more.

She looked up into his blazing eyes. "Lamont, why do you do this?" she pleaded. "I mean, I'm really trying to understand. Why do you lie to me all the time? I know you slept with Emma. Everyone knows." She pointed toward the bathroom. "And she almost died right in there."

"Who said that!"

"*Everyone!*"

"Everyone who?" He wanted specific names so he could deal with them.

"That is beside the point. The point is I know you slept with her and then you insist that you didn't."

"Yes, she came back here one night," he said, sitting bolt upright on the bed. "Yes, she overdosed in my bathroom. Yes, we had to revive her." He ran down the counts like he was submitting a plea in court. "But I never had sex with her. She passed out before I could."

"So why didn't you tell me that?"

"It was before I was with you. It didn't concern you."

"That's not the whole truth," she said, wondering why he could not just come clean. "I know you slept with her. And if it was before we got together then you should just say that. But I don't think it was just one time. You're always trying to hide something."

"I have nothing to hide," Lamont said, swelling with hubris. He'd done nothing wrong. So what if he'd lied about fucking Emma? If you gave a woman an inch, she'd take a yard and hang you with it. So what if he'd been getting the happy ending massage from Olga twice a week for the past three years? He'd always said that was his only time to really relax and that was the truth! Didn't he deserve that small pleasure? And didn't everyone realize by now that oral sex was not sex? It meant nothing. He didn't know Olga's last name and he didn't fucking care. He didn't know how old she was, if she was married, if she had kids, and that's why they got along so well. She showed up on time, did her job—very well—and left. That's what he called a model employee.

After Mimi got all upset, Imani had told Olga her services were no longer required. He didn't have to do that. He didn't *have* to do anything. He ran this show. But he *chose* to do it for Mimi. Because he cared so much about her feelings.

And so what that he'd slept with Kendra a few (or more) times while Mimi was away on tour. Kendra fell under the category of "been there, done that." Kendra was no threat to their relationship. She was his sidepiece and, as Mimi was so fond of saying, "It didn't count."

"Do you know I ran into Paola the other night in L.A.?" Lamont said. "She was all over me. I ditched her and she came banging on my door in the middle of the night. And you know what I told her?"

Mimi looked at him like she didn't really care.

"I told her, 'I'm getting married next week, honey. *I'm taken.*'"

"Do you want a round of applause for that?"

"This was the same night you were spreading your legs at The Four Seasons," he pointed out viciously. "Ironic, isn't it?"

He looked at her cowering at the end of the bed and expected to hear another denial. But this time she said nothing and that silence cut him like a knife. He realized he wanted to hear a denial. He desperately needed to hear it. He didn't want to believe it was true. But it was. Olga was nobody and those slip-ups with Kendra meant less than nothing. But this thing with Gemini . . . that was clearly more than sex.

How could she do this? he thought. *How could she do this to me?* She'd embarrassed him in front of his mother, his employees, and now the whole world would know.

Had she had *unprotected* sex with that chump? He hadn't even thought about *that*. A disgusted shiver ran up his spine and he was on the verge of heaving. He thought he'd finally found a sweet, pristine angel, a woman worthy of being his wife. And now he looked at her and all he saw was another filthy common whore. How could he marry something like that? He didn't even want to touch her.

"I have nothing to hide," he repeated, bile stuck in his throat. "You, on the other hand . . ."

"You get rid of anyone who shows even the slightest sign of disagreeing with you. They disobey and that's it, they're gone," Mimi said.

"People have to realize their actions have consequences," he said.

"What happens to me when I don't want to sing the songs you buy for me? I hate almost all the stuff I've recorded for this second album. I hate it," she said. "No one respects me as a musician and I don't blame them. I'm just this wind-up doll that sings on cue. People call me a low-budget Beyoncé!"

"That was one person," Lamont insisted. "One stupid critic."

"I want to write my own songs," she said.

"You think it's that easy?" Lamont sneered. "You think every debut artist comes out and gets the heat that you got? I orchestrated every detail and made sure you got the love you deserve. Mainstream love. You just prance through doing all the fun stuff while I'm getting my hands dirty laying the foundation, then doubling back to clean up the messes."

"I want to do my own work," she said firmly. "I want to write my own songs."

"We'll see about that," he muttered.

"Will we? And what if I want to dress myself and wear my hair curly? Do I have to ask permission for everything? I don't like that arrangement anymore."

Lamont leaned back against the pillows and rubbed his eyes.

"You want me to be your precious little baby girl, but sooner or later the baby has to grow up."

"I know," he said.

"When we were in St. Bart's you pointed out that woman on the beach and said, 'She's too old and has had too many kids to be wearing that bikini.' Do you know how awful you sound when you say shit like that? And then it turned out to be someone you knew and you went right over to her and acted like her best friend!"

He sat, brooding.

"What happens when I'm over thirty and I've had kids? You gonna talk about me like that?"

Stiffly, "No."

"Or maybe you're not planning on being with me when I'm thirty. Maybe you'll get rid of me and find another twenty-year-old who's willing to listen to everything you say. But when I get married, I plan on staying married. Do you?"

Feeling wrongfully accused and missing the sweet girl he'd wanted to marry (without a prenuptial!), he mumbled, "What's happened to you?"

"How much money do I have?" she said.

"What?" Lamont said, thinking that every time he was sure this conversation had hit rock bottom, it somehow took another step down.

"How much money do I have?" she repeated. "Every time I ask you for an accounting of my finances, you just tell me you're handling it and brush me off. With all these deals you're making for me, am I still broke?"

"You're not broke," Lamont offered vaguely.

"Well, let me see the paperwork," she said. "You got me out here working like a slave. I think at the very least I should know how much money I have."

"Why?" Lamont snapped. "Are you going to chip in for our million-dollar wedding? Are you going to contribute to our daily expenses? No," he said before she had a chance to answer, "you're not. I take care of everything so you have nothing to worry about."

"No, I wouldn't contribute to this wedding because you're the one who wants it to be a circus. I would have run away with you any day or night and gotten married like Vanessa and Alonzo did. This wedding is not about us, Lamont. It's about everything but us. Fuck *InStyle!*"

Fuck InStyle? What was this blasphemy he heard her speaking?

They sat in silence for a while, at an impasse. Then Mimi got up and put on some clothes. Casual clothes.

"What are you doing?" Lamont said. "We have to get dressed for the rehearsal dinner."

"Are we going?" she said, tying her hair back.

"Of course we're going," he said.

"Lamont, maybe..." she said, then trailed off, coming to the full realization that Lamont was a man who'd always lived his life a certain way and he probably was not going to change. Not even for her.

He grabbed her hand. "I forgive you the Gemini thing," he said.

"There's nothing to forgive," she said.

"Okay, I was going to do something with Olga," he said. "But it was only that one time." She wasn't going to back out of this on him. This wedding was going to happen. It had to. What would they tell all the guests? What would they tell Rev. Jackson? "And I know nothing happened with Gemini. I believe you."

She gave him a long, appraising stare and suddenly all her regrets and conflicting emotions evaporated. Daryl had always said you can't teach an old dog new tricks. And he was right.

"But I don't believe you," she said. "I don't want to marry you, Lamont. I'm sorry."

Lamont stood there, stunned, as she brushed past him and walked out of the bedroom. "Listen to me," he said after a moment. "You're talking crazy." But he realized she was gone and he was talking to himself.

He came out of the bedroom and saw Mimi slipping on her sneakers by the front door.

"Where are you going?" Lamont yelled, hurrying down the stairs. "Listen to me. Come back here!"

But she didn't listen to him. She scooped up Bezel, opened the door, and didn't look back.

◆

CHAPTER 56

Life After Death

LENA'S SISTER, Alexandra, arrived at The Grand Hotel du Cap Ferrat in the south of France in the early afternoon. After settling into her room, she found Mimi and Lena lounging poolside.

"Hello, girls," she said.

"*Bonjour!*" Mimi sat up on her chaise to give Lena's sister a kiss and a hug. "How was your flight?"

"Fine, thank you," Alex said. She was still fully dressed and lugging a large tote bag that bore her initials.

"Hi," Lena said obligingly as she slathered Bain de Soleil tanning oil on her legs.

"It's great to see you, too," Alex replied. "And not in handcuffs," she added with a snort of disgust.

Lena rolled her eyes underneath her shades.

"I brought all the papers and magazines you requested," Alex continued bitterly, dropping the heavy bag with a thud on the floor near Lena's chair. "No need to thank me."

"Thanks, Alex," Mimi said genuinely, reaching for the bag.

"Did you see Daddy yet?" Lena asked.

"No," Alex said. "Where is he?"

"I don't know," Lena said. "But he was waiting for you to get here. You should go find him." Alex looked like she wanted to rest in the sun for a while so Lena added, "Right now."

As soon as Alex left, Lena grabbed a few of the newspapers and magazines that Mimi had spread all over the bottom half of her lounge chair. "Oh God, I need a cigarette for this," Lena said, slipping one out of her pack and lighting up.

The day that Mimi walked out on Lamont, she'd jumped into a cab downstairs. The driver said, "Where to?" and she had no idea. Then she gave him Lena's address. It was the only place Lamont wouldn't think to look. It was the only place she'd feel safe.

When Mimi arrived, Henrietta, the housekeeper, was there and she said Lena had gone to the police station with Mr. Whitaker. Henrietta explained that she had slept at the apartment one night the week before ("Because my corns was killing me, I couldn't make it to the subway…") and she had been woken up by what she thought was a burglar breaking in but had turned out to be Lena and "that rapper boyfriend of hers." "I overheard them talking about dumping a gun and getting their stories straight," Henrietta said. "Talking all kinds of foolishness. If Lena had been my girl, I would have knocked some sense into her fast ass a long time ago." And so, even though her corns were aching, Henrietta had surreptitiously followed them down to the incinerator room and she had fished the gun out of some trash bag after they'd gone. Then she called Mr. Whitaker in L.A. and told him there was big trouble.

By the time Marlin arrived in New York and confronted Lena, she'd learned that Billy had been killed. It took her two minutes and twelve seconds to flip on Daryl. Marlin got her a criminal attorney and they went to the police with her full story. The police confirmed that Daryl's gun had fired the shot that killed Billy.

When Lena returned to the apartment, she and Mimi had a tearful reunion. Mimi told her she'd left Lamont and she didn't know what to do, where to go. So she stayed with Lena that night and they talked all night about whether she was doing the right thing.

Lena made the cover of the *Tribune* the next day and the story reported that the cops were looking for Da Mack, who was now on the run. The story of Mimi and Lamont's broken engagement had not hit the streets yet but Marlin saw the maelstrom beginning to gather around both girls. Since Mimi said she was sure she wasn't going through with the wedding, Marlin decided they both needed to get out of town until all the press blew over. They were all on the night flight to Paris.

"This is horrible," Mimi said, holding up the copy of *Us Weekly* Alex had bought. The headline read: SHATTERED FAIRY TALE.

"This is worse," Lena said, holding up yesterday's *Tribune*. Daryl's picture was on the cover under the headline, DA MACK: IT WAS AN ACCIDENT!

They'd already seen some of the news about Mimi's canceled wedding and Daryl's arrest on CNN. And they had called Jordan and gotten some inside scoop on what was happening from her. But Alex was given the task of bringing over all the past week's press coverage so they could see it for themselves.

Lena leaned over and they gaped at the *Us Weekly* cover. "They always gotta run the picture-torn-down-the-middle shot," she said, shaking her head at the picture of Mimi and Lamont in happier times. "You look good there, though. When was that?"

"Ugh, I don't remember," Mimi said, opening to the story. "'Sources say Jackson called off the million-dollar nuptials after learning that the singer had a fling with Gemini, the superproducer behind such hits as...'" She stopped reading and looked at the picture of Gemini at the top of the page.

"That's a damn shame," Lena said. "What did Gemini ever do to anybody?"

"And he's so private," Mimi moaned. "He's going to hate me for putting him in the middle of this."

"He'll be annoyed," Lena admitted. "But he won't hate you. You should definitely call him, though, to smooth things over. Or just make a statement saying that it's not true."

"Make a statement through who?" Mimi said, still scanning the piece. "Ally C. is Lamont's publicist and I can't use her anymore."

"Yeah, well, you need to find someone new," Lena said, checking out the *Tribune* story on her involvement in Daryl's arrest. "My dad is your lawyer now, he'll find you someone else. He'll take care of everything."

"And wait, listen to this...'"Lamont is devastated by this betrayal," says a source close to Jackson."' Mimi closed the magazine. "I really want to know who these sources are!"

"I can tell you," Lena said. "Lamont and Ally C."

"You think so?"

"Please, Mimi, you've been in the game long enough now to know how it works," Lena said, picking up *Us Weekly* to skim the article for herself. "And was he so devastated that he had to go on *your* honeymoon with Kendra?" Jordan had told them that.

"I know, I can't believe that," Mimi said, welling up. Over the past week, she'd been prone to spontaneous bursts of tears.

Lena was ready with a tissue, the tears had become such a regular occurrence. She whipped one out and handed it to Mimi while continuing to read the article. "You dumped him," Lena said, all of sudden sounding like the sensible one.

"I know," Mimi said, sniffling. "But he goes away with Kendra a week later. I mean, he's over me already?"

"Good that you didn't marry him then, if that's the kind of asshole he is," Lena said.

Marlin appeared and pulled up a chair. He noticed Mimi was crying again and did not comment. He'd done more parenting in the past week—for Lena and Mimi—than he'd done in his lifetime. He ran his eyes over the screaming tabloid headlines and sighed. He was thinking of taking a vacation after this vacation.

"So, Mimi, I spoke to Irv Greene," he said, leaning back under the umbrella of a nearby table for some shade. "And he wants to sign you as the first artist on his new label."

"He does?" Mimi and Lena said in unison.

"Yes," Marlin said. "I told him you didn't like the material you had already recorded for the second record. You had some other ideas. He wants to talk to you when we get back. Maybe you'll have to start over...but he's willing to hear what you have to say. How does that sound?"

"It sounds great," Mimi said hesitantly. It made her suspicious that she wasn't going to have to fight with anyone. So far, everything had been a tug-of-war. How could anything be this simple? "But what about Lamont? He's just going to let me out of my contract?"

"Well, Irv is buying out the contract," Marlin said carefully because he didn't want to trigger more tears. "And Lamont is fine with that."

"Lamont is fine with that?" Mimi said, angry, not weepy. "He'll let me go just like that?"

Marlin cleared his throat. "*You* let *him* go," Marlin noted. "Am I correct?"

Lena had another Kleenex ready, just in case.

Mimi nodded. "Yes," she said quietly.

"You know how he is," Lena said. "When something is over, it's over."

"This is the best situation for everyone," Marlin said.

"Yeah," Lena said, wholeheartedly agreeing with her father for the first time in a decade. "You'll see."

The pool waiter came by and asked if they needed anything.

"Banana daiquiri," Lena said. As Marlin picked up one of the papers, she added, "A *virgin* banana daiquiri."

"Same for me," Mimi said.

"I'll take one, too," Marlin said, skimming the story about Lena's former boyfriend, who had accidentally shot and killed this poor thirteen-year-old boy. "But I want alcohol in mine. And, please, make it a double."

Lena leaned over to grab *Star* magazine and his eyes fixed on the small of her back. "Marlena, is that a *tattoo*? Oh my goodness," he moaned, squinting hard. "What does it *say*? C-R-A..."

CHAPTER 57

◆

I Used to Love H.E.R.

WITH LAMONT IN THE BACKSEAT, Carlos drove through a pair of wrought-iron gates and eased the new Range Rover up the long, tree-lined driveway. The 20,000-square-foot castle in the leafy New York suburb of Bedford was a home befitting Lamont's new status as the chairman of Augusta Music. He'd recently purchased it after receiving $95 million for the sale of Triple Large Entertainment. The TLE office was closed down, all of the TLE artists (except Mimi) were re-signed directly to Augusta's black music division, and Lamont's first official act as chairman was to fire hundreds of Augusta employees.

Carlos parked by the side entrance. Before heading inside, Lamont grabbed the envelope that had arrived at his office this afternoon. He walked through the kitchen, where his personal chef was preparing dinner, and dashed upstairs to the master bedroom suite, passing the butler and one of the three full-time maids on the way, speaking to no one.

"Hi, honey," Kendra chirped as soon as he set foot in the bedroom.

"Hey." He kissed her on the cheek and pulled his tie loose. Kendra could be smothering, especially now that they were living together, but she had proved her loyalty. When they'd gone to Hawaii after the cancelled wedding, he'd chewed her ear off about what a disloyal bitch Mimi had been. Kendra had never complained. On the last day of the trip, he had apologized for going on endlessly about it and for all the times he had hurt her in the past. He had told her that he had never appreciated her the way he should have and sworn that was going to change. Her eyes had lit up and she had smiled bigger than he'd ever seen.

"How was your day, babykins?" Kendra inquired as Lamont undressed.

"Wonderful," he said. "Busy. And yours?"

"Very busy. I went to the gym and..."

Kendra went into details about her leisurely day and Lamont tuned her out. It had become their nightly routine. Kendra had given up on her acting career. Being Lamont's live-in girlfriend was a full-time job. Days were spent beautifying herself, keeping Mama company, and managing the large staff required to ensure things at the mansion ran smoothly. Nights were spent attending industry functions with Lamont and satisfying him sexually... sometimes with the help of one—or two—of her beautiful, disease-free friends.

"Great," Lamont said curtly, which was a signal to her that she should shut up. He looked at the envelope he had brought home from the office. It contained a copy of Mimi's new CD, which was coming out soon on Irv's label, Greene Music. He was anxious to listen to it. But he needed some privacy.

"Olga is waiting for you down in the spa room," Kendra said and handed him his silk Sulka robe.

Lamont headed downstairs, smiling. He'd forgotten Olga would be here today. Kendra had recently surprised him by hiring Olga back—even though Kendra had always known about the "happy endings." And that was why Kendra was the best girlfriend in the world.

While Olga kneaded his back, Lamont got a chance to listen to Mimi's new album. The first song was called "Listen to Me" and it sounded pretty good. The second, "On the Inside," was even better. It was just his kind of music. The third song was called "Nothing Is Something" and he didn't care for the lyrics. After the fourth song, "Do As I Say," he felt he'd heard enough.

On the floor, he noticed a slip of paper that had fallen out of the envelope. It was a note from Irv and he squinted to see the words scribbled on it. *Business, never personal,* it read.

He had Olga change the disc.

He wished Mimi well, but would this record sell almost two million copies as *his* had done? Probably not. As New Age music filled the room, he tried to put Mimi out of his mind for good.

"Turn over," Olga said, and he did.

◆

CHAPTER 58

Ladies First

AS THE NOMINEES FOR ALBUM OF THE YEAR were announced, Mimi squeezed Gem's hand. When they got to her name, Gem squeezed back.

Gem had been her sole producer and cosongwriter on her sophomore album, *Listen to Me*. She'd spent six months at The Funk Shack recording songs with him and, in that time, a romance had blossomed. She was living in L.A. now and he was still in Georgia but, somehow, between her hectic schedule and the distance between them, they had been able to make the relationship work.

She had been up for three Grammy Awards, and already she'd lost two. So when the envelope for Album of the Year was opened and a name was called, Mimi began to clap and smile as she had done for every other award. But then Gem was looking at her. He was smiling. Everyone was looking at her. Everyone was smiling. She saw Irv jump up in the front row, clapping very hard with his hands almost over his head.

Gem pulled her to her feet, hugged her, and said, "Go!" He stepped out of the row so she could get to the aisle.

And only then did she realize they were clapping for her. She managed to walk up to the stage, hugging Irv on the way up, but she couldn't hear anything. It sounded like waves crashing against rocks. All she could see was a white light. It really did feel like going to heaven. Afterward, she couldn't remember what she had said but she knew she'd at least managed to thank Gem and Irv.

Backstage, Deb, the publicist for Greene Music, was waiting. She ushered Mimi through a ton of interviews and Mimi couldn't remember a single thing she had said in those, either.

By the time she hooked up with Gem again to go to Irv's annual Grammy after-party, it felt like two weeks had passed. Though Mimi was physically and emotionally exhausted, she worked the room with Irv because this was his moment to shine as much as hers. He'd given her free rein to do what she wanted on the album and his team had done a stellar job in helping her transition her image from ghetto-fab hip-hop princess to alternative soul singer–songwriter. He was so happy, he looked like he was floating around the room. "I guess old Irv's still got it," he crowed, with his arm around Mimi's shoulders. It seemed like the photographer's flashbulbs would never stop.

When Lamont showed up, Irv went over to speak to him and Mimi went back to her table with Gem. She hadn't seen or spoken to Lamont since the day she'd run out of his apartment. And this was not the place for that to happen the first time. As far as she was concerned, it didn't need to happen at all.

But as she left, she stopped in the ladies' room. And as she came out, she ran right into Lamont, who was heading into the men's room.

"Hey," he said warmly. He pecked her on the cheek as if she were a friend he hadn't seen in a while, not his former fiancée who'd walked out on him two days before their million-dollar wedding.

"Hello," she said, standing awkwardly in the dark corner of the restaurant.

"Congratulations," Lamont said. "You deserve it. I thought you should have gotten best song, too."

"Thank you."

"Hopefully, by your third joint, you'll have somebody new to write about," he said, making a playful jibe about her autobiographical lyrics.

She laughed and just then a photographer popped around the corner and yet another flashbulb exploded before she and Lamont both hurried away in separate directions.

That single picture of them together earned the lucky photographer $150,000. It ran on the party pages of *Vibe, Vogue, Harper's Bazaar, Us Weekly, People,* and *New York* magazine.

Mimi looked stunning, her long brown curls hanging loose, her shoulders bare in her strapless Zac Posen dress, her makeup flawless, an inviting half-smile on her face.

Lamont, however, got caught out there. He was squinting at her, his mostly obscured face in profile, and the unflattering angle gave the whole world a perfect view of his triple large chin.

◆

Outro

DARYL WENT TO JAIL for aggravated manslaughter after admitting that he'd accidentally shot Billy. Despite all his arrests for gun possession, he had never fired a gun in his life until that night. He is currently holding daily rap seminars at Sing Sing Correctional Facility and planning to release a hip-hop/gospel album called *Praisin'* upon his release. But he will have to find a new record label because Hitz, Inc., despite its name and hardcore reputation, dropped him following his conviction.

LAMONT, making hits at Augusta and still living with Kendra with no plans to marry, finally got his chance to be in *Vanity Fair*. They called him to get secondary quotes for their exposé on Daryl's meteoric rise and fall.

VANESSA divorced ALONZO (she got hefty alimony payments, he got custody of Pedro) and moved to L.A. where she hooked up with

Margeaux Prescott, an outspoken, openly gay, middle-aged but well-preserved white actress who was starring in her own reality television show. With filming of the second season of the cult hit just beginning, Vanessa is determined to get a lot of air time.

IMANI had always harbored an obsessive crush on her boss but knew she didn't stand a chance with him since she wasn't a) a model; b) a light-skinned black girl with long hair and longer legs who looked like a model; or c) white.

But then she got the next best thing. His brother. She consoled Alonzo after Vanessa abruptly dumped him and they started dating. And she realized this was much better than being with Lamont, because Alonzo was gorgeous and sweet and faithful!

MAMA developed a line of very real-looking wigs and add-on hair pieces and hawked Mama Jax Custom Hair on QVC. When Lamont was informed that *Black Enterprise* was planning to do a one-page story on his mother, he shook them down for two.

Mama, who hadn't been known to date in years, fell madly in love with a widower whom she met through her church. Lamont didn't trust the guy. At Mama's birthday dinner, he pulled the sixty-nine-year-old, mild-mannered, retired pediatrician aside and told him to "watch his back."

JORDAN, now editor in chief of *Sistah Girl*, indefinitely put off her wedding to Nate after reading a feminist manifesto called "Here Comes the Bride" that convinced her that marriage was an antiquated institution that enslaved women.

But she agreed to let Nate impregnate her because she didn't want to become one of those forty-year-old career women who found out too late that their eggs were all dried up or defective.

LENA relocated to L.A. and gave up hard-partying to focus on her career. Marlin gave her some start-up capital and found additional investors for her business venture—a line of tees and athletic apparel called "Whit." Lena's sister, Alexandra, helped with the business plan and Maryslesis Gonzalez was named design director. First year's sales projections are two million dollars.

MUSTAFA followed Vanessa to L.A. and lived in Margeaux Prescott's guest bungalow, Kato-Kaelin style. He is a consultant for Lena's clothing line.

LAMONT signed Emma White to Augusta, saying she would be "the next Faith Hill." Except her voice didn't even come close. Though completely devoid of musical talent, everyone at the label loved Emma because she hustled like a pro doing promotional appearances, she came ready-made with corporate affiliations, and she looked amazing in her videos.

WITCHY, now the senior vice president of black music at Augusta, got engaged to Theresa Dearborne, the *T* in PYT. Though the group was hugely successful, his family said they'd never heard of her and refused to meet their future daughter-in-law, who they privately referred to as "the colored girl."

Then Theresa dumped him for cheating on her with none other

than Emma White. The Mann family was overjoyed when Witchy disentangled himself from sweet, talented, clean-living Theresa and moved in with Emma, a vapid former junkie who did not even have her GED.

ALLY C. married a nice Jewish dentist from Great Neck, whose last name happened to be Cornbluth, so she could continue to go by the nickname Ally C.

SUM WUN came out on the Wendy Williams show. Lamont was furious! But once he saw a spike in sales, he pimped Sum out to the media, touting him as "hip-hop's first homo-thug." Sum became a gay icon and was named one of *People's* "50 Most Beautiful."

Lamont was named "Man of the Year" by GLAAD (The Gay & Lesbian Alliance Against Defamation).

GRIMY converted to Islam, as BEAUTIFUL had been encouraging him to do for years. Brotha X, as he now calls himself, shuns drugs, cigarettes, alcohol, and pork. And he does not use cuss words in his rhymes, a decision Lamont is trying to get him to reconsider.

Beautiful keeps herself covered at all times.

DON GAMBINO and ENVEE became the proud, unmarried parents of a baby girl. Their daughter has bright blue eyes, white-blond hair, and skin paler than Casper the Friendly Ghost. Ebony Jones is her name.

SUPA PHAT E and his wife, RENEE, also had a visit from the stork. Triplets, thanks to the fertility drugs. Phat E gained sixty pounds in "sympathy weight" during the pregnancy. But the happy couple worked out together afterward and he has lost almost one hundred.

FLO$$'s unimaginatively titled fourth album, *Flo$$in'*, tanked. But Eugene was making enough in film—six million per—that he didn't sweat it.

He and his sexy costar, Lysa Richards, are currently Hollywood's black "It" couple.

RADICKULYS was diagnosed with dyslexia and saw a therapist, who helped him manage his disability. Lamont promptly got him a deal with Scholastic to put out a line of educational rap CDs. Dicky is currently on a world tour, promoting literacy and his first educational rap-along CD, *Radickulys Rhyming*, accompanied by a band of groupies known as Da Silly Hoes.

A newcomer to Augusta Music, NASDAQ finally has an album, *Bull Market*, scheduled for release next year. Daryl's ice-jacking is a secret he and Alonzo swore to keep to themselves.

CRAZY G's debut album, *Mayhem*, fizzled. He is living in Miami with his round-the-way girl, the one he'd always kept on the side while he ran through every hip-hop and R&B chick in the industry.

BRADLEY BROWN III left ANNE "PRISSANNE" BROWN for his longtime mistress, who dressed like a stripper and knew how to drop it like it was hot.

Anne got half and the kids. She is seeing a therapist four times a week.

RAYSHAUN ATKINS broke his leg in a car accident and had to sit out an entire NBA season. He spends all his free time "in the lab" working on his debut rap CD. Lamont will not take his calls.

JERRY MORELLI ran out on Angela after stealing the car Mimi had bought her. Angela is now the president of Mimi's fan club and happily spends her weekends mailing off Mimi's signed headshots to her daughter's devoted fans.

KEESHA is a stay-at-home mother to her two kids in Toledo, and she still believes that one day her fiancé is going to quit dealing drugs of his own volition.

TOYA moved to Los Angeles, where she opened her own hair salon, which Mimi financed. Mimi and Lena threw her a star-studded opening party and it does a booming business.

MIMI is happy with her personal life—her long-distance romance with Gem continues to bloom—and her career has never been better.

The Grammy win bolstered sales of *Listen to Me*.

It did *quadruple* large numbers.

Six-million sold . . . and counting.

Bling!

SHOUT OUTS

◆

Ira Silverberg, my fabulous agent, for schooling me on everything from first serial to world rights; being available to me 24-7-365; alerting me to sample sales and watching my back end. You're the shit.

Tad Floridis for "discovering" me and being oh so cool as well as Anna, Neil, and everyone at my agency, Donadio & Olson.

Hilary Bass, Kathy Schneider, Kristin Powers, and the whole Miramax gang for being open to my endless list of ideas and giving so much time and attention to this project. And especially Jonathan Burnham for having so much faith in me. Love ya, sweetie!

Peter Borland for becoming so immersed in the book that you started using "shorty" and "yo" in everyday conversation. Every time I exfoliate, I'll be thinking of you.

Lloyd Boston, my style guru, for this conversation—Lloyd: "I came up with a title." Erica: "What is it?" L: "Are you ready?" E: "I'm ready." L: "Bling." E: Stunned silence. L: "Do you hear me? Not bling-bling. Just 'Bling.' One word. It's stronger, cleaner." E: "Oh my god. That's brilliant. How did you come up with that?" L: "C'mon, this is Lloyd Boston you're talking to." You are The Man and one day you will be my baby daddy. Be patient.

Tatiana Siegel for taking it seriously from day one.

Aisha Steiner for being a true friend. Lobster Theory's come full circle, baby. Watch the breakfront!

David Netto for being the coolest motherfucker I know.

Kimora Lee Simmons, for ten years of jokes; for being the ultimate diva...go on, girl. And, most of all, for giving me the smartest, sweetest, most beautiful godbaby I could ever dream of in Ming Lee—and a bonus sweetie in Aoki Lee. Love you, Mama!

Mogul/Yogi Simmons, for scoffing at my dreams of bestsellerdom thereby motivating me to prove you wrong. Now get off my dick, nigga!

Luke Hoverman, for recovering from your fair-weather status to become a great sounding board and support system. We'll always have Vegas. Latte, anyone?

David Thigpen for being a great friend and a mentor in my bid for global domination in all writing genres.

Dwayne Johnson-Cochran for the cheerleading.

Robert Lawrence for always telling me to soldier up and for the chocolate-covered strawberries.

Eisa Ulen and Nikki Prescott for that special SLC love.

Dominique Neblung for hooking a sista up with luxury goods on the cheap when she was poor and being thrilled when said sista could finally afford the shit retail.

All my babies Ashante, Tyson, Dylan, Alannah, Bryson, Schyler, Noah ("the Raven"), and Toby for bringing me laughter.

James Patrick Herman (aka Sasha), Hyun Kim, Serena Kim, Mimi Valdes, OJ Lima, Nina Malkin, Amy Barnett, Orla Healy, and all the other editors over the years who took the time to say "Nice job" when I turned in a piece.

Joanna Milter for encouraging me and hooking me up with Tad and Ira.

Tommy Hilfiger for being the best boss in the world and for always looking out.

Gennifer Eliot for the critiques and encouragement.

My family especially Kirk, Kevin, Kenard, Dawn, Dwayne, Kenyon and Kim "La Diva" Lopez for always asking how the book was going.

Joan Adams for not accepting any excuses and telling it like it is!

Big Poppa for teaching me many lessons including the greatest of all: Never count on anyone but yourself.

And to all da haters, I still got love for ya! (Just kidding—I don't.)